THE
LEAST
AMONG THEM

THE
LEAST
AMONG THEM

A Novel

Rolf Goerke

SUNSTONE PRESS

SANTA FE

Sunstone books may be purchased for educational, business, or sales promotional use.
For information please write: Special Markets Department, Sunstone Press,
P.O. Box 2321, Santa Fe, New Mexico 87504-2321.

Cover art by Pedro Lobatos, Creel, Chihuahua, Mexico
Book and cover design › Vicki Ahl
Body typeface › Contantia
Printed on acid-free paper

Library of Congress Cataloging-in-Publication Data

Goerke, Rolf, 1938-
  The least among them : a novel / by Rolf Goerke.
    pages cm
  ISBN 978-0-86534-926-1 (soft cover : alk. paper)
  1. Self-actualization (Psychology)--Fiction. 2. Self-realization--Fiction. 3. Psychological
fiction. I. Title.
  PS3607.O335L43 2013
  813'.6--dc23

                    2013015701

WWW.SUNSTONEPRESS.COM
SUNSTONE PRESS / POST OFFICE BOX 2321 / SANTA FE, NM 87504-2321 /USA
(505) 988-4418 / ORDERS ONLY (800) 243-5644 / FAX (505) 988-1025

I dedicate this book to—

My wife Eulalia,
who introduced me to the Tarahumara and their canyons.

And also to Enrique Madrid, border scholar and longtime friend,
who introduced me to life along the Rio Grande.

1
Voice in the Desert

A blood-red sun touches down behind the brown desert hills.

The 16 year old Lorenzo lets fly a stone at a lagging goat, one of the twenty he is herding in a direction away from the Rio Grande and back toward his house—a .22 rifle in his other hand, on the chance he might see a rabbit.

They are winding among the thickets of mesquite that line the river when he is suddenly startled and stopped by the sight of something dark and strange in some dense bushes ahead of him—what looks like a shaggy-haired, monster-like creature. Or could it be the very Devil himself? Flooded with a fear verging on terror both hands instinctively clutch the rifle.

Taking a few steps to one side to see better, he experiences a roar accompanied by a blinding light and something exploding in his chest.

And he not at all resisting—slides gratefully down into a black hole of nothingness.

It was soon revealed that unknown to the local populace, and for a week now, American soldiers had been positioned—hidden and camouflaged and moving only at night—on private lands on the Texas side of this part of the river for the purpose of apprehending whomever they saw crossing drugs.

Such as the young man the soldiers maintained they had shot after he had fired at them.

The outraged and grief-stricken farming people of El Polvo, all of whom knew that Lorenzo had never had anything to do with drugs and would not harm a fly, and finding their lands were now occupied territory, went berserk.

Jesse—a short, skinny wiry man with a moustache—called a meeting in back of the Catholic church under the community's largest cottonwood tree. And there—it a good 110 degrees in its shade—he immediately announced his plan for everyone to grab shot guns and deer rifles and oust the invader-trespassers.

"US soldiers stole this soil we are standing on from Mexico with canons and guns—and us who had been living here for hundreds of years they begrudgingly made Americans—but they still treat us like dumb dirty lazy Mexicans—the likes of which they don't want in their white spic and span country—and now they have come back—this time dressed like the devils they are to murder our children."

Carlos, who raised bees and sold desert wildflower honey from a roadside stand, spoke, "Yeah—but our music is brighter and prettier—and our tortillas and beans and chile and roast goat taste better than the packaged stuff they eat—and our women are prettier and spicier and taste better too—I am with you."

And then Julio, a big powerful man, the father of Lorenzo, speaking very quietly, said, "Our homes and families are tighter and have more soul—they are warm—like a thick wool blanket on a cold night—they are sweet-smelling—like the desert after a rain—and those others have come to destroy that—by yes—murdering our children—I will fight with you—and the wife says she will too."

Pablo, an ancient, bent-over man who as a boy had fought with Pancho Villa, said, "We have bigger balls too—and as you all know the first shots of the Mexican Revolution were fired not far from here—by men just like us—over in Cuchillo Parado—a small village very much like this one—and afterwards we threw the Americans out of Mexico—and took back our oil."

"But I tell you that if we are not very prudent in this matter—they with their angry machine guns will mow us down like we do our fields of alfalfa—and then rape our women."

Carlos said, "We will put an encampment in the mountains—and come down quietly on a dark moonless night and set the brush afire to confuse them—and slice their jugulars—just like we do with our goats."

Right then Carlos' vivacious young wife with a baby in her arms appeared out of somewhere and swinging her hips as she walked up under the cottonwood announced that she just found out that all the soldiers had climbed into the back of a large canopied brown truck and cleared out an hour ago.

Javier spoke, the only one of them who had graduated from college, "We will begin legal proceedings against the government—challenge the constitutionality of the army occupying our community—and try to establish a case for murder."

Someone shouted, "Ay-ay-ay."

"And we will demand a million dollars for each family in El Polvo—which is the least they owe us after a hundred fifty years of walking on us."

There were several yells of "Ay-ay-ay.

"First we will need to find the right very good lawyer—and who will work for us who have no money to pay him with—and there will be many meetings—and investigations—it will take time, maybe months—I will start making inquiries tomorrow."

This time all of them yelled their approval. And the meeting dispersed.

And driving home in their old pickups they all felt a tingling in their skin, felt much better and proud of themselves.

Even knowing that not one of them would ever have dared fire a shot, much less cut a throat.

The village of El Polvo—which is the Spanish word for dust—spreads lazily along the north bank of the Rio Grande where that river begins its wind through a beautiful mountainous desert region known as the Big Bend. The river's fertile flood plain irrigated with water brought by canals from the river can produce several crops of alfalfa a year. Behind the fields, what strikes some eyes as a harsh and totally inhospitable desert—dominated by shiny green creosote, catclaw, prickly pear, and tall whip-like, spined sticks of ocotillo, along with various species of small cylindrical ground-hugging cacti—produces enough sparse grasses and other small plants to support a few goats and cows.

The community consists of about 30 families, along with a Post Office, a Catholic church, an abandoned primary school, a huge abandoned cantaloupe shed, and an abandoned cheese factory. Although these days everyone knows English, only Spanish is heard.

Just across the river lies the Mexican farming community of Las Palomas where everyone is related to at least someone in El Polvo—since historically the two have been one community with a magical life-giving river flowing though its center.

In the early 1600s, Spanish priests accompanied by a few settlers established a mission at what is now El Polvo in order to convert and civilize the concentration of Jumano Indians who were farming both sides of the river as well as hunting the then plentiful deer, antelope and buffalo. As a consequence the genes of the present population are still overwhelmingly Indian. And also still Indian are some of its ways of seeing the world—which are perceived by the Anglo-European minds to the north as backwards, or even crazy.

A few years ago a white retiree from Massachusetts moved into El Polvo and organized those with goats into a Cheese Makers' Coop and with some grant money built for them a one-room cheese factory housing sanitary stainless steel equipment. Which building never having produced a single block of cheese now stands as a monument to the Anglo-European penchant for thinking it knows what is best for others.

Somewhat more than 150 years ago, American troops were sent into an area of dense Mexican settlement on the north bank of the lower Rio Grande near to where it empties into the Gulf of Mexico. And there, the local inhabitants fleeing for their lives, the Americans constructed a fort, and pointing their canons across the river at Matamoros easily managed to provoke the war with Mexico that so many in the United States including President Polk himself wanted.

The Reverend Parker of Boston, in speaking at that time of the Mexicans, said, "They are a people wretched in their origin, history, and character—destined to succumb as the Indians did—to a superior race with superior ideas and a better civilization."

The Americans went on to shell the civilian population of Vera Cruz. Took Mexico City. And after the surrender and in accord with the Treaty of Guadalupe Hidalgo wound up with not only El Polvo but half of Mexico.

Although that treaty established the Rio Grande as the new border between Texas and Mexico the natural ancient movement of people and goods both ways across the river continued.

Jesse taught his three kids, "Across the river in Las Palomas it's not really Mexico and here in El Polvo we are not really America—we are one land and one people—people of the border—all children of this river and of this blazing desert sun."

And Javier would at times, to those who he thought might understand him, say things like, "The border—what was once the fringe—is now the Center—the new state of mind—it is the future—that transcends fixed identities and sacred cultural traditions—and that is receptive to people of all colors—and to all voices."

"The future is *mestizaje*—the mixing together of this with that and with their opposites—like in a good soup."

Even the Border Patrol, ignoring one of its statutes, during most of its existence for the most part allowed the people of Las Palomas and El Polvo to freely cross the river at will wherever and in whichever direction they chose to—while at the same time not permitting anyone who was Mexican to pass beyond and into the American interior.

So it was that at least once a week Jesse would cross over to visit his parents who lived on the Mexican side.

Manuel and Consuelo lived in a brown adobe, dirt-roofed house without electricity or running water. Manuel grew corn, beans, and squash, as once the Jumanos had, and also some red chiles and onions and very sweet cantaloupes and yellow watermelons. Consuelo ground the corn for tortillas, as well as sometimes mesquite beans, on a stone *metate* that Manuel had found in a cave behind the house, and in the spring she went out into the desert to gather new tender prickly pear cactus pads and sweet juicy pitahya fruit—again, just as the Jumanos once had.

When the power poles recently arrived in Las Palomas, Manuel told Consuelo, "I prefer the soft friendly light from outdoor fires—and from candles—the light bulbs hurt my eyes—and make everything look the same."

Jesse told his kids over and over again, "This desert is a fountain of life—and of sanity for the spirit—to those who are not afraid of it—and who know it."

Jesse's four brothers lived within walking distance of the parents.

Each year they left their families and went north to Kansas for a few months to roof houses, working with hot tar. Wading the river with a stack of tortillas, a few cans of sardines, and some plastic gallon jugs of water, they would then head up Palo Verde Canyon for US Highway 115, a three day's walk through unbroken desert. They traveled at night to avoid the heat and to conserve the precious water, and during the day they laid up in the relative coolness of a cave or rock overhang and where a Border Patrol plane or helicopter could not spot them.

In the hot season the main worry were the rattlesnakes that also roamed at night.

"They say we take jobs and milk their social services—when the truth is that they themselves won't work for the low wages we do—and that the money they take from our pay for benefits and which we are then afraid to claim subsidizes their social services."

"Yeah—what really bothers them is that they don't want any more Mexicans in their country."

"Damn right—they are only too glad for us to give us their jobs—provided we work for a pittance and do it in Mexico—or in China."

When the river was low Jesse and his wife Juanita and the kids waded across or else churned splashing across in the pickup. And when it was high they paid the dollar a head for the round trip on Enrique's ferry—a leaky rowboat that Enrique had acquired as it had floated by from upriver somewhere. If it was a hot afternoon and the boat on the opposite shore they often had to holler loud to wake him up.

The grown-ups sitting together in the shade of the old cottonwood tree in front of Manuel's house, and their kids running around everywhere, Jesse would take a long draw from his bottle of Mexican beer, and say, "Thank you God that this little piece of Old Mexico still lives on."

A brother might say something like, "Yeah—it doesn't get better than this—the Gringos think that if they were hospitable to us—then every single one of us here in Mexico would come up to move in with them—and join them in being big shot Americans."

Sometimes Jesse's relatives crossed the river over to his place. During which visits Jesse usually fed them his specialty which was carp that he caught on a cheese-baited hook left in the river overnight. The fifteen or so pound fish he cut up and boned and cooked along with tomatoes, onion, garlic, potatoes, jalapeno chiles, and some oil on an 18 inch diameter steel disk from an old plow, the disk supported by three rocks over a mesquite fire.

All of them eating together and looking out across the river toward the 8,000 foot high Sierra Rica, its top lit by the setting sun, the sky streaked red and pink, and from which direction one often heard the howling of coyotes, Jesse liked to say, "Thank you God for making this desert such a furnace and so full of sharp spines and rattlesnakes that those other people stay up north—and point their motor homes and cameras somewhere else."

And a brother might reply with something like, "And for putting out the word that instead of a gasoline credit card we use a rubber hose siphon—and that we steal their shiny cars and drive them into Mexico and disappear them into thin air."

And another brother might say, "Fate—and their greed—and their cunning and cheating—made them very rich—and us in Mexico very poor—they need to learn to share."

❖ ❖ ❖

Up and down the river, ever since the border was created, people have smuggled one thing or another. Sotol whiskey and candelilla wax went north and refrigerators and guns crossed the other way—the goods moving mostly at night through the thick riverside vegetation, with lookouts posted to watch for government agents. From points all along the river burro trails went off into the desert. When roads were used the contraband might be hidden under a truckload of melons.

Most did not think of themselves as smugglers so much as simply ordinary folks whose job it was to outwit the demented giant who with his heel had traced a line in the sand and then said that he would make *picadillo* for his breakfast burrito out of anyone who crossed wearing the color blue.

Then during the 1960s the game changed.

Americans desperately wanting their marihuana and heroin and cocaine at the same time the possession of those substances had been declared illegal created the perfect situation for a lot of people to make a lot of money. All over Mexico poor peasants began to grow marihuana. Fields of opium poppies bloomed purple down in the hot tropical canyon bottoms of western Mexico. Remote desert air strips near the border received shipments of cocaine from as far away as South America.

Jesse told his kids, "It's all because of the Americans—they sprinkle the stuff on their cereal for breakfast—and it's making them even more loco—you guys stay away from it."

Once his oldest boy told him, "Javier says those in power in America are afraid that if too many people smoked pot—then the country would do away with wars and the very rich—and would replace oil with energy from the sun."

And he had answered, "Power over anyone or anything is defying God—which is why those drunk on power live in constant fear of everyone and everything."

The Mexicans, with generations of smuggling experience and with tight family connections across the United States, had no trouble passing the merchandise across the river and then into the interior. Tons and tons, worth billions of dollars. Mafias took control, buying off Mexico's politicians, police, and army, as well as landowners and law enforcement officials on the American side.

Carlos said, "They call us stupid—and yet they still can't get it into their heads that when people want something badly enough—one way or another they manage to get it."

Down a wide arroyo that wound through the desert from the Sierra Rica to Las Palomas rolled brand-new four-wheel drive suburbans with darkened windows and loaded with drugs from all over Mexico and the rest of Latin America.

Carlos said, "I heard on the radio that world-wide drugs generate a trillion dollars a year in profits—tell me—how does anyone stop that?"

At the Rio Grande—or the Rio Bravo as it is called in Mexico—the drugs were crossed at certain key crossing points which changed constantly and well before they were identified as such by American anti-drug agents.

Gangland type killings and shootouts occurred regularly in broad daylight, both on the streets of the Mexican border town of La Junta 20 miles upriver and in the countryside. In Las Palomas one of Jesse's nephews was shot in the head through an open bedroom window while he lay in bed with his wife.

Jesse throwing up his hands told Juanita and the kids, "The love of money is destroying every shred of human decency—and it could be that those evangelicals that tried to convert us were partly right—because what I see out there is that the Devil is indeed loose—and that the world could just very well be coming to an end."

One day Javier said to him, "Hey Jess—do you know what I learned—up there at the University of Texas?"

"Probably stuff a guy like me who barely made it to the eighth grade could not begin to understand—no matter how you explained it."

"I came to see that the goodies of civilization are drugs—for making people think they are happy."

"All of it—the sugar donuts and corn chips—the technological gadgets— the movies—the soft beds—the thousand and one varieties of truth in the form of pretty-sounding religious and political gospel."

He looked Jesse hard in the eye. "All of it addictive—distorting the brain—and leaving one craving more—because none of it ever satisfies."

Jesse said, "You mean like none of it feeds the soul?"

Javier appeared as if he were thinking, and then said, "I put some of that into a term paper—and told my philosophy professor that smoking just a little marihuana had helped me see it all more clearly—and do you know what he answered?"

"He said that I would see even better if I would just open my eyes and pay attention to things—and do you know what?—he was right."

"And that took four years?"

❖ ❖ ❖

One night the people of El Polvo, asleep in their beds, woke up to a strident wop wop wop and to the sound of bits of adobe and plaster falling from the walls and ceilings. People scurried outside—and saw a big blackish bird almost on top of them.

"It's a god damn helicopter."

Two nights later—again the same deafening and adobe and nerve-shattering wop wop wop.

The next morning Jesse returning from the Post Office barged into the house, speaking excitedly, "I just talked to Javier—he's been making phone calls—and would you believe it?—he told me that the best government intelligence has identified El Polvo as the drug capital of the Southwest—me, Carlos, Javier, Julio, old Pablo, and the others—would you believe it?—look at the dents in our pickups—and at our sagging mattresses—and the sagging doors of the houses we live in."

Soon the whole town was talking.

"My phone makes a click now and then—I would guess they have been tapping our phones for some time now."

"The helicopters have listening sensors that can pick up what you whisper to your girlfriend in bed."

"They also have something that can see through stuff—through walls—and underneath a women's clothes."

"They believe that with enough wars and helicopters and with enough laws and rules and insurance policies—and by keeping out Mexicans—they can keep life from happening."

❖ ❖ ❖

As soon as Javier found a lawyer he called a meeting in the parish hall of the church. Where the first thing the lawyer did was pass around a photograph of a camouflaged soldier as Lorenzo would have seen him.

Carlos exclaimed, "It looks like a cross between a gorilla and an extraterrestrial being—just imagine this thing—sneaking around in the mesquite—along with others just like it."

The lawyer handed around papers to sign. And afterwards Javier was elected to go to Washington to explain the sentiments of the villagers.

The Texas Rangers, who had first investigated the shooting, sought an indictment against the soldiers for murder.

Seated on the Grand Jury was the Border Patrol Agent in charge of military operations at the time of the shooting as well as several other federal employees. The soldiers were acquitted. And the Texas Rangers as well as others who understood these things contended that the Justice Department, in refusing to release information in the hands of the Defense Department, had obstructed justice.

One Sunday morning, in El Polvo, and also in Buena Vista, the American town across the river from La Junta, signs were discovered nailed to the doors of the churches, proclaiming,

Seek Justice For Lorenzo
And For All Other Drug-related Deaths
And Imprisonments—
Indict the American Way of Life.

A second Grand Jury investigation was killed when the government granted Julio a settlement of two million dollars.

The ordeal not only wore Javier out but also deflated him. He said to Julio, "Other than make all of us feel a little better—I feel our indignation has changed nothing—if anything it has likely only turned them more against us— their System is very entrenched—the next time they will be more cunning— and hit harder."

Big Julio nodded. He had lost a son. Some money had fallen into his lap.

Afterwards he told people that all he had really wanted—and which he never got—was a sincere apology and the acknowledgment that a bad mistake had been made.

Other than buying a new pickup and a small ranch on the Mexican side to run a few cows on he continued to live in El Polvo pretty much as he always had—an unassuming, quiet-spoken gentle man.

Although the government had promised the people of El Polvo that the soldiers would not return it did not give up on other methods for stopping both drugs and illegal aliens and others in their tracks at the river.

There were rumors of a string of tall listening-observation posts along the border.

And then one day came rumors of a very tall fence.

Of an impenetrable—Wall.

That night Jesse was not able to fall asleep. And then when he finally did, in the wee hours of the morning, he dreamed of the Wall.

A Wall that went down as deep as China—and rose up into the air higher than the Sierra Rica. It seemed to be made of the same stainless steel as the insides of the cheese factory—and was at least thirty feet thick.

He found himself standing on top of it and shouting up to the heavens, "They have already barricaded themselves in behind their selfish materialism—and behind all their war machinery—and book learning and nutty ideas—and now they are going to enclose the whole country behind this—this Wall—except that they still haven't figured out how to roof the damn thing—tell me—what next?"

He shouted again, louder, "I asked, What next?"

A voice said, "Be quiet—your brothers—who are roofers—will never lack for work."

At the breakfast table eating his tamales and drinking coffee, he said to Juanita, "Maybe we should join the evangelicals—because they were right—the world is without a doubt coming to an end."

"But first—what I think I need to do is ride from town to town on my burro—following the river on the American side—all the way up to El Paso—and speaking to everyone I meet of the urgent need for this country—but most of all for their own Salvation—to abolish all Walls."

Putting on his sandals and with a faraway look in his lifeless eyes, he added, "And every night I'll picket my burro close by—and fall asleep under my tarp looking out at the stars and listening to the sound of him chomping the tall grass along the roadside—and it would keep the bad dreams away."

"Because other than that—I really don't know what to do about all this."

All around town the people were speaking excitedly in rapid Spanish, "It will be like living inside a bank vault."

"All our strips of land extend to the river—the Wall will cross those lands—and we will no longer be able to get to river to water our goats—or to fish—we will never again eat carp."

"If they can so screw up a nowhere place like El Polvo—imagine what must be happening to the rest of the country."

"We will not even be able to see the river—except by climbing a high hill."

"I am trying hard to understand all this."

"For god's sake—just accept that this country that fate has set us down in doesn't make sense and is crazy—and stop trying to understand anything."

On such a beautiful December day—neither hot nor cold and with the cottonwoods along the river blazing yellow—Jesse and Javier had decided to ride their burros across to Las Palomas.

Consuelo had served them enchiladas—a stack of three corn tortillas layered with melted goat cheese and dripping with a red chile sauce and with chopped sweet onion sprinkled on top.

Javier wiping his mouth, had said, "Man—that's what American pizza ought to taste like."

Afterwards—at Gregorio's place, with its rusted, broken-down tractor without tires out in front, Jesse, Javier, and Gregorio had sat outside on cinder blocks for a while drinking beer. Then just before they had left, Gregorio had brought out his guitar and sung the *corrido* he had just finished writing—about the Wall.

A Wall—which along with all the other walls separating human beings from one another—in the next to last stanza had come tumbling and crashing down with more thunder than had the Walls of Jericho.

Gregorio had said, "I already recorded it—and the radio station in La Junta will play it and it will be heard up and down the river—just like my *corrido* about Lorenzo."

Hearing the song had put new life into Jesse.

As if a moist cleansing spirit were washing over a parched Wasteland.

And making the tall bare spiny sticks of ocotillo burst out along their entire length with small, bright green leaves.

Mounting their burros and riding away Jesse feels almost saintly.

"You know what I've been thinking Javier?—that living as we do—so simply—in this desert—is somehow like being close to the Source—and that I should maybe give up fishing for carp and instead spend my time riding around on this burro and talking to folks—and—well being sort of like a

Voice of Sanity in the Desert—like Gregorio's *corridos* are."

"Could well be your calling amigo—only with everyone these days as caught up as they are in themselves and in all their stuff—just don't take it too personally if nobody tunes you in—and be ready to duck the stones."

Riding on a little further, Javier says, "I may have said this before amigo—but I keep discovering that trying to change the world or anybody is like pushing with our hands to stop the wind—and that it's maybe smarter to just sit behind a big rock."

They splash across the river, still muddy from recent rains—heading toward where a green and white Border Patrol truck is parked on a strip of white sand.

As they approach the truck two Border Patrol men climb out, the taller and older of them saying, "You boys now just turn around and go back to where you came from."

Jesse says, "Are you guys joking?—or what?—this is my land we are all standing on—I live in that adobe house right over there—both of us are Americans."

The taller man, who seems to be in charge, says, "Well you can't cross here into the States here any more—you'll have to cross at La Junta—on the bridge—and pass through U.S. Customs and Immigration—and show a passport—it's part of the War Against Terrorism."

Jesse says. "You know damn well we are no more terrorists than you are—I've been crossing here since I was born—the bridge is thirty miles upriver—and beside—we have two hungry burros with us."

The younger Border Patrol man smiles, and says, "Well it looks like you're in for a mighty long burro ride."

Javier says, "Isn't there some alternative?"

The older man says, "We are now enforcing a law that's always been on the books—but yep—the alternative is jail."

The two men laugh.

Jesse suddenly sensing himself being filled with the Voice of Sanity in the Desert, says, "If you guys can't stop thousands of wet backs from entering whenever they want to—how the hell do you plan to keep out a terrorist?"

And Javier says, "Where was the Border Patrol when just a little ways down river from here—the American government—in violation of its own laws—and keeping everything top secret from the American people—was running arms into Mexico that then made their way to a CIA-created terrorist group in Honduras that was killing, torturing, and raping civilians in Nicaragua?"

Jesse—his eyes searching wildly for at least some tables to overturn—sputters, "And if you ass holes can't keep out the tons of dope that pass by your noses—what makes you think you can keep out the pieces for a nuclear bomb?"

The older man moving fast, grabs and twists Jesse's arm and pulls him off his burro onto the sand. Pistols come out—and handcuffs.

"You—step off the burro—real quick like."

"Either of you moves and you're dead—now lie face down on the ground—the both of you—hands behind the back—you too you little squirt—both of you are under arrest."

As Javier is handcuffed, he asks, speaking into the sand, and in a very frightened voice, "For what?"

"For being suspected terrorists plotting against the United States—that's what."

They are searched, rolled over, and searched some more. The hatch in back of the truck is opened.

"On your feet now and get into the truck."

Violent pushes help them in—and the hatch is slammed down.

The green and white truck starts up—the two burros breaking into a run toward Jesse's house, stirrups bouncing against their flanks.

2
Cooing of Doves

It light, but the sun not quite up, Lucas is driving in his pickup from Las Palomas toward the International Bridge that connects the Mexican town of La Junta to the town of Buena Vista on the American side. The wash-boarded and pot-holed dirt road he is on parallels the Rio Grande which flows in the opposite direction a few barren desert ridges over from him and out of sight. He has not seen a house or another vehicle since leaving Las Palomas—only what seems like an endless endlessness of sky and sparsely vegetated desert sands.

He is going for his mail—since in Mexico the postal system like much that is modern there does not work very well. He reaches over and rolls down the other window.

Where the road dips into and crosses a sandy arroyo he slows down to a crawl—just as six black bristle-haired javelina appear from up the arroyo. Who immediately stop. Then turn, stampeding off into the green creosote bushes.

"This desert may be just that right place for me."

It was a little over a year ago that Javier had asked him to represent the people of El Polvo in their lawsuit against the government. Having spent one of his high school years in Venezuela as an exchange student, and so knowing some Spanish, and already performing free legal services for Latinos—he said he would.

"Javier—I hear what you're saying—about the War on Drugs being a farce—many of the Mexican Americans I have represented were young first offenders—facing very stiff jail sentences for the possession of very small amounts of marijuana—and you are right that neither jailing those people nor sending in the military reduces the supply—and only helps increase the profits of the multi-billion dollar drug industries of both countries."

And it was about that time too that his wife had filed for divorce—having suddenly and for no apparent reason turned into a bundle of pure malice toward him.

Donald, who taught physics at the university, said, "It could be that Denise—as cultured and as high class as she tries to appear—and as much as she relishes her new role as academic dean—doesn't think what you have decided to do—defending people against what you see as the power of the State—is shall we say respectable—since for her—respectability—what other people think is everything."

Lucas said, "It all might also have to do with everything I am—especially anything I happen to do well—or might think is worthwhile and good—there was anger inside her when I first knew her—and somehow that part of me seems to make it worse."

"Then maybe it's just as well that the universe is ejecting you out of your vibration orbit—we call them random quantum jumps—maybe you'll land up in one that's more suitable for you."

Donald's wife, Mary, who considered herself somewhat of a spiritual counselor for the unenlightened, told him what sounded like pretty much the same thing, "All your life your soul has been in hibernation like a bear in winter—and now it's ready to emerge as a glorious butterfly—that is the energy I pick up radiating from you—an energy that would surely turn the incompatible energy trapped inside someone like your wife into a rage so intense that she does not have the slightest idea what is happening to her."

Donald said, "It's a little like matter and anti matter coming together—and annihilating one another."

When two FBI men showed up at the house to talk to him about him representing a town of drug smugglers and in a matter whose outcome could affect the government's image both within the country and abroad, he, who did not at all care for their manner, or them, had nevertheless managed to stay polite.

As they went out the door, one of the men said, "Don't push this too hard—Lucas—don't push too hard."

Returning from his office the next day a neighbor mentioned to him that the same two men had come back and had spent a long time inside the house. Asking Denise about the visit she told him that they had wanted to know more about him.

"So what did you tell them?"

"The same thing I told my lawyer—and tell my friends—that you are aloof and distant—unstable and not to be trusted—and not at all patriotic."

Working at his desk that evening he could tell that someone had gone through his files.

The next morning, starting up his pickup, he noticed it was running a little off. He got out and looked under the hood, pulled on wires, and when he undid the air cleaner found traces of a white powder that appeared to have seeped out from the filter cartridge.

And that same evening—not at all to his surprise—the police came by with a search warrant. After rummaging through the house in what appeared to him a perfunctory manner they went out to the pickup—and were soon breaking apart the brand new air filter cartridge he had installed a few hours ago.

A few days later, after putting into his pickup what he needed, he told Denise that he did not trust her either, and that the house, so befitting a university administrator, was hers.

Blue, red, pink, yellow, and white plastic grocery bags, blown out into the desert by the prevailing westerly winds and now stuck on the thorns of the mesquite and catclaw, signal that he is on the outskirts of La Junta. He drives through town and crosses the Rio Grande.

At US Customs and Immigration only one lane is open and the vehicles backed up almost to the International Bridge. After many stops and starts he enters the area of surveillance cameras. And finally is waved in to the check booth, the agent running his license plate through a computer.

He reminds himself to not say any more than asked and to tell the truth.

A stern face turns towards him and an aggressive voice asks, "American citizen?"

He hands his passport to the agent. Who goes back into his booth and fingering some computer keys calls up what is known about him, Lucas. Another agent is tapping the truck and tires with a metal rod.

"Where are you coming from in Mexico?"

"Las Palomas, " he answers, knowing he is being scrutinized for anything at all unusual and for the least sign of nervousness, hesitation, or inconsistency.

"Where is that?—and what were you doing there?"

"About thirty miles downriver from La Junta—for the time being I'm living there."

"How do you make a living?"

"I'm retired."

"From what?"

"I used to work as a lawyer."

'Pull your truck into that stall over there."

He does as he is told—guessing that it is probably because of his dust-covered pickup and living in Mexico and so close to the river that he was not wished a good day and waved along. And perhaps too because he looked far too young to be retired.

Or—who knows what the FBI may have entered into his computer data base.

He is asked to open the hood—and then to stand behind a barrier. A team of three men and a woman, all dressed in black and with pistols and radios hanging from their belts, set to work, serious and grim as they hover over the engine and climb into and under the vehicle, peering and probing where they can.

It is not so much these four dark methodical robot-like figures that bother him, as the monstrosity that has programmed their every utterance and move, a monstrosity gargantuan and amorphous and supremely controlling—and much much darker than they.

What he feels welling up within him is more than an anger of indignation—it is a primordial urge to in some way oppose this faceless creature that is sowing its dominion over planet Earth.

But he knows that even the most gentle objection or joke would only lead to the whole vehicle being disassembled, and to him being strip-searched—including up his rectum.

Both doors left open, and the hood up—he is told he can go on.

As he drives away—he is aware that his brain, his entire nervous system is out of kilter. Passing a **Fasten Your Seat Belt** sign he clumsily fastens it, his pickup for a moment swerving into the other lane.

A blinding red ball that is the sun leaps above the horizon—disorienting him even more. He pulls down the sun visor.

He sees a large road sign that had not been there before. He slows down, shields his eyes, and reads:

For Those Meeting Our Strict Criteria—
Welcome to the Homeland.
Land of a High Standard of Living

And of Invisible and Not So Invisible Daily Humiliations
And Encroachments Upon One's Personal Freedom
And Dignity.

At the Post Office, standing in line to buy some stamps, holding his mail, he spends the time studying those ahead of him and in the other line—as well as the two busy uniformed clerks so superbly impersonal and efficient.

It strikes him that all of them are so habituated to the rules and conventions of everyday life that they could not possibly have any conscious inkling of the assaults of any civilization upon the human psyche—invisible silent assaults that repeated again and again can be as devastating as the traumas of rape and war.

He is hit by a wave of compassion—and then by more waves, rolling across an arid and almost barren land and over him.

"Where?—and how?—does one begin?"

It is early afternoon by the time he crosses back over the International Bridge. He slows down for Mexican Customs and Immigration where he is waved through without having had to come to a stop.

And is immediately back in Mexico, in the border town that is La Junta with its unrepaired streets, scattered broken glass, cheaply-constructed buildings, and strange smells—back in what Donald and Mary speak of as the poverty, backwardness, and disarray of the Third World.

"How could they see it any other way?—or most Americans for that matter—who believe that their neat and ordered and expensive way of life is the natural order of things?"

Once he had tried to help Donald understand, citing a documentary film he had recently seen about the Smokey Mountain garbage dump outside of Manila in the Philippines—where on top of a mountain of eternally smoking trash thousands of squatters lived in a friendly community in huts put together from scavenged junk.

When he went on to say that according to the film's director most of those people seemed happier than the typical inhabitant of an American city, Donald answered, "My god—Lucas—it is you who do not understand us."

He parks alongside an outdoor barbecue stand under whose large blue canvas awning are some white plastic tables and chairs where people are eating off of paper plates and sipping bottled soft drinks.

After ordering, he sits down at the only vacant table, facing his chair so he can see the other customers and the street. A man at the next table asks him where he is from and he answers Texas and before that New Mexico, but that at the moment he is living in Las Palomas. He is brought a tall glass of fresh-squeezed orange juice along with a chile relleno burrito—a long green chile stuffed with melted *asadero* cheese and rolled in fried egg batter and wrapped in a flour tortilla.

At which the man saying, "Enjoy your meal," turns back to his.

Lucas says, "You too,"

He bites into his burrito, feeling himself very much an integral part of the life that is taking place around him.

Two Tarahumara Indian women appear under the awning—a girl who could be ten and her mother who is carrying an infant slung in a rebozo on her back. Both are wearing colorful full skirts, loose long-sleeved blouses, and kerchiefs over their long braided black hair. Their sandals are made from old tire treads, the soles fastened to the feet with a leather thong that ends up wrapped several times around the ankle.

They are darker than the Native Americans he has seen in New Mexico. And their eyes seem to sparkle more, and to be more alert—taking in everything.

They make their way from table to table, the girl sticking out her hand, and whenever some coins drop into it lighting up but saying nothing as the two then move on.

They strike him as different from Native Americans in the United States in other ways too, ways possibly hinted at by how they move—gracefully, and free like deer. Or possibly having to do with an aura emanating from them that one cannot see.

They come over to him and the girl putting out a dark hand, says, "*Kórima.*"

As he drops a ten peso coin into her palm and watches her excited response he cannot help but becomes aware that both of them, even hidden as they mostly are behind all that cloth, are very beautiful.

They turn, and jabbering in their sing-songy Indian language run across the street, dodging its traffic.

When he gets back to Las Palomas he will be sure to ask Polo about these people—seemingly so at ease here in La Junta, yet clearly inhabiting another world.

It is very hot, as hot as it gets a woman had told him, and many of the shops in La Junta have been closed for several hours as he turns onto the dusty desert track that heads off toward Las Palomas and ends a short way beyond. Bouncing around in back of the pickup are two boxes of groceries.

Living in Las Palomas, he too has learned to hole up during this part of the afternoon—to go into the dark bedroom of his adobe house and to lie down there on his cot and escape into sleep. For him the practice has come to seem a little like dying every day to the world. And then, at the first hint of cooling, a little before sundown—being reborn more alive and alert than he had ever thought anyone could be.

He is a bit startled when for the second time that day he sees a large sign where none was before. Which with the road so bad, and so he already going slow, does not have to slow down for to read:

Welcome To The Nothingness Of The Desert
And Thus To A Land Of Infinite Possibilities
ForA New And Maybe Better World.

Go Prepared For Rattlesnakes—
As Well As To Discover
That The Necessary Change In Consciousness
May Take A Thousand Years
Or More.

Javier, both hands gripping the prison bars, had said, "Spending two weeks here should be a graduation requirement Lucas—it would be a lot more useful than algebra—or philosophy—but now it's time to go—get us out and you get an enchilada dinner like you never tasted."

Jesse shook the bars of the door, making it clank. Then he said, "If you have power over others—and feel threatened by or don't like them—wall them out or put them in a cage—or lop their heads—and call it the Sacred Rule of Law."

"You should see the fancy courtroom they paraded us into for what they told us was a pretrial hearing—they in their suit and tie—and us in our baggy orange prison duds."

"I'm real sorry guys."

Jessie went on, "Putting on a suit and tie doesn't keep you from being a monkey—or worse than a rattlesnake—if that's what you are."

"Jesse has it right Lucas—the major acts of murder and theft against humanity—the bombings of civilian populations—the billion dollar scams—were not committed by those who are behind bars."

"Tell me Lucas—what does it say about a society?—whose incarceration rate per capita is the highest in the world?"

Lucas having come to regard these two men as the very salt of the earth, nodded. Not having checked his air cleaner he too would be wearing orange pajamas and in there with them.

As he left them, he said, "Make sure there is plenty of sweet onion on top of those enchiladas."

He made some phone calls to Washington, and also talked in person with the Border Patrol Sector Chief, making it clear that this stupid terrorist incident, and coming right on the heels of the Lorenzo shooting, could turn out very politically unwise. A week later, sooner than he had ever hoped for, all charges were dropped and the two men released.

The two Tarahumara women in La Junta had utterly fascinated him.

Desert and blue sky. And more desert and blue sky. And more heat than a person thinks one can bear. He in his pickup moving across a plain dissected by bone-dry arroyos. And far up ahead, bulging upward above the horizon—the shimmering mass that is the Sierra Rica, named that, Polo had told him, by the Indians for its abundant wildlife. And where on top, he had said, there were pine trees and still a few bears.

A high shimmering mass that just like the Enchanted Mountain of legend suddenly and in the blink of an eye transforms itself into a lovely white-robed Indian woman—her thick, coal-black hair flowing straight down to her waist.

He observes the dark brown face—the high cheekbones, straight nose, and almost lipless mouth. And then observes, looks deep into the clear bright hazel eyes—which are gazing penetratingly deep into his. As if asking, "What do you want from us indigenous people—from whom everything has already been taken?"

She possibly the most beautiful Indian woman to have ever walked the earth.

There is another instantaneous transformation—this time into a naked woman who is equally brown—she, her face featureless, in a squat position, with massive thighs, and a bulging belly as big as the rest of her.

Both her hands reaching upwards, grasp onto an overhead tree branch. And then arising from deep in her throat, comes a piercing ecstatic moan.

As appearing between her thighs—is the briefest glimpse of something about to be born.

Then suddenly again there is only the hulk that is the Sierra Rica—shimmering in the delirium of the afternoon heat.

The windows wide open, the air swirling through the cab is that of a blast furnace.

Jesse had driven his pickup, with Lucas and Javier up front and with his family in back, from El Polvo upriver to Buena Vista and then across to La Junta and back down along the river on the Mexican side to Las Palomas.

As all of them were getting out, Javier said, "It's a heck of a ridiculous drive now—just to cross the river—but you are about to eat the best enchiladas on the border—and besides—you need to experience the last bit of Old Mexico—before it's gone."

They ate their enchiladas and sipped Mexican beer in the shade of a big cottonwood tree. Lucas when he was offered a second plate, raising both hands in protest, said, "Consuelo—those were without a doubt the best enchiladas I ever ate—thank you very much—but I just can't."

Afterwards, all of them eating sweet yellow watermelon, Lucas said, "It is very pretty and peaceful here—I think I could stay here a long time."

Manuel said, "A relative has an empty house across from the school you can live in for nothing—want to see it."

The offer caught Lucas by surprise. He, Lucas, actually live here? And so he hesitated a while, before he said, "Why not at least take a look?"

He and Jesse along with Javier and Manuel all squeezing into the cab of the pickup, Jesse drove them the short way over to the house.

Climbing out, Manuel pointed to a rotted wooden structure.

"The outhouse."

They walked up to the squat old adobe house with its flat dirt roof and two very small windows—side stepping some worn-out farm machinery and other junk. Manuel pushing with his shoulder against the unlocked stuck door, they went inside.

"Just this small kitchen and a bedroom—needs some sweeping and picking up—the gas stove works—hooking it up to a tank of gas—and there's a water faucet in the school yard across the street."

It was apparent to the others that Lucas—who had not imagined anything so primitive and run down—looked dismayed.

Javier said, "Look at these adobe walls—almost two feet thick—when it's real hot or cold—this place is a mansion."

Manuel said, "You leave things to me and the woman—we'll round up a bed and a table and chair—knock down the spider webs—and do some sweeping."

Jesse said, "Believe me Lucas—this place has character—and possibilities—you just aren't seeing them yet."

Lucas' mind was racing chaotically. And the law office? And the clients he is currently representing? And what would he do here—in Las Palomas?

And then he heard himself, heard someone say, "But first I need to tie up some loose ends in the States—so how would showing up say the day after tomorrow be?—say about sundown."

Manuel said, "You do what you need to do—we'll have the place ready."

Never had it ever even crossed his mind doing what he had just so easily committed himself to.

The next morning he turned his legal files and six current clients over to a good lawyer friend.

Who asked him, "When do you think you'll be back?"

And that was when again he heard himself, someone else speaking—who said, "Never."

Donald when told of the news, said, 'My god—you've been spewed out of orbit entirely—and are about to disintegrate into the invisible dark energy of the universe."

And Mary said, "A voice predicts something magnificent for you—though for some reason I don't seem to be able to make out what the voice is saying about what that might be."

Neither of them able to understand his choice of Mexico, he told them, "It wasn't exactly a choice—it's was more like when an arctic tern just ups and starts its flight from the Antarctic to up near the North Pole to nest."

About halfway to Las Palomas he turns off into the sand and creosote bush of the desert for a hundred feet and turns off the engine. Reaches for the gallon jug that sits on the passenger seat. Gulps water.

He gets out, urinates a dark yellow stream. And then begins to walk slowly in a direction away from the road.

There is not a tree in sight, only an occasional seven-foot high yucca with a small patch of shade at its base. He thinks about how the snakes are underground, the rabbits under a clump of brush, the coyotes in their burrows, and the javelina asleep between the high vertical rock walls of some narrow sunless canyon.

And that it is only a lone crazy American that is moving around out here—where the air thick and heavy with heat along with the blinding glare off of the sky and sand soon begin to dissolve the world of space and time, annihilate part of the brain.

A crazy American not even knowing why he is here. Far out here. Existing, nothing more than existing—along with this sand and sun and cacti and sky.

A crazy American—maybe thinking he will explore the world of infinite possibilities underlying everything that he once thought of as unshakably single, solid and real.

He becomes aware of four buzzards circling darkly high overhead.

One calls down to him, "Go back to your law office—to being somebody—and making lots of money."

Looking up at them, shading his eyes with one hand, he softly and calmly says, "Laws passing for natural morality—manipulated by those who know how to manipulate them—and backed by guns and a prison system—is a poor way for making what is supposed to be an enlightened society work."

"Nevertheless it's the only way—everyone knows your ancestors evolved with clubs and rocks in their hands—which along with their newly-acquired cunningness—they then constantly and very effectively used against each other and against us wild creatures to get what they wanted."

A second buzzard shouts down, "And their gods—punishing disobedience and whatever else did not suit them with earthquakes and with fire and floods and with the thundering edicts of their voices—were no different."

"Still—I think I'd like to find another way—or to at least see if one might exist."

Another buzzard shouts down, "Ha—picturing yourself some kind of modern day Jesus and Buddha rolled into one—deluded with your own specialness and self importance—just like when you were a hot shot lawyer—and now expecting us all to clap our wings at your noble quest—"

And just then the fourth buzzard interrupting shouts down loud enough to be heard in Junta as distant thunder, "Why—when we buzzards are hard at work—with our heads and beaks buried deep inside the smelly carcass of one of you—why—we just want to laugh—hysterically."

And with that the four buzzards soar off on a current of hot air—laughing hysterically—up into the hot blue sky.

They all turning their heads in unison, shout back down, "Romantics like you give us buzzards indigestion—and so we will leave it to your fellow humans to suck dry your only water hole—and to pick your bones cleaner than we ever could."

He stands there awhile watching them become dots and vanish, then turns around slowly—and heads back toward the pickup.

Along the way he stops to examine a cactus that Polo had pointed out to him, Polo explaining that it opens its blooms—delicate and gorgeous and sweet smelling—only at night.

At the pickup he gulps more water, big drops of sweat dripping from his face and salting the taste of the water. And starting up the engine, he understands better than ever why water has been traditionally used to baptize one into life.

He drives very slowly, as if in a trance—sensing that at some point during this very ordinary yet at the same time somewhat odd day something had irrevocably changed in him, but not being able to pinpoint what.

Ahead of him the Sierra Rica looms closer. Shadows alongside the creosote, ocotillo, catclaw, and the occasional yucca have lengthened.

He tops out on the final rise—from where he can see the winding

Rio Grande along with the green fields and some cottonwood trees and the scattered houses of Las Palomas—and also, spread out along the far bank, the almost mirror image community of El Polvo.

At the ruins of an adobe house he turns into a grove of cottonwoods alongside the river. Switches off the engine.

Sitting in his pickup with the door wide open and watching the riffles where some of the river flows across a gravel bar, he sees a man appear out of a canebrake on the American side. They wave. It is Jesse—who has come to reset his lines for catfish.

He listens to the clear songs of two morning doves cooing back and forth to one another in the green canopy of leaves above him—knowing that Las Palomas in English means doves.

The sun beginning to drop earthward, he can already feel the first touch of coolness. And it is as if the whole of heaven and all of the wholeness that is life had opened.

3

A Goat Herself

About the time Lucas would have been an exchange student in Venezuela, the Tarahumara woman Felipa squatted down on a thick bed of pine needles at the edge of a deep canyon in the rugged high Sierra of western Chihuahua. And grasping with both hands a branch of the pine tree above her—gave birth to her second child.

Which child a week later, after being sprinkled with water from a sacred spring, was named Jesusita.

Now eleven—Jesusita peers down into a rocky precipitous arroyo.

There are no names for her goats, and just as she does not know she is eleven neither does she know how many she has. However she knows immediately when one is missing and which one.

Picking up a stone, she flings it down at the lone goat, the stone bouncing at the goat's feet. Which then hopping from ledge to ledge up out of the arroyo eventually joins the others as they scramble steep upward through the open oak and pine forest.

Some of them white and some black and others a mix of white and black, they nibble brush and low plants, the bell hanging from the neck of one of them tinkling—a dislodged rock occasionally rolling clattering down into the arroyo below.

Jesusita in her flowing flowery skirt, yellow billowy blouse, and faded green kerchief, and barefoot, follows along behind or sometimes to one side, balanced and quick and sure-footed, a goat herself.

Beginning when she was four, every morning as soon as she and her older sister Carmen had hung out their blankets and eaten their few tortillas and bowl of beans the two of them would head out from their one-room stone hut that was roofed with pine shake shingles and where they lived with their parents and grandfather and go over to a near-by log pen and release the goats.

And then they would herd them in one direction or another through a jumbled, incised landscape of canyons and cliffs—until shortly before nightfall.

Day after day, seeing no one, and in rain or snow.

At about age seven Jesusita began to herd the goats alone.

When feed was scarce she would have to take them very far away, over toward the Big Canyon, and even far down into it—to places near springs where long ago her grandfather Benito had built small stone corrals to hold the goats overnight.

Sometimes she stayed out for days at a time, living on *pinole,* a parched ground corn a little of which she poured into a bowl made from a squash gourd, and then adding water, stirred with her finger and drank. She would sleep in caves and under rock overhangs—and when it was very cold, tucked in among the goats.

She always threw a little of her *pinole* into the springs to feed the guardian serpent—who would often talk to her in a language she did not understand but with words that comforted her and made her feel safe.

At times—the rushing cascading waters of the arroyos sang to her melodies she had never heard before and more beautiful even than the ones her father Chelelo played at night on his violin.

All that was simply how most Tarahumara children, both girls and boys, grew up—it was life.

She comes to a pine tree with a white slash spiraling down its trunk, a tree under whose spreading branches she had once sought shelter during one of the daily thunderstorms which lash the Sierra in the summer and make the corn grow tall and the mushrooms jump out of the earth.

The sudden simultaneous crash and blinding flash of the lightning bolt that scarred the tree, along with the torrent of hail, knocked her to the ground.

As soon as the hail let up she set off in the thick fog to locate the goats, trying to hear the bell, but could not. Not even after wandering until almost dark.

Returning to the stone hut that evening without the goats her father beat her with a strip of stiff hard leather, and then pushing her back out into the night, shouted at her to not come back without the goats.

"The goats are so that all of us may live—they are more important than you or me."

The second time she lost them was when a jaguar shrieked in the middle of a very black night. For a while she could hear their hooves clattering up some almost vertical cliffs and rocks falling, and then—nothing. And so, burning one pitch-dripping pine torch after another she carefully ascended from ledge to ledge, with every step expecting to be pounced upon and raked by the big cat's claws.

Until finally, just before daylight, she discerned a faint tinkle from the ridge across from her.

She knows that jaguars do venture up from the tropical canyon bottoms to feed on Tarahumara livestock. She remembers the goat that died of a rattlesnake bite. And the two that fell off of cliffs. And how once she herself came very close to being swept into oblivion in the rushing brown waters of a rain-swollen arroyo.

She knows that all that too—is life.

For her, these steep deep arroyos and even deeper canyons, so far from anyone, are alive with what has happened and almost happened there.

She and the goats climb up onto the spine of a steep ridge that plunges downward into the maw of a canyon so gigantic that it seems it could swallow up the world. A vertical mile below her, at the very bottom, showing itself here and there, winds the Urique River, scattered along whose shores are splotches of green that indicate the small groves of oranges, bananas, and mangos, one of them, the furthest one down river that she can see, belonging to one of her uncles.

The goats wander nibbling onto a natural level terrace that juts out into the vast void of the canyon. Mill about some. Then plop down one by one among the oaks and pines. She herself assumes a squatting position off to one side. Without having to look at the sun she knows it is mid morning—and that the goats, once having eaten, will lie up here until almost mid day.

She watches some little goats, born just before the beginning of the rainy season, scamper hither and thither. She sprawls in the grass. Dozes. Wakes up.

She is content. Never has she wanted anything else, that anything be different. Never that a slope be less steep, or the rain stop. And just like she does not know what Mexico is, neither does she know what loneliness is.

She goes over to a prickly pear cactus twice as tall as she is and picks one of its egg-sized, yellowish *tunas*. Peels it, and eats the juicy, very sweet fruit. She eats six more, now looking down the ridge and toward the river.

Here and there she can make out traces of the old *Camino Real*, the mule trail, long in disuse, that once followed down the spine of the ridge all the way to the bottom and to an abandoned silver mine lying around a bend in the river where she cannot see it. Her Grandfather Benito had told her that years ago Tarahumara too would haul the ore on their backs up along this spine up to the rim of the canyon—from where mule trains would take it to Chihuahua City.

He had also told her that black people who worked in the mine would frequently run away to a certain high remote valley to join the Tarahumara who lived there.

Once, a Tarahumara, wearing a white loin cloth and white blouse-like shirt, came by her stone hut selling a medicinal plant that grew only in that valley. He was much darker than anyone she had ever seen, and very sinewy and strong. She thought him beautiful.

She herself can recognize more than a hundred plants useful to the Tarahumara. Having always watched or helped her mother, she already knows everything a woman needs to know in order to live in the world.

She wonders when her uncle will come up to visit the family, his burro loaded with two balanced crates of mangos.

Suddenly startled by a faint repetitive sound she has never heard before, she whirls around and looks up the ridge. Now she can make out a distinct clomp, clomp, clomp of something neither animal nor human.

More curious than frightened, she remains where she is, the clomp, clomp, clomp now pounding the earth, as it descends down the old mining trail no one uses anymore, and towards her.

CLOMP, CLOMP, CLOMP, CLOMP—along with the clatter of rolling rock.

And then, emerging as if out of nowhere and looking like nothing she has ever seen before, she sees what she knows must be a Gringo—a Gringo with a strange bright blue sack full of something on his back.

He now stopped at the edge of the terrace and watching two of the goats run off a ways does not notice her standing motionless and backed against the trunk of a pine tree. As he slides his arms out of some straps, she can see that the sack must be very heavy. He lets the bright blue sack drop with a thud in the grass.

She stares at the bright blue cloth of the sack and at all the straps and at the pockets with zippers. And then at the massive heavy lugged boots that go clomp clomp—perhaps for clearing the way of snakes.

And finally stares at him. He not nearly as tall as the giant who once ate Tarahumara children. Nevertheless, might he like that giant and with his massive boots gleefully kick and stamp into the dirt not only snakes but whatever else he encounters that does not please him?

He is not as white as she had heard Gringos were, not at all like her white goats. As for his hair, once in the pueblo she had seen a Mestizo woman, a Chabochi, with hair like his, the color that corn sometimes is.

More odd are each one of his movements—even just the way he stands.

She knows there are other worlds—that of Onorúgame or Father Sun, that of the departed souls, and that of the animal and plant and demon spirits— and so she suspects he too must be of another world, one which like the others must be infused with strange magical powers.

"Why hello—I didn't notice you—I'm here to see this canyon that is deeper than our Grand Canyon—that I've heard so much about—my name is Zack—what's yours?"

Although having understood most of his broken Spanish, she does not answer.

"Do you speak Spanish?"

She hesitates—and finally says, "Very little."

"Can you tell me where I can find some water?"

She points down into the arroyo up which her goat had strayed.

He takes a few steps, and looks down.

"No-oo way—there's no trail?"

"No—you can walk anywhere you want."

She is aware of his disappointment—and that she caused it.

He goes back to the bright blue sack. And as he opens it she lights up, because that is what she very much wants to know—what is inside.

The two red bags he yanks out tell her nothing. He rummages, and finally pulls out something small and block-like wrapped in shiny brown paper. Then returns the two red bags and closes up the bright blue sack—which remains as mysterious as ever.

"I have something for you to eat—it's very good—may I hand it to you— or do you want me to toss it?"

Lowering her eyes, she does not answer.

He walks over to her and holds it out for her to take. Her eyes still lowered, she quickly snatches it from him, and then, as he goes back over to the bright blue sack drops it down the neck of her blouse.

He hoists and fastens the bright blue sack onto his back, adjusts some straps and buckles.

"With the next water most likely being the river—I'd better get moving—adios."

She does not tell him the lower part of the trail where the sheerest cliffs are is no longer passable, except for the most agile Tarahumara, nor that it is too late to make it to the river today—she not wanting to again disappoint him.

He waves. Then CLOMP CLOMP CLOMP CLOMP—

Watching him swaying left and right, and skidding on the stones, and throwing his arms out for balance, struggling to stay upright, the heavy bright blue sack and big boots and not him seeming to be in charge—it occurs to her that it would be an ordeal for him to even cross her family's corn field.

As he disappears there arises within her a yearning she has never experienced before, though she does not know for what.

Clomp clomp clomp—receding into the distance.

Her hand fiddling under her yellow blouse extracts the shiny brown packet. She looks at it, and then down the trail where he and the bright blue sack disappeared.

Tearing away the shiny brown paper from what she recognizes as a bar of chocolate, she quickly eats it, barely tasting it—the shreds of paper at her feet. And only finishing it does it suddenly strike her how devoid of any human connection his giving it to her had been.

Much less relational than when she throws a handful of corn to the chickens.

While she, in spite of having for the most part looked down at the ground, feels she already knows him very well.

She wonders if he even really saw her—whether the most vital part of him had somehow not been there.

The first puffs of mushrooming clouds having appeared overhead, she knows that within a few hours, just like every summer afternoon, the sky will unleash a drenching downpour. She picks up some stones and throws one and then another in the direction of the goats, which rising onto their feet, begin to move back down toward the arroyo.

She follows behind, hopping downward with bare feet from rock to rock—an orgy of color and with her stream of long black hair bobbing and swinging in all directions.

She like fast running water flowing unrestrained and free down the mountainside.

Jesusita slides the log bars of the corral shut just as the first big drops of rain begin to spatter on the ground, fog and heavy rain already having obliterated where she had come from. Gusts of wind bend over the green corn on the hillside, whose stalks have been planted four together for mutual support so as not to blow over at such times.

Lightening strikes close by as she enters the stone hut where her mother Felipa is shoving some pieces of *ocote*, or pitch pine, into the oil drum stove. Jesusita grabs a tortilla from on top of the stove, spoons onto it some beans from a chipped white enamel pot, and sits down on a chunk of wood to eat. Some baby chicks peck in the dirt of the floor. A cat sidles up alongside her meowing for food. Her mother goes to sit in the corner on another chunk of wood, also with a tortilla with beans on it.

An occasional slantwise gust blows in some rain. There is dripping from a few opening in the shingle roof.

Jesusita moves her seat closer to the stove, takes another tortilla and more beans.

The storm passes—the sky glowing pink and red in the west.

"I saw a Gringo."

"No Gringo has ever come near here."

"One went down into the Big Canyon."

The tone of voice of her mother changes as she asks, "Did he see you?"

Jesusita says nothing.

"Did you talk to him?"

"He was thirsty—and I told him where there was water."

"And what did I tell you to do if you ever saw a Chabochi out there?"

Jesusita not answering, her mother shouts, "Hide—not let him even see you—and if he does—run off downhill—you know that—so tell me—what got into you?"

"I saw right away that he was not like the others—the Mestizos."

"And what else happened?—did he give you anything?

"Answer me—did he grab you?—did you two do it together out there?—you and the Gringo?"

For as far back as Jesusita can remember, she has been present when the neighbors drank tesguino and got drunk together often for days at a time. On numerous occasions she has helped her mother sprout the corn and grind it into a mash, which they then cooked in a wash tub over a fire in front of the hut and at the end of the day poured into tall clay ollas to ferment.

And for as far back as she can remember, at this and that tesguinada, she has seen men and women doing it together, including once her mother with their neighbor Chemo, on this very floor, her two skirts hiked up, and with her father sprawled drunk and asleep in a corner.

Her mother jumps up and grabbing a stick of firewood, strikes Jesusita across a thigh—who screaming and standing up, spins away.

Jesusita as she rushes out into the evening, shouts, "Yes I let him—just like you do."

Hears behind her, "We are Tarahumara—and once we associate with the white Chaboch Devil and his worse than devilish ways—the Tarahumara perish—you know that."

Squishing and splashing though what is almost a swamp she flees up into the cornfield—and squats down there hidden among the stalks.

After a while, shaking the rain from some stalks and then pushing them over, she lies down on them, curls up into a tight ball, and falls asleep.

The hooting of an owl wakes Jesusita up—that strange animal intimately tied to the spirit world and that every Tarahumara knows only comes to announce the imminent death of someone. And she is frightened, more frightened than she had been by the scream of the jaguar.

Falling back into a fitful half sleep, she hears it speak.

"What was most different about the Gringo was his soul—I encountered it floating up near Mother Moon—still attached to him by the thinnest of thin threads—and that same soul told me it was unwilling to compete with the trinkets the Gringo carries with him in that bright blue sack that so caught your eye—it unwilling to be humiliated in such a fashion."

A rooster crows, then again, and a third time.

"Oh—and one final thing—having to do with what your mother said—

and that is what is most important is being proud of being one's best self—and not just in being a Tarahumara—or say an owl."

"Can he get it back—his soul?"

"It is very unlikely—it is not something you just find and put back—it needs a very special place to come back to."

And with that there was a flutter of wings that brought her wide awake in the still dawn—everything still soaked and dripping from the rain.

Wet and cold she goes over to the goats that are bleating in their pen and releases them—and drives them into the woods, in the direction of the ridge that leads down into the Big Canyon.

4
Act of True Creation

When Lucas had driven into the yard to occupy his new house in Las Palomas he had been pleasantly surprised to see that except for two big pieces of farm machinery the junk that had been lying around had been carted away. The door now opened easily. And he found the inside immaculately clean. In the kitchen were a table, four chairs, a set of shelves on which were some dishes and pots and pans, and standing in a corner even two pails for hauling water. In the other room were a bed with fresh-smelling sheets and a colorful wool blanket as well as a large metal foot locker.

It took him all of 15 minutes to move in his things from the truck and to bring over two pails of water from the school yard. He had a new home in Mexico. He was elated but tired, and it getting dark, went right to bed.

In the morning he woke up to the shouts of children in the schoolyard. Soon afterwards Manuel drove up in a borrowed pickup and handed him a padlock and a key, and then unloaded a tank of propane for the stove and immediately set about connecting it. As Lucas waited for some hot water for coffee to boil, Manuel told him the only thing he owed was 30 dollars for the gas.

Lucas setting on the table two coffee cups with spoons, a bowl of sugar, and a bag of cookies, said, "You know what Manuel?—I already feel like I've always lived in this place—it fits me like an old favorite pair of pants—and with you and Consuelo being so hospitable—now I can't leave even if I wanted to."

"You find yourself a nice good-looking Mexican woman—someone like that young school teacher over there—and you will never leave."

"I counted twenty kids this morning—and someone dressed in jeans and a snug T-shirt and a baseball cap—who must have been her—she wasn't any taller than the tallest child."

"That was her—Hermelinda—she was born here in Las Palomas—but then when she finished primary school the family went off to Chihuahua

City—where she went to high school and then to the university—she married an engineer there—and left him—and now has come back to take care of her grandmother—who in return takes care of her two year old when she is teaching—all the young roosters around here knock on her door—and the not so young anymore too."

Finishing their coffee, Manuel stood up and said, "Well Lucas—welcome to Las Palomas—and let us know if there is anything you need."

"I will—here—take the rest of the cookies back to the house with you."

After Manuel left, Lucas stood there in the doorway looking over at the school and school yard, everyone now inside. He would start out his stay in las Palomas by listening to the stories of some of its people. And of course eventually he would introduce himself to Hermelinda.

The next morning, he having just emerged from the outhouse, a red four-wheel drive pickup more expensive than the pickup he himself drove pulled up alongside him and stopped, the engine still running. The driver poking his Stetsoned head out of the window said good morning and that he was Polo—the face under the Stetson browner than most and very smooth and clear-complexioned and that of someone who could be in his late twenties.

"Good morning to you too Polo—I'm Lucas."

"Manuel told me about you—that you're a friend of Jesse—and speak some Spanish—and want to get to know Mexico—so I've come by to invite you out to my ranch—going toward La Junta it's the first dirt track that goes south—my Aunt Adriana will fix you a meal that the dead would turn over in their graves for—how about this Saturday morning?"

"I'll be there."

"Good—well with your permission—I'm off—I have to take some cows to the stock yards in La Junta—nice meeting you."

"Likewise."

And pushing a button on his radio Polo rumbled off to the sound of blaring *ranchera* music—Mexican style country—for all the village to hear.

Late in the afternoon, as Lucas was washing the windows of his truck, Manuel came by again, this time with Consuelo, to make absolutely sure there was nothing he needed or needed help with. Lucas said no, especially since he would be going over to Buena Vista soon to pick up his mail and a few other things.

When he asked them about Polo they told him that he managed a ranch whose lands seemed to go on forever, all the way to the Sierra Rica, and which was owned by a rich businessman who lived in Chihuahua City. They also told him that Polo was a champion bronc rider, and that the women along the border considered him as good-looking as a man comes, and that a few years back two photographers had showed up to take some pictures of him that were to be used in a cigarette ad

Polo was also, they told him, a border legend—having been immortalized in song by Gregorio in one of his *corridos.*

Consuelo said, "Go talk to old Gregorio—he tells the story better than anyone—we're on our way to his house right now—to buy one of his small pigs."

"Tell him one of these days soon I'll be stopping by."

Manuel, as he and Consuelo were about to walk away, said, "There's maybe one more thing I should tell you—and that is that everyone here in Las Palomas knows that somewhere out on that vast ranch—Polo grows a few premium marihuana plants on the side."

As Gregorio told it to Lucas, when Polo was sixteen he had worked for a while as a wrangler at the tourist stables over in La Perla, the next community down river from El Polvo on the American side and near to where the Rio Grande enters the first of several majestic sheer-walled canyons that cut through the mountains of the Big Bend.

"These days it's mostly a sprinkling of white renegades from the big cities up north—desert rat and wild river guide and make believe cowboy and cowgirl types—tanned and burnt some of them darker than us Mexicans—living off the tourist trade or by painting pretty pictures—and all of them freedom and adventure loving—like the desert loves a long hard rain."

Reading something in Lucas' demeanor, Gregorio said, "Yeah Lucas—weirdoes like you—if that's what you're thinking."

"Anyway—what happened was that this Polo kid took a hankering for the not bad-looking blonde La Perla post mistress—an Amy—at least twice his age—such that he would keep showing up at the counter to buy a few stamps he did not need—until one day she invited him over to her house trailer for lunch—maybe even just thinking to be kind—like a mother—who really knows."

Gregorio lit up a cigarette, and then said, "Halfway through dessert Polo shoved a hand down under her blouse until he grabbed tit and right then too she kissed him hard on the mouth—and when his other hand went up under her skirt it touched a wetness like the Rio Grande overflowing its banks—and that was when she said, No, Polo, that no—in spite of which he easily sank her down onto the rug—and undoing his pants even more easily entered both her and the land of pure bliss as she moaned, Oh my God, Oh my God."

Gregorio pauses to suck on his cigarette.

"And right then something in her suddenly disconnected—and she tried to push him off—just as his body exploded with a long piecing cry that frightened the wits out of her."

"With a rage ready to kill she said in her broken Spanish—You young punk Mexican—you actually god-damn raped me—I can't believe this happened."

And violently pushing him off of her she got up and went off now raging in English to where her phone was—and began dialing. While Polo, as scared as he had ever been in his life, slipped out the door for Mexico.

The sheriff when he arrived said that he was sorry but there was nothing he could do except report the incident to the Mexican authorities.

Her version of what happened spread like wildfire through La Perla, inflaming the citizenry, whose reaction was, "Shit on borders."

And that very night, four masked adventurers from La Perla, armed with rifles and magnum revolvers, waded the Rio Grande over to Las Palomas—where they were able to find and break in on Polo asleep in his bed. And before the sea of denials could get too loud they stuffed a rag in his mouth, and then tying his hands, they led him with a rope snugged around his neck back across the river and onto American soil.

And there they stripped him buck-naked and tied him to a tree. And jeered at him—before making a phone call to the sheriff, and another to the post mistress.

"That's him all right," she told the sheriff and a small crowd of her gawking and proud fellow citizens.

But a triumph that was short-lived—lasting not even as long as a pitahya cactus is in bloom.

Because before the week was out the news spread again like wildfire that a ragged band of armed Mexicans had showed up at the Buena Vista jail at a sleepy four o'clock in the morning and without having had to fire a shot had plucked Polo in his orange prison pajamas from his cell—leaving in his place three buck-naked prison guards.

Gregorio said, "I called the *corrido* I wrote *"Paloma Blanca Ingrata"*—the guitar needs new strings—drop by in a few days and I'll play it for you—along with the ones about the Wall and the shooting of Lorenzo—I like to give people stories to live in—so they know who they are."

Lucas said, "In English it translates as *Unappreciative White Dove*—I'd love to hear it—and the other two too."

That evening, when Lucas takes a smoked ham he had bought in Buena Vista over to Manuel and Consuelo, Manuel says, "We just found out that that son of ours Jesse has set out from El Polvo leading a packed burro in the direction of El Paso—supposedly to talk to the people on the American side of the river about I'm not exactly sure what—except that it has something to do with the Wall."

Consuelo says, "For you to understand his obsession with the Wall better—I will tell you one of the stories we all grew up on here along the river— do you believe in witches?"

The question catching Lucas by surprise, he pauses, before saying, "I tend to believe that certain sensitive persons—who are very tuned to the reality of the present—can through their imagination—intuit what may have happened in the past—and what may come about in the future."

"And I also think that certain persons may have what appears to be an excess of some kind of energy inside them—which they are able to forcefully direct to help or harm others."

Manuel says, "That means he believes in them."

Consuelo continues.

"The village of El Valle—those houses you can see across the big arroyo that comes down from the Sierra Rica—gave birth about 200 years ago—to a coven of witches.

"When the border was established—splitting the world in two—the witches in El Valle became very alarmed and excited—and with the fiber from sotol leaves they collected out in the desert—braided a very long rope—it took them a year—and then with the help of burros—they packed one end up to the Sierra Rica and tied it around the largest rock pinnacle they could find—the other end they packed up to the top of Chinati Peak on the American side and tied it too around a rock pinnacle—such that the rope hung in the air with its lowest part suspended about one hundred feet in the air over the Rio Grande."

"Up and down along the river people began talking—What is this? What can anyone—even witches—do with such a long rope?"

Consuelo refills Lucas' cup with more coffee. And Lucas can tell she is already beginning to wear down from talking more than she is used to.

"Then one night—when the moon was bright and full—both towns woke up to a tremendous swooooosh—and five minutes later there was another tremendous swooooosh—and another—for almost an hour they lasted."

"The next morning the priest from El Polvo waded the river and told the people in Las Palomas he thought that he had been able to make out—overhead and silhouetted against the moon—four women strapped to seats with holes in the bottom—with their long skirts hefted above their waists—swinging back and forth across the river—from Mexico over to the United States and from the United States back to Mexico."

"That night everyone in Las Palomas, El Polvo, and El Valle was outside— looking up at the big round moon—waiting for more swooooooshes—and as the first swooooosh descended upon their heads—they all saw with their own eyes the four figures and that the priest had been right."

"Some said they thought they could also hear voices singing gleefully up there in the night sky—and words that sounded like, *Que caiga la mierda nuestra sobre todas las fronteras.*"

Manuel laughing and in some barely recognizable English, says, "Yes Lucas—more or less We shi-it on oll borthas—was what some of them heard."

On Lucas' second visit to Gregorio's place he finds Gregorio watering some tomato plants, their tomatoes still small and green.

"Let me get the guitar—and also bring out some of the bean and cheese burritos the wife made this morning—do you want chile macho in yours?"

"You bet—otherwise it's a mighty sorry burrito. "

Gregorio reappearing with the guitar and burritos, says, "You want to buy a pig?—I got one left."

"Maybe once I marry—when there will be more kitchen scraps to throw it."

Lucas grabbing a burrito, says, "I ran into Polo yesterday—I mentioned *"Paloma Blanca Ingrata"*—and we got to talking—and he told me that American women are pushovers—the only trouble with them being that when their brains want it their bodies don't—and when their bodies want it their brains don't."

"He has women and how irresistible he is to them on the brain—and it could be that it no longer works right—and that is why all his women leave him."

Lucas says, "Being born good-looking—or very smart—isn't always a blessing."

"And my *corrido* about him—blaring out of every radio all along the river—only made him worse."

Gregorio takes a bite of burrito, chews it slowly.

"Lucas—I know this contradicts what I said the other day about giving people stories to live in—but as I get older I am beginning to see that a story can turn anything into absolutely anything—and that people take their stories too seriously—deceive themselves and others with them—cry about them—and even kill for them."

"You know what Lucas?—sometimes I think I should stop writing *corridos*—and just stick to playing my guitar."

"Yeah—but before you throw them all into the fire—sing me the three you promised me."

Lucas parks in front of the long ranch house built of quarried limestone blocks and that Gregorio had told him had once been part of one of the haciendas of someone whose land holdings before the Revolution totaled many millions of acres. An elderly woman peeks out a door, who he assumes is Adriana. He waves to her. Then seeing Polo in the corral where he is shoeing a horse, he goes over to watch.

The horse's hind leg stretched backward and resting on and gripped between Polo's thighs, Polo holds a horseshoe against the hoof with one hand as with the other he pounds in a nail. With the claw of the hammer he twists off the sharp protruding tip. At Lucas' approach the horse tries to jerk its leg away but Polo shouting, *Cabrón*—holds on to it. And then does the remaining nails that he had been holding between his lips.

Polo looking over toward Lucas, says, "This is the last shoe—give me another ten minutes to finish up."

Lucas saunters over to some cottonwood trees and slides down a bank into an arroyo. Where he stands for a while by its clear flowing water that he sees has its source about fifty feet up the arroyo at a pool surrounded by reeds of cat tails. He squats and sticks a hand into the water, cups a hand and drinks. Stands back up—and follows the flow down the arroyo for a hundred yards to where it disappears in the sand.

The heat this early is already intense, a heat that has by now become for him something that simply is—like the blue cloudless sky. And like the jackrabbit that he right then scares up and that darts zigzagging through the green creosote.

When he returns to the corral, he says to Polo, " That little spring—in the middle of all this desert—it was like stumbling onto another world—and left me with something resembling—well maybe a kind of faith."

"You want to see an even prettier place?—I'll take you out to where I farm some marijuana."

Lucas a bit startled, says, "How do you know I'm not an American Drug Enforcement Agent?"

"You are such an odd ball—and so transparent—that they would never take you—also—from talking to Manuel and Jesse I know that you are not."

"Let's go then."

"I'll go grab a couple of burritos and beers—and let Aunt Adriana know we'll be back for dinner."

When Polo returns they climb into his red pickup. And set out joggling and bouncing along a desert track where a vehicle has gone before. Across flat creosote desert, across dry arroyos, and in the sandy rocky beds of others. Now and then scraping against tall spindly spiny sticks of ocotillo.

And then, the landscape changing, winding up and down and around yucca, candelilla, and sotol-covered ridges and hills—the pickup now throwing up rocks as they lurch upward, shaking Lucas' bones so that they rattle.

The pickup comes to a stop above an east-west running canyon. They climb out, pick their way past cat claw and low dark-green dagger-like lechuguilla over to the its very edge—from where they look almost two hundred feet straight down to the bottom of the vertical gash carved by eons of flood waters eroding the solid rock.

"You good at climbing Lucas?—stick close behind me but be careful not to kick any rocks down on my head—if we get to a spot where you think you might fall—well let me know before you do."

Lucas follows Polo along the canyon rim—and then down into a narrow crack a little wider than the width of a man and into which Polo has disappeared. Lucas carefully climbs his way downward over ledges and large boulders, almost every move requiring him to hold on with both hands. He is aware of the delightful coolness of the canyon's deep shade—and also that Polo with his bronc rider strength and agility is constantly having to stop to wait up for him.

Finally his feet drop onto the sand of the arroyo, where he finds himself hemmed in by two smooth red and streaked with yellow sheer canyon walls.

He a little disoriented, hears Polo say, "That is absolutely the only way down into this part of the canyon—see that high rock wall up canyon?—on top is a ten-foot deep pot hole that swirling water and sand and stones have gouged into the rock—a *tinaja*—which because not much sun gets to it holds water from when it rains all year long—the hose you see coming from it runs the water to my plants."

"There's another even higher vertical rock wall pour off right behind the pool—and just down canyon around the bend is another high vertical pour off—blocking access from below too."

Lucas' eyes follow the hose that traverses a wall of the canyon, to where—still a good 20 feet above them—he sees a cave, with some tall green plants at the entrance.

"I threw tons of good dirt and compost down into here—and then hauled it all by rope and bucket up to the cave—there was even some bat manure in the cave—the best fertilizer there is—and since the cave faces south—just enough sun gets in."

Lucas takes a good look around him—centering himself in this so new, strange, and exhilarating place.

Notices the many clusters of yellow flowers and the red blooming cacti that are growing here and there in the cracks of the rock walls.

In the utter stillness, he listens to a series of beautiful sparkling clear descending notes of a bird he cannot see, its song amplified by so much rock.

"That's a canyon wren—this is their home—they need rock walls to bounce their song off of."

"Polo—what you have going here—is beautiful—like a work of art—only real—it's—an act of true creation."

"I thought you might like it—that's why I brought you here—I enjoy working down in here better than anything else—I'm not trying to get rich—

just earn a little extra cash for a new truck now and then and to keep me in nice boots—well I'm going to climb up and check the plants—and make sure no holes in the drip irrigation hoses are clogged—you wait here because I rather doubt you could make it up there."

Lucas watches as Polo, putting his fingers and toes onto invisible holds, climbs up to the cave—disappear among the plants.

The cactus wren sings again. And again. And several more times.

Polo works his way back down the rock face to Lucas.

"I've never had anything to do with the Mafia—a cousin of mine takes what I grow to the States when he goes up there to pick apples—but you tell me—what does more brain damage?—sitting around smoking some pot with a few friends—or watching television?"

Polo as he starts back up the crack, says, "Especially when there's a pretty woman in skimpy clothes—smiling out at you—and a guy can't even exchange looks with her—much less touch her."

Lucas liked watching Hermelinda in the school yard as she played volley ball and tag with the children, she laughing and yelling and indistinguishable from them—and he liked watching her when she just stood around talking to a few of them.

Occasionally one pickup or another would come to a stop near her, the driver then chatting for a while with her through the window. From the animated way she moved her hands and body and swung her head he saw she was not at all shy with men.

He had been intentionally waiting a while before introducing himself—not wanting to appear too obvious a part of the line up knocking at her door, as Manuel had put it.

But this morning, during a moment when she was standing apart from the children, he went over and introduced himself. She immediately lit up.

"So how does someone from the big world—and an American no less—wind up in Las Palomas?

"Maybe because I very much enjoy the Mexicans I've so far met who live along the river—and who are still a part of an older way of life that is completely missing in my country."

He went on to explain how by living on the Mexican side he also hoped to be able to look at life from a vantage point different from the one he had been brought up and educated in.

"It seems that much of what I learned in school—instead of opening my eyes—mostly served to tuck me more snugly into my own very comfortable culture."

"Most of my relatives living in Chihuahua City believe that the only valuable human beings are the one's with a university education—but now that I am back where I grew up I am beginning to wonder whether through education people perhaps lose certain human qualities that are more valuable than the education—as a teacher it is something I think about often—and need to think about some more."

Two girls come up to them, and Hermelinda smiling at them, says to Lucas, "Why not come by the house tomorrow afternoon for coffee?—say about five—and we can visit some more—do you know where I live?"

"Yes—I'll be there."

"And now—Berta and Myra—what can I do for you?"

As Lucas walks slowly back to his house, he cannot help thinking, "She is not only beautiful—and nice—but alive and natural in a way that Denise could never begin to be."

The next afternoon, a little before five, Lucas drives the half mile over to the grandmother's house.

Hermelinda who is standing outside and seeing him pull up goes over to the pickup, and after a minute of small talk, takes him over to one of two chairs set out under an orange tree. Then she runs into the house—returning shortly with a tray on which are two tall glasses of what she tells him is mango-guayaba juice and also two dishes with spoons lying on top of what looks to him like custard.

"I thought you might appreciate something more refreshing than hot coffee—my daughter's asleep—and grandmother is out visiting."

Just then a bright red pick up blaring *ranchera* music approaches—and immediately turns around, roaring away toward where it came from.

"I suspect that when Polo saw your pickup—he changed his mind about showing up here—he comes by a lot even though I never invite him—he's told me he's wildly passionate—burning up for me—that I'm the only woman he's ever wanted to marry—which is what I'm sure he tells all the women."

"I've heard that that's how many Mexican men are—very—well insistent."

"That's true—in Mexico—the intense instinctual biological forces that exist for connecting men and women—and the family—was until very recently—very much at the center."

Hermelinda hesitates for a moment, as if wondering whether to continue.

"We women—in the past—have always wanted a man who radiated vitality and virility—and who was valiant and stoic—and astute—and not subservient to others."

"But now we women—who I feel ultimately do the choosing—are choosing more and more for other reasons—like me marrying an engineer partly for social prestige—and because we talked so well together about things like politics and the movies—and both liked American spaghetti."

A vivid image of himself with Denise on their first date, digging into their shrimp cocktails, which they both loved—floats slowly by in the space between them.

"Now—more than half of our families—at least in Chihuahua City—are destined for wreckage—just like in your country."

He dips his spoon into his custard.

"It's called flan—I baked it for you—do you like it?"

"It's delicious."

"I'm very sorry—I don't know what overcame me—blurting out what I did—it was so—not Mexican.

"It could be that when Polo drove up—it upset you."

They finish their flan and mango-guayaba drink in silence.

Lucas asks her how she likes teaching here in Las Palomas.

"I am trying my best—in this country known mainly for its political corruption and Mafia violence—to nurture in these children the moral character that will give them dignity and make them proud to be Mexican—and proud to be human beings—a moral character congruent with the highest ideals of our Revolution—which simultaneously succeeded and failed—but whose spirit still lives on among some of us."

"That's really beautiful."

Inside the house a child begins to scream.

"Come over for dinner this Sunday afternoon—and we can visit some more—you no doubt are living on bought tortillas that you don't even bother to heat up—grandmother and I will fix something nice."

They say good bye, and as Lucas walks to his truck he cannot help wondering whether—just maybe—she has chosen him.

5

Far Journey

A bag of *pinole* and a small wooden bowl hanging from the sash around his waist and a blanket and a gourd of water slung across a shoulder, Benito steps along in his tire-tread huaraches.

He is following in reverse a route which very long ago had been traveled by a procession of brown-skinned people speaking strange tongues and accompanying a bearded white man and a black man, both of whom may have been Gods. The bearded white God, wild-eyed and chanting and dancing, was said to have cured many that the Tarahumara shamans could not—and was also said to have passed on to the poor the many gifts that were brought to him.

So Benito's grandfather had told him his own grandfather had told him.

Benito is almost out of the pine and oak-forested Sierra Tarahumara. Ahead of and below him a broad expanse of grassland, golden yellow in the weak November sunlight, extends to the horizon. Beyond—is the vast arid Chihuahuan Desert toward which he is headed.

He has undertaken this journey of several hundred miles for the purpose of collecting peyote, which grows along with sotol and candelilla not far from the border pueblo of La Junta and on certain limestone ridges known since ancestral times to his people. On countless previous occasions he along with a small group of men had made the same journey for this plant—which would be used by the shaman in his curing ceremonies.

As he moves along it never quite leaves his mind that going off alone to collect peyote is a breach of tradition. Nor will the peyote he collects be used in curing ceremonies for the people.

However when one is very old one has a certain right to do such things he had decided.

And besides, surely having learned to read at the table of a friendly Padre and also having once worked as an interpreter for an American ethnographer has made him different from the others.

For he has read and heard many things—much more than a Tarahumara needs to know.

For example that very long ago, groups of nomadic hunter gatherers—sometimes referred to as the Basket Weaver People—migrated out of the deserts of what is now Nevada and Utah.

And that some went north into what is now Idaho to eventually become known as the Shoshone People. While others moved east and south, and picking up the rudiments of agriculture from the Pueblo People, continued southward into what is now Mexico, some of them becoming known as the People Fleet-footed Like Deer, or Tarahumara.

Those continuing even further southward became known as Huichols—and those continuing further southward yet, Aztecs.

The bearded white man who might have been a God he was told was Cabeza de Vaca, a shipwrecked Spaniard making his way to the Gulf of California to rejoin his people.

All of that could be, Benito had decided—many things could be.

He has read that other bearded white Gods walk about on the face of Mother Moon. However he, Benito, who has dream-traveled to Mother Moon many times has never seen them.

The peyote he will use to help him spend his remaining days close to the Mystery that is God-Father-Sun and that is Onorúgame. And to help him see into life more deeply and more clearly, so as to be able to continue to walk well in the world, meaning impeccably and with dignity.

In a world that for him has begun to become increasingly complicated and confusing—very cloudy.

As one step follows another it also never quite leaves his mind how tired he feels all over, more tired than he remembers having ever felt—he who once fleet-footed as a deer could have run the entire distance.

He Benito who has always considered a good man to be two strong legs and a pure soul.

Arriving at the first of the several paved highway he will cross, he waits for three roaring loaded logging trucks followed by a gleaming white pickup to go by.

He crosses, and begins thinking, as he often does, how fast the world of the Tarahumara for so long immune to what the world calls Progress is changing.

Gnarling bulldozers pushing aside trees and dirt and blasted-out rock wherever a road can be put—mainly to haul logs out on, along with tons of marijuana. More and more tourists with cameras dangling from their necks gawking at what they perceive as the exotic Tarahumara.

Tarahumara, even those from the most remote ranchos, on foot, and riding on the backs of logging trucks, sometimes families, sometimes entire communities, headed to the nearest Chabochi pueblo to receive their government payments and to buy sacks of sugar and white flour and to eat cookies and to drink cokes.

Most of his people now living in tin-roofed Chabochi-style adobe houses. Young men with a little education and with some marijuana dollars in their pockets strutting about in cowboy hats and with their giant boom boxes—and displacing the elders as community leaders.

And worst of all—*tesguino*, a beer traditionally made in tall clay *ollas* from fermented sprouted corn, the very special gift of Onorúgame to his children, gradually being replaced by *tempache*, which the people make in plastic buckets with warm water and store-bought sugar and yeast.

And without even any longer inviting Onorúgame to drink and get happily drunk with them.

Nor is there any end to this demon weed extending its tentacles in the bright Sierra sun—the delicate fine tips groping down into and filtering through the pores and cracks of the hardest rock of the deepest and most sheer-walled canyons.

And into the very soul marrow of the people.

Only among the very old do a few still know the meaning of walking well through life—and the usefulness of peyote and talking to the Gods for accomplishing that.

More than once the American had pointed out to him that it does not take swords and guns and epidemics to exterminate the ancient ways of an indigenous people.

"Benito—the Tarahumara lost most of their old ways four hundred years ago—with the arrival of the first Spanish missionaries—who brought with them oxen, goats, sheep, and chickens—and fruit trees—and the steel ax—and who taught your people how to plow and to fertilize their lands with manure."

"And precisely all that Benito—is what made it possible for the Tarahumara to retreat into these cold rocky Sierra and its rugged canyons—and to reestablish themselves where others could more or less not bother them—and so survive."

"That may well be—however the new changes that are now happening are not necessary for our survival—nor do they help the people to live better or well."

By late afternoon Benito arrives at where the last oak tree gives way to endless treeless grassland. He sits down in its shade on some matted leaves where recently a deer has bedded.

He pours water from the gourd into his wooden bowl and adds some *pinole*—which mixture he then stirs with a finger and drinks.

He glances down at some fresh deer droppings. He has heard that it was the deer who taught his people to dance *Yumari*—to move like, to be for a while deer. That could very well be, since sometimes he feels very much a wild animal—most at home wandering across the land and resting under this and that tree.

He lies down on his back, the blanket folded under his head. Closes his eyes—feeling very very tired.

He gives himself up to images from the past, of his rancho, known to his neighbors as El Divisadero—The Overlook.

In front of a small rock hut roofed with pine shake shingles a Tarahumara woman is squatting beside a smoky fire and baking thick corn tortillas on a stone *comal* that is set upon three rocks. Like all Tarahumara women she is wearing a colorful long-sleeved blouse, an ample flowered skirt over another one, a kerchief, and tire-tread huaraches, hers worn very thin.

A naked little Benito arrives and drops some sticks of firewood by her and the woman as she pats out a tortilla flashes him a smile that lights up their universe of wild rugged peaks and canyons.

The young man Benito, his head back and both hands holding the half-shell of a squash gourd, gulps *tesguino*. Then smiling broadly, passes the empty gourd back to the server. From miles around, from tiny ranchos hanging in the cliffs, the neighbors have come to drink for two days straight.

Men and brightly-dressed women—talking loudly and freely and laughing, some with arms around each other. Dancing. Singing off key. Shouting across the canyon.

At dark, a blanket under an arm, he staggers off with Mari Elena, the pretty wife of Perfecto, into the woods, she leading him by the hand until she falling pulls him down with her and on top of her.

A white-haired Benito rests two oxen from the task of plowing a rock-strewn field almost too steep to stand on—which a little before the summer rains begin he will plant to corn, beans, and squash.

His wife Luisa appears. And he leaving the oxen standing quietly in the field, the two of them go over to some tall ponderosa pines on the canyon rim. Where for a while they stand looking straight down on the tiny patches of green of the banana, orange, and mango groves of the *rancheria* of some neighbors far below.

Then they sit down together to eat the tamales filled with goat meat that Luisa has brought

A goat bell tinkles in the distant cliffs, where their granddaughter Jesusita, now seven, is herding the goats she takes out every day and in every weather.

The next day Benito and his son Chalelo leave to finish splitting roof shakes from sections of a straight-grained pine tree they have felled—leaving Luisa and Chalelo's wife Felipa to scrape away the spines from the *nopales*, the prickly pear pads they have gathered.

After a supper of corn tortillas and beans boiled with diced *nopales*, Benito, Luisa, Felipa, and Jesusita and her older sister Carmen all lay out their blankets on the dirt floor in the single small room and soon fall asleep to the repetitive strains of the atonal Tarahumara music that Chalelo is playing on his violin.

That he plays far into the night.

The Tarahumara—free and self sufficient in a way others will never understand. Having known defeat and humiliation, but never conquest and domination at the hands of the Spanish.

The Tarahumara—drinking their *tesguino*. Blissful release from the cares and obligations and the work and drudgery of daily existence. Blissful conviviality with the neighbors. The only thing one never tires of.

The Tarahumara—taught from birth to maintain themselves aloof from the corrupt selfish world of the white-bearded Chabochi Devil that surrounds them.

When Benito opens his eyes, the plain is bathed in soft moonlight from a big round moon that has just cleared the horizon.

"Mother Moon, it is time to visit you again—I have many questions—I now find it very difficult to walk over the land—and through life in the way I know I am supposed to."

"And so it is once again time to call up the big goatskin-covered drum—to help me dream travel to you—like the shaman who now lives up there in the sky with you long ago taught me—and that I then learned to do without the drum."

As Benito gazes into the night, concentrating with all his might, out of somewhere begins to sound a faint steady rapid baam-baam-baam-baam-baam that becomes louder and louder, overcoming, slowly disintegrating the plain, and the night with its moon and stars.

BAAM-BAAM-BAAM-BAAM-BAAM-BAAM-BAAM.

Suddenly Benito finds himself hurling headfirst down a long smooth winding tunnel—that after a timeless interval spews him out tumbling into daylight and gently onto soft green grass.

Smiling, he stands up, marveling at the deep purple sky he finds himself under. He hoots four times.

Is surprised when trotting gracefully toward him, barely touching the green grass, comes not the deer that had so recently abandoned her bed under the oak tree and that he been expecting—but a sleek red fox.

She exquisitely and wildly beautiful.

"Why you are huge—as big as a deer."

The fox, raising her tail high, making herself appear even larger, says, "No—you have shrunk and are now rather tiny—that way it will be easier for me to take you to Mother Moon—who will tell you—you for whom the world has turned very cloudy and swirling and unknowable—that you are now in fact beginning to see very clearly."

"If that is so—I will need to hear it from Mother Moon."

"Bah—any fox knows that its only job is to survive as best it can—and to join up with a mate—and by that means replace the foxes that have left for the stars."

"And that beyond that—there exists only the mire of human illusion."

"But as you like—Benito."

The fox dropping down onto her belly, Benito throws himself onto her back. He positions himself, gripping her solidly with his legs and with both hands the fur of her neck.

She shakes her head once, then gets back up, tenses—as Benito becomes aware in legs and crotch of being connected to an energy so extraordinarily alive and vital that it could be the same one that fires the Universe.

The fox leaps upwards into the deep purple sky that just like that changes back to dark night with its Mother Moon and stars—Benito thrilled and tingling all over, as they fly, fly, fly incredibly fast toward Mother Moon.

Who grows rapidly larger before them.

Stunned by the raw beauty of this wild fox and of Mother Moon and the stars—it strikes him forcefully that in some fashion he may have known this very fox since before the world began.

Suddenly from all sides they are joined by more foxes, and more and more foxes—until Benito finds himself in the midst of a raging churning river of foxes.

A flow that unexpectedly veers away from and toward one edge of the now looming Mother Moon, Benito now frantically tugging at neck fur to turn his fox back on course, feeling very confused and helpless.

Having never so lost control of a dream journey before.

He gives up the pointless struggle. And now, Mother Moon well behind them, dark night turns to bright day. Legs and hands relax—loosen their grip.

Benito is smiling—as he awaits his place among the stars.

In the morning, Father Sun slaps the peaceful almost blissful face of an old man wrapped in a blanket under an oak tree. And once again. But to no avail.

6

The Last Real Man

Lucas looks on as a mounted vaquero separates a calf from the cows with calves that are milling about in the corral—the horse quickly moving left or right to block the dodging and panicked animal's attempts to return to its mother. The calf is driven into a narrow holding chute.

Where it bawling, two other vaqueros vaccinate, brand, and castrate it.

Polo says, "When they grow up they get shipped to the United States where they are fattened on corn—before going to the table."

Lucas ponders the horse culture brought over to the New World by the Spanish and based on the total domination of freedom-loving wild animals—the corrals, the ropes, the steel bits in the mouth, the spurs, and the whips producing the docile well-behaved horse that does what is asked of it.

And for a moment he thinks about how the whole of civilization rests upon the domestication of human beings, they too trained to give up their freedom and to do what is asked of them.

He asks Polo what he knows about the Tarahumara.

"They live in caves in the cliffs of western Chihuahua—in canyons so deep and sheer that not even the birds make it down to the bottom—and where they grow corn and beans on patches of stony land so steep they have to hold on to keep from falling off into space."

Polo continues, "Having climbed up and down those canyons all their lives—has made the men able to run down a deer until its hooves are bloody and it drops from exhaustion."

Lucas says, "They seem like an interesting and amazing people—to have kept that kind of primitive culture more or less alive for so long."

"What they are—are wild uncivilized savages—and the darker ones—the ones that mixed with African slaves that escaped from the mines—are the wildest of all."

"Have you ever spent any time among them?"

"No way—they see us Mexicans as children of the Devil—and some of us—who they have considered to be intruders—they have killed."

"I asked only because how you describe those people does not match the impression a mother and daughter who came up to my table in La Junta left me with."

"That is because the women one sees begging in the streets have permanently broken with the culture of the canyons—now preferring the noise and bustle of towns—in La Junta an old warehouse has been donated for them to camp out in—and churches and stores give them food."

"And the men?"

"They mostly stay out of sight—drinking up the money their women and children bring home."

Polo smiling, asks, "Was the mother pretty—did you want to take her home with you.?

When Lucas does not answer—Polo says, "Because forget it—several times now I've tried to get one of them to hop into my truck—but they won't answer me or even look at me—just run off or into a store—to hell with them."

The horseman drives another calf into the chute.

"You are a good man Lucas—but damn it—you have a way of not saying things and watching that sometimes makes me—decked out as I am in my white hat and new boots and with a wad of bills in my back pocket—feel naked and dumb—as naked and dumb as some spear-throwing Tarahumara in his loin cloth—who doesn't even know what an ocean is."

Hermelinda's grandmother says to Lucas, "It's chicken mole with rice—the mole sauce is made with chocolate and chile."

Lucas seeing them eat using a piece of flour tortilla for a spoon—does the same.

"Delicious."

After finishing their chicken mole they each eat a big slice of cake with thick pink frosting.

Hermelinda says, "One of the children brought the cake to school this morning and gave it to me as a present—I had to promise to bring it home and not to eat it with them in the classroom—sometimes someone brings eggs—or a live chicken."

Hermelinda and Lucas go outside and sit down under the orange tree, looking out across the desert toward the Sierra Rica, lit golden by the sinking sun.

Lucas says, "Coming over here I passed a stake truck full of soldiers—I suppose they are here to try to stop the drug traffic."

"Only the small time traffickers—the Mafia has the money to pay off the generals—and the politicians and the police—going after the independent entrepreneurs insures that the Mafia has no competition—and at the same time makes it appear that Mexico is trying to solve the drug problem."

She pauses

"There are those who say that another reason for the army presence is to discourage another Revolution—because here in the North—with Pancho Villa and others—is where it all started—stripping the Terrazas-Creel clan of their enormous land holdings and of their control of all Chihuahua."

She takes another piece of cake.

"Villa and his Army of the North—who taught himself to read and write—and who took from the rich and gave to the poor—not out of ideology—but out of an intuitive sense of fairness—and for that labeled by some as a radical socialist—and even a communist."

She eats a fork full of cake.

"This is very good—no one ever brought me a cake before—would you like more.

"May as well."

She puts a slice on his plate.

"You are probably aware that in the south the Maya Indians rebelled not all that long ago—not only to regain their old lands—and to end the exploitation by international corporations—but also against an entire way of thinking that values money and profits at the expense of people."

Lucas says, "It's my impression that what makes Mexico unique—some Americans would say enigmatic—is precisely its indigenous past—that still lies so close to the surface."

"I think that is true—because unlike in your country—the indigenous people here—through the Church—and through marriage with the Spanish—wound up to some extent incorporated into society—and so their very different way of seeing the world was never entirely extinguished."

"Because I turned out darker than most—I am especially conscious of that heritage—I've been called *La Prieta*—the dark one—which is of course an insult."

She pauses, then goes on.

"What indigenous people have always valued most of all—is their independence and freedom to do as they please—the total opposite of the authoritarianism the Spanish brought with them to the New World—which of course made them useless for working in the mines—or for anyone."

Lucas says, "In my country—people are unaware that that kind of freedom even exists—for them freedom means being able to choose among forty flavors of ice cream."

Hermelinda smiles, and says, "Indigenous people also like to give and share—even when food is scarce—while what I see across the river to the north—is a people who believe the answer to limited resources is appropriating them for themselves—and that is a very profound difference."

"These days there are voices that support the preservation of indigenous traditions—by which they usually mean the dances, the colorful dress, and the baskets and other *artesanía*—however that is not what needs so much to be kept alive—but rather their knowledge of what real freedom is—and sharing."

Lucas decides to shut up and just listen.

"Indigenous people—living as they do in nature—are suspicious of—and one could say even antagonistic toward what others worship as Progress—or maybe I should say the form it has taken."

She takes another bite of cake.

"In Mexico the System operates very blatantly—and so Mexicans I think have a clearer sense of how rotten the System can be—and what those who control it can be like."

"Some of us are all too aware of the lies and machinations and corruption—the limitless greed—and the frivolous ostentation of our handful of very rich—and all too aware not only of their ruthlessness—and that of the drug cartels—but of the ruthlessness of all power—that looks out only for itself—while with impunity stepping on anyone and anything it needs to."

She pauses.

"Americans may consider Mexico an insignificant nowhere place—but it could be that only in such back waters is it possible for new and better ways of living to take hold—ways that are rooted in our indigenous past—and that are not purely legalistic, economic, and technological in nature—and ultimately self serving."

"And so I think your rich and your leaders are very scared of having that kind of Mexico on its border—because what your closed border—your wall symbolizes for many of us is a country that has lost its grip on the kind of power that only true integrity can give—and a country that is now living in fear."

The grandmother sticks her head out the door to say, "Cristina is asleep in her crib—and I myself for some reason being more tired than usual am going to bed—the rest of the cake I left on the table—so then—until tomorrow."

Lucas and Hermelinda say, "Until tomorrow."

The two of them sitting under the orange tree, give themselves up to the twilight hour—letting the desert work its magic.

Lucas is thinking, But might this woman—this fiery little Mexican school teacher—so passionate about wanting to change how modern society—and even the Universe itself works—just possibly be too much for me?—and might she find me just another hopeless smug and complacent Gringo?—

When right then they both simultaneously turn to look down the road—from which and around the bend they can hear what sounds like a raucous discordant singing. But which as it gets closer begins to sound more like chanting.

"Ha la la—dey hey bey—ha la la—dey hey bey—hey ley ley—da ha ba—"

There are three of them, dressed like the old hags they are—who turning up toward the house, head toward the orange tree.

"Ha la la—dey hey bey—and a good evening to you Hermelinda."

"Good evening to you Petronila—and to you Hortensia—and to you Katrina."

"Have you eaten the cake?—the one with the thick pink frosting?"

"Yes—and it was very good—but how did you know about the cake?"

"Because we baked it—ha la la—and folded in a special ingredient—dey hey bey—that as you will find out soon enough—will soon work much more magic on you than has this desert and pretty evening."

Lucas asks Hermelinda, "Who are these nuts?"

"We are the witches from El Valle—ha la la—descended from a long tradition of witches—dey hey bey—and we do not tolerate those who interfere with the public good—as Hemelinda is doing by not remarrying—the men are not sleeping well—and the furrows they plow are crooked—and they have sown beans where they should have put melon seeds—and the young girls have no one who wants to marry them."

Hermelinda says, "And what am I suppose to do about all that?"

"Why marry this Gringo—and go with him to the other side of the river where he belongs—and leave us over here alone—like life was before you returned from Chihuahua City with your fancy modern airs—and your smell that reaches the noses of all our men."

And with that the three witches of El Valle turn and run off shrieking and giggling back down the road—disappearing around the bend.

"I'm sorry Lucas—I don't feel well—and need to go inside and lie down—until tomorrow."

"Until tomorrow—I don't feel all that great myself—I'll come by the school yard tomorrow to see how you are."

Lucas dizzy and feeling very tired, not quite making it to the door of his house, lies down on his back in the dirt of the yard.

Hearing footsteps approaching, he raises his head, and sees, lit up by the moon, the tire sandal huaraches, and then the kerchiefed head of the Tarahumara woman he had yearned to take home with him.

Who dark-skinned like the night, lies down alongside him, and in a Spanish not as good as his, says, "Very long ago—Onorúgame—the Great Father of the Tarahumara people—offered them a choice between what you and I are about to do—and eternal life."

"That's interesting—in my country the people just cast their vote for eternal life."

As her hands begin to unbutton his fly, he can feel a part of himself growing big.

A part of him that arching upwards continues to grow, and grow and grow, and to grow—as it penetrates deep into the dark unfathomable mystery of the night.

Hermelinda wakes up to find herself flying joyfully through the moon-lit night sky—soaring left and right, and even doing loops. Not looking where she is going she almost bumps into something extremely long and cylindrical—which as she maneuvers to see it better, seems to have its origin in the village of Las Palomas below her, from where it rises in a gentle arc toward the Sierra Rica.

She follows along it, flying fast like a moonbeam, up to very top of the Sierra Rica. Touches down by a pine tree. And is startled to discover that what is quietly lying at rest there in the tall grass, as thick as a barrel, and animal like, soaking up the moonlight, is the virile tip of what could well be the Lord Creator himself.

She intensely curious, and on an impulse and throwing all caution to the winds, climbs on, straddles it—and begins the long smooth slide back down toward Las Palomas, soon shrieking with delight.

Faster and faster she plummets downward. And then suddenly feeling something begin to convulse under her she screams out to the night.

And screams again as she crashes onto the lap and against the chest—and into the open arms of Polo.

She jumps up out of bed—and rubs her eyes.

"Polo—what are you doing standing by the window—and how did you get into my bedroom?"

"The window was unlocked—the American comes to talk with you—I have come to take you to my ranch and to throw you onto my bed—my horse is tied to the orange tree—waiting for us."

"Men don't do that any more—rob their women like this."

"Real men still do."

"Will you promise anything?"

"The world—and then some."

"We will be—as the Bible puts it—one flesh—and if you ever even look at another woman—I will stick a knife into you and then into her—and watch you both bleed to death."

"Agreed."

"We will make children like there is no stopping."

"What else are men and women for?"

"I will do as I well please."

"Good—then you will not carry inside you a resentment that keeps you from being wild in bed."

"You will stop growing marihuana."

Polo hesitates—before he says, "Lucas said that how I go about it is beautiful—like a work of art—only better."

"You can't put it first—and me too."

"Very well then."

"Give me a minute to get Cristina—and change into a clean pair of jeans—for my man—for the last real man."

◈ ◈ ◈

When the racket of the children across the road woke Lucas up, he sat up with a start, and wondered how the hell he got out there behind the outhouse. Standing up and stretching, the first thing he noticed on this already hot June day was that there was fresh white snow on the Sierra Rica, and wondered about that too.

He walked over to the school yard to find Hermelinda.

He did not see her.

When he asked a group of children who were playing near the swings about her, they all knew that she would not be coming to teach today, since Polo had robbed her in the night. They all knew that at four in the morning he had come crashing through the main street of Las Palomas on his horse with Hermelinda behind him on its rump—both of them singing. Which meant that by now she is married, they explained to him—and clapped their hands.

Later, when Hemelinda's grandmother came by with the rest of the cake, the first thing she said was, "Lucas—I dreamed things last night that no one would ever believe a person could dream—but please don't ask me more—because not even to my Father Confessor will I ever hint at what things I did and saw."

Not until three days later did the snow finally disappear from the Sierra Rica—washed away in the rains of a torrential thunderstorm.

7

Barefoot Beauty of the Canyons

Jesusita was 12 when the soldiers came.

By then she already was known for her striking beauty and for a certain way about her that attracted men perhaps even more than just her raw beauty. Her Uncle Alfredo had already grabbed her at a *tesquinada*, pulling her down onto a blanket and clumsily rolling over onto her, which had left her with a glow between her legs that would not go away for a long time.

After that she became very adept at outwitting and foiling men—unlike her sister Carmen who had had her first child when she was 13 not knowing who the father was or even who he might be.

Carmen was now married to old Candelario, a Chabochi in his early sixties and who had lived for a good many years on the outskirts of the Chabochi pueblo of San Juan, a several hour walk away. His wife of almost a lifetime left him when he took up with her, a Tarahumara. When in retaliation his grown children burned down his very comfortable house, leaving him only the blackened adobe walls, he said, "To hell with you all."

And came to live with the Tarahumara to grow a little corn and beans and to continue his trade as a maker of guitars and violins, and also as a carver of pretty wood bowels and spoons that he took to a pueblo that was a train stop to be sold to the mostly foreign tourists.

A Tarahumara musician for whom he had made a guitar lived with his family in a cave and he had always enjoyed his visits there—sitting on the rock floor looking out at the mountains and eating beans and tortillas around a fire, and that night sleeping in the light of the stars and the moon, and on occasions drinking *tesguino* with the family and their neighbors.

Candelario himself played only a little but had ears that could tell a nice rich sound from a bad one. Bad sounds hurt his ears—just the way he told people the bad things in life hurt his soul.

The musician and the guitar, accompanied by a brother who played the violin, had gone to San Antonio Texas to play Tarahumara music as part of a cultural mission, and upon returning they told Candelario that they had found being away from the Sierra so unpleasant that they did not play well and would never again leave their canyons.

Candelario too decided to live in a cave.

He found one that was spacious, opened to the south, was a safe distance above the arroyo during high water, and that even had a spring flowing out of a crack in the rock wall at one end. From the smoke-blackened ceiling he knew it had been occupied in the past.

He rebuilt the toppled stone wall in front to keep out animals, shoveled out some goat dung, constructed against the back wall a tight rock and dried mud storage structure, lay some woven grass mats on some rock ledges inside to sleep on, and placed a few notched poles to help negotiate the almost vertical climb up from the arroyo below.

He terraced a nearby area with rocks to hold the soil, spread over it the collected goat dung, and planted tomatoes, onions, chile, and garlic. Firewood he threw down from high above onto the ledge at the cave's mouth.

Soon after he and Carmen moved in—they had a child.

Occasionally the whole family showed up at the pueblo, he on foot and leading a burro with the older child tied into the saddle and Carmen riding along on another burro behind and holding onto the other child sitting leaned against her belly.

When the men from the pueblo cracked jokes, he said things like:

"It's the most comfortable house I've ever been in—and I'm surrounded by beauty all the time besides—which makes every bite of food taste better— and doing under the stars what men and women do together makes that better too—if the Tarahumara are as dumb as you claim—it's only because many of them gave up their caves for the sealed packing crates you live in."

"I've got a good and beautiful woman—that all of you would give your front teeth to sleep with—and I love my two kids—for me that beats riding around in a brand new pick up and drinking beer with some buddies and listening to *ranchera* songs about women who break your heart."

In the old days, many of the rich Chabochi took Tarahumara women as second, third, and fourth wives, but never went off to live with the Tararahumara, much less in a cave—like that crazy hard old walnut Candelario.

As for Carmen, she told Jesusita, "He's very nice to me—adores the kids— and doesn't spend all his money on drinking."

That the two sisters were somewhat different from other Tarahumara women may have had something to do with their grandfather Benito who had known and spoken to them of many things—though it was not so much his words they remembered as the independent and moral spirit that moved those words.

Jesusita still went almost everywhere barefoot. She enjoyed feeling the subtleties of the connection with rock, pebbles, dirt, pine needles, and oak leaves.

It was half of life.

Today Jesusita, Felipa, and Chalelo are up well before sunup.

It is the birthday of Alfredo, he having several days ago invited the neighbors for miles around to his rancho to celebrate—and also to help him build a new and larger adobe house.

His rancho—part of a *rancheria* of several other nearby ranchos—was near the bottom of Arroyo Hondo, a side canyon of the Big Canyon. More steep-walled than the Big Canyon and in stretches almost inaccessible, the Tarahumara living there had recently turned away from their thousand-year heritage of growing corn and beans in order to grow opium poppies—made possible by the half mile of black plastic hose that ran water from upriver into the fields.

The independent enterprise having so far escaped Mafia control, Alfredo was a relatively rich man.

Jesusita remembers how just before her Grandfather Benito had left for the journey he never came back from he had said about Alfredo, "My youngest son is lost—like a goat to the coyotes—which is what happens when one learns to live and to work like the Chabochi do—for money and wanting to be looked up too—and for that willing to do absolutely anything."

And so she saw it as only natural that when one day Carmen quietly informed their mother Felipa that she had married a Chabochi, Felipa kicked her hard in the butt and then as Carmen fled from the hut with her child threw rocks at them.

That Carmen lived in a cave, like the most traditional of the Tarahumara, did not help. But time did. And also that whenever Carmen came to visit she left a little money.

Jesusita reluctantly fastens a pair of tire tread huaraches to her feet—

since they will be going down into thorn country. Then her father grabbing a pick and her mother a shovel, they start out.

And almost immediately are descending the steep switchbacks down through the pines.

And now down down through the oaks. And down down even further—into the desert-like tropics.

Here and there huge, spined saguaro cactus rise out of the thorny brush like giants from another world groping their way back skyward—a few of them, now late in June, still retaining a few purplish pitahaya fruit.

Arriving at the rancho—almost a vertical mile below their own—they find at least ten other families already there, some having come from much further away than they have. People are standing and drinking coffee around a fire over which a cauldron hangs from a tripod while others are sitting on the ground eating from clay bowls held in a hand or on their laps.

On a long hewn plank supported at the ends by rocks are baskets of tortillas and some pots of goat stew as well as bowls and cups. Those finishing eating go over to a hose which is dribbling water with which they wash their bowls and cups which they then set back onto the plank since there are not enough for everyone.

Chalelo, Felipa, and Jesusita go around with their right hand extended, exchanging a quick brush of fingers with the others, even with the two year olds, for whom this manner of greeting is among the first things learned. They exchange no words, not even with Alfredo, or with Candelario or Carmen.

Dolores, the wife of Alfredo, offers Chalelo a gourd dipper of *tesguino*—who head back, empties it in several gulps, and who then, licking his lips and smiling, hands the dipper back. Dolores goes over to a large tin wash tub, submerges the dipper, and returning, hands it to Felipa who gulps hers down as well.

Jesusita sits down on a bench—another hewn plank set on rocks. Although she does not yet drink she has of course helped Felipa make *tesguino* countless times at their own rancho—and has drunk it in small amounts, and on a few occasions when everyone was too drunk to notice she too has gotten a little drunk.

People pick up their tools and drift to behind the house to work, a few of the women with children slung in *rebozos* on their backs. Dolores sets out among them a five-gallon plastic bucket of *tesguino*.

They work hard and well. Picking loose the soil. Carting it in a wheel barrow. Mixing mud. Packing the mud into a wooden form for shaping the bricks. Rolling and dragging rocks down the hillside for the foundation. Excavating the trench in which the rocks will be set. Piling the rocks alongside the trench. Setting them with mud mortar.

Soon everyone is talking loudly, some non stop, and joking and laughing, pausing in the work only to wipe a brow or to gulp down another dipper of *tesguino*. Dolores refills the plastic bucket. Someone lets loose a wild yell.

It is for the Tarahumara a day *bien bonito*—very very nice—that can only get nicer.

The children have their own world apart—they sometimes watching but mostly running and fooling around, the older ones caring for the little ones, a few of whom are asleep in hammocks improvised from rope and a folded blanket.

Jesusita knows that work will stop a little past mid day when the heat down here in the canyon bottom begins to become intense, and by when everyone will be too drunk to work anyway. And she knows that it is then that the serious drinking will begin—and not end until every drop of *tesguino* is gone.

She thinks of the times when her parents were drunk for days at time—the vicious fights between them, the pushes and punches and the thrown rocks, and sometimes her mother on the dirt with other men, and once her father with another woman, the only food in the house being what she or Carmen put together.

She remembers once accompanying her wise Grandfather Benito homeward—he staggering, bloodied from having fallen off the trail and rolled into an arroyo, yelling nonsense, and falling again and again, and finally crumpled up for good. And then she leaving him to pass the night there.

Once out of anger she ran away all the way to the bottom of the Big Canyon, to her uncle who grew mangos and papaya, and was there a week before Chalelo found out where she was and came to bring her back.

She notices that Valencio is already running around in circles, naked from the waist down—no one paying any attention to him.

Suddenly she becomes angry again—at Chalelo and Felipa and at Alfredo—at all of them, since they are all the same. She does not know any adult that does not drink—though she knows a few women who drink only a little.

In another year, she knows, she too will be doing what she has learned is most Tarahumara.

Once—a Gringo had momentarily lit in her what may have been a desire and a possibility for an indefinable something else. Every time she herded the goats over to the ridge on which she had encountered him she felt the presence of something that still lingered, still dripped from the trees like after a rain. Many times she had herded the goats that far when she did not have to—always listening for the clomp, clomp of his boots and looking for him and the bright blue sack to emerge from out of the trees.

And once—she saw him, climbing back out of the canyon, he so very tired and thirsty. But when she went over to him to take him by the hand to water—he was gone.

Jesusita and her cousin Marta who is her age go off together, Marta with a slender 12 foot cane pole with a hook and a small basket woven from sotol fastened to one end. They climb up onto a mesa—an occasional drunken shout challenging the Gods reaching up to them.

Marta manipulating the cane pole, snatches a purplish pitahaya, then another, and lowers them down. And she and Jesusita eat them, they deliciously juicy and sweet.

They watch a long thin black snake winding its way over and between the spines up one of the saguaros—it searching for eggs in the cavities where cactus wrens sometimes nest.

For her, Jesusita, it is the sheer delight of eating pitahayas which ripen at the very time of year when other foods are very scarce, and not *tesguino*, that is most Tarahumara.

They continue gathering, from this and that saguaro, the last of this June's pitahayas—until they can eat no more.

The day by now intensely hot, they start back down to the rancho.

Jesusita is suddenly struck by how quiet it is in that direction, as if everyone might have gone off to do the serious drinking at someone else's rancho, and mentions it to Marta. They decide to sneak up quietly and find a good place from which to see the house.

Jesusita follows Marta through the boulders and the brush to a place Marta said was close to the house and from which they would not be seen—and where she said she had sometimes gone to hide from her father Alfredo when he was drunk.

They are startled at seeing as many uniformed Chabochi soldiers as most Tarahumara have goats.

And then they see the women with long ropes around their necks, all tethered to the same rock, and see off to one side and facing the women, the Tarahumara men, their hands tied behind their backs, their feet bound, and each one tethered to his own bush. Among the women are several girls younger than they are who had not managed to run off along with almost all the boys.

It was probably no more difficult for the soldiers to corral this group of drunken Tarahumara than for her, Jesusita, to corral her goats.

She watches as three of the soldiers approach Carmen, the prettiest, two of them each grabbing a leg and the other one both arms, then flipping her onto the ground, as another soldier approaches unbuttoning his pants. Even with her legs held spread wide, it is not until he pushes up her two skirts and straddles her that she realizes what is happening and tries frantically to move but cannot.

Some of the soldiers cheer, and others, both soldiers and Tarahumara, yell things—in the midst of which rises a long piercing wail.

Several of the Tarahumara joining in the wailing, Jesusita is both terrified and fascinated as she watches the soldier withdraw his glistening and still swollen *bisaka*—another soldier already pushing him aside.

Neither of the cousins having had to say anything, they wind rapidly back through the brush and the boulders. And then rapidly uphill—just as someone who must have been Candelario begins shouting drunkenly and wildly in Spanish a string of words that makes no sense to either of them.

High up in the cliffs, where the first pines begin, and at a spring where Marta has watered her goats, they stop—too frightened to go to any house, anywhere.

It strikes Jesusita, who has witnessed many *tesguinadas*, that the soldiers now far down below them are just men doing what most men would probably do if given the opportunity. Just as billy goats are billy goats.

For a long time now she has known that that impulse is what keeps life going. Keeps life spewing out new life, and that life, spewing out yet more life.

She knows that she is spoken of by some as the barefoot beauty of the canyons—the most lusted after of them all.

❖ ❖ ❖

She that night wanting desperately to fall into the deepest sleep she has ever known, tosses and turns.

She becomes aware of men lurking behind trees, bushes, and rocks.

And of billy goats, jack burros, and muscled bulls eyeing her. And that snakes have stopped slithering and toads have stopped hopping—eyeing her.

And that in every rancho, jealous and envious women are conspiring and concocting herbal potions and hexes to harm her.

Looking up at the sky she watches as a star transforms itself into Alfredo, and as all the other stars become transformed into men too—all of whom drooling, then begin to descend in a horde out of the suddenly blackest of nights down upon her.

She panics. And as she attempts to stand up, the Black Devil himself, father of the Chabochi Devil, and wielding a large flashing knife grabs her and plunges it into her lower abdomen, again and again.

Until finally breaking free, she hurls herself off her ledge—to slowly float off, hurting and bleeding, into the welcome welcoming immensity of the canyon.

Shortly after sunup they are brought awake by the sputtering wop wop wop of a helicopter. They watch it swoop past them like a monster black bird down into Arroyo Hondo, and there swoop some more, dropping something that falls glinting onto where they know the poppy fields are.

From stories she has heard, Jesusita knows that the soldiers before they leave will burn down all the houses and cut into pieces the black plastic pipe.

She tells Marta she will never go back there—not even after the soldiers leave.

"Did you hear me Marta—I said never."

"Never."

8

Man Who Never Was

Early in the morning a few white puffs of cloud appeared scattered across the blue sky. By late afternoon, above the Sierra Rica, a high towering cumulus had formed, glistening white in the sun—that kept on billowing and towering higher and higher as it turned purple and then black underneath. Soon bolts of lightning darted downward, producing distant thunder, the flashes soon swallowed up behind a grey curtain of rain.

Half an hour later the lightning and thunder and rain were gone, leaving only a dark purplish sky and the diminished thunder head, which now glistened even more brilliantly in the slant light of the sinking sun.

And it was then that Lucas saw the two glorious rainbows that arched over the Sierra Rica, one above the other—from indigo to red, and again from indigo to red, across the sky.

The next day, he walking over to see Gregorio, Polo pulled up in his red pickup alongside him, with Hermelinda snuggled close at his side. Both of them as they made small talk with him seemed incredibly happy.

When Lucas mentioned the storm over the Sierra Rica, Polo said, "Though it will rain very little—it's the beginning of what we call the rainy season here—which will cool things off some—and green the desert up a bit."

"Watch out for the arroyos—sometimes it rains very hard far away where you can't see it—and so you can be standing in one that's bone dry—under a clear blue sky—and suddenly hear a sound like a freight train—just before a five foot wall of muddy water and rocks slams you and carries you off."

Hermelinda said, "There is nothing more beautiful—and that makes a person feel more alive than the desert after a rain."

"Hear that Lucas?—she wants me to put her first—but for her it's wet sand and dripping cactus."

Just before they drove away, Polo hooking an arm around Hermelinda's neck, said, "She's worth more than all the marijuana fields in Mexico—the last sprouting of true Mexican womanhood—like Mexican women used to be."

Polo squeezes her.

"We've talked about you Lucas—and we haven't been able to agree on the how—except that in some odd way you may have changed both of us just that little to have made this possible."

"More likely it was simply life spontaneously erupting in its own unpredictable way—but regardless—my heartiest good luck to the both of you."

During the next weeks, Lucas went about visiting the people in Las Palomas he did not yet know—and also some of the neighboring villages.

The men were not always easy to find since it was customary for them to absent themselves from the house for the day even when as was often the case they had nothing to do. They liked to drive around in their pickups, beat up to be sure, but which with the help of Mexican ingenuity and baling wire and whatever they managed to keep running.

As for their women, one of the men told him, "For their own good—they belong in the house—with a child in the belly or at the breast—and as for the young pretty ones—best with a broken leg."

It soon became apparent to Lucas that the Old Mexico life style that Manuel and Consuelo lived, and Gregorio, was not the whole of Las Palomas— some of the families having adopted more modern ways and having in the process become somewhat less openly friendly, less hospitable and helpful.

Most houses now had a second hand refrigerator, a fan, a light bulb in each room, and a few a television. The original dirt floors had concrete slabs on top of them and some of the original dirt roofs sheets of lamina over them. The adobe walls were plastered inside and out with a cement mixture and painted, often blue, pink, or green. There were even bathrooms, although the flushing mechanism might be a bucket of water.

The older men told him they had grown up with outhouses and walking in the fields behind horses and oxen, and growing a variety of foods, mostly for the family table. Seeds came from last year's crop and fertilizer from their animals. Then at some point all that had suddenly changed to growing only the few crops that were most profitable and to buying seeds and fertilizer with loans from the bank. At first they grew cotton—and after that went bust, alfalfa.

He found many of the houses vacant and was told that most of them belonged to those who had left permanently for the United States—not so much because of poverty but rather to get ahead and for the status of living there. They sent back dollars to their relatives in Mexico. Now and then they returned for a few days to eat barbecue with those relatives, and the men to sit in their pickups parked under a cottonwood tree along with a dozen other pickups, everyone drinking beer and listening to *ranchera* music played so loud it shook the town.

About one of those Mexican Americans, he was told, "He still sees himself as very attached to his Mexican roots—except that he now considers himself a very superior being to the us burros who still live here and have remained poor—I think he just comes back to show off his brand new pickup and expensive stereo."

The men who stayed, many of them having bought up and now farming the lands of those who had once been their neighbors, now sat shaded by large umbrellas high up in the seats of old tractors which like their pickups they kept running, barely.

Yet in spite of the changes—Las Palomas remained a small rural village off the beaten track and a place where all belonged who were born there. Where everyone knew each detail of everyone else's life. And where everything that happened was significant, to be talked about by everyone for days.

People identified with their extended families—and with the land, the animals, and the weather. Everyone turned out to bury the dead.

Lucas began to experience life as an uncomplicated whole whose few simple parts could be accommodated easily into the brain—such that he began to wonder whether he might even one day understand human existence so far as it could be understood.

Each village had its own distinctive character. Some were much friendlier than others. Those he talked with in Las Palomas told him that those who lived over in El Valle just across the big arroyo were not to be trusted. And that some were malevolent witches.

One very old woman as she was wetting down the dirt floor of her porch told him, "They were the ones responsible for the snow in June on the Sierra Rica—they were partying up there with the Devil—and wanted to slide down the slopes on their bare behinds."

Stopping her work, she went on to tell him, "The head witch is Petronila— when she was young and beautiful she worked as a prostitute in La Junta—and would tell everyone that if it were not for her profession all the men would leave their wives for other women."

The woman's neighbor, who had been standing to one side, listening intently to every word, approached and said, "But the worst of the them is Katrina—who insists they consort not with the Devil but only with God—who they call their Earth Mother—and that she Katrina is a descendent of nature goddesses who very long ago lived in golden temples."

Then the neighbor made the sign of the cross, before saying, "Katerina once told me it was the womanless perverts ruling the Church—and wanting to rule the world—who gave the Goddesses and all women a bad name—began calling them harlots and witches—and burning them—millions of them."

And she made the sign of the cross again.

One man in response to one of his questions told him, "Americans always want to know—but I assure you young man—that you will never know this village by just listening to us—because half of what gets said is pure gossip—what never happened that way—or what never even happened at all."

Lucas remained silent for a while, thinking about how in the courtroom too, even with witnesses and cross examinations and the so-called rock-hard evidence, all one could do was put together a reasonable-sounding argument for what happened. One never knew.

He also knew that among human beings, and governments—the fabrication, the intentional lie was endemic.

"More than really find out anything—what I am really trying to do—as best as I can—is connect as best I can to the people—given I haven't lived all my life here—nor have any relatives here."

And it was then that, for the first time, it occurred to him that possibly only by connecting—by connecting totally—can one really know anybody. Or anything.

The same man also told him, "Manuel's family has—let us say—more or less adopted you—but be careful with the others—particularly anyone under sixty and who has spent a little time away from here."

"One of the first things all Mexicans learn—is that outside of one's family—no one is to be completely trusted."

"Oh—and one more thing—and I don't know how to put this nicely—but no matter how much you do things the Mexican way—or how good your Spanish—or how fine a person you are—in many people's eyes you will always be an intrusive Gringo."

❖ ❖ ❖

Time seemed to evaporate. And Lucas felt himself sinking into an eternal Now—a Now that had absolutely no consequences for a tomorrow that did not exist.

He learned that to do something *mañana* means never—or at best when one feels like it.

What had at first bothered him somewhat was the junk scattered about outside the houses—the strewn every-which-way devastation of old farm machinery, refrigerators, stoves, bedsprings, vehicles, tires, armless dolls and everything else that over time breaks down or wears out.

But then at one house he noticed that a truck chassis had been utilized to bridge an irrigation ditch. At another, a car body sheltered some small goats, and stacks of tires served as a terrace to hold back a hillside. And at yet another he saw a doorless refrigerator laid on its back that had garlic planted in it.

He wondered whether these people, in not frantically surrounding themselves with what is new and shiny, might not have a clearer view of the world—a world in which there is absolutely nothing that does not pass away and that in one way or another nature does not eventually recycle into something else.

What he often heard was, "The younger ones want to buy things and to be seen as somebody important—so they go off to where there are jobs and life is fancier—and those with children go off to where there are better schools—and others to the States."

"They call it finding a better life—*saliendo adelante*—getting ahead."

"It's mostly just us older ones now—and all that's left for us is to die off."

On one of his trips to La Junta to buy groceries Lucas wandered into its only bookstore, and came out with *México Desconocido—Unknown Mexico*—by the Norwegian ethnologist Carl Lumholz, and first published in 1904. Lumholz had spent five years in Mexico's Sierra Madre, most of that time with the Tarahumara Indians among whom he and one or another bilingual guide had traveled on foot and on horseback.

Lucas was surprised to discover that Lumholz' portrayal of the Tarahumara resonated with the image of them his own very brief encounter with the two women in La Junta had left him with.

Lumholz too had noted the strong aura those people radiated—and their confidence, quiet alertness, and noble bearing. All of which he attributed to them living with *"the electricity that emanates from the very heart of nature."*

Lumholz wrote that the Tarahumara women were equal to men and independent. They worked in the fields, owned property, made decisions together with their husbands, initiated courting, and had complete sexual liberty except with Mexicans.

He also wrote that the Tarahumara were not only *"disgustingly healthy"* but also the best endurance runners in the world, the men easily running more than 150 miles without stopping.

Lucas doing some further research at the library in La Junta discovered that the Tarahumara had once been a fierce warrior people linguistically tied to the conquering and empire-building Aztecs to the south and sharing with them such customs as sun worship, human sacrifice, and collecting the skulls of those they killed in ritual and war.

Their small farmsteads, their wild beer drinking and wild fierceness in battle. and their success in occupying a wide territory by conquering and assimilating the original populations reminded him of the Vikings.

In the seventeenth century, rather than fight and be decimated by Spanish swords and cannons, the Tarahumara chose to retreat into the most rugged and deepest canyon country of North America. Where, having never been conquered, they still live today—more or less still like when the Spanish first came.

What particularly caught Lucas' attention was how Lumholz described those Tarahumara who had had significant contact with the white Mestizo society surrounding them:

"Civilization, in the form that it reaches them, offers no benefit ... it tumbles their religion ... they have learned the arts of deception and stealing, and don't know any more how to keep their promises ... knowing money, greed is awakened in them and they look out only for their own self interest ... it is the same history repeating itself all over ... the simple Indian becoming victim of the industrious white man."

It caught his attention because on the wall of his old law office there had hung an artist's portrait of a Mohawk War Chief called Thayendanegea, who without deep canyons to retreat into had fought bitterly so that his people might remain free. At the bottom of the portrait was one of the Chief's statements to the white invaders, *"In the government you call civilized, the happiness of the*

people is constantly sacrificed to the splendor of empire ... we have no prisons ...
we have no written laws ... we have no robbery under the pretext of law."

It was the portrait of a human face that revealed an utter inner dignity and integrity.

More than once it had occurred to Lucas that it was very likely that at some point the FBI had broken into that law office. And might have even, for the record, taken a photograph of the portrait—as the Mohawk Chief looked the agents straight in the eye.

Lucas when he had mentioned to Hermelinda his desire to look at life from another vantage point had not at the time realized the profound implications of that almost casual statement.

As he gradually became aware of absolutely everything he had taken so for granted being changed in subtle and often not so subtle ways, he came to realize that what was happening was that he was learning how to See—and via a path much quicker and easier than the Buddha's.

Looking at Mexico with American eyes and at America just across the river with his newly adopted Mexican eyes—as well as by delving into the culture of the Tarahumara—he began to See what until then he had only known intellectually.

Which was that any culture was but one possible way for structuring human life—and that each culture had its own story, which as Gregorio had suggested, could be made to say anything.

He began to See how much of what people do and hold most sacred is consensual illusion, and how much of that could even be considered consensual insanity. And that it was precisely the human capacity for living in a world of illusion that kept the societal scripts pasted together and made them work.

Although continuing to walk in the familiar world of culture, he felt himself to be less and less of it. And simultaneously he began to feel a much greater integrity, a greater sense of freedom, and to intuit that perhaps by simply totally lifting the cultural veil—one is There.

Like the enlightened Buddha—or a wolf loping through the forest.

Almost always, passing by one of the houses in Las Palomas, Lucas would see a young woman who was attached to a long blue and yellow rope, its one end fastened to an ankle with a small lock and its other end attached to the high branch of a huge cottonwood tree.

Sitting with her back against the tree, in its shade, and watching the road, each time she saw him she would emit an unintelligible yell.

When one day he decided to knock on the door of the house, she picked up a rock—but then just held on to it, watching him. An elderly woman came to the door and said good morning and asked in what way she could help him. He introduced himself and said that he was living in Las Palomas and just wanted to get acquainted with everyone. She invited him in, asked him to sit down, and then began fixing coffee.

"I feel I need to explain Norma—my daughter—and that rope— something happened to her mind a few years ago—as if it just broke—I could keep her locked in a room—but she loves being outside—except that free she would go off out into the desert in a minute—without water—even with the sun hot enough to cook any rabbit not under a bush—several times I had to call the neighbors to help find her—and she is very good at hiding—so we all decided together on the rope."

"I'm very sorry for her—and for you."

"She was mostly perfectly fine before—except for maybe being too sensitive when something in life was not right or went awry—God must have decided that this is how things need to be—for his Plan for all of us to work out."

"Would you mind if I visited with her?—being she is as much a part of the village as anyone."

"She doesn't talk—or give any sign that she understands—and will likely only throw rocks at you."

"I will stay well back."

"You may then—as long as you do not upset her—here the coffee is ready—I apologize that we are out of sugar."

"The only people who want to see her are those who consider her to be like some strange animal in a zoo—but she is not at all stupid—and can spot them from far away—and so maybe she will not throw rocks at you after all."

"Having someone like her in their midst bothers most people—does more than just bother them I guess—because once the authorities took her away—and it was when she returned that she started throwing rocks at people."

As he stood up, she said, "I feel I need to say—that although she is not at all what is thought of as pretty—I am well aware that there are men who would like to do things to her—but I somehow trust you—I don't know why."

"Thanks—and for the coffee too."

"It was nothing."

He went over and sat down in some shade cast by the standing wall of a tumbled adobe house and beyond the reach of the rope. He noticed for the first time that off to one side there was a chair that he had never seen her use, and behind it some vertical poles stuck in the ground, around which were draped some old torn blankets, the structure probably serving as an outhouse.

The rock she had picked up still in her hand, she made no motion to throw it. Nor did she look directly at him—though he knew she was acutely aware of his presence and perhaps even knew that he had come to be with her. Her brown hair was cut short and she wore a plain dress that looked like it might have been put on fresh that morning.

Once she let out her strange yell which this time sounded more like something involuntarily unleashed from far back in her throat, and not at all of her doing or directed at him.

Sitting there, Lucas Saw as he never had before that people such as her were as much a part of the human scheme as anyone, a vital part of an evolutionary process that constantly gives birth to a variety of forms—tall with short, straight with curved.

Saw that intellectual giants owed their existence to people like Norma—as did saints to criminals.

When after about twenty minutes he got up to leave, she still clutched the rock. He waved and called over to her, "Until the next time Norma."

And so now and then he would come by, and sit by her off to one side, saying nothing—just being with her and Las Palomas and the desert. And he came to rather enjoy visiting like that, with no expectation of anything more. The two of them like two animals.

Soon he was sitting down inside the circle of the limit of the blue and yellow rope—close enough to see the constant slight fear in her eyes. Whenever he picked up more than that—a sudden odd gesture, a tension in her body—he moved slowly back.

And over time he came to feel himself more connected to her than he found himself connected to most people he knew.

And also found himself, in some unexpected and odd way, more connected to the Mystery that underlies the Universe and all of life. And wondered whether that was why certain Indian groups have considered persons like Norma to be Holy, a special gift bestowed upon them by the Great Spirit.

Although he himself did not see her in quite that way.

Because for him, trying hard to See, nothing anymore was a gift or a curse, or more holy or less holy—it simply was.

One night walking back toward his house through the dark empty silent main street of Las Palomas he thinks about how he happened to be in this place, remembers the enchilada dinner, and Jesse and Javier—it all having commenced with two terrorists behind prison bars.

He begins thinking about how desperately striking out at America—the modern world—with an act of terrorism, although it might destroy a few lives and building, has the ultimate effect of only hardening and making more rigid the societal script that prompted the terrorism in the first place.

Whereas just one person who Sees—has the potential for providing the seed that inspires the total rewriting of that script.

He wonders whether the enemy of Seeing might not be almost everyone.

Jesus left many villages needing to shake their dust from his sandals.

Was crucified and humiliated not by order of the Roman authorities but because of the clamor of a populace that despised him.

And perhaps it was not so much the words he spoke that so aroused those people—but rather that by Seeing he found himself so apart from them that not even doing and saying nothing would have saved him.

There is a hissing of soaring wings in the darkness overhead.

"Lucas—your blasphemous thoughts woke us up in our very comfortable roosts in the ash trees behind the school—and we had to laugh so hysterically as not to be able to get back to sleep—imagine—you a Seer—when the truth is you cannot see past your own big fat nose."

Then he hears their hysterical laughter—it now receding into the distance.

The next evening, as the sky in the west is turning bright crimson, Lucas follows the main road out of the village and in a direction away from La Junta to where it ends at a bright pink house partially hidden by mesquite and perched on a knoll overlooking the Rio Grande. The first house he has seen with a red tile roof.

Going up to the house, he sees a new white pickup like Polo's parked under a ramada, from whose vigas, hanging by ropes, are two nicely-embossed saddles. He knocks—and stands there waiting, looking down on the flood plain of the river and at the two horses and bunch of mules grazing on the Mexican side. It is a luscious evening.

A man wearing a yellow cap with Caterpillar Tractor printed on it approaches from around the back of the house. Who before he gets to Lucas, stops.

"Good evening—what can I do for you?"

Lucas after saying good evening introduces himself and then explains that he is just out walking getting to know the village and its people—as the man's eyes dart left and right, as if looking to see if there might be others hidden in the mesquite.

Lucas says, "A pretty place you have up here."

"It's plenty nice here—well enjoy your walk."

Lucas saying adios, turns back toward Las Palomas—the man standing there watching him.

Some interactions are pure gold—and now and then there is one like the one he is walking away from.

The last tinges of the fading sunset go unnoticed.

And yes, generals, police chiefs, and politicians eat steak every night—in return for ignoring signs like the one nailed to the front door of the pink house with the red tile roof, and the ones dangling from the nearby mesquite bushes, all announcing:

Major Drug Crossing

Back at his house, lying face up on his bed, his running shoes underneath it with the bad taste of the evening still stuck to their bottoms, Lucas begins thinking some more of how Lumholz described the Tarahumara.

They had very few myths or stories.

And the predominant tone of their religious fiestas is wordlessness—as they the Tarahumara, lit up by the light from several fires, dance all night long under the stars to the gravelly beat of gourd rattles the dances given to them long ago by Turkey and Deer.

Lucas imagines himself one of the dancers in the flickering firelight—

stamping his feet on the hard earth—stamping and stamping to the beat of the gourd rattle. All through the night—as time and the ordinary, everyday world dissolve.

And in doing so, he has an inkling of another consciousness—one that permits the soul to break free and travel to the stars. Free. Free.

But immediately is surprised to suddenly discover himself wedged tightly inside what appears to be a box. He can barely move, or breathe, and it is very lonely in there. He hears what could be the shuffling of a strange wind or footsteps approaching—and begins kicking and banging with his fists, shouting, "You whoever or whatever you are out there—I am someone trapped inside a box—the box you see is not me."

"The box you are in are the illusions that hold what your society's calls Reality in place—that you want to escape—to reach the stars—but still can't."

"Well get me out."

"I can't—only you can do that—by not marching to those illusions."

"I am already a man without a country—but I promise to not watch nor cheer at any more hockey games—or believe that a special diet or information from the Internet will save me."

And with that the box he is in vanishes.

Standing up straight and breathing the ocean of fresh air so deeply that it rushes down into him and tickles the soles of his feet, and stretching both arms out toward the stars—his two fists bump with a thud into something very solid.

"Hey—I'm still in a box."

"It's another box—you were inside a box inside of a box—this one holding in place another illusion—the special identity you have created for yourself—the personal story you live in—and think is you. "

"I am already a man without a wife—and without his own house—and without a career—but I promise to replace my Toyota pickup with a dented clunker—and to stop reading books that only intellectuals read—and to quit showing off my swan dive."

And with that the words making up who he had thought was Lucas go poof—they just like that returning back to being the bubblets of air that they always were.

"Congratulations Lucas—you are now—almost nobody."

"I sense I am still in a box—a different kind of box—that is more stretchy and like an invisible balloon around me."

"Yes—and one that is somewhat more substantial and real than the other two—in that it is not so totally a fabrication of the human mind."

"Then how do I get out?"

"For the time being it's best that you remain there—so you can go about the task of beating off and placating the dragons—big and tiny—that lurk behind every tree and bush and in every hollow log and under every rock—just waiting their chance to pounce on and devour you."

"What you are telling me then is that this last box—is my body—with its ancient instincts for survival—and whose archetypal story is its perpetual struggle to keep from getting ground back into dust and quarks."

"Exactly—and the rest of that story is that if you proceed from your heart—and honorably—and with a faith that banishes all fear—the princess who is right for you—may find you."

"To bring new bodies into the world."

"More or less."

Lucas closes his eyes. Words. So many words have tired him enormously. Like words—even during an excruciatingly long court trial—had never tired him.

And hearing even more words—something about the Man Who Never Was, and about him and everything being only blips in the energy distribution of the Universe—

He feels a tremendous urge to rid himself of them—to run neighing out into the desert like a stallion trying to shake off a cloud of pestering flies.

He sits up. But no matter how much he tries to take the first step—all he can manage is to fall careening backwards and exhausted into sleep.

9

Old Mexico

One day in early August, when Lucas answered a knock on his door, there stood Jesse, and behind him tied to a bush, a packed grey burro.

"What a surprise—I thought you'd be up in Utah by now."

"It's a long story Lucas—and so complicated I don't know if I could ever get it right."

"No story ever gets it right."

"Yeah—but I'm going to try—I haven't even been home yet—I wanted to swing by my folks first—and drop in on you too—sort of keep moving a while longer—even though when Juana finds out she is likely to slip a scorpion into my boot."

"You don't need a lawyer?"

"I may need something—but a lawyer no."

"Let me bring out some chairs—do you want a lemonade?—something to eat?"

"I just came from my folks—but maybe later."

The two of them settled on chairs in the shade of a wall of the house, Jesse says, "I discovered I like it here on this part of the border better than any place in the world—life is somehow more clear and down to earth here—and at the same time—well—more magical too."

"I'm pretty comfortable here myself—especially among the last remnants of Old Mexico—like the way your parents still live—and the kind of people they are—but tell me—how did it all go?"

"Well I put some things on the burro—a blanket—a piece of plastic to lie on—a tarp to rig over me to get out of the sun and for when it rained—an extra shirt, pants, and pair of socks—a pot and frying pan and a plate to eat off of—a flashlight to help me see the snakes—some jugs of water—and some food—and of course oats for the burro."

"Yes I know—Jesus and the Yogis would have said it was way too much."

"And so I set off following as many back roads as I could—toward El Paso—sleeping not far from the highway—picketing the burro where he could eat the tall roadside grass—cooking over a fire with sticks I picked off the ground."

"Cars would stop and people ask me where I was going—and I said, West—and when they asked for how long I said, Who knows—some of them gave me money and sandwiches and apples—and sometimes they would drive off and come back with some burghers—and most of them said they wished they could do something like that."

And then, a faraway look coming into his eyes, he says, "Some of them I invited to eat with me around the fire—out there in the desert—I tell you Lucas—it was a very good and free kind of life."

"Yes—but what about your message about Walls?"

"I never gave it—not once—and this is where the story gets complicated— whenever I was about to speak about the Wall—or any of the other goings on in El Polvo—I could not make my mouth open—and at the same time—and this is the strangest part—something about me—and it may have been the Spirit of Pure Freedom glowing inside me—encouraged people to tell me their own sad tales—and there was no end to them—I was like a magnet—that extracted only Sorrows."

"Lucas—do you have something to nibble on?—I'm not hungry—but I need to nibble on a little something."

"There's a bag of corn chips dusted with hot chile powder."

"That would be perfect."

Lucas goes inside—and comes back out with a bowl of the chips and two glasses of lemonade. And for a while they sit there drinking the lemonade and eating chile corn chips.

"Well what I did was to shove each Sorrow into a one of those large black trash bags—I called it the Bag of Sorrows—and kept it lashed on top of the burro—and we traveled along like that—and instead of collecting aluminum cans—we collected Sorrows."

"One guy used up his life savings and then took out a bank loan he couldn't pay back—for an operation for his wife—who then reaped the benefit of suffering on for six months longer than she would have otherwise—and then the bank took his house."

"A woman's son had both legs exploded out from under him by a land mine across the ocean somewhere."

"A devout Christian couple had been putting their daughter through college—and she demanded more spending money—which they told her they did not have—and so out of retaliation she married a Turk and now lives in Istanbul—mumbling prayers on her knees four times a day."

"And you would not believe how many had been tossed out into the seven winds by employers and spouses they had spent a good part of a lifetime being loyal to."

"Am I right Lucas?—that you have heard more than enough?—because it's really the same story over and over and over."

"Anyway—soon I didn't feel so free anymore—and the Bag of Sorrows soon got so heavy that the burro finally said to me, "Just one more Sorrow Jesse—and I stop taking steps—either forward or backwards.""

And as I turned him around—back toward El Polvo—the burro said, "And besides—telling one's Sorrow just makes it more real—and sometimes one even turns into that Sorrow—and it winds up being—well—like having a Wall around one."

"I left the Bag of Sorrows at the first roadside park we came to—leaned against an overflowing trash barrel—what else could I have done with it?—tell me Lucas—was that the right thing to do?"

"Beats me Jesse—a world so haywire might not have any answers."

"You are very astute Lucas—that is exactly what I've began thinking too—give it up—and let Divine Providence take care of all this—or God—or Mother Teresa—or the Big Bang that my oldest boy coming home from school one day told me started all this."

As Jesse finishes up the last handful of chips, Lucas says, "A famous writer once wrote that the truest man is the Man of Sorrow—but I've always thought that would make for one very sorry man—you know—somewhat like a bean burrito without a good chile sauce."

"Right on Lucas—most of us dumb *Mexicanos*—along with our Indian friends—come with lots of chile sauce—with *aguante*—which means saying I can take anything you dish out—to the heat and to the cold—and to the bad tooth that does not let one sleep at night—and to when it does not rain and people grow so gaunt from eating nothing but leaves off of bushes that they no longer recognize one another."

"And you know what Lucas—it works a whole lot better than hope—which always lets you down."

"And it works better than listening to *ranchera* music and crying in your tequila—and hooting ay ay ay."

"Damn it Lucas—that's what life is—fighting to stay on your feet while everything else is hard at work trying to knock you on your ass—being one tough piece of rawhide."

Jesse reaches for more chips, but pulls back his hand when he sees the plate is empty. He says, "One evening a hitch hiker showed up at my camp."

"And he mistaking me for Jesus—and saying he was thirsty for justice—asked if it would be okay for him to help me out by chopping down all the fig trees that weren't bearing figs—and also by driving off a cliff and into the Rio Grande all the pigs he could find."

"I didn't know what to say—but finally I told him that that work had just been completed—and gave him a plate of spaghetti—and then the seconds I was hoping to eat myself."

"I'm not the same man I was Lucas—and it hasn't all come together for me yet—and so that's why I didn't go straight home."

"As the hitch hiker was leaving he apologized for eating so much—saying he knew that life was more than eating spaghetti—but that he had been very hungry."

"As he left he asked if he was on the right road to the Kingdom—I handed him five dollars and said it was—did I do an okay thing Lucas?"

"I doubt anyone could have done it better."

Jesse standing up says, "I'm off to see Gregorio—maybe he can put all this into a *corrido*—so I can understand it."

They walk together over to the burro. Tightening up the cinch, Jesse says, "If you really want to see Old Mexico—go up the big arroyo which is Arroyo Grande until you hit Barranco Azul—which is nothing more than six worn-out adobe houses all out of sight of one another—walking you can get there in a day—and there's even water always running in the arroyo—here and there."

Jesse unties the burro.

"I spent a lot of time there when I was a kid—helping my grandfather—he'd send me out alone into the desert with the goats for two weeks at a time—I lived in a cave with a sack of beans—some flour and lard—and a rusty twenty-two."

"Ate a lot of burnt tortillas—but I wasn't confused like I am now."

❖ ❖ ❖

Lucas sets out on foot up Arroyo Grande as soon as it is light enough to see snakes, Manuel having last evening told him that August being their mating season it was then that they were most about, and most aggressive.

Across one shoulder he is carrying a thin rolled-up blanket, the two ends tied together with a length of rawhide. Inside are a spare T shirt, an empty 2-liter Coke bottle for when he might need to carry water, a flashlight, and a plastic bag containing a mixture of raw oats, milk powder, and raisins, another bag of nuts, and a plastic bowl and spoon—Manuel having assured him that among the people of Barranco Azul he would never go hungry.

The arroyo which winds serpent-like down from its source in the Sierra Rica is wide and flat and he is making good time up its bed of hard-packed sand and gravel. Here and there he encounters patches of scattered rocks and splotches of dried greenish algae and also uprooted trees left there by flood waters. Small willows and some cottonwoods and ashes line the occasional stretches of clear running water. It is already pink in the east.

A blinding edge of the sun pokes up over the eastern horizon—and Lucas can feel the heat of the day begin.

He sees tire tracks and is reminded that this arroyo, out of the way as it is, is a route for drugs going to the border. Has several times seen one or another suburban with darkened windows passing down its bed between El Valle and Las Palomas.

He sees his first rattlesnake, wound in a resting coil and warming itself in the early morning sun—it not moving as he goes by. Walking now on loose sand he begins to slow down. He passes another coiled snake, this one lifting its head and flicking its tongue in and out.

About midmorning he stops to drink some water, scooping it up in a cupped palm from a four-inch-deep pool. He glances at the fresh javelina tracks and droppings—and moves on. It is very hot, and he knows that by now the snakes have glided into holes and under bushes and rocks.

The sun at mid day is intense. He is very thirsty, and drinks again, as well as fills his water bottle. He takes off his T shirt, soaks it, and puts it back on.

Here and there, the arroyo's high perpendicular cut banks expose the roots of a mesquite tree up above him on the arroyo's rim—roots that make their way downward deep into the earth in their eternal groping for water, sometimes, Polo had told him, to a depth of eighty feet.

At the base of one of those high cut banks, a north-facing one, he plops down in its thin strip of dense shade. He pours some water into his bowl, stirs in some of his oat, milk powder, and raisin mixture. Eats. After which he lies down and goes to sleep—as the desert shimmers and bakes.

When he wakes up—the sun on its way down—it is still as hot as ever. He drinks the rest of his water. Gets up and walks on.

Soon he can see some hills in the distance, between which hills he is guessing must lie the blue cliffs of Barranco Azul.

He arrives at the first hills as the sun is touching the horizon, and does in fact find that the arroyo having narrowed there are now on both sides of him low cliffs of blue-black rock and shale, the waters of the arroyo here running strongly and in places shin-deep.

It has cooled down.

The hills are low and rounded and there is absolutely nothing that could be called spectacular in sight—yet he is overcome by the feeling that he has never been anywhere more soothing and beautiful.

It strikes him how the true beauty of a place has to do with being immersed in the middle of it and fully experiencing it with all the senses—and very little to do with just visually looking at it from afar.

Ahead of him perched at the edge of the arroyo on a bluff, in the middle of what appears to be nowhere, is a small brown weather-eroded adobe building with a flat dirt roof. Moving on he looks for the way up to it.

Soon comes to a well with a pole structure from which dangles a pulley over which runs a rope that goes down into the well. And right behind the well finds a very steep trail—which he keeps sliding a little back on as he climbs up on the loose blue shale.

The rancho he arrives at smells of goat, their pellets everywhere, but he sees no person or animals or other sign of life. He knocks. And is surprised when the door is opened by a pretty eleven or so year old girl.

He says, "Good afternoon."

And she smiling and her eyes brightening, says, "Good afternoon—*pase*."

Which *pase*, Manuel had told him, in Old Mexico means not only to come inside to rest but is also an invitation to eat something and to spend the night, and to have breakfast too. He goes in.

The girl brings him a chair, saying, "Rest—you must be very tired."

And then she runs outside—and comes back with some sticks of wood which she shoves into the wood stove which already has some fire in it.

"My mother is visiting my grandmother up the arroyo—and my father and brother are bringing in the goats—we have forty-seven of them—everyone will be back before it gets dark."

She stirs a pot that was already on the stove. And putting some white flour and water and salt into a red plastic mixing bowl, starts kneading the dough for tortillas—some of the flour having splashed onto her blue and in some places torn dress.

Lucas sitting in his chair, a little disoriented, the door opens and who must be the mother comes in. Who says, "Good afternoon."

"Good afternoon," says Lucas as he stands up and shakes her hand.

The barks of a dog along with the baaing of goats and the tinkling of a bell are heard from the hill behind the house.

The mother disappears into the other room. And her daughter pats out round tortillas and lays them on the stove, while turning others. The mother comes back out wearing what could be her nicest dress and with her hair freshly combed—and immediately begins sweeping the floor.

A big tall unshaven man and a boy come in and come over to shake Lucas' hand and there are more Good afternoons.

Lucas tells them that he is a friend of Manuel and walked up from Las Palomas because he wants to see more of the Old Mexico.

The wife says, "You've come to the right place—we are very poor here—a few goats—and a small field a half mile away we farm some corn and beans on—we plow with a burro—pull your chair up to the table and we'll put some food in you—Anita—run over to Marcela and tell her we have a guest and need two eggs for the morning—I am sorry that there is no coffee—we are very poor here—nor was there lard for the tortillas—but they are hot—and there are beans."

Lucas is thankful that there is no lard in the house, knowing that to honor guests Mexicans like to put enough lard into the dough and the beans to choke a hog. And he is thankful for the beans, knowing from Manuel that when a family is poor, many times there is only tortillas and salt.

He sees that he has been served half of the beans that were in the pot, leaving the other half to be shared by three people. But he says nothing and eats, as he knows guests typically do which is first and by themselves. He notices there are only three chairs in the room.

Anita comes in with two eggs and a long green chile. Her mother putting them in a basket, says to Lucas, "You must be very tired—I'll go put some clean sheets on the bed."

Lucas knowing they are going to put him in their bed and they themselves sleep on the dirt floor here in the kitchen, or else outside, says, "I brought a blanket and shelter—I'll be absolutely fine out in back of the house."

The husband says, "There are mountain lions—and the snakes are very active at night this time of year—and sometimes there is a heavy dew—or a fierce wind that blows sand."

Ill at ease with this new kind of hospitality and much preferring to sleep outside, Lucas says, "You've already given me a very nice meal—but I'll do whatever you think is best."

The wife says, "The bed will be ready in a few minutes—you kids come along and help move some things into the kitchen."

"Aren't you folks going to eat?"

"We'll eat a little something before we go to sleep."

At the barest first light Lucas wakes up to the errr-er-errr-errr of a rooster from somewhere up the arroyo—which is then answered by other roosters. A dog outside the house begins barking and so does another one off in the distance. There are voices in the other room, and a doors opens and closes several times. Someone begins to chop wood. A burro brays behind the house.

For breakfast he eats two eggs scrambled with diced green chile, and tortillas.

When he says he would like to visit all the houses in Barranco Azul, the husband says, "But you will do that while you stay with us—we already sent Anita out to find a chicken for dinner tonight—and some lard for the tortillas and beans—she will take you to all the houses—some of them being tucked away are hard to find."

His wife says, "All of us in Barranco Azul are related in one way or another."

Lucas thinking he does not want to spend another night in their bed, and also recalling the Mexican proverb, After three days house guests and the dead stink, says, "What I would really like to do is build a very simple shelter nearby—a small *jacal*—and eat with you—I like looking out at the desert."

The husband says, "There's no need for that—we do fine sleeping in the kitchen—and the kids always sleep on the floor anyway."

The wife says, "From the point—one can look up and down the arroyo—he might like it there—and there are lots of rocks to put up some walls with."

Lucas says, "That sounds like it would be great—by the way—my name is Lucas."

The husband says, "They call me Chapo—little man—because I'm the tallest one around here—and my woman is Mara—our son over there is Ricardo—he doesn't say much—we will all help."

They go outside and over the edge of the arroyo, where Lucas giving his approval they begin hauling and placing rocks in a three-quarter semi-circle. Anita back from her errand joins them. When the wall is four-feet high and almost done, Chapo leaves on his burro for somewhere. For a while there is the sound of an ax. And then he comes back with the burro loaded with mesquite poles, a large piece of plastic, and a shovel and some other tools. They set four mesquite posts into the ground around the wall. Then Chapo goes off again, this time returning with a load of old rotten boards.

By noon they are placing the plastic over a slightly sloping board roof and weighing it with stones. The *jacal* is up—and Mara sweeps inside as well as the surrounding area with a broom.

Chapo says, "Something like this only bigger is sort of what everyone in Barranco Azul once lived in."

"We six families are an *ejido*—this was once part of a hacienda whose lands had no end—after the Revolution the government gave our great great grandparents and some others this little piece near water to be owned by all of them in common—in perpetuity."

"But then just a few years ago it complained we did not grow enough to sell to the rest of the world—were inefficient—and not doing our part in making Mexico prosper."

"So now one is permitted to sell the land one has worked to anyone— soon all the *ejido* lands will be gone—and again in the hands of those with money."

Mara says, "We are poor—we can barely feed ourselves—but we do not want to live any other way—we were not put on earth to work hard in order to make ourselves rich—and a handful of others even richer."

Ricardo says, "I want to live in the *jacal* too—with Lucas."

As Lucas follows Anita through the creosote bushes and over a hill to her aunt's house, her long brown hair swinging from side to side, he already feels as connected to her as he was to Norma.

The aunt and her four children receive him like a long lost relative. While he is eating his tortillas and *pipián*—boiled ground squash seeds—the children ask him about the United States, and ask how certain Spanish words are said in English. Anita tells her aunt about the *jacal* and says that she had wanted to live in it too—like Ricardo—but her mother had said no.

"And a good thing too—and you Lucas—you be careful with this young woman."

Each day Anita took him to visit a different neighbor—each one apologizing for being so poor, and having had so little or no schooling. Yet he had never before met a people who gave so much of what they had, or who were more helpful, or more relational. He had never before been in homes that were so permeated with human warmth—and life. More than just the salt of the earth, these people in their simplicity and naturalness were the earth itself.

He wondered if they might really feel superior to him—even while publically mocking their condition.

Thinking about Manuel and Consuelo, Jesse, Gregorio, Polo, Hermelinda, and Norma, and now the people of Barranco Azul, it struck him that neither in English nor in Spanish was there a word even remotely capable of describing the quality of his interactions with those people. Which perhaps meant that they, the interactions and the people, were somehow—for want of a better word—more real.

Anita at her young age seemed to already know all the things that everyone in Barranco Azul knew.

She told him that sometime before she was born everyone in Barranco Azul had stopped growing corn and beans and began to plant marijuana and that then the soldiers came and held people's heads under water in the arroyo and did other bad things that the ones who stayed and went back to growing corn and beans still remembered.

As they walked among numerous low candelilla plants, each one resembling a mini-forest of very thin waxy candles, she said that one of the families had once made its living uprooting those plants and afterwards boiling them with sulfuric acid in a big vat to release the wax which then floated to the surface.

She went on to say that one day the father and son, having waded the Rio Grande to cross some wax illegally, did not return. And that a week later their bodies were found entangled in the roots of a tree along the Mexican bank down river from Las Palomas and that everyone immediately knew that crossing back across the river with their money they had been robbed by Mexicans and their heads held underwater and murdered.

"My cousin Raquel when she was thirteen fell in love with Anastasio—who was married to my father's sister—and they both ran off together to La Junta."

"And my father—who almost never gets mad—told everyone that if Anastasio ever showed his face here again—he and the other brothers would bury him alive where no one would ever find him."

Those stories—ones the others of the *ejido* never would have told him—clearly revealed that Barranco Azul, isolated as it was from the rest of the world, was in no way isolated from greed, envy, gullibility, stupidity, and uncontrollable passions.

When he asked about some huge very old bones lying scattered across a large flat valley they were traversing she told him that everyone had always said that they were the bones of the giants that once ate people—which giants the people finally succeeded in tricking with a delicious goat stew and poisoning.

"But then a few years ago a man from Mexico City came to look at the bones—he told us they were the remains of gigantic reptiles that once ruled the earth—dinosaurs—and he showed us pictures of what they looked like—telling us they had all suddenly died off a very long time ago."

"When I asked him why—he said that it could have had something to do with a drastic change in the weather—but then he said that a more correct answer might be that it is in the nature of all things—even what appears to rule the earth—to eventually die off."

"I asked him if that meant everything that was most beautiful too—and he said yes."

Lucas was more at home in his *jacal* than he had ever been anywhere. It being open to every bit of breeze, and to the stars, and not holding the heat from the day as did the houses—he began to sleep deliciously.

Part of each day he spent wandering alone through the desert, carrying with him only a bottle of water and wearing a wide-brimmed straw hat he had borrowed from Chapo. Almost everywhere he found marine fossils. And on one hilltop, the petrified wood remains of an ancient forest.

Near an edge of many of the arroyo as well as on some of the terraces and hilltops he came upon old Indian sites with partially tumbled circular rock walls similar to the one forming the base for his *jacal*. And at those sites he also found perfectly-round, eight-inch-diameter vertical holes in exposed bedrock—that would once have served for grinding mesquite beans and other foods. At some of the larger sites—where there were as many as 20 house structures—rocks had been placed over an expanse of ground in intricate geometric arrangements, no doubt speaking a sacred language.

The hilltop sites, which were the smallest, were most likely lookouts for spotting the game in the valleys below.

From his research in the library in La Junta, he knew that nomadic hunter gatherers had roamed the area at least 12,000 years ago when it was a lush grassland with forested peaks and many flowing creeks and the home of buffalo, deer, and antelope. As the climate became drier, the forest disappeared, creeks dried up, and the grass became more sparse. And as game too became scarcer, people began to eat more lizards, rabbits, and rodents, as well as more seeds, greens, and roots.

Then about 2,000 years before the time of Christ, as domesticated wild corn made its way northward from its origins far to the south, some of the hunter gatherers began to take up farming in the vicinity of La Junta de los Rios, where the Rio Grande having its source in the Rockies joins the Rio Conchos that descends from the Sierra Tarahumara. The new sedentary farmers maintained close cultural and commercial ties with those who remained nomads—trading for example corn and at a later date also beans and squash for hides and meat.

La Junta de Los Rios became a commercial nexus. One trade route led to the urban center of Casas Grandes, and from there crossed the Sierra Tarahumara to the Gulf of California. Another trade route led up to the Anasazi settlements in what is now New Mexico. And so the people in the area of La Junta de Los Rios decorated themselves with sea shells as well as with turquoise.

With the arrival of the Spanish, the goats, sheep, cattle, horses, and burros they brought with them began to overgraze the fragile grasslands. The thin sod cover washed away, and water no longer soaking into the ground, springs and creeks dried up, and more spiny plants took over—and the land became stark desert.

Eventually—La Junta de Los Rios split into the sister towns of La Junta, Mexico and Buena Vista, Texas.

And not long afterwards, the very last of the nomadic hunter gatherers—as they defended their lands and raided the ranches and towns—disappeared in a puff of gunpowder.

Lucas on his walks would now and then imagine himself one of those earlier people—as they continually roamed on silent feet and in very small groups across an ever changing landscape, houseless, and carrying with them the very few things they had, and finding here and there for the taking the plants and wildlife they subsisted on.

Leaving almost nothing in their wake for future archeologists to conjecture about.

Lucas the Aboriginal, marrying at fourteen, and trekking along with his wife and children and a few others across the sands, free as the breeze brushing his face, filling his belly with prickly pear pads, mesquite beans, and agave, and occasionally a piece of roast rabbit, day after day, full moon after full moon—until the time came to leave his bones there.

Theirs would have been an extremely socially intimate, healthy, fit, and adventurous existence—and one free of boredom.

An existence vibrant with deep connections to just a few other human beings and to the land with its plants and animals, and to all that was up in the sky. Connections so deep that in every moment and with every step one felt an integral part of something beautiful beyond words and infinitely greater than oneself.

For them the world would have appeared generous and perhaps even almost perfect—unmarred by the sense that anything could be or should be any different, should be improved.

This evening, Lucas, sitting in his *jacal*, and looking out up the arroyo and towards the Sierra Rica, rolls over in his mind that nowhere does there really exist a nowhere place, a backwaters—that all the workings of the Universe pass through Barranco Azul.

Where a once lifeless chunk of rock became an inland sea that became forest and grassland and then finally this desert in which he now finds himself.

Where dinosaurs once wandered and raised families and fought ferociously for territory and for food and basked in the sun. And where much later dark-skinned humans from Asia did more or less the same.

And he Sees that nothing was a failure, or lost out—that nothing played a more major or minor role than anything else.

And that nothing even really struggled against anything else—everything having simply reacted and unfolded in the only way it possibly could.

Nothing triumphing, or harming—or sinning and needing to be forgiven.

He watches two horsemen coming down the arroyo, they talking back and forth and driving ahead of them six burros—one of the men gesturing wildly with one hand.

After they have passed—he listens to a mockingbird flawlessly imitate one bird song after another.

What remains, he has decided, is to go off alone into a totally peopleless part of this desert for a night or two—in order to be with it totally, and so know it better.

Also, he feels a need to let the experience of these last several days in Barranco Azul settle out—penetrate fully into his bones and brain.

10

Seven Dancers

From Barranco Azul, Arroyo Grande continues to wind southward and gradually upward toward the Sierra Rica. About halfway to those mountains, and a little to the west, a long high ridge rises solitary and abruptly out of flat desert and runs perpendicular to the arroyo and finally out of sight.

When Lucas mentioned to Chapo he wanted to hike along the top of that ridge for a few days Chapo told him the ridge was called the Sierra de la Mula and that getting to its base would take him a whole day and that once he left Barranco Azul he would see no water, not even in Arroyo Grande.

"You'd need to carry a ton of it along with you—and you could also very easily die out there—just like once upon a time a white mule did."

That same evening Lucas filled four gallon jugs with water, wrapped the stack of bean burritos that Mara had made for him in a cloth, and went to bed early. It seemed like the Sierra de la Mula had the remoteness he was looking for.

In the morning, at barest first light, with his bedroll, and with a jug of water slung over each shoulder and one in each hand, he makes his way, half sliding down the shale into the arroyo.

During the hottest part of the afternoon he sleeps in the shade of a north-facing cutbank in a bend of the arroyo. Waking up, he finishes off his first gallon of water. And then he climbs up the cutbank and out of Arroyo Grande.

He trudges along winding up small arroyos and through foothills toward the Sierra de la Mula. On whose flank he can now plainly distinguish the deep gashes cut by several major arroyos. He heads towards the base of the closest gash. Drops into a major arroyo. Follows up its bed—and soon finds himself at the mouth of a rock-walled canyon.

He proceeds, more slowly now, upward between the canyon's red rock walls, scrambling up rock ledges, picking his way past thorny brush, negotiating the jumble of boulders some as big as houses that have broken away and tumbled from the cliffs above. Climbing higher and higher.

The canyon narrows—and he is thankful for the intermittent dense shade.

He hopes he will not encounter a high, unclimbable vertical rock pour off—like the ones above and below Polo's marijuana cave.

He comes to a ten foot high wall. With a long stick he maneuvers each of his three almost full jugs up onto its lip. And then manages to climb up himself. On top he hears the familiar crystal-clear descending notes of a canyon wren. He sits down in deep cool shade to rest, drinks some water, and remains there for a while listening to its song a few more times.

He sets out still feeling exhausted from the constant uphill, the weight of the water, and the scrambling over boulders. He begins to gulp more and more water.

The canyon, its two sheer walls towering up out of sight, narrows even more, and the floor of the arroyo becomes solid rock. He feels he is in a tunnel.

"This is what I came for—to find the key hole to another world."

Rounding a sharp bend he comes upon a pool of water lying in a deep depression in the bedrock—a *tinaja*—more than half full from the last major thunder storm. Even with bright green algae floating in it, the water is clear and beautiful. Scooping it up with his plastic bowel and pouring it into one of the jugs, he is as content as he has ever been.

A half mile further on the canyon opens up and he again finds himself hiking up a sandy arroyo that winds up through some low hills toward what he sees must be the top, which is now very close—the vegetation at this higher elevation consisting of mostly sotol, agave, and yucca, and even some grass green from the summer rains.

Seeing three tall Spanish Dagger yuccas on the edge of the arroyo, he decides to spend the night there—and to make this and their patch of shade his base camp to explore from as well. Unrolling his blanket and spreading it on the ground—he has his new home. He sits down. Looking out into the distance, he can make out the glint off the roof of one of the houses in Barranco Azul.

The silence strikes him as more profound than any human utterance or music.

The red ball of sun touches down, sinks out of sight. He eats a bean burrito. Then curls up and goes to sleep.

He opens his eyes to a perfectly still and moonless night and to more stars than he has ever seen—all of them striking him as very alive, and as beings like himself.

He begins thinking how connecting to the stars—or to people or to anything—ultimately has to do with connecting to silent, invisible energies.

His mind turns to some of what Donald has told him:

That modern science points to every subatomic particle being in continuous and instantaneous communication with every other subatomic particle of the Universe.

That as recently as 20 years ago, scientists were totally unaware of the existence of the most abundant form of energy presently in the Universe—the invisible evenly-distributed dark energy, which fills what until then had always been thought of as only the vast nothingness of the empty space separating galaxies.

And which energy drives the accelerating expansion of the Universe, doubling its size every billion years.

Lucas soothed by the thought of floating in a pulsing sea of mysterious dark energy, and by his roof of star friends—falls back to sleep.

He opens his eyes and immediately sees hovering by his feet, and about two feet above the ground, three distinct amorphous white shapes—their presence overpowering the night and the stars.

When he, still lying motionless on his back, asks with perfect calm, "Who are you?"

They flit away into the nothingness.

"Where are you?—or did I only dream you?"

"No—I couldn't have—your energy was too strong for a dream—it's what woke me up in the first place."

He stares up at the barest sliver of moon for a while, then turns onto his side—and onto his back again. And finally again falls asleep.

In the morning he looks for foot prints, but finds none on the hard gravel earth. He eats a burrito. Then grabbing a full jug of water and sticking a burrito into a pocket, he heads for the crest of the long ridge that is the Sierra de la Mula.

Is soon hiking along on top, able to look out across the vast expanse of lowland stretching out to the horizon on both sides of him. Here up high it is not as hot as yesterday.

About mid day he dips down into a saddle grown thick with brush and prickly pear cactus—looks around, and then sits down in the scant shade of a fat yucca, his back against it. Where he drinks from his jug and eats his burrito.

Almost asleep, he hears a rustling, and twisting around sees a large black javelina emerging from a clump of brush, it followed by six somewhat smaller ones, none of whom paying any attention to him, move about sniffing, before plopping down one by one, here and there around him to rest. He smells their strong skunk-like odor.

Five more come out of the brush and lie down around him, the closest about fifteen feet away. He very slowly repositions himself to observe them better.

He feels accepted. Totally connected. He too one of them. He thinks of Norma. And that this is how human beings, lying about outside together, related to one another for more than a million years—long before there was spoken language.

Among these javelina, the connection has a quality and intensity he has never experienced before—a palpable physical presence charging the air and penetrating every cell of his body.

Rooting him into the Universe.

Recently he has become more aware of the vast chasm separating nomadic hunter gatherers from those who began to live in houses and farm. But what an even greater space must exist between those humans who lived without language and those among whom language arose and then became necessary.

Looking one by one at the dirt-covered, black-bristled, muscled bodies, it is clearer to him than ever that long ago there would have been no sickly or otherwise unfit human beings—only a well-tested toughness of body and mind.

That must have given them a remarkable kind of spiritual power.

With the rise of civilization, human beings began to think of themselves as having a more highly developed moral sense and as being wiser and more noble than animals—while primitive peoples have always seen it the other way around, that the highest knowledge came from watching the animals.

How presumptions of modern human beings to believe that their role in the world is in any way different from that of these javelina—that using symbolic language, and having constructed great cities, and meaning, places them in another and higher plane of existence.

The javelina get up. And wander slowly together out of the saddle and down the north side of ridge.

Heading back along the ridge to camp, Lucas begins to sense that it may not be totally chance that he is here—first the *tinaja* with water in it, then the apparitions, and just now the javelina. Senses that perhaps it is in fact true that a certain consciousness makes the Universe appear to work in a different and very special kind of way.

He is almost to where he will drop down off the ridge to his camp when he sees not far below him, jutting out from the other flank of the ridge, a flat terrace that he had not noticed coming the other way. And simultaneously sees, scattered here and there and moving across its flatness, six white-clad figures. He watches them for a while.

Seeing they are clearly human beings, he heads down toward them—toward what appear to be six very dark-skinned men all wearing white floppy blouses along with skirt-like garments that hang to their knees.

Several of them see him and stop moving—watching. As he approaches the nearest one, only when he sees the tire-tread sandals does it dawn on him that this man standing before him is a Tarahumara Indian—dressed just like the ones pictured in *México Desconocido*.

Face to face with the Tarahumara, he stops—the other five all now converging toward the two of them.

Lucas says, "*Buenas tardes*."

The man says, "*Kwira*."

Lucas assuming that *kwira*, just like *buenas tardes*, must signify hello, goes on to say, "What are so many of you doing here?—so far away from the Sierra—and from anything."

The man just stares at Lucas.

One by one the others arrive. An older man with white-hair to his shoulders and with more bearing than the others asks in an odd Spanish, "Why have you come here?—to us?"

"I only came to know this mountain—that they tell me is the Sierra de la Mula."

"That is very good—we ourselves have always known this mountain—

we are very happy to be here—with the rocks and the wind—and the lovely plants—can you hear one who is very small and who is God—singing?"

Lucas becoming aware that he and possibly the others too are drunk, says, "No—but maybe I do not hear as well as you."

"He sings so beautifully I sometimes cry—he is singing—I want to go back with you to your land—to learn your songs."

The Indian who had not answered Lucas says, in an equally odd Spanish, "That is why we are here—to take this God back with us to our land—so that he may purify the faltering bodies and hearts of our people."

The white-haired Indian who first spoke says, "He who is singing is Jículi—and sits to the right of Farther Sun."

It dawning on Lucas that these Indians have come to collect peyote—mescal buttons—he asks the white-haired man, "Are you a shaman?"

"Ah—for a white man you See very well—Jículi helps one to See—and right now I am Seeing you very well—for some reason you are very easy to See."

The other Tarahumara stand silent and motionless, watching and listening.

"Who Sees—can See can see into the heart of things—and into the past and future—and into other worlds—and in doing so—heal those who need healing—and himself also."

Lucas is aware that a kind of sympathetic magic, an energy resonance with these men, is making him too a little drunk.

The shaman swaying and catching his balance, says, "Or do you not believe a shaman can heal?"

Lucas pauses—then says, "Some probably can."

The shaman remains silent. Finally says, "Let's you and I walk over to that bush and talk—and yes—I know very well I am drunk."

The shaman laughs, as the two of them, leave the others and walk together toward the bush.

"I See you very well—and that you are not like the others who are not Tarahumara—and the God tells me I should tell you some things—help you."

The shaman laughs again—burps.

"As I See you already know—I heal partly by trickery—I pretend to suck worms and filth from bodies—and I act in bizarre ways—and so you are rightly skeptical of me—but those things I only do so the people will have complete faith in me—because just faith alone—no matter how acquired—can do half the work of healing."

The shaman seems to be looking at the sky for the words that are to follow. He spits on the ground. Looks over his shoulder—watching for a moment his companions as they fan back out into the terrace.

"The other half is healing from a place of Seeing—which is nothing but total connection—while energies from the Unseen World flow through one and into the other."

Lucas is quiet for a while—before saying, "Yes—and without the utter belief and faith in you that you spoke of—an ordinary person would probably resist those energies with all the force of his or her being."

The shaman lights up, smiling broadly, "Come along my friend—at dark you will dance *dutuburi* with us—to honor Jículi—it is sad—that very few Tarahumara honor Jículi anymore."

A bonfire lights up a circle of desert and the seven ethereal shapes that move about within it, one of which is shaking a gourd rattle—to which fourteen feet do a turkey-like hopping motion. Stuck into the ground is a cross at the foot of which is a sack containing Jículi—the collected peyote. Now and then one of the dancers takes some sticks from a high heap piled nearby and throws them into the fire, making it blaze up.

On and on through the night—a dancer now and then lying down at the edge of the firelight to sleep for a while. Then rejoining the dance—that never changes.

The stars and the sliver moon now shining much brighter than in the world the dancers have left behind.

"Thank God—it's Lucas," says Chapo.

Heads turn to watch Lucas coming down the arroyo—and as he climbs up the trail from the well.

And finally, lo, there he is before them—Lucas. Who says, "*Buenas tardes.*"

After Chapo, Anita, Roberto, and Mara all say *Buenas tardes.* Chapo says, "All of Barranco Azul was about to go out on horseback looking for you—the sun has burnt you darker than us—and you look as if you haven't eaten since you left—to be honest—you hardly look the same person—come into the house so we can put some food into you."

A week or two or three passes. And Lucas is by now as much a part of the landscape as the blue cliffs—the people naturally assuming he will be here forever, his bones one day buried on the hill where piles of rocks lie over those whose spirits finally did leave Barranco Azul.

So it took all the effort of which he was capable, to one morning, finishing his breakfast, pronounce the words communicating that tomorrow, at first light, he would return to Las Palomas.

Eyes misted over—and Anita began to cry.

The next morning he left $100 under his empty coffee cup.

They all asked, "When are you coming back?

And he always answered, "As soon as I can."

And as he was walking away, he heard Anita say, "Mother says I can sleep in your *jacal*—I will take very good care of it—so that it will always be here waiting for you."

11

May No Scorpion Sting You

When she was 14, Jesusita married Pancho who was twice her age.

Before the marriage, except for an occasional *kwira* and brush of the fingertips Jesusita and Pancho had never interacted with one another. Nevertheless by word of mouth each knew all there really was to know about the other.

Pancho knew that Jesusita was a hard worker, responsible, tended to not drink very much, was less prone to anger than the typical Tarahumara woman, and that besides going barefoot was different in a way people seemed unable to specify.

Jesusita for her part knew that Poncho's wife, taking the two children, had left him for someone from a distant community with whom she had become intimate at one of the fiestas.

She also knew that through hard work he always produced good crops not only of corn, beans, and squash but also of potatoes, peas, and lentils, that he was not one of the ones who when he was drunk might beat his wife, and that he had spent three years in the Mestizo pueblo of San Juan attending a Tarahumara boarding school for grades 7-9.

Within a two hour walk of Chalelo's rancho, down into a steep-sided arroyo and back up again on the other side, there was a *primaria*—an elementary school comprising grades 1-6. About half of the Tarahumara families sent their children to the school, encouraged by the free lunches for the children and by the monthly food allotments and cash stipends that they themselves received. Students from distant ranchos boarded with relatives who lived closer.

Jesusita had never gone because she had been needed to herd the goats.

Prompted by the government, the Tarahumara at one of their Sunday community meetings had voted to construct a playground behind the two-room adobe school building.

On the specified day, families—each adult with a tool and carrying on a shoulder a seven-foot peeled wooden post—arrived from all directions. Although the government would pay them for their labor the people did not come for the pay, or even so much for the sake of the students, but rather to be together and to drink.

Men and women dug holes for the posts and set them and strung chicken wire to enclose the area, carried rocks for terracing the sloping ground, and pushed wheelbarrows of dirt to fill in behind.

Among the workers were Chalelo, Felipa, and Jesusita—and also Pancho.

Marta who had come up out of the *barrancas*—as the big canyons are collectively known—leading a burro loaded with two crates of ripe yellow *guayaba* fruit, was selling them.

At about the same time the hole for the outhouse struck bedrock and had to be restarted in a new location several women began serving *tesguino*. People began to talk loudly and to laugh and to tell stories—and the day turned very *bonito*.

It was the first time that Pancho had seen Jesusita since she had bloomed as a woman—a change which even beneath two flowing skirts, a billowy blouse, and a kerchief was obvious.

The two of them became very aware of each other's presence, exchanged looks from afar, and smiles—and with no more than that a connection was established. Out of all the men of the community equally aware of her—those her age and those somewhat older, the married, and the very old—she had in this way chosen him.

Mid afternoon the work stopped—but not the drinking.

At dark several fires were lit, with afterwards people standing and sitting around them. Chalelo began to play his violin and another man a guitar. Jesusita and Pancho danced together for a while, hopping and stamping their feet, not touching, nor looking at one another.

Until suddenly Jesusita grabbed Pancho by the arm and led him away beyond the reach of the firelight—where in the dark she pulled him onto the ground and on top of her.

In the morning those not too drunk noticed that Jesusita and Pancho were now married as the two of them walked together over to where a caldron of *posole*—a stew of corn and goat meat—hung over a smoking fire. After Jesusita served Pancho and then herself, they stood there for a while along with some others in silence—eating *posole* and tortillas and drinking coffee.

Jesusita went to live with Pablo at his rancho which was a three hour walk from the rancho of Chalelo and Felipa. Alfredo sent his daughter Marta to live with Chalelo and Felipa to herd the goats. He now a poor man would have one less mouth to feed.

He and his neighbors in Arroyo Hondo had received food and other assistance from the other Tarahumarat to help them deal with their bad fortune at the hands of soldiers.

Which was in keeping with the tradition called *korima*—by which those who have more are obligated to give to those who by the inscrutable turns of nature wind up having too little to live on.

Jesusita had grown up hearing her Grandfather Benito say, "The Padre repeated to me over and over that the good person is whoever cares for the least and most unfortunate among us—we the Tarahumara have for the most part always lived that way—like the Padre's God wants people to live."

And sometimes he would add, "Except that instead of wine—we drink *tesguino*."

Pancho farmed his few acres to produce enough food for himself and Jesusita and a little more—for *tesguino*, and also to sell so that he could buy a few things such as coffee, sugar, white flour, and lard. And occasionally a length of stove pipe or a hoe blade, or other item.

Jesusita decided that as a married woman she would wear huaraches—so Pancho bought some tire rubber and thong leather and made her a pair.

And since Tarahumara women all competed with one another in looking nice, Jesusita now and then asked for a cut of cloth from which to sew a new skirt and blouse, or for a new kerchief. Then there was the soap powder for keeping both his and her clothes spotless.

Grandfather Benito had sometimes complained that all those bought items were creations of the Chabochi Devil—explaining that until very recently Tarahumara woman had woven their cloth on a loom with the wool of their own sheep, and that for soap used the mashed roots of a yucca plant, and that the women down in the *barrancas* went bare-breasted.

Nevertheless—he had always liked his coffee, and with lots of sugar.

Pancho, to live well, needed to spend very little time doing the work of farming.

In the spring, walking behind and guiding his two oxen and now and then poking them with a goad and yelling at them he plowed up his fields. Then as the summer rains began he and Jesusita walked in the furrows poking holes into the ground with sharpened sticks and dropping in grains of corn and packing dirt over the holes with a heel. In another field they scattered beans.

When it was time for the corn to be weeded and for mounds of dirt to be put around the base of the young stalks to help support them against the gusty winds unleashed by the violent thunder storms, Pancho invited the neighbors over to drink and to help.

And so on those occasions Jesusita made *tesquino* in a large wash tub, cooking the corn mash outside all day over a fire.

A few days later, the *tesguino* properly fermented, the neighbors arrived early in the morning for breakfast—after which they pulled weeds and mounded dirt around the plants as they drank and talked and ranted and joked and laughed.

Another day Pancho and Jesusita went off to work and drink in a neighbor's field—and a few days later to another. And then to another.

In late fall, the rains having ended and the corn mature, Pancho again invited the neighbors, this time to drink and to harvest. After which he and Jesusita went around to the neighbors to drink and to help them harvest.

Now and then Pablo repaired fence, searched for a missing cow, or shifted the location of the corral for the goats in order to help distribute their manure over his fields.

All of which—added up to maybe two months of field labor during the year.

At his boarding school in San Juan Pancho had had difficulty understanding the turbulence and seeming senselessness of Mexican history.

Nevertheless one thing he did manage to grasp was that when those who work the land are forced to support a ruler—as well as priests, soldiers, government functionaries, and a wealthy landed gentry—their work never ends. And that they become peons or slaves.

He also managed to comprehend that much of the 500 years of Mexican history in some way reflected an entire country's struggle for the freedom and independence and dignity that he and all the other Tarahumara had always had and around which all of Tarahumara life still revolved.

In San Juan he saw that the Chabochi—even the ones driving around in late model pickups with an elbow out the window and the ones pulling out a fat sheaf of peso notes in stores—having become in his eyes slaves to money, could not possibly have an inkling any more of what real freedom was or felt like.

Nor therefore ever understand the Tarahumara.

For him and for most Tarahumara, freedom from the drudgery of endless work and the freedom to do what one wanted when one wanted was much more important than any amount of money—even more important than one's tortillas and beans.

He came to see that such freedom ultimately rested on being one's own master economically, which for him and the other Tarahumara increasingly meant holding tightly onto one's lands.

Ten months into their marriage Jesusita gave birth to a girl.

She squatting on a blanket and breathing hard but not making any other sound, after about 15 minutes pushed out the child. Pancho wiped the little girl with a towel, wrapped her in his jacket, cut the cord with his large pocket knife, and handed her to Jesusita who put her on her breast. The afterbirth he buried under a peach tree.

They did not bother to inform anyone. For them just as life was not seen as a special blessing, neither was a child. Each simply was. One's life to be lived out—and now a child to be raised.

They named her Zenaida.

And so it was not until after Lolo, Pancho's widowed father, had come over to borrow an adze and saw Jesusita with the child in her *rebozo* that people began to find out.

After Lolo had finished his coffee and plate of beans and left, Pancho as he was shoving one end of a four-foot long log into the mouth of the stove, said, "Before he hardly spoke to me—now he comes over all the time—to just sit here."

Jesusita said, "He makes me uncomfortable—but he's your father—we have to make him feel welcome."

Pancho grabbed his ax and headed out the door for more wood.

"Wait—Zenaida and I are coming along to watch."

Almost every day Pancho and Jesusita took Zenaida to the *divisadero*, a rock ledge overlook from which one could look down on a vast expanse of forest and canyon country. Here they would sit or sprawl for an hour, saying nothing—just looking out, or playing with her.

Whenever Pancho left for somewhere by himself for more than a day he touched Zenaida's head and said a prayer asking that all go well with her—that she not get sick, or fall, that no snake bite her, no scorpion sting her.

He still vividly remembers shoveling dirt on the home-made coffin of his little three year old brother. Who asleep on a blanket spread on their dirt floor and stung by a scorpion—died four hours later.

By age two Zenaida could be trusted to walk by herself along the edge of the *divisadero*, whose cliff plunged straight down almost a thousand feet.

Jesusita felt that in Pancho she had chosen well.

Pancho and Jesusita went drinking about twice a week. When it was not to work at some task, it was for a fiesta, or to celebrate a birthday or saints day, and sometimes it was for no other reason except to drink.

They drank to be with the neighbors, as well as to break up the sameness of a sedentary and isolated agricultural existence with entertainment that occasionally verged on sheer spectacle.

Married to Pancho Jesusita now had much less fear of the other men, even the very drunk ones. She danced with them, let them put their arms around her, exchanged sexual banter and squeezes with them—knowing they were now unlikely to try to drag her off into the woods or behind the house.

One evening, sitting by the stove, with Zenaida asleep at their feet, she says to Pancho, "I haven't seen the Devil in a very long time—not since we married."

"What Devil?—the big stuffed Chabochi doll—the Judas we pummel with sticks during the festival of *Semana Santa*—Holy Week—until he's just a pile of straw?"

"No—the huge black one—the real one—who when you touch him there is nothing there."

This morning the neighbors had helped Pancho ax down trees and drag them over to reinforce the fence that had not been holding his two oxen and six cows—the cows being for him as they were for all Tarahumara his money in the bank.

It is now the middle of the night. A dwindling fire throws light across the patio in front of Pancho's house. Everyone is to some degree drunk and the *tesquino* is almost gone. A few strewn bodies are already dead to the world.

Marciano has brought to the gathering a bottle of the *sotol*, a liquor a Chabochi recently taught him how to distill from the base of the same plant from whose long leaves Tarahumara women weave the baskets they sell. The bottle is now open and being passed around among the men.

Lolo is ranting against Chemo who is not present and who with 15 cows is the richest Tarahumara in the community

"He's always running his animals on other people's lands—and saying they broke through."

Lolo stumbling, falls to his knees, and staying like that, says, "When his first wife left him and was never seen again—that may be all that people said— but what he did was throw her off a cliff—and then buried her in a hole he dug there at the bottom."

"Who said that—that I'm a liar?"

Reaching for a stick of firewood he falls on his face. Grabs it. And gets back onto his feet with the stick in hand.

"Who said I'm a liar?"

"You Pancho—give me the bottle—damn it—I said give it to me."

And he stumbles over to Pancho who, head back, is finishing off the bottle.

He whacks Pancho with the stick—who in trying to step back falls over, the bottle rolling clinking away.

"You think you're better than the rest of us because you went to school— well you are nothing—I said nothing—do you hear?"

Then looking around, as if for something, he finds it. And dropping the stick lurches over to Jesusita whose arm he grabs as with the other hand he rips loose her two skirts.

"Now we'll see what this whore of yours is like."

And throwing himself on her they both crash to the ground, Jesusita shrieking.

Someone calls out, "Hey Pancho—what are you doing?"

And right then Lolo as he is struggling with Jesusita, screams and throws himself twisting and rolling to one side.

Jesusita gets up and runs off wailing. And someone says, "Look—he's bleeding like a slaughtered goat—and he's got a long fat jack knife stuck in him."

"Hey—where's Pancho?"

"Let's shove something into those holes."

And so they stuffed pieces of cloth into the holes and two men carried Lolo into Pancho's house—where they left him on a blanket to be attended by two somewhat sober women.

While Chalelo and Felipa headed back toward their rancho—Jesusita with Zenaida in her *reboso* right behind them.

The next day about noon Marciano came by to inform them that Lolo was dead and that the body was right now being carried in a litter by four men to his rancho where that evening there would be a wake along with the usual feast of fresh-killed goat and dancing in front of the coffin which a neighbor was already making. Chalelo said he would bring his violin.

Marciano also said that no one had seen or heard from Pancho.

Felipa said to Jesusita, "Just like a drunk knows better than to stick his hand in a fire—Pancho knew the time was right to disappear—he's gone for good—three or four years in prison he could have handled—but not the shame of facing the neighbors."

"For now—I can't either—I will not be going with you this evening."

Felipa had guessed right. Nobody ever heard from Pancho again.

12

Terribly Awry

About mid September, the thunderstorms having let up, the desert began to cool down.

Lucas told Polo that very soon he was going to set out walking across the desert, following along one bank or the other of the Rio Conchos up toward the Continental Divide to where its thinning tributaries, branching out, penetrate into the very heart of the Sierra Tarahumara.

"But Lucas—we wanted you to be the *compadre* for the baby who will be here in a few months—we are thinking of naming him Lucas."

"I want to get to the Sierra before the snows do—I'm real sorry Polo—not being able to be the godfather of your child—and I know that leaving good friends is like uprooting a tree—but I feel I need to live with those people for a while."

"Live with them?—those people are not like you and me—they used to eat their enemies and dance around a fire with the heads stuck on long poles."

When he told Manuel and Consuelo, Manuel said, "But why walk across the whole state of Chihuahua?—when you can take a bus and be there in a day."

"Dropping into such another world riding a bus—or in a helicopter—would somehow feel—how should I put it?—very discordant with why I am going there."

"But why—besides wanting to live with those people—are you going there?

"It could have something to do with my love and fascination of what I think of as Old Mexico—people like you two—and those in Barranco Azul."

"The Tarahumara are an even older Old Mexico—who go back a thousand years."

Consuelo brushed an eye with her finger.

"We in Las Palomas will miss you very much—Manuel and I were hoping you would marry here—a nice Las Palomas girl—who would fatten you up with tortillas and give you blonde brown-skinned children."

Manuel looked at Consuelo.

"He is looking for their wisdom—and their magic—it is perhaps too ordinary for him here."

"No Manuel—there is wisdom and magic here along the river—and there are no better people anywhere than you two and Jesse."

Gregorio told Lucas, "A number of years ago a young American hippie couple came among us—dressed as Apaches—with moccasins and beads and feathers—claiming to be healers—and I tell you—the whole romantic Indian business can easily become an aberration—a disease."

"Do you know what Gregorio?—maybe all this really has very little to do with Indians—or with Old Mexico."

"With what then?"

"I don't know—that's what I'm hoping to find out."

The last person he spoke to of his plans and by far the hardest for him— was Norma. She had never given any sign that she understood anything of the very few sentences he had occasionally spoken to her. Nor did she this time. But he sensed she could read the message his body transmitted—and reacted by becoming somehow even more silent than a silent person usually is.

Soon everyone in Las Palomas knew that soon he would leave them to begin a two month walk up the Conchos to the Sierra Tarahumara.

On a trip to the States for his mail and to arrange some matters he visited Donald and Mary.

Donald said, "That slippery tunnel you seem to on the verge of sliding down is the one through the fourth dimension to the other universe parallel to this one—you will never find your way back."

Lucas, aware of it feeling very odd sitting on a sofa, said, "There is never a way back from anywhere."

Mary said, "You seem much more of a—what shall we say?—well maybe a spiritual warrior—than when we last saw you—you continue to amaze me— and I am very happy for you."

Then she said, "I defended you against Julie—our psychiatrist friend—who when I described you explained that living in another culture is symptomatic of a character disorder."

"I've faced them in court—the trained people experts—who thinking that by fitting someone into their mental paradigm they then understand and know that person."

"And that that then makes them intellectually and morally superior to that person—with the right to control his or her destiny."

A massive white thunderhead billowing upward. And soon—towering over the Sierra Rica.

Then suddenly, the world exploding with wild crazy bolts of lightning and crashing thunder, as thousands of waterfalls cascade from the sky, falling on and obliterating the villages of Las Palomas and El Valle.

After two hours—the storm turns to a light steady rain.

That evening, the rain done, Lucas stands on a rise that overlooks Arroyo Grande and watches as entire trees are swept along in the wide brown roiling waters—the branches, trunks, and tangled roots of trees rolling in the waves and somersaulting in the air.

He walks through the mire of sticky adobe mud and puddles back to his house. Where he lies down on the bed, and lulled by the dull distant roar from the arroyo, falls into a deep sleep.

A loud knocking on the door wakes him up, and wondering who could be about in such darkness and muck, he goes to the door and opens it.

"Why good evening Petronila."

"Hey tey wey—I am flattered you remember my name—wey tey hey—I have come to visit you."

"Well you just come right in and make yourself at home—here is a chair—and I will fix you some hot coffee—you look like you are soaked two times over."

"It's nothing—it's just getting wet—hey tey wey—what is important is that the others have elected me to come here to apologize for wanting to banish the Gringo back to his own country—and to let him know that if he were to stay in Las Palomas—we would all clap our hands."

"Why I really appreciate that Petronila."

Lucas goes over to the stove, lights a burner, and then stands there, waiting for water to boil. There is silence, until Petronila says, "You did not act superior to us who live on this side of the river—you did not try to teach us anything—and like us—though in your own special way—you shit on borders—and on boxes and conventions—that hide what is Real. "

Lucas hands her a cup of steaming coffee and sits down in a chair across from her.

"But you are still very far from perfect—you think we are nuts—just like the others do—and that we are old dry wrinkly hags—and that we don't dress and talk properly."

Lucas does not know what to say. He notices for the first time that she—like Hermelinda—is much darker than most Mexicans, more Indian looking, and that her eyes are as alive and alert and penetrating as any he has ever seen. He guesses her to be anywhere from 50 to 80.

Laughing, she says, "Come—I will take off these wet clothes—and then let us two climb into your bed together—in Mexico we have a proverb which says, The dark ones—even the ugly ones—are very good under the blanket."

Lucas freezes.

And again she laughs, "See—you think that because I am old—that the Fire of Creation out of which arose the earth and the stars is no longer in me—you hesitated—and now the opportunity is lost and irretrievable—you would have come to know things you never knew before—and to know them with more certainty than you have ever known anything."

Lucas suddenly likes, feels connected to this woman.

"Nevertheless—I and the other witches of El Valle are going to give you a going-away present—and since we know we cannot trick you again with a cake—we will dance and frolic around a bonfire—and invoke the beautiful Tonantzin—once an Earth Fertility Goddess of the Aztecs—whose Temple was torn down by those pious Franciscans—and who herself was torn apart by snarling Spanish mastiffs—but who still lives—wandering alone up in the mountains people call the Sierra Rica."

"And so now—with your permission—I am off for El Valle."

Petronila gets up from her chair and goes to the door. Opens it to the dark wet night.

"How can you possibly cross the waters of the arroyo?"

"I will take a running start and leap—hey tey wey—and hold my feet and skirt high—so as not to get tangled in the branches of a swimming tree—wey tey hey."

"Are you sure you don't want to stay here until morning?"

But before he finished the sentence she was gone.

◆ ◆ ◆

Several nights later—Lucas finds himself flying toward a huge round white moon, he enjoying immensely sweeping sideways to the left, and then swooping upwards and down and around—and now and then turning somersaults like a cottonwood tree in the swollen waters of the arroyo. For the first time in his life he knows the joy of pure freedom.

From his left, flying in a narrowing spiral, comes Anita, and right behind her, Norma, a long golden string attached to an ankle, which nobody has to tell him is to keep her from flying off to a far star and hiding out there. The three of them do loops around each other, all of them laughing, and the two women emitting shrieks besides.

They are joined by Petronila.

"Hey wey tey—tey wey hey."

And then they are joined by who might possibly be the most beautiful Indian woman who ever walked the earth—she of the Enchanted Mountain, Tonantzin.

And the five of them do loops around each other, in silence now, out of respect for the Goddess, and with skirts staying magically and decorously in place.

Except for Petronila's, which suddenly wraps itself around her head—causing her to collide with a thud against Lucas.

Who clutching her tightly against him, whispers in her ear, "Hey tey wey."

The flood waters having receded, Lucas walks up Arroyo Grande looking at the newly deposited piles of sand and gravel and debris with here and there an uprooted cottonwood or ash tree lying on its side.

"Look down there guys—it's the albino Indian—without his bow and arrows—heads up Lucas—here come some buzzard feathers to stick in your sombrero—to help make you even more ludicrous."

Lucas stops—and looks up at the four circling buzzards.

"Go back to being a lawyer—and accept your slice of society's pie."

Four long black feathers come to rest near his feet.

And another buzzard shouts down to Lucas, "There is no equality in nature—just as there are no perfect circles—what holds society together is not understanding and compassion—and pretty ideas—but *los chingones*—those who impose their strength and will with impunity on the weak—every burro—even the dumbest Mexican knows that."

And yet another shouts down, even louder, "Whenever the *chingones* come across honesty and trust and humility—they lick their lips."

And then with all the vehemence of which it is capable, spits out, "And as for you—who obstinately refuses to join the other sheep going meekly to slaughter—you can be sure that when the *chingones* go up your ass—it won't be to search you."

And the fourth buzzard spits down, with even more vehemence, "And we buzzards when we find your carcass—will begin with you right there too."

And they soar upwards chanting, "Ludicrous Lucas—even more ludicrous than a rich man on his 90 foot yacht uncorking a two-hundred-dollar bottle of champagne—Ludicrous Lucas—even more ludicrous than—"

Lucas shuts his ears and eyes and mind to the black creatures, and stepping over the four feathers, returns to walking and being with the beauty of the arroyo, its recent waters, still muddy, sliding snaking downhill toward the nearby Rio Grande.

On the morning of Lucas' departure a small group is gathered at his house for breakfast. Polo and Hermelinda. Manuel and Consuelo. Gregorio. And Jesse. Tied outside are two saddled horses and a saddled burro. Lucas' pickup with a few things in it is already parked in back of Manuel's house.

They file out, Lucas last with his blanket roll over a shoulder. He padlocks the door—gives the key to Manuel. Polo and Hermelinda climb onto the horses and Jesse onto his burro. Lucas adjusts his brand-new American Teva sandals—his answer to blisters and also, given the many anticipated river crossings, to water-logged boots.

And they are off. Move on through the village, Lucas waving to someone here and there. At the last house he shakes hands with Manuel and Consuelo. And then with Gregorio, who says, "Be sure to come back—and with a good story—for a *corrido*."

Manuel and Consuelo say nothing.

Lucas says to them, "Go into my house and lift up the coffee cup in the middle of the table."

Then everyone waving, Lucas and the other three head out into the desert, Polo riding up ahead. Wind up arroyos and across a ridge—and down an arroyo. Cross an expanse of flat basin. Enter a maze of rocky hills.

On a beautiful, not too hot October day.

Mid afternoon, passing through a line of cottonwood and salt cedar trees, they come to the bank of the Rio Conchos—smaller than the Rio Grande, and more beautiful than Lucas had imagined. The three riders dismount and tie their animals.

They and Lucas walk down the sandy bank and to the edge of the river.

Polo tosses a stone that goes plunk.

"That's was you Lucas—disappearing into who knows where—and leaving only ripples—and then not even ripples."

Polo continues.

"When you hit a wall go up and around above it—or cross over to the other side—in many places you can wade—always put your camp on high ground where a big water can't get you—there are houses and tiny villages here and there along the way."

Hermelinda says, "When you get to some houses that go by the name of La Paz—ask for my Aunt Modesta—and tell her I said to send you away with enough tortillas and whatever else she has to last for several days."

Jesse says, "I'd come with you—but Juana would give me hell."

Lucas says, "You inspired this Jesse—and a lot of other things."

He looks hard at each of them. And then shakes their hands, Hermelinda asking when he will be back.

To which he gives the Mexican answer, "*Quién sabe?*—who knows."

From out of somewhere, he faintly hears, "*Que te vaya bien*—good luck."

As he turns away, and takes the first step of his walk up along the Conchos, he hears, again from that same unreal place, but now even more faintly, "*Que Diós te cuide*—May God look after you."

And feeling in the pit of his stomach that something is terribly awry with this beautiful river and this beautiful October day, that seems to be spinning out of control all around him and under his feet, he takes another step, and another, and another—

Not looking back.

Knowing in his heart that early human beings—the ancient nomadic hunter gatherers—did not, were not meant to walk away like this from their band.

He had brought with him no map—and the very little food he had brought soon ran out. But what he needed always turned up.

Whenever he came to a house he asked the best route to the next house. And was received by the very poor Mexicans with the same hospitality that he had known in Barranco Azul.

"*Pase—pase,* " they all said.

And so he never lacked for food or for a place to stay for the night—or even for a few days if that felt right. In those small villages in which there was a small store he bought a few cans of tuna fish, some crackers, and oranges, for along the way—and afterwards sat out front drinking a warm bottled soft drink and visiting with whomever happened to be around.

The people in the occasional larger villages were much less likely to want to relate to him or to say, *Pase*—although there always seemed to be one person who did.

Twice he came to villages whose weird invisible wind he could feel even before he entered. Who knows what the people there were up to or what had happened there. And so like Jesus more than once had done, he too more or less stamped the dirt of those places from his Teva sandals and moved on.

Whenever he could he slept under the cottonwoods by the shore of the river or on a nearby rise overlooking it—delighting in the feel of the raw earth and in waking up to the sun giving birth to the new morning. He bathed every day—as well as washed out his clothes, squishing them without soap in the river until they lost their smell.

Now and then there were high walls on both sides of the river and he had to head inland to find a way around. Once he got lost. But then in the middle of what seemed like nowhere came upon two burros, and then their owner who was harvesting candelilla nearby. Who acting not in the least surprised to see him took him to the river.

Another time, he contemplating a wade through deep fast dangerous water, a man on horseback appeared on the opposite side, crossed over to him through the churning water that came to his stirrups, and took him across sitting behind on the animal's rump.

Everywhere and in every weather—he felt totally at home.

He thought now and then of the houseless ones—Jesus, and the yogis of India, and the bag ladies, and the birds in the field. And how for most of human history everyone had lived somewhat like he now was—moving onward from one day to the next and finding one's daily bread wherever one happened to find it.

He began to feel that something comparable to a Divine Providence was walking with him—nudging him along and guiding him. It was a feeling deeper than faith.

Walking a little every day, day after day, following the Conchos—yesterday and tomorrow ceased to exist.

And soon he even forgot that he was headed for the Sierra Tarahumara.

13
Among the Boulders

Felipa pushes the burning log further into the stove. Then sits down on a stump, looking very worn out, older, her tautness and quickness to anger diminished. Chalelo takes down the violin hanging on the wall, and tunes the strings.

Felipa says,"You Jesusita have lost a husband—but I want to repeat again to fix well in your mind what I have already told you more than once—my story—and the story of the others—of when the measles came—and when for a week I did not have the strength to stand on my feet—when we had to bury my younger sister and two of my brothers in back of the house where the three piles of rocks are—and how all the neighbors shut themselves in their houses but still almost half of them died too."

"So that afterwards—it seemed to those of us who were left—that we had to start up the world all over again."

"Neither Lolo nor Pancho—nor the drinking—did this—it's just that life sometimes happens in that kind of way—no matter what one does."

Jesuista accomodates Zenaida into her *reboso*, walks out into the night, hearing behind her the repetitive strains of *pascola* music.

Jesusita asleep on some heaped-up pine needles, with Zenaida beside her, comes awake to a round moon shining on her face.

Never has she ever wondered what the moon was, or made of, the moon being simply the moon, as grass is grass.

Bathed in its light, and feeling soothed and that the moon is trying to heal her, she digs her bare feet down under the pine needles.

She remembers how her Grandfather Benito had told her that Father Sun is a harsh master who if angered can punish and destroy by burning up the people or by not returning in the spring high in the sky to warm them, or by withholding the rains so that the corn withers, or by sending too much rain and drowning the corn and sometimes the people too. And so it was important to dance to honor Father Sun and to share with him the best of what one has—thick tortillas, the meat of a fat cow or goat, and of course *tesguino*.

He went on to tell her that to the contrary, Mother Moon in the dark of night is gentle and comforting, accessible and intimate—as she grows round and wanes and grows round again. And that she will listen if one talks to her—and care. She too wants to come down to the fiestas of the Tarahumara, though not so much to be honored as to just be with her children.

All which had echoed much of what she herself had already intuited from having wandered through the canyons for days at a time with her herd of goats, sleeping with the moon shining down upon her like a caring mother and in the morning waking up to the rising Father Sun as shattering the darkness of light he lit up the small far-off patches of green corn on the hillsides.

Honoring the Sun and the Moon, those two from whom life emanates, as well as relating in a deep and caring way to everyone and everything, and sharing—it seemed she already knew all that. And she told him so.

"That could well be—because the forces driving Sun and Moon are the same ones that flow within all of us"

Her Grandfather Benito had gone on to say, "Not listening to and heeding those forces—people flounder and err at every turn—like the Chabochi—and those Tarahumara too who no longer think and live like all Tarahumara once used to."

"It is no longer enough to be just a reverent and honest Tarahumara—one needs to stay alert and strong—very alert and strong—and resistant—because every day the world is a more dangerous place—more full of seductions to become like the Chabochi."

"And because the old good ways are very fragile Jesusita—very—very fragile."

She had always seen that Father Sun was more necessary for the sheer survival of the people. But tonight, soothed by Mother Moon, she wonders, "Is sheer survival at any cost—at the center of life?

"Might not Mother Moon—who helps one to heal—and to become a good person—and who is a good friend—be just as important as Father Sun?"

"Might not—she be more important?"

❖ ❖ ❖

Jesusita once again took charge of the goats. And Marta took over the housework as well as helping with bringing in the wood for the fire—only going out with the goats when Jesusita, Chalelo, and Felipa went off to drink.

It seemed to Jesusita that all the men now wanted her—her body—more than ever.

When one day she came face to face with a Chabochi on the trail who tried to grab her, she darted downhill, knowing that absolutely no Chabochi could catch her.

A Tarahumara she knew would probably have caught her. But they, unless drunk, were too timid to grab her.

Once at a gathering, when a drunk Tarahumara managed to drag her by the arm beyond the fire light, she pleaded having to urinate. Then went off a few feet, squatted down—and was suddenly gone.

Another time, when the man wasn't paying attention, she picked up a stone and heaved it behind them and as it crashed, yelled, "Someone is coming."

And when he turned, she darted off and hid quietly behind a nearby pine tree.

"Where did you fly off to?—you witch."

In the direction away from the Big Canyon the land where Jesusita herded the goats abutted the land where Esteban and María herded theirs. They being neighbors and thus often drinking together she knew both of them well.

Esteban was the most beautiful of the Tarahumara men, and the best runner, always part of one or another team that competed in running along together and with a foot hurling a small wooden ball ahead of them—the teams covering a distance of 100 miles and with torches of pitch pine carried by spectators helping to illuminate the way once it got dark. Jesusita always bet one of her pretty skirts on his team and over time had won more skirts than she had lost, most of which she then gave as gifts to her mother and sister.

Esteban and María had two children, the oldest still too young to go out alone with the goats. So María and Esteban took turns herding them. Now and then Jesusita when she saw María with the goats would herd hers that way and the two women would visit—at which times María, who was also pretty, seemingly enough so to hold any man, never failed to complain to Jesusita that Esteban drank too much and went off with other women at the *tesguinadas*.

But everyone knew that—and also that María had often fought with the other women—once drawing blood with a hoe.

Although Esteban had never grabbed her, twice he did try to get her to leave a *tesguinada* with him and a blanket

Late one afternoon, the sun almost down, Esteban herded his goats so that they were closer to hers than usual, and for a while kept them like that, so that he and she were in view of one another.

And she watching him bounding from rock to rock marveled at how incredibly quick and agile he was—and how incredibly beautiful. He darker and taller than most Tarahumara. With long flowing hair.

And watching him become as if one with the grey rock cliffs, the pines and the maguey and the sky—so did she. And in this way and in spite of the distance they each kept, they mingled—such that she felt they were now connected forever.

And so with Zenaida slung in a *reboso* on her back, she threw some stones at her goats and herded them toward his.

When she arrived back at the house in the middle of the night she casually mentioned to Felipa that the goats had run off and that it had taken her several hours to find them.

Then two weeks later she announced to Chalelo and Felipa that she and Esteban were married and that she would now be living with him on the rancho of his brother since where he had lived with María belonged to her.

As she wraps three skirts, two blouses, and a comb in a *rebozo*, Felipa says, "And the two children?"

"They will stay with María."

"You know that some of the women say she is a *hechicera*—a *bruja*—a witch."

"That is what they say about anyone they don't like."

She knots the *rebozo*, and with another *rebozo* attaches Zenaida to her back, knots it, and picks up the bundle.

"It's been very hard—very—without Pancho."

Jesusita and Esteban moved into the adobe house in which Esteban's mother had been living until she died a year ago. The brother Faustino and his wife Matilde and a daughter Claudia who was 14 lived nearby across some fields.

And so she again began to live the life of every Tarahumara wife—making the tortillas, ridding the beans of stones and dirt and then boiling them all morning, hauling water up from the arroyo in a bucket balanced on her head, scrubbing and beating the soiled clothes on a large flat rock, throwing corn to the chickens, starting the fire in the stove and keeping it burning, chopping firewood, working in the fields, and gathering in season the wild greens, mushrooms, prickly pear pads and their sweet *tuna* fruits, And of course took care of Zenaida, who at three was now speaking a little Tarahumara as well as some Spanish.

Somehow it was not as easy for her to settle into being married again as she had imagined it would be. She was quick to make comparisons with Pancho. Esteban was critical and demanding, and when he was drinking they fought a lot. And so it was not long before her intense joy in the two of them sleeping tangled together throughout the night began to diminish.

Then suddenly Esteban began sleeping in a corner on his own blanket.

One night she hears something rattling on the roof—and her first thought is that it is the scraping of the Black Devil—coming for her. She pulls the blanket over her head.

But then right away stands up, and looking about her sees that Esteban is not on his blanket. She goes cautiously to the door, opens it, and stepping into the moonless night catches sight of the hulk of what must certainly be the Black Devil—just as it disappears down the trail into the arroyo from which she carries up their water.

She hesitates. Has the Black Devil carried off Esteban?

Feeling dizzy, and herself falling into a world of weirdness and confusion, she begins to feel herself being pulled by a strange force effortlessly and silently down the trail toward the arroyo.

At an overlook from which she can hear a trickle of water, she stops. And watches as two shapes—a smaller one and a much larger one—sink down together among the boulders.

She throws a rock hard, and another one, and still more into the night—until long after the shapes are gone.

Suddenly remembering Zenaida—she turns and runs frantic back up to the house.

When Jesusita opens her eyes to the bright light of the morning she knows immediately that it was Claudia who Esteban had followed down to the arroyo. And that it was she who had thrown pebbles on the roof. She knows as only a woman knows. In response to a whine, she turns over and gives Zenaida a breast.

As she is gathering together her few things, she hears a woman's voice.

"Jesusita—it's me María."

She opens the door, and they exchange the *kwira* greeting.

"What a surprise—sit down."

Jesusita shoves some sticks of *ocote* into the stove to revive the fire.

"No don't bother with anything—I just came from Faustino's house where I left off some dried cow meat in return for a favor—and where I ate very well—here's a little meat for you too—as a gift—and to let you know I have no anger toward you—yesterday the cow fell and broke a leg."

María hands Jesusita a small flour sack and Jesusita puts it with her small pile of things.

"Faustino said that Esteban is drinking at the house of Shimino—and that it looks like they will be at it for another two days—and so I knew this would be a good day to stop by."

"Yes—it is a good day."

"Well I am going now."

And as María walks away, Jesusita says, very softly, "Yes—it is a very good day."

She puts her things and the meat on a *rebozo*, which she folds and knots. Then fastens Zenaida to her back with the other *reboso* and walks away from the house—leaving the door wide open.

Arriving at her parent's hut, she finds no one there—the stove cold.

"Yes—it is a very good day for everyone—they are all off drinking with Shimino."

She lays some sticks in the stove and starts a fire. Roasts the meat in some goat fat in a fry pan. Eats, giving some pieces to Zenaida. And puts what is left back in the flour sack, and again ties up the *reboso*. Then lies down on the dirt floor and sleeps for a while alongside Zenaida.

It almost dark she sets out with Zenaida in the direction of the Big

Canyon. And only when she arrives at a tiny rock structure she has stayed in before when she was herding the goats does she stop.

At Shimino's house that night, some of the drunks heard from far off in the direction of the Big Canyon the occasional faint howling like none they had ever heard before of a sick coyote.

And the next night too—of what was probably the same coyote before it died.

14
Killing Stone

Lucas has so far found the Tarahumara more often than not both fearful and hostile to his presence, and at best not very open and friendly—to the point that he has more than once considered abandoning his goal of living for a while among those people.

Their shed-like log houses have for the most part been located well away from and usually high above the main trails. For him to negotiate the barely distinguishable very thin paths that led up to them often required grasping with both hands onto rocks or trees.

These tiny ranchos were located not far from water and where there was a small patch of ground on which to plant enough corn and beans to feed a family. Hardly ever were they in sight of one another.

Most of the women upon catching sight of him ran off into the woods. Or if in their houses they shut themselves inside, not coming out even at his request for a glass of water, as he stood there surrounded by vicious yelping dogs looking for the opportunity to bite a leg from behind.

Not once has he been invited to eat a tortilla and a plate of beans. One woman, who did not run, offered to sell him a liter of water for ten dollars.

Most of the men he encountered—some of whom were dressed in traditional knee-length skirt and loose fitting blouse-like shirt and others of whom were dressed like Mestizos in long pants, long-sleeved shirt, and vaquero hat—greeted him with a Kwira, touching their fingertips to his.

But although all the men, unlike all the women, spoke some Spanish, it was difficult to get information from them—about anything. When he asked where the next rancho was the typical answer was, Over there, accompanied by an equally vague wave of the hand. Twice he was deliberately pointed in the wrong direction.

It was much more than the noble reserve which Lumholz described, or a fear of outsiders—it was, it seemed to him, their version of a closed border, of a Wall, for keeping intruders like him out.

Nevertheless, in spite of their fear and hostility, with persistence and a willingness to accept rejection, and by learning to read what was unspoken in a people who spoke very little, and by presenting himself very humbly, he managed to find Tarahumara here and there who did interact with him—sold him some tortillas and beans, or *pinole*, let him put up his tarp lean-to nearby, did make the effort to indicate to him which fork in the trail to take.

Whenever he asked if he could buy some food he rarely got a yes or no, the man or woman simply disappearing into the house. But he learned to hang around or to go off a ways and set up his camp—and that after a while someone from the family, often one of the children, would come over with a filling and delicious meal.

He became completely comfortable with their almost silent way of being with each other and with him—finding it more relational and connective than asking and answering questions and telling stories.

And so by simply being among the Tarahumara on their isolated ranchos, and by being aware and watching everything—the men and the women, the children, the goats and the oxen, and the arrangement of their houses and fields—he saw he was in fact beginning to assimilate, little by little, the essence of these people.

This essence, reminding him of the remnants of the Old Mexico he had experienced along the Rio Grande, he decided was again an expression of an uncomplicated way of being in the world, a world of a few fully comprehensible parts understandable by everyone.

However in the case of the Tarahumara, that essence was also an expression of living outside in nature—working in the fields, and with axes in the forest, walking everywhere, mostly up or down, and often cooking on an open fire in front of their houses, and weaving their wool blankets and doing most of their other domestic tasks there too.

And it was that, he decided, which gave them the aura of being charged with what Lumholz had referred to as the *"electricity of nature."*

He soon saw them as not at all exotic, but as people just like himself—only happening to live another way.

By far the most welcoming were the drunks, who throwing an arm around him or extending a gourd of *tesguino* toward him insisted he drink and meet the neighbors sitting and sprawled nearby on the ground, the men and women and children looking like a band of ragged amiable gypsies, all of them talkative and wanting to be friends with him.

However very quickly he learned that at any time during such gatherings, simply his presence alone was often sufficient to incite insults from someone, then to being pushed, and finally to that person wanting to fight with the Gringo.

So he found ways to avoid all situations involving drinking—knowing that politely refusing to join in could also lead to nastiness. Now whenever he heard loud talking or yells he made a wide detour. Whenever offered a drink he claimed a bad stomach.

The hostility toward him that went far beyond the hostility of most groups toward outsiders was quite understandable.

Several of the first Spanish missionaries arriving in the early 1600s had described the Tarahumara as supremely hospitable and generous, and as a people incapable even of lying, and who quickly and easily identified with the person and teachings of Jesus.

However others—miners, farmers, cattlemen, and merchants—followed right on the heels of the missionaries.

As a consequence, the Tarahumara soon found themselves losing their best lands, cheated at every turn, put to forced labor in the mines. They saw their women violated.

When the Tarahumara resisted, they saw the heads of their shamans skewered on the tops of long upright poles.

And so the Tarahumara rather than face further violation and humiliation, and even extermination, began a gradual withdrawal into the most inaccessible and rugged parts of the Sierra and into its deepest canyons, taking along with them not only some European agricultural practices but also an intense hatred of the Chabochi invader.

Who—white and bearded and with a long penis—they incorporated into their religion as the personification of the Devil. An effigy of which they would once a year beat with clubs to a pile of loose straw.

This morning, from his camp on a low knoll, he looks down on two small fields of mature corn and beyond them at a log hut from whose pine shake roof smoke filters upward through the cracks. His eyes follow the bright colors of a

Tarahumara girl as she releases some goats from a pole corral—and then with her dog drives them up a valley.

As soon as they disappear from sight he slings his bedroll over a shoulder—and continues his walk along a branch of the Rio Conchos in a westerly direction towards the Continental Divide. Once on the other side, he will drop down into one of the several very deep canyons—three of them deeper than the Grand Canyon—which channel the waters of the steep western slope of the Sierra towards the Gulf of California.

He no longer has any doubts. Somewhere in one of those canyons he will stop walking. And there, indeed live for a while with these very different and fine people—no matter what.

The next morning he follows a little-used trail and the river into a high gorge. With barely room for him along one of its walls, he picks his way, the waters cascading from one greenish pool to another. Twice he has to step into one of the pools, the water reaching to his waist.

Where the gorge opens up the land flattens and the river meanders through a valley planted in corn, the tawny stalks and leaves of late autumn more than head high.

Coming to a black two-inch hose that crosses the trail he stops, and notices at the edge of the river a red Pacific Marine pump similar to ones he has seen in the States. Curious, he follows along the hose in a direction away from the river and into the corn field.

And almost immediately comes upon another field, this one planted in marijuana, and like the corn ready to be harvested. He guesses there could be as many as 100 acres.

On two occasions, in the States, the prosecution had introduced entire plants just like the ones before him into the court as evidence.

Now nervous, he decides to backtrack through the gorge and to look for another trail parallel to the river but away from it.

"Freeze Gringo—and put your hands on your head."

Putting his two hands on his head, and slowly turning, he sees there are six of them, with their low-slung black machine guns pointed at him. Although all wear dark green uniforms, visored black caps, and combat boots, Lucas knows they are not the Mexican army. They all look nasty.

"We've been watching you since you entered the gorge—drop that blanket contraption to the ground—and return your hands to your head."

One of the men pat searches him—then picks up the bed roll.

"Good—now come along with us—you in the middle—you can put your hands down now."

They all walk back the short way to the main trail—and then continue up river on it.

Lucas well aware that a few US anti-drug agents have disappeared for good in Mexico knows that right now is not the time to protest anything.

They turn onto a side trail. And soon come to a small brown adobe house encircled by a barbed wire fence. One of the men undoing and holding open the gate, they pass through and go into the house where there is a small table around which are three stumps for sitting on, a counter with some dirty dishes on it, and a wood stove made from half of a rusty oil drum.

Lucas stares at some clothes strewn in a corner on the dirt floor along with a few children's toys. And is overcome by the strange feeling that a Tarahumara family very recently lived here—a wealthier and more Mexicanized one—and then very suddenly left.

"Into the next room Gringo."

Lucas going through the open door finds himself in a room in which there are two beds with torn rumpled Tarahumara wool blankets on them— and on one of the beds a blonde-haired doll without arms.

One of the two men who has entered with him, standing by the door, the barrel of the machine gun cradled in the crook of an arm, says, "Take off your clothes."

"Everything?"

"Everything—make a neat pile on that bed."

Lucas does what he was told.

The other man scoops up the clothes, and they both leave, closing the door on Lucas.

Lucas lies down on one of the beds, pulls the blanket part way over himself—waiting for what will be next, very resigned, having given himself up totally to what increasingly seems to him like a dream. Finding himself strangely calm and unafraid, and wondering why, he falls asleep.

He is woken by the door opening, through which a single man enters, his only arm the revolver at his waist.

"Here—you can put your clothes back on now—we sent some people down river asking the Indians about you—it appears there is just you—and from what they could make out you are no more than a loco Gringo."

Lucas gets up and dresses.

"Even though we went through everything and found nothing that might indicate otherwise—our associates over on the coast—using the personal data we found—are running a background check on you—to help determine for sure whether you do or do not work for the government—or a newspaper."

There is a tapping at the front door.

"Come in."

A small Tarahumara woman looking to be in her early twenties enters with a basket of tortillas and an earthen bowl of beans, looks around, and sets the food on a bed.

"Thank you Petra—this is Lucas—he'll be staying with us a while."

The woman not acknowledging Lucas moves hurriedly back outside.

"The house is for your use—don't go beyond the fence—there are thirty of us near by—better trained than the army—and familiar with every inch of ground—even on a night so dark you yourself would get lost returning from the outhouse—and we have dogs and Indian trackers who can find anyone."

The man looks at Lucas.

"What we do with you will be up to The Old Man—who you will meet when he comes by to chat with you—it could very well be that we—you know—"

And the man finishes by drawing his index finger at right angles across his own throat.

When he is gone, Lucas takes the bowl and basket to the table in the other room and sits down on a stump to eat the by now very familiar meal of boiled beans and thick hand-patted tortillas made with corn ground on a stone *metate*

He goes to bed as it is beginning to get dark, and lies there.

He knows that these people live in constant fear—of rival cartels, the government, and betrayal from within their own ranks. And he knows that they could very easily perceive him as equally dangerous. And kill him.

He is aware of their penchant for throwing severed heads on the dance floor at fiestas, and for placing them in the beer coolers. And that during the Mexican Revolution, all factions—all of Mexico—partook of variations of this same custom.

Yet he has never felt so totally unafraid of anything as he does now—of what still seems to him like a dream, a dream in sharper focus than wakefulness.

It becomes clearer to him than ever before that the ultimate purpose of anything is not survival, but rather to play out its small part in the totality of the flow of mysterious energies constituting the Universe.

Most seeds do not take hold. Forests are leveled by fire and plagues. Sometimes obliterated by a slowly moving sea of ice.

Of all known species, 99.9% are now extinct.

Every civilization has eventually crumbled. And the Hopi elders are waiting patiently in their brown sun-baked pueblos for the American Dinosaur too to finally crash earthward of its own weight—for the White Man too to pass.

According to Donald, the Universe at some point in the very far future will have become a highly energy-diluted and uniform nothingness.

Leaving no trace whatsoever that anything ever was.

Suddenly—he finds himself high up in the sky in the south of Mexico and looking down on the hundreds of pyramids that once comprised the soul of Mesoamerica.

Virgin princesses and virile young warriors, as well as a sea of others, are climbing the steps up to the sacrificial killing stones. Where black-robed priests with sharp obsidian knives are slicing open chests and ripping out the hearts and holding them, dripping blood, up to the Sun.

And then just as suddenly—he finds himself in a long line of Indians at the base of one of the pyramids.

Waiting his turn to begin climbing the steps.

Up to the bloodied place—to help move the Sun across the sky and to nourish the green head-high corn swaying in the wind in the surrounding valleys below.

From somewhere, something invisible swishes through what could be tall green corn stalks—toward him.

"A fine pickle of fish Lucas—you escaped from the box of cultural-illusion—and from the box of the illusion of the personal I and its story—and now I find you here—inside this chintzy box of adobe bricks—a prisoner of the infamous Mafia."

"Yes—and now it could be that I am about to leave the world of boxes—and return to being what never was in the first place."

"Are you are ready for that?"

"Yes—I have spent some time with the Tarahumara—all of us just sitting around together on the ground—saying nothing—just being with each other—and with the corn and bean fields—and with the trees and the rocks and the grass—and the breeze and the sky—"

"And?"

"It was like coming home—to the zillions of thread-like connections that constitute Reality."

"And so?"

"And so that confirmed what I already suspected—that it is the likes of you—the pure disembodied bundles of words—that needs to be vanquished—and not the specter of returning to being the Man Who Never Was."

And with that the Presence went clunk and vanished.

A tapping on the front door wakens him at dawn. When he opens the door, the same Tarahumara woman, Petra, handing him a dish covered with a piece of cloth, says, "*Kwira.*"

"*Kwira,*"

He takes the dish without saying thank you—having learned that a Tarahumara even if given a thousand peso bill does not acknowledge the gift.

Petra remains standing there. He is aware that alone she seems entirely at ease with him.

"Where did the family go that used to live here?"

A wild look contorting her face, she says, "They—they killed him—and Juani too—his grown son—for making trouble—they—they buried them behind the outhouse—his wife was able to run off taking their girl—I have to go now."

And she hurries off through the gate, forgetting to close it.

Lucas closes the gate, brings the dish of food into the kitchen, and immediately goes back outside to look behind the outhouse. Where he sees the disturbed soil and vegetation and out of place rocks where not very long ago a large hole had been dug.

He seemed to have known all this from the moment he set foot in the house.

In the States he had come across an article in the *El Paso Times* describing the intrusion of the drug cartels into the most remote parts of the Sierra Tarahumara and how in some areas Tarahumara resisting the occupation and seizure of their lands were being murdered.

Back in the kitchen, sitting on his stump, he eats his beans and tortillas, along with a hard-boiled egg and a hot red chile.

The door opens and a white-haired man wearing jeans, a torn and faded red T-shirt, and Tarahumara tire-rubber huaraches enters, he is perhaps around 80, but moving like a much younger man. There is no visible sign of a pistol.

"*Buenos días* Lucas—no—stay where you are and finish your egg."

The man goes over to Lucas, who as they shake hands, says, "*Buenas días.*"

"I'm Luis—The Old Man—whatever—I've come to chat with you—and to ask you a few questions."

The Old Man sits down on another stump across the table from Lucas. Who finishes his egg—The Old Man studying him.

"So tell me—how did you decide to become a lawyer?"

"To tell it right would take a while."

"We have all day."

"My father—when he was a college student—was part of what is sometimes referred to as the counter culture of the sixties—a time when there was a surge in grass roots citizen democracy—in a country increasingly perceived by many to be run by corporations, banks, law firms, foundations, the media, and the government bureaucracy."

Lucas pauses, self conscious—aware he has never told this story before.

"His part in all that was helping African Americans show that the freedom and equality that defined America was a myth—in Alabama he was clubbed and jailed by the police while the FBI looked on—are you sure you want to hear all this?"

The Old Man smiling, says, "In the sixties—one of Mexico's best known muralists—who painted the noblest aspects of our Revolution—went to jail too—for many years—for the crime of social dissolution—and also in the sixties—on our Plaza of Three Cultures—during a student protest—the government massacred three hundred persons—but please continue."

"My father described to me how the FBI infiltrated the universities in order to destroy all movements questioning and challenging the authority of the establishment—how it worked secretly with certain professors and paid bribes and burglarized offices—blackmailed—sent forged letters and planted evidence—"

"Yes, yes—I know how all that works—but excuse me—do go on."

"A high level report came out of Harvard about how too much democracy contradicts the interests of the governing elite."

"The struggle for equality—along with the questioning of capitalistic exploitation and the profit motive—as well as the opposition to the Vietnam War—were all linked to drug use."

The Old Man laughs, and says, "And one of the things that eventually came out of all that was the War on Drugs—directed for the most part at us poor Mexicans just trying to make a living."

Lucas continues.

"And also something even more ominous—the planned move toward a less free and less democratic society—and toward a more totalitarian one— which means—ultimately—the surveillance and control of everyone and everything."

"And so I am guessing that you Lucas—as a lawyer—wanted to oppose that."

"Yes."

"And how opportune for your government—in consolidating that control you spoke of—that some towers came crashing down in New York—was it not?"

"There are those who do allege there was some sort of complicity."

"And you?"

"An experienced lawyer knows that almost everything is uncertain—and that it is impossible to get to the truth of anything."

"Very good Lucas—very good—and do you feel that through your work you have made a difference?"

"I may have helped a few individuals—while what I have worked against— what some have referred to as the Apparatus—has tripled in size and ferocity."

"And I found that trying to change its structure—or the direction and spirit driving it—and especially from the inside—and by legal means—is futile—I am no longer a lawyer."

"So how do you intend to fight back—change the world—besides wandering through the Sierra in your funny American sandals?"

Lucas looks down at his black Tevas—thinking hard. And finally says, "Fight or actively oppose or try to change anything no—but maybe plant a seed—by myself trying to live another way—maybe one that spontaneously manifests itself—when it can—in something like—shall we say—as much understanding as I can come up with—and in acts of total honesty and compassion and kindness."

The Old Man roars with laughter.

"Lucas—you loco—you have made my day."

The Old Man shouts, "Pablo—come in here."

The soldier who had been stationed outside, kicks open the door, his machine gun pointed at Lucas.

"Pedro—this you have to hear—tell him Lucas—what you intend to do to oppose the American government—the Apparatus—the System."

Pedro having lowered the machine gun, Lucas says nothing.

"Lucas here says that he is going to beat it over the head with acts of total honesty and compassion and kindness—and I am sure that next he will tell me to quit the drug business and to do the same."

Pedro smiling, The Old Man nods for him to go. Who turning his attention back to Lucas, says, "And I suppose that you came here among the Indians to find a wise shaman—a Don Juan—full of the ancient knowledge that will assist you in some way in all this."

"I don't believe there are any really wise men—only ordinary people who struggle along as best they can—each with his or her own special perspective and knowledge of the world."

"Are you one of those missionary folks?—they speak moralistic nonsense and pop up wherever there are Indians too."

"I think the place I am now at—may be just wanting to spend some time where life is simpler—less intricate and tangled—and more intuitive."

"If you really want to know those people I suggest you find yourself a Tarahumara woman—they are very good—much better than Gringas—and even better than our reputed hot Latinas—take my word for that."

The Old Man smiles at Lucas. There is silence.

"Do you know that you are on a terrorist watch list?"

"It doesn't surprise me."

"Why aren't you a registered voter?"

"Because it seems to me that both political parties—when it comes to what most matters are not all that different—and that they work primarily for themselves—and for the same corporate and financial interests—and not for the well being of the people."

The Old Man says, "Isn't' it ironic—that nowadays—even in corrupt Mexico—our three parties represent a wider range of choice than yours do."

He pauses.

"Except that when American contribute dollars and campaign expertise to help our business-dominated party win an election against a socialist candidate—our choice turns into something of a joke too."

The Old Man again pauses. Then his expression turning grim, goes on.

"Your country pushed our Senor Presidente into the presidency—and as part of the bargain our Senor Presidente launched the government's war on the cartels."

"And that war—my good friend—in disrupting what until then had been a more or less gentlemanly and harmonious and stable arrangement for us Mexicans—then precipitated yet another war between the cartels themselves."

"Just imagine Lucas—already 60,000 dead—and another 20,000 desaparecidos—and the Americans merrily smoking their marijuana."

"If a cartel buys off the Mexican government it is corruption—if the Americans do it—it is good clean humanitarian foreign aid."

"And now all that unleashed violence could well serve as a pretext for the US to intervene in whatever way necessary for the purpose of preventing what it fears more than even drugs."

The Old Man looks hard at Lucas.

"Which is Mexico turning toward a mild form of socialism—even if it's just the government subsidizing better education and better health care for the people."

"As your government well knows—our Revolution had strong socialist and even Marxist leanings—in the noblest sense of wanting to restore dignity to the common people—a sentiment still very alive in many Mexicans."

For a brief instant, Hermelinda's face replaces the face of The Old Man.

"So now this cartel has its own soldiers—some of whom you have met—all of them superbly trained in guerrilla warfare—ready to resist—not only our competitors and the government—but also an invasion by your countrymen."

The Old Man seeming to catch himself, stops. Stands up.

"Well it's been a pleasure Lucas—good talks used to be a regular part of my life—a very long time ago—we'll chat some more tomorrow."

The Old Man goes out the door.

Lucas feels worn down by the tension of someone assessing him as a person and probing for cracks in what he said. He had tried to not say anything antagonistic—or too much.

He had not mentioned his increasing sense that a high capacity for morality could very well be innate in human beings—who had lived together in families and other small social groupings for more than a million years without the language from which one day would arise laws as well as the moral precepts of religion.

Had not mentioned his belief that once people needed the laws of kings, or commandments from God, or the teachings of Jesus for telling them how to live—the world was by then already lost to the possibility of natural morality. Which cannot be prescribed or inculcated.

Nor mentioned that legalistic thinking and obedience to the law would have been part of the process that drove natural morality underground in the first place.

And perhaps most significantly, he had not mentioned his belief that only by living in harmony with the inner promptings of one's natural morality can a person ever hope to feel whole and walk with dignity and true well-being in the world.

Instead—he had let The Old Man laugh his head off at him.

Lucas answering a tapping at the door, the now familiar Petra without looking at him hands him a dish with some tortillas on top—then turns and leaves.

He sits down at the table. Underneath the tortillas he discovers what seems to be a yellow squash soup. He feels very lonely. And imagines how nice it would be to have Petra sitting across the table from him, the two of them in silence, and dipping their tortillas in their bowls of squash soup.

"Lucas—you still in there?"

Lucas comes wide awake. The sun is already up. He jumps up and in the kitchen finds The Old Man standing there—and his bedroll on the table. The Old Man says, *"Buenos días*—you sure didn't bring much with you."

"Buenos días."

"Well—I just finished talking to the outside on the radio—you are not to continue up this river—however a helicopter is due here about noon to take me out for a meeting—you can ride with me—I will leave you with a thousand US dollars—for a hotel—so you can take a shower and eat a good meal."

Lucas saying nothing, he says, "Or I can arrange that a Tarahumara go with you back through the gorge and then take you up to the Divide through country where there are no people—the tortillas in your bedroll are moldy—Petra can put together a bag of *pinole* and some dried apples for the both of you."

"Walking would be great."

"If any of this shows up in print we will track you down and have you killed."

"I understand that."

"Oh—and by the way—should you ever need to make more money than you probably ever have—get word to me—we can always use a good American lawyer who knows how to deal with the government."

The two of them go outside together. The Old Man stops, hesitates—begins to speak.

"Would you have ever guessed that I helped channel funds and arms from Mexico to Fidel Castro—when he was fighting that bastard Batista—who was working not for the Cuban people but for the United States which controlled him as well as more than half of Cuba's economy?"

"No."

"I was once an idealist—and like you deluded in thinking I could make the world a better place."

"I got to know Fidel fairly well—we drank the finest Cuban rum together—watching naked black women shimmy—and laughed hard together when the CIA-backed invasion of exiles from Florida fell on its face in the Caribbean mud—and then laughed some more at the string of lies that poured out of Washington afterwards."

"But very soon—the direction the revolution took—its regimentation and ideological rhetoric—its authoritarianism got to me."

Lucas says, "I question whether any form of social engineering can create a better world."

The Old Man appearing not to have heard, continues.

"I became a negotiator for this cartel in its international dealings—cocaine from Columbia was coming to Cuba—and Fidel loving the prospect of inundating the US in dope was landing boat loads up and down the Florida coast—cocaine was also arriving on desert airstrips in Chihuahua near the US border—Noriega down in Panama was involved."

"Like you Lucas—I too am opposing an establishment and a government that mainly serves a privileged few—we provide jobs and some prosperity in what would otherwise be a very poor country—and for that many not only respect us but see us as heroes."

"Drugs—at least a trillion dollars a year business—is now on a par with banking and oil—and you can be sure that it is no longer just the cartels that are involved."

The Old Man stops, suddenly looking tired, worn out—older. Goes on.

"Life took me by surprise when one day I suddenly woke up an old man—and then my wife died."

"And so when the young bloods—with their flaming cowboy shirts, alligator skin boots, gold-handled pistols, and fancy showpiece women—put pressure on me to retire—I negotiated a deal and left all of it—the mansion, the rodeos, discos, cock fights, and horse racing—and the cocaine too—for this."

"Was that a too crazy thing for an old man to do?"

"I was born in another part of the Sierra—and have returned to it to die—and to be laid to rest under a pile of rocks—and not in a cemetery of narcotumbas—all of them costing more than houses for the living."

"Some people say I am responsible for the killing of judges, soldiers, police, journalists, rivals, informers, and who knows who else—but it was not me—it was life."

"Look at this sagging skin—hanging from my chin and from my arms like old unwashed drapes."

The Old Man pauses. His eyes turn toward somewhere very far away.

"Extinction—that is what life—in one way or another—for some sooner and for others later—does to every one of us."

He snaps a finger against a thumb.

"During the Black Plague—a third of the population of Europe—just like that."

"Lucas—have you heard about the Aztec's sacred killing stone?"

Lucas is startled. And wondering if the other night The Old Man too might have been waiting his turn at the base of the same pyramid—the two of them connected in some mysterious fashion—he nods.

"Mexicans live closer to the truth—we accept the fact that not just warriors but everyone—everyone needs to go off to the killing stone to make life work—or as the Aztecs saw it—to make the corn grow tall and to keep the Sun moving across the sky."

"I grew up killing pigs, goats, and chickens—to feed the family—to keep it going—and saw that there was nothing at all bad in that."

The Old Man pauses again, the eyes looking so intently at something that they seem to be oblivious to him, Lucas.

"When others vehemently oppose one's own best interests—it is sometimes easiest to just kill them—like Mexican caciques and our noble *presidentes* and other politicians and our glorious generals have always done."

"And like the Americans have done for their tin and rubber—and oil—and for their bananas—and cleverly calling it saving civilization—and nation building—and winning the minds and hearts of the people."

"Yes my friend—killing can be something very natural—as natural as squashing the flies and mosquitoes that annoy us—as natural—as running to the outhouse."

The Old Man laughs a strange laugh.

"The United States didn't get rich and powerful by being dainty or noble—how many civilians do you suppose died in the fire bombings of Dresden?—and at Nagasaki and Hiroshima?—how many indigenous bones lie strewn under your cities and highways?"

Lucas walks quietly away back into the house. Inside, he can still hear The Old Man.

"And if bombing Bagdad to send Sadam a powerful message wasn't terrorism—I guess I don't know what is."

"A United Nations report blamed American bombings for the death of tens of thousands of Iraqi children—economic sanctions indirectly killed another hundred thousand—and on a flight to Mexico City I watched a film about Iraqi children without arms and legs who had been blown up by US land mines"

"Mexico as you no doubt know—did not bow to US pressure to support that aggressive intervention—you tell me—you the shining moral light—which society is the more violent one?"

"You hear me Lucas?—why is selling drugs criminal and selling more arms than the rest of the world combined perfectly okay?"

"I say it all depends on who writes the rules—and has more guns—and can talk the cleverest dishonest talk."

"Do you hear me Lucas?—no American can be a shining light."

Lucas goes into the bedroom, closes the door, and sits down on the bed.

"A lot of us give to the poor—we are celebrated in *corridos* Lucas—just like Pancho Villa."

Lucas feels dizzy, done in—not just by The Old Man, but by life, by everything. He can feel his mind racing out of control in all directions.

The Old Man can do no more than play out the role in the grand scheme of Creation that has been dealt to him—dealt to him by his genes, by the social-cultural context that is Mexico, and by all the other accidents of chance that produced him.

Just like the rest of us.

People believe that by ridding themselves of the likes of The Old Man, that by ridding themselves of the radicals, the depraved, the lunatics, and other undesirables—the good and just society will jump out of the ground and flourish and flower.

The Bolsheviks as they went about eliminating sixty million of their fellow citizens believed this.

And Lucas now feeling even dizzier, suddenly senses that the fundamental problem facing the twenty-first century is not this or that group or ideology or madman. Nor is it the Apparatus—that impersonal machinery of laws, bureaucratic rules and guns for controlling billions of human beings.

Rather the problem is nothing less than the whole of modern civilization in all its gargantuan complexity.

A civilization which built up of material objects and intricate abstractions—seems suddenly to Lucas to be floating upward into the sky like some gigantic unpiloted rudderless blimp broke loose from its mooring.

Sensing its upward acceleration in the pit of his stomach, Lucas reeling and stumbling reaches out about him, groping frantically in all directions.

Knowing that what he urgently needs to grasp onto at this very moment—is the lifeline to a new Creation.

And does.

And violently yanked and brought to his knees his eyes lock onto the dark barbarian inhabited forests far below—where he can faintly make out, here and there, in the murky swamp waters, glimmering bits and pieces of something reddish emerging, and coalescing.

That now rises up—whole and unrecognizable and glowing.

And looking like what he knows must appear to other beholders to be some lunatic and dangerous scarlet creature from the netherworld.

Lucas barely able to keep up is following along behind a Tarahumara more silent than any he has so far encountered. He has seen no sign of a trail, but knows they are heading west, toward the Divide. Anxious now to reach the canyons he does not really mind that they are going so fast.

Whenever Lucas suggests they rest, or eat, the Tarahumara without a word complies—the two of them in their unspoken way getting along amazingly well.

At nightfall, Lucas wrapped in his blanket against the chill notices that his guide, without a blanket or jacket, is already fast asleep nearby.

Moments later, he sees the red-tinted, rounded edge of the moon—poking up silently from behind a far dark mountain.

15

Tónachi

Lucas is in the Sierra uplands west of the Continental Divide in the midst of a wild jumble of rugged canyons cut by the Verde, Batopilas, Urique, Oteras, and Chinipas Rivers and their many tributaries as all those waters flow down toward the Gulf of California. He is almost to the rim of the Urique Canyon, one of three that are deeper than the Grand Canyon.

It was almost a week ago that he had first begun to hear talk of an American couple that lived somewhere near a place called Téparabo and who told the people they had been sent by God.

And then yesterday, coming to a dirt road, and walking along it past some fields of tawny corn stubble and a scattering of crumbling Tarahumara log houses, he had come upon a very American-looking but modest house with a white van alongside it and with two blonde-headed boys playing in the yard.

John and Brenda greeted him with a hospitality that reminded him of Barranco Azul, right away offering him the room of one of the boys for as long as he wished to stay.

It was they—both of them missionaries supported by an alliance of churches from Kansas—who informed him that he was now in the Tarahumara Baja, or Low Tarahumara, a region culturally distinct from that of the headwaters of the Conchos River where he had come from and which was the Tarahumara Alta, or High Tarahumara.

As they explained it, as the Tarahumara migrated away from the Spanish and out of the plains of eastern Chihuahua and into the Sierra, some continued to wander westward beyond the headwaters of the Rio Conchos, crossed the Continental Divide, and went down into lands occupied by other tribes— Guazapares, Chínipas, Tubares, Cuiteco, Cerocahui, Témoris, and Wajiro—and which tribes through a process of war and intermarriage they displaced, all but a few Wajiro eventually becoming extinct.

Those of the Tarahumara Alta looked eastward toward where they came from, even as far east as Chihuahua City. While those of the Tarahumara Baja looked westward toward the tropical coastal lowlands of Sinaloa and Sonora as had the tribes they had displaced.

Over time, several Mestizo towns—Urique, Batopilas, Uruachi, Morelos, and Moris—took root in the heart of the Lower Tarahumara in order to mine its gold and silver.

And as a consequence of all this, the cultures and also the languages of the Tarahumara Baja and the Tarahumara Alta had diverged.

During supper Brenda said, "We believe in living as Jesus would—with Him in our hearts to guide us—and we believe in the family—and in home schooling—and in living somewhat apart from those who the Tarahumara refer to as the Chabochi—those having spider webs over their eyes and so are unable to distinguish what is true and real from the lies and seductions of the Devil."

"It really surprised us how many of them see the outside world the same way we do."

Lucas said, "I guess I probably tend to see the world somewhat that way too."

Brenda and John smiled. Then John said, "It is precisely this period in history—this Information Age—and not the Middle Ages—that should be labeled the Dark Ages."

Taking some more potatoes, he said, "People these days live very comfortably and are super busy with what they consider to be supremely important things—but they are—well—*despistados*—not only on the wrong path—but totally clueless."

Pausing as if wondering whether to continue, he then said, "What is supposed to be man and woman being as one flesh—has turned into perversion."

"Would you like more meat John?"

At that point he Lucas had turned the conversation back to the Tarahumara.

Brenda explained that in the Tarahumara Baja the men had never worn the down-to-the-knee skirt garment, the *taparrabos*, characteristic of the Tarahumara Alta. And that in the Tarahumara Baja the women remove the roughage from the corn when they make their *pinole* so that it will mix better with water and not stick in the throat—those of the Tarahumara Alta maintaining that such *pinole* is tasteless and does not fill one up.

John said that here in the Tarahumara Baja they refer to themselves as

Tarahumara and to the others as *weris.* And that although the two groups speak different dialects they more or less understand one another, though not always.

He Lucas enjoying his peach cobbler desert made with home-canned peaches, John said, "Without you telling us—I can tell you are not a Christian—but it strikes me that you are someone very ready to accept Jesus into his heart—and to be reborn an entirely new person from who you were before—it would not take very much—it is so very simple Lucas—it is all in just one book—and it is so much better than wandering about and being—well maybe lost."

That night he had had a dream.

"John—this is Lucas the theologian—who has come to speak to you on Genesis."

"And?"

"When people stopped heeding the natural Voices inside their heads that told them what to do—and then stopped hearing them altogether—the world changed profoundly"

"To know what to do—they divided up the Universe into Good and Evil—and said—We will do only what is Good."

"And also—not wanting to live anymore like the giant armadillos did—but rather like Gods—they forsook the plump berries and fat mammoths that had always been there for the taking—and began to bend their backs to hoeing corn and beans—and to building great cities—and temples—and churches that soared to the sky."

"Lucas—stop right now."

But like a big river boat churning downstream, he had continued.

"But without the original Voices to guide them—in spite of all their temples and churches—the only Good they could manage was to live helter skelter lives of ignorance and iniquity."

"Everything that was once natural and spontaneous and holy—now became something to be dominated and controlled and reshaped—or destroyed."

"Or else its existence denied."

"So that even childbirth—what had always been a cosmic orgasmic experience—became excruciating pain."

"Lucas—my God—I said stop."

"And then one day—to top it all off—they murdered one of the last persons still capable of hearing the Voices."

"Lucas—I in this very moment—see revealed before me a giant foot descending straight from Heaven to grind you against the hard earth and back to the fine powder the Devil concocted you from."

And it was then that Lucas, watching the sole of the monstrous foot that was descending down upon him—it getting larger and larger and he even smelling it—woke up.

As soon as he finished breakfast the next morning, he packed his bedroll, explaining to John and Brenda that he was already long overdue in arriving at the Urique Canyon—where he planned to live with the Tarahumara for a while.

As they all shook hands, John said, "For someone who was a lawyer you don't say much—and for an American you don't dance to superficialities—you'll make a good Tarahumara."

The sun is sinking out of sight in the west as Lucas walks up to the very edge of the Urique Canyon.

He peers down into an abyss so immense that he cannot quite assimilate its reality. He stands there for a while looking down into it. Then stares across it, barely able to make out a few ranchos stuck here and there on the far wall—so far away as to be another world, even for a Tarahumara.

He turns away and walks over toward a nearby pine tree. Passes by a gigantic maguey plant from whose base green, dagger-like blades thrust up as high as his head. And sits down against the pine tree—the prickliness of its fallen needles and their smell, as well the nearness of the maguey, it now etched against the sky and catching the last rays of the sun, all helping to convince him that it is indeed he Lucas who is actually here on the lip of this canyon.

It crosses his mind how easily the brain's sensory apparatus for perceiving and interpreting the world is roiled.

John's reference to the Dark Ages comes to mind. And Lucas thinks of how for many hundreds of years many of the most sensitive, intelligent, and educated Europeans chose to seclude themselves in monasteries located away from the temptations of the larger society, some of them high up in the cliffs—not unlike the Tarahumara homesteads across the canyon.

Churchmen, who besides praying to God, devoted themselves to trying to live a more moral life—one characterized by poverty, humility, and charity. Again—a life not unlike that of the Tarahumara.

A hummingbird darts toward a patch of red on his shirt and darts away.

He thinks about the Franciscans, Dominicans, Augustinians, and Jesuits who later came to Mexico to establish missions and to live among and to save the souls of the native people—and who in doing so probably prevented the total extinction of the native populations that took place in some other parts of the New World.

Churchmen whose humble style of living, lack of pretension, and kindness and helpfulness toward the Indians—harked back to, and was already the Indian way.

He undoes his bedroll. Then with his knife, he slices around the top of the large can of beef stew with potatoes and carrots that John and Breda sent him off with. Dipping into the can with his spoon, and thinking some more about those two, he begins speaking quietly to the maguey.

"Knowing in one's heart that there is another and more moral way of going about in the world—one with the power to radically transform one—that's certainly a start."

And then addressing the abyss just behind the maguey, its nothingness, he says, "But I wonder if then weaving such knowledge into a story—said to be sacred—and thereby turning it into what is in effect ideology—only gets in the way."

In the morning as he is taking down his tarp he notices that two Tarahumara boys who seem to have appeared out of nowhere are quietly watching him. Except for their tire-tread huaraches they are dressed like Mestizos, in long sleeve shirt and pants. They look to be about eight and ten.

He goes over to them, says, *"Kwira,"* and brushes fingertips with each of them as they too say, *"Kwira"*—so softly he can barely hear them.

He says, "Where are you going?"

The older boy says, "Just walking around."

"Where do you live?"

The same boy motions with his head away from the rim of the Urique Canyon.

"Over there."

Lucas looks at the steep-walled side canyon with its side canyons, "over there" appearing to be an impenetrable maze of almost vertical rock walls.

The three of them stand in silence for several minutes.

"Is yours the only house?"

"There are several."

" How does one go to get there?"

"We will take you."

"How far is it?"

"It is very close."

It took them four hours—the two boys spending almost half that time waiting for Lucas—to reach what they told him was Tónachi, a *ranchería* of ten or so houses all out of sight of one another and most of them in open pine forest on top of a mesa. Three times they had had to wade waist-high across the same arroyo. And in several places a notched log leaned against a rock face had provided the only foothold.

The boys telling him that their Aunt Reyna had lived for a while in the Chabochi pueblo of San Juan and so spoke very good Spanish, they left him off at her two-room adobe house that was separated by a corn field from a tumbledown log hut in which they said her son and his wife lived.

Reyna, a talkative woman probably in her forties and with a long black braid hanging down her back, invited him into the house. She served him coffee, tortillas, and potatoes fried with red chilies and onions—which he ate, as he was now well-accustomed to, sitting on a chunk of wood with the plate on his lap and using a tortilla for a spoon.

Her son Gavino, she told him, had recently married Marta, a girl from down in the *barrancas*. Who did not keep the house very clean and who played around too much at the *tesguinadas*.

Reyna said that besides Gavino she had also raised another boy that a young unmarried neighbor had given to her and who when he was about 14 left for Sinaloa to pick tomatoes for a month—but was then never heard from again.

"I often wonder if we Tarahumara have hearts of stone."

"Sometimes—when one wears out—and is gone—it is even hard to find relatives willing to help carry the coffin to the cemetery—it's a very long way."

"My father—with twenty cows—was richer than many Tarahumara— he sold peaches and wheat to the Chabochi in San Juan—but he worked too hard—harder than a poor burro—even transporting from very far away all our water up to this place that has no water during the dry season."

"He was very strict with his children—and had children with other women too."

Lucas noticed she was wearing new white tennis shoes, and that lined up on one of the shelves there were two more pair of shoes along with a pair of huaraches. A cardboard box in the corner was filled with what looked like skirts, and another cardboard box with blouses. She seemed to have more than she needed.

"I make a lot of *tesguino*—and so my son and I always have plenty of help from the neighbors—most of the other women now make only *tempache*—with sugar and yeast—because it is less work—it's taste is very ugly compared to *tesguino* made from sprouted corn—Tarahumara women are becoming very lazy—and that Marta is the laziest one of them all."

She never mentioned a husband, nor did he ask.

When he asked if he could put up a shelter out in the pines nearby, take his meals with her, and stay in the area for awhile, she lighting up, said, "Of course—and I will teach you Tarahumara words—and by watching very closely you will learn how to live like we do."

He finished his coffee, marveling at this stoke of good fortune—at having found a friendly hospitable Tarahumara who not only spoke good Spanish but who also had had just enough dealings with the outside world to understand it a little in the way that he did..

"Come—I will take you to meet Gavino and that woman of his—a little beyond their house is a small arroyo that still has some water in it this time of year—and across it and a little above it would be a very nice place for you to camp."

She placing a heavy sack of beans on her head, he preceded her out the door, which she secured with a piece of cord, and then he followed her into the rocky cornfield, he now and then tripping in the deep furrows, while she never once touching the bundle on her head flowed along proud and erect and without a lurch.

Dogs barking and running in circles around them and some chickens squawking, Gavino and Marta appeared at the door and greeted them. And then they all went inside, Gavino receiving the sack of beans and telling them to sit down on one of the chunks of wood.

Reyna began speaking in Tarahumara—most likely telling them that he would be living nearby—while Gavino and Marta out of what seemed to be fear looked down at the floor.

He watched Marta go over to the large metal pot on top of the barrel stove and take out two ears of corn. One of the *elotes* she handed to Reyna and without looking at him the other to him.

He and Reyna nibbled their corn.

When Reyna said something sharply to Marta, he saw Marta momentarily stiffen.

Although the top of Marta's head would probably barely reach his chest, she did not in the least strike him as tiny, but only as would any woman—a woman who could be 15 or as old as 25.

When he asked Gavino how old he was, he mumbled what sounded like, "*Sí*—yes."

Gavino struck him at first as one of those nondescript people one sometimes tends to pass by. But then observing more closely the brown thin body of this very young man, who probably knew nothing of the world beyond where he could walk to and back from in a day, he realized that this was someone who could, if he had to, go into untamed forest, and with little more than an ax, a borrowed ox, and some seed, build a house and put together a farmstead that would maintain himself and a family.

And who could probably step out the door and run for a hundred miles through these canyons without stopping.

Damn it all, thought Lucas, Not by hook nor by crook—will I ever know what it is really like to live like a Tarahumara.

The campsite Reyna took him to was very pretty, on a pine-studded knoll overlooking the mesa and the arroyo as well as the two houses about a quarter mile away. Across the arroyo were some apple trees on which a few yellow apples still remained.

"Tarahumara like to put their houses in nice places where they can see out—and where it makes one happy and strong to just be there—even if it means carrying wood and water from far away—or a loaded burro sometimes rolling down into an arroyo just getting things up there."

"I've come to feel that way too—and to question the priority that we Americans put on what we think of as ease and comfort."

He was aware that Reyna had not fully understood his way of putting it.

Pointing with her finger, she explained to him that this mesa—the Mesa of Tónachi—fell off abruptly on four sides into deeps canyons, all side canyons of side canyons that led into the major Urique Canyon, or as people called it, the Big Canyon. And then pointed to what she said was a narrow neck of land that connected the island-like Mesa of Tónachi to some higher more rugged-looking country.

"A few of us live up there."

"We Tarahumara live very spread out—only here and there is there a patch of land suitable for growing corn on—and that also has a little water nearby."

"Not having neighbors nearby gives all of us room for our cows and goats—it is very strange living all piled together—the way the Chabochi do."

"Come down to eat something before it turns dark—and again for breakfast—or anytime just to sit by the stove and visit—especially should it rain or snow."

"I will."

And then she turned and was off in a shuffle-like run down to the arroyo—her flowered skirt and long braid swinging as she hopped across on the rocks.

He had done it—or maybe it had mostly just happened. Whichever—he was now living on the Mesa of Tónachi. With the Tarahumara.

16
Dark Brown Belly

Reyna served him other foods besides just tortillas and beans—goat cheese, squash, chili sauces, eggs, potatoes, watercress greens, peas, tamales, walnuts, dried apples and peaches, and once even stewed chicken. They had never discussed payment but he knew she knew that she would be reimbursed for her efforts—though he could not help wondering if somehow she thought all this might make her rich.

She told him she had worked for more than a year living in the home of a well-to-do Chabochi family in San Juan, doing the cleaning and cooking and taking care of the children.

"Once they took me with them to Los Mochis—where they often locked me in a room so I would not stray out and get lost—the city frightened me terribly—even walking through it with them."

When he explained to her that he wanted to know all the families on the Mesa of Tónachi and that should some be too afraid of him he would ask her to accompany him to those houses, she said, "Everyone here already knows all about you—but even so—you are right—I am sure one or two will hide or run."

"Be extra careful with María—she is a *bruja*—a witch—a number of years ago she put some *bakano*—a small cactus that grows down in the *barrancas*—into some meat and out of spite gave it to another woman—once a very nice and hard-working woman—who went *loca*—and now can't make tortillas or baskets and wanders about barefoot in the canyons with her parent's goats as best she can."

He resolved to meet them all, the *loca* too, aware that relating to just the friendly, fluent and talkative ones—like Reyna—would not be knowing the Tarahumara.

❖ ❖ ❖

Lucas walks down to the arroyo to fill his water bottle. He sits down by a clear pool, looking at its sandy bottom—listening to the trickle of water and smelling the rich smell of fermenting yellow apples that strew the ground across from him.

A sharp slap slap slapping makes him look down the arroyo, where he sees Marta kneeling at its edge alongside a small pile of clothes and beating a green garment on a rock. Now with a cupped hand she throws more water onto the garment and then with both hands pushes it back and forth against the rock.

She is washing just far enough away that although verbal acknowledgment of each other's presence was possible, it would not have been natural. And yet just close enough to announce that they, and only they, the two of them, were at this moment sharing this part of the Universe together.

It seems to him that he is more aware of each of her movements than if she were sitting here alongside him—and senses that she is aware of him in the same way, even though she has never once looked at him directly, as he is looking at her.

Had she from her house seen him come down to the arroyo—and then herself come here?

He becomes aware of a change in all of his body, a physical glow of well being. As if a powerful energy field flowing through her and having its source in the whole of Nature were provoking in him an exactly matching and equal response.

The two of them creating about them a charged landscape so powerful as to overwhelm any third person who might happen to find him or herself nearby.

And Gavino?

Slap slap slap.

He feeling giddy with a kind of weird peace and joy, fills his bottle of water and heads back up the hill toward his camp.

He wonders if trying to see life more clearly only makes it more incomprehensible. But perhaps that is as it should be—and that the other trap besides installing oneself in too much comfort is installing oneself in too much coherence and clarity.

And Gavino?

❖ ❖ ❖

He found Shimino sitting out in front of his house leaned against a wall. He was maybe about 80. His young wife Rosa was nearby pressing down on a block of cheese in a wooden mold. A boy about 10 was making tortillas on a comal set over an open fire and another slightly younger boy was walking about with a baby in his arms. They were the same two who had brought him to the Mesa of Tónachi.

Lucas sat down on a rock.

Shimino said, "Without sisters—boys learn to do what girls would do."

When Rosa finished with the cheese she served him a piece on a tortilla, and wrapped the rest in an embroidered cloth. Then she took the baby, lifted her blouse. and putting it to her breast sat down across from him on another rock.

It struck Lucas that relating to him like that she was now more at ease with him than before—even more centered and confident in who she was.

The two boys took off into a field running and yelling and laughing.

Rosa told him that a few years ago when the soldiers came they took away Reyna's husband to a prison somewhere, and that he never came back.

"He was much younger than her—and she left her first husband for him."

Shimino told him that his son Marciano had recently married Rosa's sister María.

"Their two girls aren't his—María had them with Esteban—but he went off with another woman."

"But it was me who got the younger and better looking of the sisters— what do you think of that?"

"That you look to me like someone who will make it to a hundred years."

"In the old days many of us made it to a very old age—unless a pestilence or a year without corn got us."

The two boys swooped by still running and yelling and laughing but now each of them with a stick and whacking and rolling ahead of them a black hoop they had made from a section of black water tubing.

Shimino called over to them, "Enough—it's time to go out and bring in the goats."

As Lucas left, Shimino asked him, "Did you marry her?"

"Who?"

"Reyna—she hinted that maybe you had."

Approaching the house of Marciano and María, Lucas saw three women running into the woods. Marciano who had been chopping up some firewood stayed put alongside the house, ax in one hand, watching him approach. They greeted each other. Marciano sat down on a log and indicated to Lucas that he sit down on another.

After about fifteen minutes of mostly silence and he about ready to leave, María appeared and greeted him. She went inside, and came back and handed him a glass filled with water and with some *pinole* at the bottom. Which he stirred with his finger and drank.

María began talking about Reyna—how spending so much time with the Chabochi in San Juan had made her a Chabochi too, which as María then explained meant looking out for oneself and getting ahead and being important at the expense of others.

"My mother told me that when Reyna was young she was the wildest one of all—she married the two men she did because they were rich—she was a slut and still is—and as old as she is."

"She has twenty pairs of shoes—and always dresses nicer than the rest of us—she has some money—from her last husband—that she has buried somewhere."

"There are stories going around—you be very careful with her."

He found Faustino and Matilde sitting in front of their house and visiting with Faustino's brother Esteban who lived nearby and who had come by to castrate a bull that was to begin a life as a plow ox.

Matilde brought him a plate of tortillas and beans on top of which were four red pea-like berries.

"They are *chiltepines*—they grow wild on bushes down in the *barrancas*— our daughter Claudia who lives down there brought them up to us—they are very hot."

"I've had these chiles before—and yes they wake one up—I love them."

And then as he was crumbling one of the tiny red balls between his thumb and index finger, the pieces falling on his beans, he heard Esteban say, "I hear you and Reyna are married."

"No—she helps me—we are just friends."

Lying on his bedroll waiting to fall asleep, he thought about Reyna.

From the very first he had been aware that she liked him. And now by him doing what seemed to him to have been doing nothing, and even though he had been extra cautious to avoid any gesture whatsoever that might be interpreted as a romantic intention, it appeared he might have wound up married to her—or almost so.

He realized he had been very naive. For a Tarahumara was not living on a woman's land and having her cook for one being married?

He has come to see that Reyna was not just any Tarahumara woman. Whatever her past, she was good-hearted. Hers was not what she had referred to as the Tarahumara's heart of stone. He had even come to see her wanting nice things and to stand out not as a vice—but rather as an unconscious craving for what one might call love.

Nowhere, apparently, was life simple and straightforward. He would try to flow with the complication as best he could. And continue in small ways to be nice to her.

When he wakes up in the middle of the night the glow from his interaction with Marta is still in his body—only now more intense. And it strikes him that she too is not just any woman. That no woman is just any woman.

Lucas has just returned to his camp after having eaten a breakfast of eggs and tortillas at Reyna's house. Having for the first time during a meal felt somewhat awkward, he is wondering whether maybe he should leave the Mesa.

Hearing a noise, he turns and is surprised to see Marta—who is standing against an oak tree a couple of arm lengths away. She is dressed more nicely than usual and in one hand holds an unfinished green basket along with some strips of *sotol*. She is very nervous.

He says, "*Kwira.*"

And she too but very softly says, "*Kwira.*"

Neither of them move to brush fingertips.

"You startled me—where are you going?"

"To the *divisadero* to weave a cover for the basket."

He looks at the almost completed perfectly round sotol basket with its intricate design of lighter-colored sotol, all made by eye.

"It's going to be very pretty."

They stand there for a while in silence, she now more nervous than before, her free hand fiddling with her red kerchief.

Then the hand goes down to her waist, up under her blouse a little—and begins to make slow small circular motions against the revealed dark brown belly.

Lucas notices the large safety pin at her hip that holds her two skirts in place, and knows that if he took several steps and undid the safety pin, the skirts would fall to the ground, for her and him to lie on.

His whole body aching to do that—does nothing.

The hand leaves the belly, the blouse falling back over the dark brown skin. And she continues to stand there—for what seems to him like almost forever.

Finally she says, "I am going now—to finish the basket."

And hurries off quickly into the pines.

Lucas stands there motionless for a while—acutely aware that his campsite feels extraordinarily empty.

"Ha la la—dey hey bey"

"Petronila—how did you get here?"

"Not by being so silly as to walk up the Conchos you can be sure."

"How did you find me?"

"I and the others danced in the sky with you—and so now we are all permanently linked to you—watching you—we are now your Guardian Guiding Spirits—and you can't get rid of us—dey hey bey."

She begins to hop up and down with her long green skirt moving up to her knees and back down again with every hop. Comes to a halt.

" I was once young and taut-bellied and smooth-skinned just like her—me you certainly would have grabbed—but you are grossly mistaken—she did not come for that."

She hops up and down some more, higher and higher, talking to him.

"Did you ever feel really alive Lucas?—sometimes I feel I might just burst open like a flower and fly off through space as a beautiful comet."

Suddenly she seems to Lucas as young as Marta.

"No of course you haven't—how could you?—or any man?—once men discovered the craziness that passes for power and fame and took over the world—crushing the sexual vitality right out of us women—and began collecting the skulls of their enemies."

Lucas interrupting, shouts, "Yes I have felt alive—flying up there in the sky."

And just as Lucas is about to cry out with intense joy from an electric current surging up from his feet and himself jump up off the ground—Petronila comes to rest.

"She came to be your woman—not to do what you wanted to do with her—and with what courage she came up this hill—frightened and putting one foot forward—and then the other—until she got here."

"And finding that she was your woman—then yes—gladly would she have lain down with you."

"Why me?"

"You have no one to do your wash—or to keep you warm at night in bed—and you have no children—and she sees herself as much better for you than Reyna—who in her opinion does not even make good tortillas."

"But—what about Gavino?—why me?"

"Why? why? why?—why anything?—why do I sometimes hop up and down?—or hop along on one foot singing Ha la la—dey hey bey?—why you are so incredibly—so?—why there's not even a word for it."

"Having one's woman is not munching wedding cake—or just frolicking in bed—it is total transformation—just like we witches practice—when we turn people into trees and pigs—when I was young and beautiful like Marta I tried to teach men this—but could not—not to one."

"There are very few like me left Lucas—aliveness and brightness has given way to blight and decay and dullness—and the Goddesses for restoring the old Natural Order are gone."

"So dey hey bey to you Lucas."

And with that she swings herself around and with her long green skirt dragging along behind her hops off on one leg into the pines.

Which her electricity igniting them—burst into the sacred bright flame they always were.

The rest of that morning, and that afternoon, and all the long night, he wonders whether Marta will return. And the next morning too—as he glances repeatedly over at the pine she had been standing against.

He now sees that the shyest Tarahamara woman knows exactly what to do once the eyes of society are not upon her. That Marta did not need *tesguino* nor any ploy to help her. That the Universe simply put her here at his feet.

He thinks some more about Reyna. And then wonders whether Petronila too may have spent an entire life looking for what might be called love.

A woman's voice calls out, "Lucas—Lucas."

He looks about him for the source of the voice—which is clearly not Marta's. Nor Petronila's."

"Lucas—I am up here—high in the sky above you—where once you and I and the others danced together among our brothers and sisters the Moon and the Stars—only because it is day you cannot see me—I am both the white-robed one with the cascading black hair—and the one staring out over an enormous belly."

Lucas says, "Tonantzin."

And looking up, he searches the sky, trying to catch sight of who he remembers as maybe the most beautiful Indian woman to have ever walked the earth.

"No Lucas—you did not arrive in a roaring helicopter—nor filling your solitude and poisoning the Sierra air with loud *ranchera* music—nor along with a flock of tourists chatting about what they will eat when they get back home."

"You have come alone in your quiet odd American shoes to watch and to listen—and not to dominate the Holy Space—and that is all very good."

"But—in spite of all that—you have nevertheless dropped out of the sky like a beached floundering whale among these people—and they will never again be the same."

"I am sorry—I did not know how else to do it—but I do understand."

"That will suffice."

"And another thing—it seems that ever since you set foot in Mexico you have been destined for a Tarahumara woman—but as you will soon find out—there are persons—who will want intensely to destroy what you and she may have together—as well as the both of you."

Lucas scans the sky wanting desperately to see her, so incredibly beautiful.

"It may be that some Indian women think they see in you—whether correctly or incorrectly—something they think they want."

"What?"

"It may have to do with the ancestors of their own men—once proud warriors—watching brutal gold-hungry Conquistadors and others taking for themselves—not out of love and respect—but out of lust—the most beautiful of us Indian women."

"A strange race of men from across the ocean—focused only on themselves—and knowing only force and absolute authority—and never hearing or even really seeing the other—and needing to dominate and humiliate."

"The defeat and humiliation of our Indian men continues—in a variety of new forms—day after day—at every turn."

"People who are treated as if they are nothing—learn to act toward others—and even toward their spouses and children—as if they too are nothing."

She pauses, and then goes on.

"It may be that some of these Indian women may be hoping to find in you something that is neither defeat—nor the perverse urge to dominate and to crush what cannot be dominated."

"And they may instinctively sense that something better can come only from what is totally different from what they have ever seen or known."

His eyes again sweep the sky.

And suddenly rest upon a dark brown belly.

Huge, and bulging out towards him and pushing aside the sky, to make room for the new creation that seems to be at this very moment bursting out upon the world.

Then just as suddenly—there is again only the sky—uniformly blue.

"Lucas—the fecundity of life—is not reproduction—not replication—it is the constant shooting forth of an array of possibilities—out of which a very few take hold—in the form of new creations before then unimaginable."

"It was not replication that gave rise to mastodons—and to spiders and lily pads and mango trees—and to condors—and to people of different colors."

"Will what you and a Tarahumara woman put into the world be something new—and even extraordinary?"

"And then actually take hold—meaning for a short while have its heyday in the sun?

"Who knows Lucas—not even I know that."

Lucas stands there for a while. Watches as out of nowhere a white puff of cloud appears in the now silent blue sky.

17

La Loca

From Reyna especially, Lucas kept on hearing more stories about the neighbors.

Where Rosario and Natalia lived was once the rancho of Natalia's brother Pancho who had killed their father with a pocketknife, the both of them drunk, and who had then fled to who knows where.

"Because of what happened—Natalia has forgotten how to do numbers and sometimes is confused about the day of the week—but otherwise is a good wife."

"It's sad—what we Tarahumara sometimes do to one another—and with life being as hard as it is."

She also told him Rosario had had María bury something on the rancho to keep away the ghost of the dead man.

One morning after breakfast, Reyna told him more about La Loca.

"She hasn't worn huaraches for years now—nor washed—nor combed her hair—and sometimes smears food over her face—the tortillas she makes are lopsided and either burnt or raw—so no man will marry her—and those that try to come close to her for other reasons she drives off with rocks—or else runs away downhill into places where our best runners couldn't catch her."

"If you hear a howling in the night that's louder than a coyote's—it's her—the children are terrified of her—and when they misbehave they are told La Loca will snatch them and carry them off."

Just then Marta and Gavino walked in. Other than greet him, Marta acted as if he Lucas were not there. The couple sitting down and beginning to talk about something to Reyna in Tarahumara, he excused himself and left for his camp.

Crossing the arroyo at where Marta had washed the clothes, he became aroused. And Gavino? Might he drunk stick a knife into him—like Pancho did to his father? And into her too?

❖ ❖ ❖

Lucas had been careful to not appear superior to his new neighbors—either by bestowing this and that or by acting in any other way that could be taken as patronizing.

When Rosario had asked him for a new ax he had seen right away the problems that buying him one could lead to, not only the envy of the others but to him in the eyes of Rosario being turned into who knows what. And even to maybe Rosario ultimately resenting him.

However for a while now he had been wanting to be able to bring some small gift to the houses he visited—possibly some peanuts, or *chiltepines* or other appreciated food item not grown on the Mesa.

Yesterday Reyna had arranged with Gavino that he take him to San Juan—so that he could buy a a few such things.

And so this morning he is following Gavino as they drop off the Mesa on a trail so steep that three times already he Lucas has landed sliding on his butt. Twice he has to ask Gavino to slow down.

At a major arroyo, after first watching Gavino hop across like a bird from rock to rock, he himself wades across, the cold water to his waist.

In spite of not having said anything to one another, to Lucas they seem—connected .

At an overlook Gavino stops to redo a broken thong on one of his sandals.

"We will go by the cave where Candelario and Carmen live—Marta wants Carmen to bring us the leg of a goat the next time they kill one—they are first cousins."

"Candelario is a crazy Chabochi—there are a few who say that he is nothing but an old lusting billy goat—and that they are going to kill him for marrying a Tarahumara."

Which were the most words Gavino had ever spoken to him.

They set out again. And soon hear the tinkle of a goat bell, smell smoke. A dog barks.

The cave—with its openness and spaciousness and view of the canyons—does not strike Lucas in the least as the holdover from the Stone Age he had imagined. Bright clothes hang on some bushes nearby and several thick white and black wool blankets are draped over the low rock wall at the mouth of the cave. A woman is squatting on the ground patting out a tortilla. Now lays it on a stone *comal* over a fire.

She looks up smiling and stands up to greet them, after which he and Gavino sitting down on the stone wall she returns to her tortillas. She and Gavino begin talking back and forth in sing-songy Tarahumara.

Lucas loses himself in the aesthetic harmony of this place. Sometimes he finds he prefers not being able to understand.

A clatter of rock announcing him, who Lucas guesses must be Candelario arrives from out of somewhere, he wearing a straw cowboy hat, a dirty white bandana around his neck, and with a long tear up one pant leg. He shakes their hands, saying to Lucas, "We've never had a visitor here before who wasn't Tarahumara—and we haven't had that many of them either—the women don't like Carmen because they are envious—and the men don't like me because I married one of their women—and one of their best looking ones at that."

"Carmen—where are those dried peaches?—and roast them up some pieces of goat jerky."

Lucas eating his hot tortilla, roast goat, and peaches, tells Candelario that he put up a camp on the Mesa because he enjoys being with the Tarahumara and for a while wants to share with them the simplicity in which they live. To which Candelario says, "I have my problems with them—but they are a fine people—a very fine people—better than the ones I moved away from—who think they are superior and know everything."

"And let me tell you something—their women make the best wives in the world—as long as you don't try to push them around—because if you do they will whack you with a hoe—or else grab their extra skirt and blouse and leave running faster than you can catch them—right Carmen?"

Carmen turning over a tortilla, smiles.

"We and the two boys stay to ourselves here—like the Tarahumara themselves generally do anyway—in San Juan when they talk to Carmen it's pure insult—*mi hija*—my daughter this and *mi hija* that—and you will see that when Gavino walks into town they will call him *muchacho*—boy—and if someone invites the two of you in for a tortilla—for desert they might give you a piece of cake but not him."

"For the Chabochi the Tarahumara are not a people—they are a social problem—when the truth is that it's the other way around."

"I grew up in San Juan—in those days a tiny Mestizo community you could only get to by burro trail—we didn't live all that different from the Tarahumara—except that we put any extra dollars into other things besides all that drinking—and worked harder—and so had nicer houses and all of us rode horses and had burros—instead of walking and carrying everything on our backs—we were all as poor as you could find—but honest and helpful and tough—like back country people tend to be."

"Then the marijuana came—and at a hundred dollars a kilo—came the money—then a road—and outsiders—and a store that even sold seafood from the coast—then more stores—and right away every family had a truck—or a suburban with smoked windows for moving out the sacks of marijuana to the buyers."

"The machos threw their empty beer cans out the windows and forgot how to walk and turned big-bellied—and everyone fancied up their houses and filled them with expensive furniture and you name it—and wires were strung from poles for electricity—and so soon instead of visiting—people were staying inside watching soap operas—and getting filled with nutty notions."

"It still amazes me—how quickly—almost overnight—the new ways changed how people were—as if they had been waiting all their lives for just this moment."

"The wife I had fit right in—and for some reason I did not—and when I took up with Carmen she moved out to live with her sister—and turned our sons against me—who burned down my house."

"I told folks that when I watched my house and everything in it become a roaring whoosh of flame—I had shouted burn burn burn—because a home is love and a warm human presence—not fancy furniture and sanitary ceramic tile floors and pictures hanging on the walls."

"Soon the word went around towatch out for that crazy old walnut Candelario—who would just as soon burn down the whole town."

Lucas laughs and says, "I've heard that in a few cultures people used to burn everything they owned every so many years—to purify their lives."

"Lucas—they all thought they had discovered Paradise."

"When the truth is that good decent down-to-earth people stopped being people altogether—just walking masks—wind up toys—not seeing you—just wanting one thing or another out of you."

"And sometimes making me want to knock them on the head with a stick and shout—hey, anybody there?"

Lucas smiles, as Candelario goes on.

"It's as if only way to exist in this new world is to be what one isn't—to the point that before long one forgets what one once was in the first place—and one is left with only the mask."

"So tell me Lucas—how does a person talk to something that is not really there.?"

"Look at her—my Carmen—making tortillas for herself and her family—because that is real—and that is dignity and freedom—not living for money and strutting around in a pair of brand new alligator hide cowboy boots."

"She grew up very far back in the canyons—very poor—and where the people are more like the old Tarahumara than are the ones on the Mesa—where you are."

"She has a sister even prettier than her—Jesusita—the barefoot beauty of the canyons I call her—except that she turned *loca*—and that now having grown so thin and looking like a wild animal—her beauty is a little hard to see."

"But even as *loca* as she is—she's real."

"I'd like to know that area—and meet the sister too someday—if that's possible."

"Come by again anytime—stay a few days—and Carmen and the boys will take you to her parent's house—what do you think Carmen?"

Carmen not turning her head away from her tortillas, smiles.

"In San Juan—what has always been most important has been lost Lucas—and much sadder than that is that people do not care—or even know it."

Candelario picks up a small rock, holds it for a moment in his two hands, and then like a wild man throws it hard and far across the arroyo at something only he can see. He stands there a moment. Then turning back toward Lucas, he says, "Society—the government and soldiers it has produced—took turns raping this woman you see Lucas—along with some others—and do you know what I think?—that their modern uppity Paradise is a mask for Hell."

Candelario had reminded him of Jesse—the native unschooled intelligence, and wanting desperately to fix the world but not knowing where to begin. For Candelario, Carmen was not the object of an old man's lust, but his salvation, she and the two boys keeping him calmed down and rooted into the rocky earth of these canyons.

He had come to like Gavino, feeling a certain bond between them, and in San Juan had bought the two of them a chicken dinner and some beers. Gavino had bought a red kerchief for Marta, and for himself some new leather thongs for holding in place his huaraches.

Now when they ran into each other, Gavino greeted him with less shyness. If Marta was with him, she continued to act as if he Lucas were not there. Just as she would whenever she came over by herself to Reyna's house and found him there.

One morning, going down to the arroyo for water, he encounters Marta, she too having come for water, and she lights up as he has never seen a woman light up. And then, the two of them standing there facing each other from opposite sides of the arroyo, it trickling quietly, she with a boldness he has not seen in her before, says, "When you go to San Juan again—bring me a pair of white shoes—like Reyna's."

He says nothing, just standing there, looking at her, and feeling excruciatingly connected to her.

Turning, he walks with his plastic jug of water back up the hill, giddier than the other time, the earth reeling under his feet. Bringing her the shoes he intuits would marry them.

Or are they already married?

Carmen's two boys, about seven and nine, walk up ahead, and after them Carmen, with him last. The land is more abrupt than any he has yet seen, with rock cliffs everywhere, and many of the arroyos cascading downwards in long thin waterfalls.

"Who knows if we'll find Jesusita there—sometimes when she is least well—she runs off for days at a time—and finally shows up at the house only because she is desperately hungry."

At an overlook, she and him looking straight down into what she has tells him is Arroyo Hondo, she says, "The shiny spot you see is the tin roof of my uncle Alfredo's house—Marta grew up there—he and the others down there used to grow a lot of opium poppies—but don't anymore."

As she was talking he had noticed something darken in her, and her voice shake.

"These days—besides corn and beans—he grows some very nice chiles, onions, and papaya."

She too, with Candelario not there, is not at all shy.

They continue, now along the rim of the Arroyo Hondo Canyon, where the tropical heat rising up from below has produced a profusion of maguey, prickly pear, and sotol among the scattered tall pines.

"People used to eat a lot more maguey than they do now—you have to roast the part that is underground a day and night in a deep rock-lined pit covered with dirt—it's very sweet."

He knows that maguey was a staple of the Mescalero Apaches of the American Southwest—and that in the south of Mexico tequila is made from a variety of the same plant.

Two dogs start barking. They see a rock hut. Goats in a pole corral. As they approach closer, two women and a man appear standing in front of the door watching. The boys run ahead.

The dogs dash out circling him, snarling furiously as Carmen orders them away in Tarahumara. And then one of the dogs having ripped his pants leg she picks up a rock. The dogs back off—still snarling

"They smell you are different."

The younger and thinner of the two women disappears back into the house.

Chalelo and Felipa greet Carmen and then him. And immediately begin talking to Carmen in Tarahumara as he follows them all inside and into the dim light of a cramped room in which there is a small table, some chunks of wood for sitting on, and a stove made from half of a metal barrel.

Pressed into a corner, hiding from him, is a woman holding a tortilla against her face, her blouse ripped in several places and her black hair in disarray, her bare feet and thin calves caked with dirt.

The two boys come in laughing, and each grabbing a tortilla off the stove run back out the door. Carmen and her parents have not stopped jabbering.

The wild-looking woman, who is obviously Jesusita, still holding the tortilla against her face, with her free hand picks up one of the chunks of wood, comes towards him and sets it down by him.

"*Asagá*—sit down."

Then returns to her corner, she the only one having noticed that he a guest has been forgotten.

He sitting on his chunk of wood and leaned against a wall, stares at her, and sees that Candelario was right—one has to search for the beauty.

She lowers the tortilla and suddenly smiles at him the best she is able, a distorted smile, that almost breaks out into a laugh. And to which he spontaneously responds, smiling back, his whole body wanting to smile back, almost wanting to laugh too.

And the three others still talking, oblivious to them, he vows to see what it will take to turn this woman, this very odd barefoot beauty of the canyons, this Jesusita into his woman.

18

In the Heart

In early December, a few red trumpet flowers still blooming on south-facing slopes, the last of the corn was being harvested, and on two occasions Lucas joined in, stuffing the ears he picked into old flour sacks, stamping down the stalks, and now and then plopping down on them to drink some *tesguino*. With all the talking and laughing and shouts—instead of being repetitive, mechanical, ornery work, and deadening—it was more like a party. Although he was not a drinker, he had decided that drinking now and then with the neighbors was absolutely the only way to be accepted by them and to hear their stories.

At these work parties his neighbors told him everything they never would have had they been sober. How a woman had taken her daughter's very white-looking baby and abandoned it on the plaza in San Juan. How when the soldiers used to show up looking for marijuana they would hold heads under water in the arroyos to get people to talk. And how once old Shimino, drunker than a crazy hoot owl, had shoved that cocky equally-drunk Esteban off a rock ledge, which battered him up badly enough that he had to be carried out on a litter to the clinic in San Juan.

He found drinking an occasional gourd of *tesguino* while working under a hot sun tasty and refreshing. He managed to drink much less than the others, usually by saying that too much upset his stomach. Sometimes he simply passed the offered gourd on to someone else—or poured it on the ground when the attention of the others was focused elsewhere.

Drinking in this way never made him more outgoing like it did the others, nor otherwise changed his behavior. And just at that certain point when he noticed he was beginning to slur his words, or noticed the slightest befuddling, he quit.

He saw how when the others began to stumble and sometimes fall over it reduced all of them to a condition of utter equality—Chemo who had recently been elected *gobernador*, Esteban the best runner, the shaman Don Corpo. And he saw how all of this would have accustomed everyone from a very early age to the crazy and sometimes outrageous things that human beings are liable to do or say—and so in that way probably helped make people more tolerant and compassionate.

Always as everyone became too drunk to do useful work, and the serious drinking began, he left—well before any real trouble was likely to arise because of him being an American. Even though they all would have liked that he had stayed—would have liked to have seen the American wobbling and finally toppling over into a heap too.

He told Candelario, "How they spend their free time seems socially healthier and no less nutty than say yelling at the fate of a little ball being moved around by big grown men on a football field—or spending a good chunk of one's life swimming back and forth in a tiny pool of water and with one's head submersed in order to win a medal to hang around one's neck."

"I don't like some of what sometimes happens at the *tesguinadas*—but then bad things happen when people zip around in their nice cars too."

One evening he said to what may have been the deep canyons and to the sun and the sky, "The Aztecs with their Killing Stone—the Tarahumara with their *tesguino*—Mexico—the United States—tell me—is one essentially any different from the other?"

By now, whenever Lucas walked to somewhere he ran into people he knew also going somewhere. Men, women, couples, the very old, children, and entire families—some driving cows and packed burros ahead of them. Along with the greeting there were always a few additional words exchanged—as well as an energy that helped make walking on effortless.

He began to feel himself one of the neighbors. Immediately recognizable. Significant. An undeniable part of the landscape.

One day on his way to Marciano's place to help him split shingles for roofing a new room he was adding to his house he saw coming up the trail toward him a young girl who in her blue jeans and pink sweater and who with her light-brown uncovered hair did not appear at all Tarahumara.

"Anita—how did you get here?

"By leaving behind all of society's ideas of what an eleven year old is—and by throwing myself fearlessly headfirst into the unknown and giving myself up to God—and it turned out that it was not so difficult find you—given that most of the state of Chihuahua knows about the crazy American going off to live with the Tarahumara."

They both stop, and stand there two arm lengths apart—looking at one another.

"Back in Barranco Azul—a turkey vulture—late in heading south for the winter—circled above my head and nastily spit down at me that you had found a woman."

Lucas saying nothing, she goes on, "So very calmly—surprising even myself—I dismantled the *jacal*—the wood posts and the boards will make good firewood and soon go up in smoke—and the rocks I rolled one by one over the edge into the arroyo—the next flood waters will take them very far away."

Lucas staring hard at her thinks he can detect in her small thin body the slightest hint of budding womanhood.

"I came because I love you—and although almost all the *ranchera* songs speak about nothing but love love love—I do not think people know what it is—they couldn't—and still be the way they are."

"I love you too Anita."

"Love is not a word you say to try to make someone feel good—a person who really does—does not leave."

"But—"

"But but but—that is what everyone says—and why their kind of love does not work."

Lucas is stunned.

"I sometimes think I don't want to ever grow up—and find out there is no one out there for me—and begin to do ugly things—that make me ugly too."

"I came because I want only the best for you Lucas—even if that means you being with someone else—and so I came to tell you that I feel Jesusita will be very good for you."

"Growing up she was very much like me—and then something happened to her—awful yes—but perhaps that saved her from becoming like—well maybe like the rest of us—you will have to work very hard and be very patient to reach her—and what she still has."

"She was not put into the world to be like everyone else—so you must always be kind—and never get angry at her—never—no matter what she does."

Her eyes moistening, she turns, and as she walks slowly away, Lucas says, "Maybe what you speak of is still there in everyone—and looking hard and patiently for it is what one needs to do with every person—and yes—of course—at the same time be kind—always."

She stops, and turns back around.

Now a sleek tan deer, her shining eyes looking directly into his—intently curious.

He takes a step toward her and she wheels off the trail, and kicking up rocks and dirt bounds off uphill through the pines. Bounding higher and higher. And higher, and higher still—until she melts into the wild blue of the sky.

It was time to leave the Mesa of Tónachi.

Carmen having gone to speak with Felipa, had returned saying that there was a partially tumbled-down rock structure from very long ago nearby that he could put some kind of roof over and stay at.

"Mother said that either she or Jesusita would bring food over to you twice every day."

As he was leaving the cave, Candelario had mentioned, "By the way—do talk with Jaime—the school teacher—because his story I think you would find extremely interesting—that around here only he and I know about—I told him your trustworthiness was impeccable."

"I've been meaning to go by."

When he told Reyna, saying nothing more other than that he wanted to spend some time up by Chalelo and Felipa, she nodded—and then beamed when he handed her more pesos than probably she had expected.

When he told Gavino, Marta who was making tortillas did not look up. Nor did she when he went back out the door.

Lucas gathered up his few things and headed for the narrow neck of land that connected the Mesa with the more rugged mountain and canyon country where Chalelo and Felipa lived, as well as Antonia, and Chemo and Niceta.

Chalelo took him to the rock ruins which were halfway between his rancho and the rancho of Antonia, and in leaving invited him to come by the house anytime.

In three hours those rocks that over the years had fallen were back in place and the structure had a tarp roof laid over some poles and held done on the edges with rocks. Where a door once was served as his picture window through which he could look out into the distance at the undulations comprising the other rim of what Chalelo had referred to as the Big Canyon.

He sits down outside against one of the rock walls.

He tries to imagine having been born here, on the dirt floor inside, and spending a lifetime growing corn and beans on the rocky hillside behind the house, and then growing old and finally dying here on the same dirt floor.

He feels very comfortable with the Tarahumara, a people with no pretenses, no ideology, and very few illusions.

They had no oral history, few stories, and no religious rituals and beliefs any more for maintaining their culture intact—only their *tesguino* and isolated existence.

Along with what he has come to see as a very agreeable way of life. They got up when they wanted, worked when they wanted, served no boss, ate a varied and nutritious diet, never rushed, were as Lumholz had put it *"disgustingly fit,"* never felt the need to explain why they did anything, did not meddle in the affairs of others, and loved lolling around outside in nature in the company of their family and neighbors.

Having the skills and the wood for crafting beautiful furniture, they were happy sitting on chunks of wood and sleeping on a dirt floor. And he suspected that living in a house full of nice furniture would feel so strange to them that they would end up burning the furniture for firewood.

They had no government and military and elite to support. No road system or pyramids to build and maintain. No laws backed by guns telling them how to act and what to do. They had no concept of a nation, or of the State as the overriding entity that makes it possible for a society to function.

They were like the societies from which Engel learned that dependence on an all powerful State was not the natural condition for human beings and that started him thinking of ways to again make the State superfluous so that it might wither away and people again take charge of their own lives.

And he begins to see the threat that the mere existence of the Tarahumara and other indigenous cultures might present to the privileged and powerful few who utilize the State for their own materialistic and selfish ends—and also begins to understand more clearly the State's need to define indigenous people as ignorant children and as Candelario had put it a "social problem."

He picks up the plastic bucket that Chalelo had lent him and picks his way down to the arroyo. Dips the bucket into a clear deep pool. Then stands there awhile looking at nothing in particular. He makes his way back up to his new house. Again sits down against the same rock wall as before.

His thoughts turn to the many Tarahumara couples he has seen doing things outside together—working in a field or bringing in firewood together, scooting down a trail off to somewhere together, or just sitting and being with each other at an overlook or under a tree.

Suddenly he sees the eyes of Jesusita looking into his, her distorted smile, and the thin legs ending in the bare feet, and the tear in her blouse that now and then reveals a momentary glimpse of a breast.

Is he the loco? How would Donald and Mary view him should he show up with this woman at the university?

Yet—yet Anita had come to assure him that yes, this Tarahumara woman, who had hidden herself behind a tortilla, was in fact the right woman for him.

He hears the tinkle of a goat bell coming toward him. Listens intently as the tinkle gets closer.

A black and white goat bursts out of the trees, followed by others—and now they surround him, nibbling brush, at least 20 of them roiling the day with the confusion of their hither and thither.

Then he sees her, she Jesusita standing nearby off to one side against a pine tree, holding a white enamel plate in one hand—in all her strangeness and shyness. And it startles him a little how she had managed to approach so close without him having noticed.

She squats down there, hovered over the earth, the brown legs and bare feet disappearing under her skirts, her eyes lowered, the plate in her hand.

He becoming oblivious to the scrambling and scampering of the goats—now sees only her and nothing else.

He gets up and goes slowly over toward her.

But sensing her increasing fear, her wanting to run off, he stops. She glances up at him as she sets the plate on the ground.

Then springs up panicked and bolts—kicking up her bare feet and wildly waving both arms at the goats as they scurry off.

Something, or someone, who could be Anita, speaks in his ear, "The deer needs to be stay wild—it needs its space—it needs to feel safe."

And as he stands there watching her and the goats run uphill, he is aware of a kind of waddle in her motion that seems to be a physical manifestation of what may be changed in her brain, yet somehow so right for her—somehow so her.

Disappearing with the goats over the rise she is not gone—because she is now lodged in his heart.

In the morning Felipa came by to pick up the plate and to leave another. When he asked how Jesusita was she told him that right after corralling the goats last night she had gone off somewhere and had still not returned.

"Sometimes she is gone for many days—that is why she is so thin."

"Zenaida is the one out with the goats—she is still a little young so we don't let her take them far away—Chalelo and I are really the ones raising her."

"I am afraid I frightened her."

"No—it's the world that frightens her."

He eats his tortillas and beans, the beans a variety called *ojos de cabra*—goat eyes—and more tasty than any other he has ever eaten.

He is content. He is on a path for which he knows there are no precedents, no rules, and that requires no wisdom or special knowledge to follow—only the ability to respond and flow spontaneously and without calculation to whatever happens.

And faith—not in the certainty that he will win her, but simply faith that this path is for him the right one.

He knows that by actively pursuing Jesusita, or trying to figure her out, or trying to convince or impress her, or in any way push—would be leaving the path.

Setting out for Antonia's house, he feels an unusual strength in his legs. He runs up a hill and finds it does not tire him. And marvels at how quick-footed he is running and hopping over rocks back down the other side.

It occurs to him that never has he met a grown Tarahumara running to somewhere, only walking. And that it must not be running but rather walking every day down into and up out of these steep canyons that enables a Tarahumara to easily run along kicking a wooden ball for more than 100 miles and to arrive at the finish line of a race not even very tired.

Catching sight of a house with smoke wafting out from the under the shingled roof he slows down to a walk. Dogs bark. A woman appears at the door.

She, Antonia, with her blazing eyes and who could be as old as 90 has a dignity in her erect bearing that he has not encountered before.

"*Asagá—asagá.*"

He sits down on a block of wood and watches transfixed as she lays some sticks of wood onto a raised rock hearth, blows to revive the fire—her every unhurried and confident movement appearing as if entirely new to him.

She tells him she must be wearing out because now when she hikes down to visit Alfredo who lives down at the bottom of the Arroyo Hondo Canyon it leaves her legs tired—and that coming back uphill takes much longer than it used to.

At one time all the Tarahumara women must have been like her.

He continues to watch her as with a gourd she dips water from a clay olla and into a tin can, breaks off some twigs of laurel that are hanging overhead, adds them to the can, and places the can on top of some red coals she has pulled away from the flame.

When he mentions that most of the older women he has met did not know any Spanish she says that long ago she and her son Benito lived for a while near a mission center.

As he drinks his laurel tea from a clay mug, absorbing the presence of this woman, it becomes obvious to him that it is partly Jesusita in his heart that is somehow helping to make possible what seems to him to be an almost unworldly connection to Antonia.

She tells him that living alone when one is old is not bad because it gives one the time and space for readying the soul for its most solitary of flights to another world.

"To far beyond the stars—to where before anything began."

"What is it like there?"

"*Quien sabe?*—who really knows—but maybe it is where you are so happy you want to cry."

"And what is life here like?"

"It is very hard—the people are only happy when they drink—I stopped drinking many years ago—we Tarahumara when we drink forget our mates—and our children."

"Ahh—but how you ask things—I am worn out with so much talk—like when I arrive from the bottom of the canyon."

They sit there on their chunks of wood in silence. He stares at some squashes piled in a corner, at a piece of dried meat hanging from a rafter, at a sack filled with ears of corn leaned against a wood structure that supports the stone *metate* used for grinding the corn.

Getting up, he wanders outside and sits down on a rock. Watches six chickens pecking at some corn kernels that lie scattered on the dirt.

He looks up at the steep corn field, its low stubble poking up through the natural layer of stones and rocks that blanket the field—a field of stones and rocks, yet they helping to keep the soil from washing down into the arroyos when it rains, and also helping to hold in moisture, as well as discouraging the growth of weeds.

He thinks about how some Native Americans have practiced carrying a power animal—sometimes a wolf, or eagle, or bear—in their hearts, believing that without such a power animal one flounders about in the world, disordered, confused and, as John had put it totally clueless.

It occurs to him that it must be primarily the holding of something in the heart that gives one power, and not the animal itself. And wonders if maybe that something—during the long blurry period in human history preceding the rise of symbolic language and of a culture involving power animals—could have been one's mate, and thereby making possible the pair bond so necessary for raising children.

And might this original holding in the heart also have engendered an intimate and loving way of relating to those of one's group—a natural spontaneous morality that helped people live together cooperatively in a world that was extraordinarily difficult to live in?

And might this holding in the heart, along with an authenticity of being that enables one to speak from the heart, and Seeing too, and even human freedom in the sense of not being subservient to any authority—all be part of the same single constellation comprising what human beings in their essence once were?

An essence having its source in the old mammalian-emotional brain?

If so, the Golden Age—that ancient time when human beings were presumably better people and lived more harmoniously and happily—may well not be quite the poet's myth it is usually made out to be.

Standing up, he goes over to the opening that is the window and says, "*Ma shimea ne*—I am going now."

And hearing the response, *U go bá*, he turns and begins to walk back toward his rock house.

He thinks about the brawny Neanderthals who 50,000 years ago wandered about glaciated Europe, taking along with them as best they could their old and the sick. They the first people to bury their dead.

Was their extinction at the hands of the newcomers who arrived from Africa due to those people having brought with them a more cerebral brain? One capable not only of symbolic language and imagination, but also one that was more cunning and more unfeeling and ruthlessly voracious in pursuing what it wanted?

He thinks about some modern roosters, who bred for fast growth and meat, have in the process lost their ancestral mating dance, and now rape and murder their hens.

Almost to his rock hut Lucas hears a familiar swishing through tall grass, only this time sounding more like a gigantic whoosh.

"My dear Lucas—twice now you have wanted to banish me to oblivion for being the clever manipulator of words—the huckster you perceive me as—in spite of which I have come once again—this time to let you know that you are nothing but a hypocrite."

"You don't say much—and you appreciate the silent Tarahumara—but you think far too much—far far too much."

"The whole of civilization—clanking around inside your head—so loud it sometimes drives me crazy."

"I'm real sorry—but it's not me—it' the old clutter still slowly leaking from my brain—and that I'm patiently waiting for to finish leaking out."

"If I were to enlarge the holes—the too sudden drop in pressure might do me in—but thanks anyway—for your concern."

There is a silence—until finally the voice says, "Well—okay then."

And with that there was another whoosh.

That evening it is again Felipa who brings him his tortillas and *ojos de cabra.*

"It has not been easy with Jesusita—once the baskets she wove were nicer than mine—and now she cannot even make a tortilla—and there are the constant problems with the men who come around—wanting her as much as ever—but never to marry."

"I'm very sorry."

"Life is very strange."

"Yes it is."

"It is even stranger than my dreams—I'm going now."

"*Hasta mañana.*"

"*Hasta mañana.*"

In the middle of the night he wakes up to the joyful yipping and howling of coyotes. He listens to them—until suddenly and all at once they quit.

And it is then that he hears the pitiful wailing howl of what he immediately recognizes as Jesusita.

Thinking how the power animal, for it to stay, has to at every moment be put first, and not the chasing after one or the other of the glitzy chimeras that civilization has unloosed upon the world—he falls back to sleep.

19
Planting A Seed

When Lucas arrived at the two-room adobe school, Jaime was standing outside beside another teacher, the two of them watching the children playing inside the fenced school yard—some of them running around yelling and others standing quietly in groups, maybe 30 in all.

After introducing himself to Jaime, Jaime introduced him to Margo, a young Mestizo woman from Chihuahua City who told him she was performing her year of obligatory service in a rural area.

Jaime said, "When I first came here seven years ago there was no school—classes were in that grove of pines over there."

Children shyly approached, soon encircling them but standing back. Lucas waved and said, *Kwira,* and two of them said, *Kwira.*

"Candelario mentioned you'd maybe be by—hang out with the kids for another half hour—and then I'll have all the time in the world for visiting."

Sitting across the tiny wood table from one another in Jaime's half of the teacherage, drinking coffee and eating cookies, Jaime told him his father was Tarahumara, but that his mother was Wajiro, a group of about 2,000 who bordered the Tarahumara to the west.

"My wife is Wajiro too and lives with our three girls in San Juan—but every weekend we all go to visit and help my mother who after my dad died went back to live with her people—and we visit my wife's parent's too—I want my family to stay very Wajiro."

"They are a more warm-hearted and open people than the Tarahumara—and that may have had something to do with why there are so few of them and so many Tarahumara."

He said that even with his schooling and having left the land he felt he had stayed very Wajiro inside, more so than many who though still farming with oxen their corn and beans were nevertheless slowly becoming more and more like the Mestizos around them.

"All the State's efforts towards indigenous peoples are aimed at charity and cooption—and not at autonomous self development—as promulgated by the Constitution."

"In accepting payments—as well as free food, clothing, and building materials—in return for complying with government programs in health care, education, and agricultural practices—and along the way becoming dependent on the State—indigenous people here in Chihuahua are gradually losing not only their culture—but what has always been their essence—their independence and freedom and dignity."

"The money the Tarahumara receive they use to drink more than ever—and now besides—because their drinking is no longer a sacred act honoring Onorúgame—they are ashamed of it."

"Selling their forests—working all day in a marijuana field for a Chabochi—riding to somewhere in back of a truck instead of walking—and consuming so much sugar and white flour as they now do—does nothing for them either."

"So what do you teach these children?"

"I can sense you are thinking that we teachers are a major part of the processes destroying their culture—and you are right—but if I do not teach them someone else will—and in my small way I try to subvert those processes ."

"What I try to teach is the meaning and value of true freedom and dignity—as well as the importance of helping one another—and of sharing—and honesty—and a respect for what is different—and I encourage the students to carry those notions with them always—as a kind of touch stone to measure everything else by."

"In other words—I try to teach the old indigenous way of being a person and walking in the world."

Lucas was reminded of Hermelinda wanting to instill in her pupils what was noblest in the Revolution—a spirit of equality and justice, and also, just like Jaime, the freedom and dignity of the individual.

Jaime said, "Very early in my career I learned that the purpose of most education is to solidify the prevailing norms of society—and not to open eyes—or to encourage viewpoints that challenge those norms."

And then Jaime began his account of how some 15 years ago he had left his first teaching position in order to join Subcomandante Marcos and the very poor indigenous peoples of Chiapas in their armed insurrection against the Mexican government.

The indigenous peoples of Chiapas he said had never received the lands promised to them under the Constitution. And then the cattlemen and other large landowners began employing para-military gangs to terrorize the communities in order to appropriate even more of their lands. Simultaneously giant corporations from elsewhere were making a small elite from beyond Chiapas very rich as they extracted what they could of its oil, gas, uranium, hydro power, coffee, bananas, melons, coco, avocados, and mahogany and cypress.

And when indigenous leaders protested in any way whatsoever—whether through organizing, legal channels, or even with just dialog—the rich and powerful abetted by the government responded with lies and when that did not work with even more terror and injustice in the form of jail, evictions, and murder.

"It is the way Mexico has always worked and still works—the people kept dirt-poor and serving a handful of very rich—and where anyone addressing what might be even a simple question to someone holding political power—to a municipal president—to the omnipotent Father—is punished."

"Among Mestizos—the measure of a person is the power he or she holds to control and step on others—without power one is nothing—and that has always been Mexico's problem."

And so, Jaime continued, the EZIN—the Zapatista Army of National Liberation—came into being, a third of whom were women—and what was at first primarily a struggle for lands became a struggle to change the political structure of Mexico—and eventually also the course of the world.

Jaime's job had been to instill in the local people some of the greater implications of what they were fighting for.

"What Marcos wanted for Mexico was what the power elite and government were most intransigent in not wanting to grant—namely an open forum for dialog—and available to all the people and all points of view—in which everyone is treated as significant and heard and taken into account."

"And the indigenous people could understand that—better than anyone—because that has always been the indigenous way."

Lucas was reminded of the Iroquois Confederacy—for Benjamin Franklin the model for an authentic democracy.

"Jaime—having spent so many years as a lawyer—I tend to think that the indigenous way works because of something more basic—because again and again I have seen how what is termed dialog is no more than cleverness in justifying and arguing one's own position—and in attacking and ridiculing that of the other person."

"Also I have seen how the rich and the powerful become very adept at manipulating what the people believe to be democracy and open dialog—at engineering public consent—for example by such means as buying the backing of experts and other important people—controlling the media and the policy think tanks—intentionally causing events to happen that affect public opinion—and even setting up mind control institutes."

Lucas paused—continued.

"And so I feel that more important than the dialogue itself is something else you referred to—about everyone—and I emphasize everyone—being seen as significant—and listened to—and taken into account."

"In other words a willingness to see the other person as a fellow human being—whom one wants to open one's heart to and to treat honorably and help—even if it means—as it almost always does—doing with less of or without something oneself."

"Yes—except how does one open one's heart to American helicopters and Swiss planes dropping bombs on one's village?—and rodents into the corn fields?—how does one open one's heart to sixty thousand soldiers occupying half of Chiapas and with their bayonets and tanks terrorizing and displacing families from where they have lived for generations?"

There was a silence. Until finally, Lucas swallowed, and said, "Once things go so far that something with deaf ears is intent on stamping us into the dirt—and we can't get away—I guess the options are either to let it—or else try to incapacitate or destroy it."

Jaime went on to say that the war against the government had been launched the day NAFTA went into effect, and as a powerful statement against global capitalism—against an economic system ballyhooed by the media as the harbinger of a New World Order, one of productive efficiency and of promised prosperity for all.

But which in reality was a system in which the measure of all value is the profitability of a few megalith-like international corporations and financial institutions—and not by any means the well being of the people or of the environments in which they live.

"Chiapas has been raped ten times over—its beauty and its fruits and the very life and sacred spirit of the earth itself having been stolen—and all of it sold—at the highest price the market would bear—and the people left bleeding and poor and of no account."

"Just as one day—most of the people of the world are liable to be left bleeding—and hopelessly poor and of no account."

"While here and there—in Mexico City—in London—in Geneva Switzerland—a small handful of individuals sit with impunity on their mountains of loot and crimes and lies—and call it productivity—economic health—Progress."

"Imagine Lucas—a faceless Marcos in his black ski mask—and a bunch of poor nondescript Mayan Indians from the mountains and jungles of a nowhere place like Chiapas—working together in planting a seed for the vision of what humanity needs to return to—if it is to survive."

"Which is restore the dignity innate in every person—the only thing anyone can really have—and what makes one most human—and that one can only acquire by respecting the dignity of others."

"And so much better than money—or social programs—or drugs—for countering all the modern forces bent on wearing down and ultimately extinguishing the psychological and spiritual strength of the individual."

It struck Lucas that the human dignity Jaime seemed so almost obsessed with had much in common with what he himself had been thinking about—namely the capacity for natural morality and integrity that he felt still existed at some deep level in everyone

"We knew we could not bring down the Mexican government—but we knew we might to some extent wake up the Mexican people—and others—all over the world."

"And it was precisely that—our message—highlighting the injustices and depredations of their New World Order—which most likely prompted your government to immediately bestow upon ours a generous loan as well as military aid for the purpose of quickly extinguishing what we were trying to do—from the face of the earth."

"All of that is now many years ago—but the conditions that ignited what flamed up in Chiapas continue to exist—only more so—and in even a more terrifying kind of way—not only in Chiapas—but all around the world."

"And I wonder whether maybe many of those flailing out at the symbols of arrogance, power and luxury—many of the ones called terrorists—might not in their own desperate fashion be fighting for human dignity too—refusing to conform to being dumb sheep—and slaves to a soulless productivity— expendable and disdained nobodies."

"And I also wonder whether more surveillance and force and control— in making the world even more unlivable—only increases the propensity to rebellion—not just by a few—but by many—by entire populations."

Lucas suddenly again feeling overwhelmed by life—just as he did listening to The Old Man—said, "You could be right—and which could be why many of the more advanced industrialized nations—including my own—for a while now have had in place elaborate martial law contingency plans for dealing not just with isolated riots and acts of terrorism—but with armed mass rebellion among their own citizens."

There was a silence. To Lucas it seemed there was nothing more one could say.

It was all too overwhelming—dizzily overwhelming.

"It could be Lucas that even Marcos did not see it all—possibly because of him having spent so much time in a big city—and at the university."

"He would cry if he saw the shack I grew up in—he wants galvanized metal roofs to replace split shake shingles—the clatter of tortilla machines to replace the sound of patting hands—and considers it a disgrace that a four year old chops and carries home firewood for the family—instead of being in preschool."

"I think that old Candelario—living as he does in his cave—sees it better—because he—not even born an Indian—understands the value of the old Tarahumara and Wajiro ways—and how they have helped nourish dignity and integrity—and wants to see all that—at least here—way back in the canyons—continue forever."

"I realize as well as anyone that globalization and technology are irreversible—the inevitable future as people say—however as I see it—I feel it still remains to be seen whether the total extinction of what it once meant to be a human being—is also the inevitable future ."

"For me—Candelario and indigenous peoples are significant not just for being who they are—and not like everybody else—but also because they are symbols—living beacons that point to a shift in direction that the future—its guiding spirit—can still take."

"I see them both of those way too Jaime—as I also do a few people I know who live along the Rio Grande—a culture I have come to think of as Old Mexico."

"One of our Mexican writers called what you are maybe talking about *México Profundo*—in the sense of inscrutable and so most real—and with roots deep in what was ancient Mesoamerica."

Lucas stood up and said, "I'll come by again sometime—I'd like to hear more about the Wajiro."

As he headed toward the door, Jaime putting a hand on his shoulder, said, "The Tarahumara and the Wajiro—and also the Tepehuan to the south— are sitting on a fortune of prime drug lands—along with forests—and I never underestimate the readiness of the cartels and the corporations and the government to shoot us all in the back and throw all of us in a hole."

"You watch yourself too Lucas."

20
Not Yes Not No

Lucas is brought awake by the tinkle of a goat bell.

Stepping outside he sees goats bursting out of the forest, and running behind them Zenaida. Behind her is Jesusita, barefoot and in the same ragged clothes he remembers from before, with a plate in one hand.

The women stop running. And Jesusita, now holding her other hand in front of her eyes, walks toward him—Zenaida hanging back.

Jesusita drops the hand from her face to brush his.

"*Kwira*—here is your breakfast."

"*Kwira.*"

She returns the hand to in front of her eyes and stands there looking at him between the partly open fingers.

"Zenaida is too scared to come nearer."

He looks over at Zenaida, dressed like her mother but more neatly in her brightly-colored skirt, blouse, kerchief, and huaraches. She appears to be about seven, and like almost all the Tarahumara girls her age that he has so far encountered she radiates the poise of a young woman.

"That's okay—I see she is watching us very hard—and that she is very much with us."

"Yes—I have told her all about you."

He is aware how soft spoken Jesusita is and how broken and accented and minimal her Spanish. However that he and she would be able to communicate only about the most basic things and in only the most basic way seems somehow entirely irrelevant.

"You have a very nice daughter."

Jesusita smiles, looking pleased.

He noticing how the tear in her blouse now exposes more breast than before, becomes aroused, feels the surge of electricity between them. Jesusita drops her hand from her face Smiles a weird smile—which he responds to.

She speaks something to Zenaida in Tarahumara, who picking up rocks hurls them at the goats driving them back into the forest. And disappears behind them.

As he goes hard, she smiles more weirdly than before—then suddenly laughs.

Wondering if he dare touch her—she suddenly wheels, and runs with her distinctive waddle but like lightning off into the forest too.

There is something very sane about this woman—so without pretense. Because with her goats, with Zenaida, with him, and with the sky and the trees, she seems more relational and more sensitively aware than anyone he has ever known.

And it becomes clear to him that it is precisely this animal-like naturalness, an innocence, that makes her more beautiful than other beautiful women—that no nicer clothes or way of fixing her hair or any amount of sophistication could improve upon.

Which could be why from the moment they saw one another—he knew she was his woman.

When she came again just before nightfall with his dinner, she was wearing another blouse with no tears. And this time after handing him the plate she moved off to one side and squatted down there, silent—watching him eat.

After he handed her the empty plate she remained squatting there for a while, with neither of them saying anything. Until finally, as if sensing when the length of the visit was exactly right, she said she was going now, and left.

Several days later she asked him if he had brothers and sisters. And if he had a wife.

He named two brothers. When he said he had no wife, she answered, "*Mentira*—a lie—I know you have one waiting for you where you came from—and that you are married to Reyna too."

He tried to explain the nature of the relationship he had had with Reyna.

"Everyone says you and she are married."

That night he heard her long howls, not very far off—but there were only two.

In the morning, when it was Felipa who brought him his breakfast, she told him, "She is asleep in the house and not hiding out in some canyon—something has changed in her."

Just as the sun went down, he heard the tinkle of a goat bell—and moments later was swallowed up by the herd of milling goats, several entering his rock hut.

As he ate, Jesusita sat nearby on her *reboso*, she having carefully positioned her two skirts to cover even her ankles. Zenaida for the first time becoming child-like, played at catching bugs, laughing, as she and her mother now and then jabbered back and forth in Tarahumara.

Jesusita just before she left, said, "Come by our house in the morning and eat with us."

And it was then that she, looking no less beautiful than the beautiful Tonantzin, smiled a smile that was not at all askew, and that lit up the darkening night with an exquisitely beautiful soft green glow that could only have originated in another world.

In the morning when he arrives at the house only Jesusita is there, she blowing on the smoky fire. When he asks where the others are she says that Zenaida is with the goats and that her parents had unexpectedly left very early to drink tesguino at Chemo and Niceta's place. She pointing to a a block of wood tells him to sit down.

Watching her somewhat uncoordinated movements he sees that the log ends she has inserted into the stove are too big, and wonders if maybe this is the first time she has started up a fire in a long time. He notices the pile of old ashes on the dirt floor in front of the stove. And the unwashed plates on the small rickety table in the corner.

"Is there an ax around?"

She points outside.

He goes outside, sees an ax lying on a pile of logs, and with it chops off two chunks from one of the logs, which he then splits into small pieces. He carries an armful inside.

Jesusita sticks some of the pieces into the stove—and soon the fire jumps to life.

He feels very married to her.

From a badly-dented pail full of corn that has been soaking in a mixture of water and lime she scoops up a handful and drops it into the mouth of a metal grinder set on a post and begins turning the crank, the mashed corn or *masa* falling into another pail with some holes in it that is hanging from the post. As he watches her face and the jerkiness of the turning he can see that it is an effort for her.

He is acutely aware that she is doing her utter best to do what everyone said she could no longer do.

She is grateful when he takes over the turning of the crank. She takes some of the *masa* from the pail, shapes it into a loaf, and places it on the stone *metate* for the second grinding. Now with both hands and with downward motions she pushes a cylindrical stone over the *masa*.

From outside comes the sound of voices. And Chalelo and Felipa enter the hut.

Felipa begins speaking to Jesusita in Tarahumara, and Chalelo says to Lucas, "We are a little drunk—but only a little—welcome—sit down my friend—soon there will be food."

Jesusita picking up a shovel that is missing its handle moves stiffly and zombie-like over to the stove where with a piece of firewood she pushes some of the ashes onto the shovel. Carries them outside. Felipa begins to grind at the metate—and soon is patting out a tortilla, which she then lays on top of the stove. Jesusita makes two more trips with shovelfuls of ashes, not having said a word since her parents arrived, and now looking very black, not even acknowledging him—she no longer of this world.

All the ashes cleaned up, she takes a ragged blanket from a pile in a corner and slumps down there on top of the others, the blanket over her head.

Felipa putting a large pot of something on the stove, says, "That is how she is—and what it has been like for us for many years now."

Chalelo had invited him to the Fiesta of Guadalupe, which was to take place behind the school, saying that everyone would be there, and that there would be meat.

He arrived at the clearing as the sun was touching down. People were bringing in wood and stacking it besides two fires over each of which hung a large metal cauldron. Women were cutting up the meat of a cow as well as all its other edible parts. Men were standing silently in small groups. A few individuals were sitting on hewn plank benches at the edge of the clearing.

And others, mostly women, were sitting on the ground. Children were here and there.

He went around and greeted every single person, all of whom he now knew. He was told that Chemo, being rich, had donated the cow—and immediately saw that the fiestas also served as a means for redistributing wealth.

The stewed meat which they called *tónari* they would all eat along with some tortillas at sunup. After which everyone would receive a portion of the leftover meat and then spend the rest of the day drinking *tesguino*.

As it gets dark the shapes of people blur, become otherworldly as they move about in the firelight and in the shadows. Overhead the stars flicker. What impresses him most is the quietness.

Chalelo seated on one of the planks begins to tune his violin. Alongside him, Faustino tunes his guitar. And soon they are playing the distinctive Tarahumara music, lilting and slightly intentionally discordant, but most of all repetitive—a mantra of sound to relax one, and to transform consciousness.

Now and then he can pick up a hint of the Celtic strains that some Irish priest must have brought with him from Britain along with his violin—which instrument was soon adopted by the Tarahumara who until then had only known the drum, the rattle, the rasp, and the flute.

One by one, people begin to dance to the same melodic bars repeating themselves over and over again. A line of men and another of women, stomping and hopping.

The Sierra winter night turns cold.

The musicians stop—shift into another melody. And Reyna walks over to them with a shovelful of red coals from one of the fires and dumps it by their bare huarachied feet.

Although Felipa had told him that Jesusita had run howling down into a canyon, he is hoping she will magically appear, knowing he is here.

He walks over and joins the men's line of dancers. He now stomping and hopping—just as he had once before, high up on the ridge of the Sierra de la Mula.

There is a pause to drink coffee. Drinking his, he scans the shapes for one that might be Jesusita.

As he dances on through the night, in communion with the others and with the cosmos, he continues to push on—beyond sleepiness and physical exhaustion, and to that part of him that preceded human consciousness.

To that primordial place where there was no longer a Lucas.

He arrives back at his rock hut in the early afternoon, having left the others to do their drinking.

After a while—he takes the tin can of *tónari* he had been given and goes over to Chalelo's house to see if Jesusita might be there. Not finding anyone, nor the goats, he picks up the ax and begins cutting up a log for firewood.

The wood cut and stacked and he about ready to leave he hears the familiar tinkle of goats ascending from out of one of the canyons. Watches them appear one by one at the canyon's edge and behind them Jesusita and Zenaida. Who herd them not toward the house but off to one side and to the top of a low knoll.

He knows that the two women are as intensely aware of him as he is of them—yet they do not come closer.

He chops some more wood, wondering if it might be time to leave the Sierra and return to the border—leave what is turning out to seem more and more like a fool's errand.

The sun touches down.

And then he sees the goats coming down off the knoll toward the house and the two women waving their arms behind them, At an oak tree near the corral Jesusita grabs onto an overhead branch with both hands and swings her slender brown legs up high to another branch and then pulls herself up onto it. And balanced up there throws down to the milling goats below her some of the corn stalks that are hanging high in the tree so that the animals cannot get to them.

She like a tree snake slides back down onto the ground among the frantically eating goats, and leaving Zenaida with them, walks slowly over to him. Her face is flushed. And she very beautiful.

They brush fingertips, say *Kwira*, and then, the words spilling from his mouth without him having intended them to, he says, "I want to marry you—I'll build you a pretty house—either here or wherever you like."

They stand there for a moment, she saying nothing, her face expressionless.

He takes two steps and picks up the can of *tónari*.

"I brought you and Zenaida this from the fiesta."

She spits on the ground. And then more forcefully a second time. Then quickly grabs the can and without looking into it or at him hurries back to Zenaida.

The two talk together in Tarahumara—for very long time.

Finally he goes over to them.

"Well—yes or no?—if yes—tomorrow I will speak to your father Chalelo—if no—then I will be leaving here and the Sierra very soon."

They stand there in silence for another very long time—the goats eating their corn stalks. Now and then Jesusita spits.

He wonders if he has just done the most stupid thing anyone has ever done.

Jesusita turns away. And the two women shoo the goats into the corral for the night. Jesusita puts up the bars. She says something to Zenaida.

And then they both run—run like he has never seen a Tarahumara run, Jesusita with the tin can in her hand, back up to the knoll they had come down from.

Where they disappear over the crest.

That night in his hut he listens for her howling—but the night with its stars and the half moon are silent—like the silence beyond the grave.

Toward morning he is shaken awake by Donald and Mary, both of them shouting in his ear.

"My god Lucas—face up to it—the looniest one out there is you—you—you—come back to the States where you belong—and leave these people alone—alone—alone—alone."

He wakes up in his rock hut with the sun already up. He wonders whether Chalelo and Felipa are still drinking. And whether he has frightened Jesusita off for good.

He regrets having pressured her with an ultimatum—she perhaps understanding at a deeper level than he does that life is not yes or no, not this or that.

From now on he would do nothing—simply wait. He has expressed his intention, and now all that is left is to see what happens.

The sun is high when he sees the two women emerge like shy deer from out of the trees.

Zenaida stops. At which Jesusita, a plate in one hand, stops too, and says something to her. And then they continue toward him, Zenaida this time following along, although well behind her mother.

Jesusita is wearing what look like her nicest clothes, and she has bathed and washed her hair, and is wearing tire-tread huaraches.

Her eyes looking down, she hands him the plate—on which there are tortillas and also all of the meat he had given her yesterday.

She looks up at him and into his eyes, and smiles. Then turns her head.

"Zenaida come closer—it is only Lucas."

"Your mother is right—how can you take a tortilla and some of this meat standing so far away?

21

Two Pails

Lucas knew that among the Tarahumara it was not the custom to ask the parents for permission to marry their daughter—not even if she were only twelve.

However in the case of Jesusita, she not being well, Chalelo and Felipa controlled her like they would not have another daughter, guarding her, and Zenaida too, against the nightmare of lusting drunk neighbors and outsiders like him.

Moreover he knew that the Tarahumara exerted tremendous pressure on their women to avoid liaisons with those who were not Tarahumara—one reason why the culture had remained so intact for hundreds of years. Reyna had told him that very light-skinned infants were sometimes abandoned—even if both parents were Tarahumara.

No one in the Tónachi area had ever heard of any Tarahumara having married an American. Nor did they have any concept of where or what the United States was. All they knew about him for sure was that he was light-skinned, had facial features that were different from what they had seen before, spoke an odd Spanish, was not from nearby, and did everything another way from the way they would.

What was he really up to back here—this Chabochi-Gringo who did not even know how to plant corn and beans? Who could have full confidence in such a nebulous being?

Nevertheless, in his favor was the fact that everyone considered Jesusita to be hopelessly *loca*, and not marriageable—she the least among them.

He did not want to in any way alienate Chalelo and Felipa. Were he to live with their daughter he would need their constant help—with building a house, for acquiring food, and with a multitude of other necessities which were part of the daily life of this culture. And perhaps would need their help with Jesusita too.

When he mentioned to Chalelo who had just finished cutting up some firewood that he wanted to marry Jesusita Chalelo responded as if he had not heard the question. And began to chop at another log. The log breaking into two, he stopped.

"Jesusita and Zenaida are pure expense—and we are very poor—not like Chemo with all his cows—I work hard—very hard—how long will you be staying up here?—with us?"

"I don't know—it depends."

They stand there silently for a while.

"I enjoyed listening to your violin at the Fiesta of Guadalupe."

"It is much more talkative than I am—and never speaks nonsense—like I do when I am drunk—and like sometimes I do when I am not drunk too—come inside and eat a tortilla."

The two of them ate their heated-up beans and tortillas in silence. Again—it seemed to be not yes, not no.

Afterwards, he watched Chalelo yoke up his two oxen to a handmade wooden plow—and then continued to watch as he walked behind them, now and then shouting, the oxen slowly trudging back and forth across the steep rocky hillside turning over a patch of the stony earth.

The Tarahumara had all the time in the world. There was absolutely no urgency to give away one of their women to someone who might very well be a fly-by-night—leaving her with a white baby, and possibly more *loca* than ever.

That evening, Lucas sitting against a wall or his rock hut, waiting for the first stars to appear, hears a very soft humming in the air around him, a humming that seems pregnant with meaning. He twists this way and that trying to locate its source—now feeling in what could be every cell of his body a pleasant tingling.

"Listen well Lucas—but not with your ears—because I have come to tell you a story that Gregorio never put into a *corrido*—not only because it was too horrible—but because it spoke too honestly about things that people do not want to hear or see."

"Who are you—are you one of the witches—a friend of Petronila—Katrina?"

"This is Norma—now listen closely."

"A few years ago—someone from Las Palomas or from elsewhere—we don't know who—complained to the authorities in La Junta that I spent my days dirty like an animal—and tied up like one."

"Four police came—with machine guns."

"They cut the rope—handcuffed me—and also Mother—and took us both away screaming and crying in the back of a pickup—with one of the police with his machine gun riding in back with us—and in La Junta they put us in a very ugly jail."

"Some of the people in Las Palomas submitted a signed statement explaining the rope—and the judge declared Mother innocent and she was let go."

"I was taken to Chihuahua City—and turned over to the State—and put in what they called a hospital—but which was really just another jail cell—with a tiny high window that only by hanging on the bars and pulling myself up could I see out of—and they injected drugs into me which made it difficult to think or stay awake."

"The doctors were the worst—I can't begin to explain what they were like—except that I saw them as angular and twisted out of shape—I always groped around for something to throw at them—but there was nothing—they were the ones who could least accept who I was—always using the words help and cure and fix—but really only wanting to feel powerful and important—and to control me."

"Like they themselves were controlled—jiggled like puppets—every moment of their lives—only not aware of it."

"I discovered a hatred I did not know I was capable of—there was absolutely nowhere to run to—or hide—at first I screamed a lot—and finally it seemed I died—but found myself somehow still alive—in my black aloneness."

The humming and the voice cease—leaving in him only a lingering tingling. Extending his arms overhead, he tries to reach into the blackness to her—to her utter aloneness.

He recalls how in the 1930s, some of the most distinguished psychiatrists in the world had come up with the cure for severe mental disorders—gas chambers, which the Nazis afterwards appropriated for their own final solution or cure for the disease of Jewishness.

Norma's use of the word twisted—was as good as any.

People are beginning to wake up to the destruction taking place to every aspect of the physical environment—to the forests, the rivers, the air, the oceans, and to all the wild creatures—and to their own physical bodies. Yet remain oblivious to the even much greater devastation that has taken place to the human psyche—to its balance, wholeness, and to its capacity for sensitive awareness.

A devastation that begins even before one is born—in everyone.

And so probably what Norma had pointed to was on the mark. That those most to be feared are the experts on what a person and a society should be like. As well as anyone else wielding power, along with an image of unimpeachable correctness and respectability, over the lives of others.

They much more dangerous than the officially-declared mentally ill, most of whom are at worst at times only a nuisance and a bother to take care of.

The air about him hums again—the tingling in his body now more intense than ever.

"In spite of Mother's pleading—and then protests—they just did not want to give me up."

"Eventually—she and the people of Las Palomas found a lawyer—a nephew of Consuelo who lives in Chihuahua City—and with his help I finally returned to under my tree in the desert."

"Mother had to sign a paper promising to keep me very clean—uncontaminated by the soil and dust of the earth in which people grow their corn and beans—and from which they build their adobe houses—and from which we all come from and return to."

"Since the desert has no grass—she put a chair under the tree—but I never sat in it—because I like sprawling on the ground—and sometimes rolling over onto my belly—and back again—it makes me feel alive."

"No one in Las Palomas told you any of this because they were ashamed to—ashamed that they were part of such a world."

"Lucas—be very very careful with Jesusita—she and I are very simple and totally defenseless creatures—and society cannot tolerate our presence—it makes people too uncomfortable—it throws into their face that the world is not what they have made it into and pretend it to be."

"I have also come to tell you that in knowing you—something about us connecting—has helped anchor me—like the blue and yellow rope did—against being swept away in the confusion and craziness."

"I no longer need the rope—I still roam out into the desert—but no longer very far—and never to run away."

"The other evening—out on the desert—a herd of javelina came by and invited me to join them—one of them said she knew you—part of me wanted very much to go with them—but thanking them I said no."

The soft humming suddenly turns into a loud hissing whirlwind. Then he hears—barely able to make out the words, "Lucas—the one they will most want to fix—is you."

The tingling throughout his body intensifies—until barely able to stand it, feeling he is about to explode, and closing his eyes, he defiantly screams, "No—no—I won't let them—never."

Which hushes the whirlwind.

When he opens his eyes—Lucas finds himself floating just above the bottom of a deep clear pool of utter calm.

He holds out his hand—and brushes fingertips with a golden-haired mermaid. And says, "Kwira."

In the morning, when Jesusita came with his breakfast, she asked him to buy her two metal pails, a cut of red cloth for making a skirt, and a kerchief. He replied that he would go to San Juan the next day.

And then she stood there—watching him eat until he was done.

Whenever she was with him, except for some odd mannerisms, there seemed to be very little *loca* about her. He suspected that whenever she ran, disappeared, or hid, it was because something did at those times go awry in her brain—she not wanting him to see her like that.

She was trying her best to be a good woman for him.

Lucas and Candelario are sitting on the low rock wall at the front of the cave, both of them watching Carmen who is deftly weaving a perfectly round basket from the strips of sotol beside her. At Lucas' feet are two galvanized metal pails, one stuck inside the other, and stuffed inside are a folded red cloth, a blue kerchief, and a large plastic bag of green jalapeno chiles. The other bag of chiles he bought sits on a rock ledge behind Carmen.

Carmen, her fingers tucking a strip of sotol into place, and without looking up, says, "They will gladly accept the pails—but never let you have her—and Jesusita with her illness will not be able to help you."

"I'm inclined to agree with her Lucas—Chalelo and Felipa are nice to me to my face—but when they are drunk both of them try to pick a fight with me—

and twice we've had to leave—that Jesusita is a lot better and happy just is not what is most important to them."

"The world is a strange place Lucas—everything backwards."

"People still get on me for having left my wife—when it was she who left me—taking a job in the Presidencia in San Juan as a secretary—five days a week—stroking like a lover the keys of her computer—crisply answering the phone—telling people to please have a seat—and all behind a mask of self importance—deluded that she now was somebody—and that is still who she was when she arrived home—and like with all the others I wanted to beat her on the head too—and yell, Where did you go?—and this went on for a year or two—until finally I said, Enough."

"And in retaliation—she turned our children against me."

Candelario brushes a fly from his nose.

"People don't like it that at my age I started another family—but hell—I'm in perfect health and more alive than most people I know—which just might be a sign of some damn good genes—and I think women can sense that—and that with me they may improve the human race."

Lucas smiling, says, "Candelario—you certainly are an old hard walnut—but I understand what you are saying—how these days it is other things—such as piling up money and wanting to be important—that is now driving the direction of human evolution—and not the animal-like vitality that has driven it for millions of years.."

"You got it right Lucas—you always hear me real good."

Lucas heading towards Chalelo's house with the two pails, the red cloth, the kerchief and the chiles, sees Jesusita and Zenaida and the goats by the corral.

Jesusita spotting him, shields her eyes with a hand and with her waddle-like run and rolling her head moves the goats in a direction away from him, Zenaida following. When he yells that he has pails and the cloth, she runs even faster, not even glancing back.

He continues to the house and sits down on a log, from where he watches the two women who have stopped running and who appear to be keeping the goats more or less in one area, chasing them back whenever they try to roam further.

After almost an hour, and he is about to leave, Jesusita begins walking toward him, having left the goats with Zenaida.

Almost to him, she smiles a smile that lights her up.

He hands her the pails, which she sets on the ground. Then turns very serious as she immediately unfolds the red bundle of cloth and carefully examines it, stroking it here and there. After which she neatly folds it back up, unfolds the blue kerchief, and examines it too.

As she removes the faded kerchief she is wearing, and ties on the new one, he notices a single grey hair which stands out against the coal blackness of the others. And it strikes him that a woman is beautiful for a very short time—only long enough to help attract a man with whom to have children, one who will then willingly sacrifice himself for the well being of her and them.

And that when some day Jesusita too, like Antonia, is grey-haired and wrinkled—that is exactly as it should be.

"Come into to the house and drink some *pinole*—and we will roast some of the chiles you brought as well."

He follows her inside. Jesusita puts two green chiles on the stove that still has some fire in it—and then prepares two glasses of *pinole*.

Felipa and Chalelo enter and greet him, ignoring Jesusita. Chalelo lies down on his back on a goatskin. Felipa pours some corn into the grinder and begins to turn the crank, not acknowledging the two shiny pails nor the pile of chiles on the small table beside her.

Jesusita handing Lucas his chile and glass of *pinole* squats down alongside the chunk of wood he is sitting on, their shoulder touching. He feels very married to her.

Suddenly she gets up and goes out the door.

When she does not come back he goes out to look for her, a half-eaten chile in his hand.

Catching sight of her standing at the edge of the corn field he goes over toward her. She moves away to hide behind some head-high stalks.

"Come by the day after tomorrow—early in the morning—it is my mother's birthday—and there will be others coming too—my father is going to kill some chickens—and Antonio will bring potatoes—but now—go."

He turns away, and taking a bite of his chile, begins the walk back to his rock hut.

❖ ❖ ❖

Arriving at Chalelo's house he finds that everyone is already there and drinking and eating tortillas and chicken-potato stew. He goes from person to person greeting each one. And then he goes over to Jesusita who is squatting at the edge of the group, she wearing her new blue kerchief and a new red skirt. He sits down on the ground next to her.

"The skirt is very pretty—did you sew it?"

"Yes."

Felipa comes over to them with a white plastic bucket of *tesguino*, and scooping with a gourd dipper, hands it to him. He drinks the *tesguino* slowly, pausing several times.

Jesusita, her head far back, empties the gourd in a fraction of the time it took him. Wipes her mouth with a sleeve as she hands the dipper back. She stands up and disappears into the house.

People are joking and laughing. Chemo has his arm around Shimino's wife Rosa. Matilde is dancing by herself to her own music—ta taa ta ta taa, ta taa ta ta taa. Alfredo is making squeaking sounds with Chalelo's violin.

Jesusita returns with two plates of chicken-potato stew with some tortillas lying on top, and handing him one ot the plates, reassumes her squatting position. They eat, spooning up pieces of chicken and potato with a piece of tortilla, now and then tilting the plate to drink the broth.

Chemo's wife Niceta comes over and begins to chat with Jesusita in Tarahumara, while now and then glancing at Lucas, she always before having acted toward him as if he did not exist.

Niceta takes hold of one of his hands and says something to him in Tarahumara. Jesusita spits hard at the earth and then also says something in Tarahumara. Niceta wheels and leaves, and Jesusita takes hold of the hand that Niceta had been holding.

When Chalelo begins to play his violin she stands up, and still holding onto his hand pulls him up. And the two of them dance.

The music stopping, Felipa appears before them with the bucket. He declines the gourd and passes it on to Jesusita. Who her back turned to him, and drinking from the gourd, scrunches the softness of her hips against his body, swaying from side to side.

Felipa says, "Get away from him—enough of that filth."

Jesusita taking a step forward, hands Felipa the emptied gourd. But then as soon as Felipa leaves she moves backwards again, scrunching her hips against his body—against his now hard *bisaka*.

Felipa returning yanks her away.

"Don't you have any shame?"

He follows Jesusita who has withdrawn into her black unreachable place off to one side of the gathering, where she lies down on the ground and curls into a ball. He sits down beside her. And soon she is asleep.

It is getting dark. The noisiness of the others continues unabated. Alfredo and Faustino are pushing one another—until Faustino moving backwards stumbles over a log and falls to the ground. And continues to lie there, dead to the world.

Lucas wonders whether the cultural custom of drinking is basically a way for a sedentary people to escape from the routine dullness of farming the same small plot of land year after year, generation after generation. For hunter gatherers, always on the move over a vast, ever-changing landscape, daily life may have been hard, sometimes extremely hard, but rarely boring.

Candelario had told him that a while back he had stopped drinking—and had convinced Carmen to stop too. For him it had to do with the soldiers falling upon Alfredo's rancho and the ensuing rage and humiliation leaving him no longer the same Candelario.

"It was a little like a rattlesnake frightening a horse crossing a bridge—after that the horse will not cross any bridge."

It dark now, he looks down at the sleeping Jesusita. He knows that society will always consider her *loca*. But that does not matter. Because what she and he have predates society—and language with its categories and definitions.

He hears the loud drunken voice of Alfredo talking with someone.

Jesusita jerks herself up into a sitting position.

"They are talking of beating us with sticks—and killing us—you for being a rich gringo—and me for being with you—come—follow me."

And without giving him time to answer she is gone in the night. He rushes, stumbling, after her, and then almost runs into her, she having stopped to wait for him. Taking his hand she leads him off through the pitch blackness.

Letting go of his hand, she says, "Faster—they are coming after us—I can see the glint of their long knives."

He follows at her heels knowing it would be useless to try to assure her that no one is behind them. Just when he can no longer keep up, she slows down to a walk. And together they traverse what seems to him a dreamscape, made even more unreal by the altered state, the *locura* of Jesusita, A strange wordless dreamscape—that only dissipates when they arrive at the door of his rock hut. He goes inside.

And comes right back out with the old blanket he brought from Las Palomas and also a much thicker one woven by a Tarahumara that he bought in San Juan. He spreads the old one alongside a wall of the house and sits down on it, while Jesusita remains standing, tuned to and melted into the silence of the night.

"They are saying that I am a disgrace to the Tarahumara—and that they will push both of us off a cliff—for the coyotes and the jaguars to grow fat on."

"They are now far away and too drunk to do anything to us tonight—they would be the ones falling off a cliff."

"They will send the Black Devil to do it for them."

"Come—sit down—the blankets will keep us warm."

She remains standing. What could be an hour passes.

Then without him having noticed, she is suddenly beside him. Pushes him down so that they are lying side by side and pulls the thick blanket entirely over them, blotting out the stars—the two of them not touching.

He feels an energy emanating from her and an identical energy taking hold of his own body, can smell her wetness, as with both hands she pulls her two skirts up to her waist. She finding his hand, rubs it on her warm belly. With his other hand he undoes his fly. And then, the blanket still over his head, he straddles her and enters her liquid smooth readiness for him, his body already moving of its own impulse and in a way it never has before.

Hears emerging from out of the depths of his being the beginnings of a strange howl that rises in unison with another corresponding howl, the two as one and increasing in intensity and filling the night for what seems forever.

Those at Chelelo's house, hearing the howling that pierces their drunken stupor and the night, whoop in reply, and joke about how they need not fear the stupid gringo—that the howling of La Loca will of itself soon drive him back to where he came from.

22
Blue Corn Tortillas

Waking up at first light, Lucas finds that Jesusita is not at his side. Several times he calls her name, not expecting an answer—and gets none. Maybe this is the reality of life with this woman—never quite knowing what she will do.

Mid morning, neither she nor Felipa having brought him breakfast, he opens a bag of *pinole*, pours some into a cup along with some water, stirs with a finger, and drinks it.

That night from the direction of the Big Canyon he hears howl after howl after howl.

He feels very much with her, and her desperation, and terror.

And not until the howls cease does he fall asleep—at peace and with her alongside him.

The next morning Lucas watches as Chalelo and Felipa emerge out of the trees followed by Jesusita and Zenaida. After they all say *Kwira*, Chalelo says, "Yesterday we forbid Jesusita to have anything more to do with you—making it clear to her that the last thing we needed was another Chabochi in the family."

He pauses, looking at Lucas.

"However we hadn't realized how stubbornly determined she is to be with you—no strong words or harsh whip can convince her otherwise."

"She ran out into the night saying that this time it was to die out there—Felipa and I went to where we thought she might be and brought her back to the house—as we have done many times before."

"So we have decided to give her to you—you can now go anywhere you want with her—and the two of you can live with us until you build your own house."

Felipa says, "Although she is less sick than before you came—she is still far from well—she continues to do many foolish things—and she sometimes gets very angry and one cannot do anything with her."

"Zenaida will continue to live with us—she and I will do the goats—very soon she will be able to do them all by herself—it will be enough for you taking care of Jesusita."

They all stand there in silence, Zenaida distracted by some raucous birds in an oak tree, and Jesusita as if none of this concerned her in the least.

Chalelo says, "Gather up your things and then come to the house for breakfast—we will go now."

They all lived together in the one small room. When they ate there were only three wood chunks for the five of them to sit on, so usually the two women ate squatting. At nightfall they laid out some goatskins on the dirt floor to sleep on, along with blankets they brought in from outside and that had been hanging over a line exposed to the sun. The fire in the oil drum stove was almost always going and the door of the house almost always wide open.

Felipa and Zenaida prepared the tortillas and beans—and on some days the additional diced prickly pear cactus or wild mustard or water cress greens. There was always tea made with laurel leaves, the bushes growing nearby. Jesusita because of her illness never took part in the affairs of the kitchen other than to bring over to where he was sitting his plate of food and cup of tea.

However she worked assiduously at washing her clothes and his, more than she really needed to. He himself brought in wood from the forest and cut it up for the stove.

One day he bought a male goat from Chalelo, who then cut its throat and skinned it. The first meals were the cooked blood that had flowed from its neck and that Zenaida had caught in a pan. Then for the next week they ate its meat including that from the head and also the intestines.

Now and then Niceta brought over a block of cheese made from milk from Chemos's cows.

Living with the family had a human warmth that Lucas had not experienced before. He got used to the conversations in Tarahumara that sometimes occurred in the middle of the night, and to people getting up and stepping over him to go outside, and to someone lighting up the room with a pitch torch and eating a tortilla. And over time even got used to the fleas that crawled over him and occasionally bit him.

He had known that in marrying Jesusita he would also be marrying her family. It surprised him how graciously and warmly Felipa and Chalelo now treated him, as if he were another person entirely.

Jesusita almost always slept holding tightly on to him. He was content.

Which changed during the first *tesguinada*—when people wandering noisily in and out of the house throughout the night and sometimes even plopping down by him and Jesusita made sleep impossible. And then someone standing above them in the dark urinated over them.

In the morning Jesusita said, "Rosa told me that you are no good for me—none of them knew I still existed—and now they all want to help me."

That same afternoon Lucas began work on improving his old rock hut a half mile away, chinking the cracks in the walls with mud, and chopping down, limbing, and peeling some trees for *vigas* to lay across the walls to support a roof. He then hired Shimio's son Marciano to set out on the first of several trips to San Juan for sheets of tin roofing.

Each sheet, rolled up and tied so as to form a twelve foot long tube, Marciano carried on his shoulder down into and up out of several canyons to the reconstruction project.

A window was made from hewed wood and a piece of clear plastic. And the old blanket was hung over the door opening.

And here they slept—and also retreated to to escape the wildness of the *tesguinadas,* and also at other times to simply be alone. And eventually, because Jesusita liked to sleep late, Felipa, usually accompanied by Zenaida, began to bring over to them their breakfast.

Since he arrived in the Tónachi area he had tried his best to get along with everyone—to be helpful, kind, and generous, to always more or less agree, to never try to convince, to accept whatever anyone did. Which has always been the Tarahumara way, when people were not drinking.

He knew that even if he were cheated, or lied to, or insulted, the best response was say to nothing, and to instead simply try to minimize further dealings with that particular person.

And he also knew it was best not to stand out in a way that might make anyone envious, or in any way make anyone uncomfortable—and that people's capacity for retaliation, for resorting to witches or to some other form of terrorism to do harm, was enormous.

But even doing his intelligent best, could he, a Gringo, now married to a Tarahumara woman, and to a beautiful one, and living with the Tarahumara in a place that was not his, continue to get along—with everyone?

He saw that even Zenaida would still not come over to them alone. And that she was now identifying almost totally with Chalelo and Felipa, the image of her mother now actually living with an American undoubtedly making her more uncomfortable than ever. And maybe Chalelo and Felipa had foreseen that, insisting she stay with them as they had.

About every other day Jesusita suffered an attack of whatever it was that seemed to torment her. Usually she simply disappeared during a slight lapse of inattention on his part while he was engrossed in some task or in some thoughts. Suddenly she was not there, but rather who knew where, hiding behind a rock, or out in the forest.

Sometimes he would wake up in the night and she would not be there.

Once he managed to grab her by the arm as she was leaving and she becoming furious began to spew words at him in Tarahumara that sprinkled with a few Spanish words—such as police, long knife, poison, hanging rope, and son of a bitch—made it obvious that what he was hearing was a barrage of delusion, cursing, and paranoia.

When he released her she hit him and fled howling into the darkness.

Always after a few hours she returned as if absolutely nothing had happened. Whenever he asked her what thought or sensation in her body might have provoked her unusual action she did not answer.

Now and then he thought of Marta, who he had not seen since he had left the Mesa, she still lodged in his mind and as bewitchingly enticing as ever, maybe even more so and in a way that Jesusita was not. But he knew that he was now entirely immune to whatever it was she might want with him.

One morning after Felipa and Zenaida had left, Jesusita said, "Buy me a coffee pot and some pretty cups—as well as coffee and sugar and some cookies—and pile up some sticks to make some fires with—so we can always offer whoever comes by something nice"

In early July the monsoon rains having their origin somewhere out in the Pacific Ocean began. Day after day of cold hail and heavy showers. The billowing mushrooming clouds began to form about noon. Then parts of the sky turned black, pierced by bolts of lightning and thunder—and soon one found oneself ankle-deep in water and the rushing roaring arroyos impassable.

Sometimes a clear sky would produce a torrential rain in an hour. The land turned green. Here and there waterfalls cascaded for a thousand feet down a cliff. Rainbows arched across the sky. Corn, beans and squash shot up from the earth. And almost overnight—beautiful mushrooms as big as grapefruit.

While it stormed the Tarahumara lay sprawled on the floors of their houses, or sat silently against a wall, the fire going. And waited—sometimes for an hour, and other times for many hours. And occasionally for several days.

One day Blas, who was a nephew of Alfredo, walked drenched into Felipa's kitchen, sat down near the fire, and ate a tortilla with chile and beans as he chatted. Then he went back out into the downpour to where his burro loaded with a crate of mangos from down in the *barrancas* was tied to a tree, and undoing some ropes, brought the crate inside.

Jesusita wanted to buy them all, but Felipa said that some would ferment and go rotten before that many could be eaten. So Lucas bought only half the crate, Blas saying he could probably sell the rest to Chemo.

Immediately Jesusita picked out the biggest ripest yellowest mango, and without peeling it bit into it as its juice ran down her chin and onto her white blouse.

The next morning after breakfast and under a clear blue sky, Lucas and Jesusita set out through the dripping wet woods with a bag of mangos to visit Antonia who Jesusita said she hadn't spoken with in years.

She points excitedly to what she says is a cow on a hillside. They stop, but as hard as he tries, he cannot see it. They go on.

Several minutes later she jerks his arm such that he almost falls over backwards and at the same time scolds him for having almost stepped on the long thin green snake that is lying across the trail.

Almost to Antonia's house, Jesusita breaks into a wildly joyful run down a steep slope. Climbing back up to him she holds in one hand an exquisitely-shaped pale yellow mushroom larger than a grapefruit. She is glowing.

It occurs to him that all the instincts of the hunter gatherer are very much alive in her—as maybe they still are in every Tarahumara, now farming corn and beans.

Antonia accepts the bag of mangos and the mushroom and asks them in as if their visit were an almost everyday occurrence. On the small table in a pan is a loaf of blue dough ready to be patted into blue corn tortillas and baked. The two women talk back and forth in sing songy Tarahumara.

Antonia goes to the stove and blows into it to revive the flame. And

Jesusita sticking a hand into the blue *masa*, begins patting out a tortilla. Which she then gently places on the stove.

As Jesusita continues to make tortillas Antonia grinds some dried red chiles on the *metate*, the two of them still now and then chatting back and forth.

"Antonia says that she raised her four children in the rock house you and I are in—and that back then everyone lived in tiny rock houses and cooked outside—like you and I sometimes do."

As Jesusita sets the perfectly round blue corn tortillas one by one on an embroidered cloth which lies on the table he notices that they are also all perfectly cooked, and as nice as those that Felipa makes.

He is transfixed by what is transpiring in this kitchen—and by the intensity of the connection between these two women.

Although he knows that Jesusita is Antonia's great granddaughter, he is aware that that is not what he is witnessing.

But that it is Antonia herself, her natural bearing and dignity, and her aura, totally enveloping and embracing Jesusita—that has precipitated the transformation in her.

Along with the round, blue corn tortillas.

When Jesusita runs outside to respond to a call of nature, Antonia speaks to him in Spanish, "People say that María gave her *bacano*—that could be—or maybe not—the real curse may have been her beauty—I say that because I too was once almost as beautiful as she was—and maybe too the curse may have had to do with her seeing and feeling many things others do not—that jar with the world as she thinks it should be."

"My son—her grandfather Benito—was like that."

Lucas says, "I have more or less put together her story from pieces people have told me—and you may be right—that at a certain point it became quite natural for her to run off to another place."

Antonia continues.

"People say many spiteful things—can say anything—and like to blame someone they already do not like—like poor María—who already has enough troubles of her own."

"Keep her safe from the spiteful ones."

And handing him a hot tortilla, says, "By which I mean—with Jesusita—watch out for almost everyone."

❖ ❖ ❖

Returning to their rock hut, with a black sky and lightning and thunder moving toward them from the direction of the Big Canyon, Jesusita bounds off like a deer into the trees twice—each time bringing back a giant yellowish mushroom.

"I will cook them for us for supper."

The words psychosis and schizophrenia come to mind. Those are the labels most psychiatrists would be quick to pin onto Jesusita as a way of explaining what they would consider to be an abnormal, illogical, and non functional way of going about in society.

But is not the world a very dangerous place for the non-cunning and innocent? Might not in some cases an animal-like fear of predators lurking who knows where be justifiable?

Old Candelario put it well. A horse having a frightening experience will learn to fear the entire context surrounding that experience. For Jesusita might not that context have been everything comprising Tarahumara and Mestizo society? And might it not have been natural and logical for her to want to avoid such a place—and to construct another one that felt safer to her, even if unintelligible to everyone else?

Is it a sign of irrationality that frightening events once wired into the circuitry of the brain and changing its chemistry cannot be extinguished by rational explanation?

Or that soldiers—or the police—dressed in black, with their clubs and guns and jails, and the impunity with which they sometimes act—can appear as diabolical servants of the Devil?

Might some variant of Jesusita's peculiar brain structure, in ancient times, even have served to help human beings to survive and flourish?

Yet how many Jesusitas have been accused of housing demons? Or these days, of manifesting an aberration of the human heart defined as criminality?

Jesusita is no longer in front of him. He stops and calls out her name but is answered only by rolling thunder. He runs for a while down the trail—slows back down to a walk.

And then just as a few drops of rain begin to fall—she runs out from behind the pine tree she had been hiding behind.

She wildly waving the two big mushrooms and laughing at her joke.

❖ ❖ ❖

That night, under the sound of rain falling on the tin roof, and she beneath him, wearing her blue kerchief, and he moving along with her in a way that is beyond his control and with a joyfulness more volcanic than any he has ever known—it flashes into his consciousness ever so briefly that out of this particular wild flurry will emerge a new being.

Afterwards the two of them lying together embraced, the rain still drumming on the roof, he feels a profound peace. And knows it will be a boy.

Knows.

Jesusita falls asleep, her breathing now seeming to be coming from some spirit world.

It occurs to him that the orgasmic coming together of man and woman in a way that is totally spontaneous and simultaneous may be the only thing in life that really feels good—and that gives one true confidence, and a sense of absolute knowing.

A free-flowing energy transaction that is cellular and cosmic. And prior to consciousness. And that cannot coexist along with erotic fantasy or any other mental imagery.

How many of the ills of civilization, as Freud and others have maintained, have to do with the repression of that primal energy flow and with diverting it toward other so-called higher, more civilized endeavors—and into seeking illusory happiness in control, power, status, money, and the glitter and easy comfort of material things?

The rain stops. Jesusita sighs.

He had assumed that Jesusita, although having been poisoned with a vile peyote-like cactus, was nevertheless, as Lumholz might have put it, of disgustingly healthy and resistant Tarahumara stock.

However now it appears she may have a genetic disposition toward schizophrenia, or emotional instability and trauma, or whatever one wants to call it—which would make her more prone to give birth to similar constitutions. And perhaps to mutations as well.

Still wrapped in each other's arms, Jesusita sighs again.

Suddenly he is startled—as once again he sees the shapeless reddish creature, slowly rising up out of the depths of the barbarian forests and swamps, taking on form.

Whoever—whatever—they may bring into the world, he will love, and care for, along with this woman alongside him.

Love and care for—those his people.

23

Arctic Seal

It is a blue morning with billows of fog from last night's rain rising out of the Big Canyon as Lucas and Jesusita make their way to the house of the shaman Don Corpo.

A few days ago Chalelo had told him that Don Corpo had recently returned from San Juan where he had a second house and which he used when he performed his cures.

"These days he heals mainly Chabochi—which has made him famous and rich—some of them come from as far away as Chihuahua City—and even from across the ocean from a place called France—we poor Tarahumara can no longer afford to be cured by him—so we never took Jesusita."

"I will see what he is like—I happen to think there are as many different varieties of shamans as there are people—and that a very few probably do have a certain gift for healing."

At an arroyo running with abundant water Jesusita says, "I want to bathe."

And before he can say anything she has dropped her two skirts. She removes her kerchief, blouse, and huaraches, leaving a naked brown woman, in all her innocence, as if freshly arisen from the earth like the mist billowing up out of the canyon behind her.

Who when he first met her had not bathed in years.

She steps into a shallow pool and sits down in it, the water encircling her waist, and with both hands splashes water over the rest of her body including her head. Begins gently rubbing a leg to clean it.

He has never seen her so content and happy.

Lucas sits down, and leaned against a rock, waits.

As he had walked out the door of Mary and Donalds's house, Mary had said, "Bring me back a real shaman—or better yet—come back yourself a shaman."

The practice of shamanism rising as it did simultaneously with the murky beginnings of human consciousness and culture had always fascinated him too.

His encounter with the herd of javelina and right afterwards with the peyote shaman up on the high ridge of the isolated Sierra de la Mula had prompted him to mull over his perceptions of that twilight period in human history.

The old primeval world of javalina—and of wolf and bear and the first human beings—he saw as instinctually structured and solid, as if carved in granite. For the most part only genetic mutation could radically change behavior.

But then with the rise of symbolic language another and a much more insubstantial kind of world arose, a cultural and pliable one flimsily constructed from words, imagination, and dreams, where anything could transmute from one thing into another—or spring just like that out of nothing and into existence.

As he saw it, the shaman's primary task became to help hold that new world together—to with his immense prestige and authority solidify its reality.

And part of that task was to heal anyone whose soul wandered out of that reality—or who had been invaded by the wild untamed forces that lay beyond it.

And so now and then the shaman, entering a trance-like state of wakeful dreaming, would journey down into the underworld and into the chaotic archetypical cultural imagery of his own unconscious. Where he found the spirit allies to help him battle against devouring snakes and worms, sucking whirlpools, and other terrors for the purpose of retrieving a sick individual's soul.

Or with spirit allies and energized by his trance state the shaman would drive the demon spirits from the sick individual's body.

It particularly struck him that although the shaman journeyed mainly among animal spirits, talked to them, and even sometimes himself assumed a non-human form, he nevertheless did not step out of the human cultural drama. Never journeyed further. To that earlier place—to before the stories of the Creation and of the animals and of the other beings within it began.

Never journeyed into the actual world inhabited by javelina and wolf and bear.

As maybe has Jesusita—who with both hands forming a cup and throwing more water onto her head appears to him at this moment to be some inland variety of Arctic seal.

She stands up, goes over to her clothes, and dripping wet puts them on—runs the fingers of both hands through her hair for a while.

Then they go on.

Lucas from a distance seeing there is no smoke coming from the house ahead of them and that the door is shut, says, "It looks like no one is there."

"He's inside asleep."

At the house, Jesusita calls out, "Don Corpo."

They wait.

After a few minutes the door opens and a short man in cowboy boots and wearing a purple shirt and with jet black hair streaked with grey hanging to his shoulders steps out.

As they take turns greeting him, Lucas notices that the shirt is silk.

"I'm Lucas—I met you at a *tesguinada*—but we never got to know one another."

"Yes—the American who married our prettiest woman—Jesusita—in spite of her being very much a madwoman—and you now want to see if I can cure her."

Don Corpo smiles. And they stand there a moment. Then he puts both of his hands on her head, and holds them there, his eyes half closed. He moves his hands away to just above the head, now passing them slowly back and forth across it.

"I See things—and See that there is too much vital current on one side and not enough on the other—there is a blockage—probably caused by the terrible envy she still has of a woman."

As he massages the back of Jesusita's neck he comes more alive, the eyes sparkling.

Lucas is aware that Don Corpo, except for having responded to Jesusita in a sexual way, has in no way connected to Jesusita the person. That he knows nothing of her condition and who she really is, and apparently could care less.

How can technical expertise, total disconnection, a strong sense of one's self importance, and the itch for payment possibly tune itself to the innermost of another?

Don Corpo removes his hands from Jesusita.

"I can cure her—she will need to bring a few things—the first time six eggs—and the next time a live chicken."

He begins to talk to Jesusita in Tarahumara. At one point he looks over at Lucas, who right then notices an abrupt change in Jesusita. And although he did not understand a single word it is immediately clear to him that he is telling her that she must leave this Gringo.

Lucas tells Don Corpo that he will think it over and that they will go now so as not to get caught by an afternoon storm.

As they leave he is aware of Jesusita falling into her strange waddle walk, her head cocked to one side.

He recalls a saying from a shamanic culture, "When the people get sick the shaman fattens."

Aware that Jesusita is straggling along far behind him he slows down.

Where is the Healer, he wonders, who can reconnect human beings to that innermost that lies buried under thousands of years of culturally-ordained illusion and repression—to that deep-down core self in which all true sanity and well being must surely be rooted?

Maybe it should fall to the stunned woman waddling along behind him—with nothing but her naturalness and authenticity of an Arctic seal—to heal Don Corpo.

Has she not already healed that crazy Lucas who walked all the way to the remote canyons of the Tarahumara not even knowing why?

And has she not healed Chalelo and Felipa too—the both of them now softer, and warmer and wanting to be helpful in whatever way they can, and no longer speaking harshly of Candelario, nor drinking as much?

Hearing steps running towards him, he turns.

"Run—I saw them—the police coming up the arroyo—and their sharp knives flashing—run as fast as you can."

Chalelo told Lucas, "There is some talk against you—and now against us too—but I tell the others that what happens on my land is not their concern."

Lucas said nothing, just stood there frozen—as Chalelo walked off.

He thought about how much better Jesusita seemed, and content with again being the daughter she had not been in years.

But in spite of that, might she still do even better away from the Sierra and its associations? And might not he, who would never plant corn and beans, nor drink seriously with the neighbors, never be one of them, do better somewhere else too?

One day when he mentioned to her the possibility of them going to his house on the Rio Grande, she did not respond with either yes or no.

Another day he told her a little about the area, that some of the people raised goats, but that there were very few trees, and no Tarahumara.

That same evening she told him about an American who broke the backs of rattlesnakes by stamping on them with his heavy boots.

"I wanted him to stuff me into his shiny blue sack and to take me with him far away—I still don't know why."

"But the sack was already full and heavy with other things—and it was so hard for him walking with it and he was so thirsty—and so busy looking all around him for what I later realized must have been his soul—that he did not hear me—or even see me I don't think."

When he then described a few of the people he knew who lived along the river—Jesse, Manuel and Consuelo, Gregorio, Polo and Hermelinda—he could sense her brighten.

And himself brighten as well.

Candelario came by as Lucas was descending a slope dragging a large dead branch. After greeting each other, Candelario asked where Jesusita was.

"She went off with Felipa and Zenaida—to look for mushrooms."

"That is maybe just as well—I have come to let you know about some crazy things that are happening—as if this world weren't crazy enough."

"Let me get some coffee heating first."

Lucas arranges some sticks, lights a piece of pitch pine with a match, and shoves the flaming torch among the sticks. He goes inside and returns with two white enamel cups and a shiny aluminum coffee pot. Positions the coffee pot on three rocks over the flame. And then sits down on a log across from Candelario.

"First of all—and this is what I managed to get out of Carmen—Gavino and Marta had quite a row—that ended in her taking a pot of boiling water off the stove and throwing it at him—after which she grabbed a few things and ran out the door."

"The last words she yelled at him were that you were going to bring her some white shoes and take her to the United States."

"She is with her folks down in Arroyo Hondo—and Gavino is with Reyna and limping around with a blistered leg."

"He has told a few people he is going to kill you—telling them that you are a *brujo*—that you possess something similar to what we Mestizos call the evil eye—with which you bewitch women—and that you consort with María at night when the moon is full—and so her husband Marciano too is sympathetic to Gavino."

"And also Esteban—who is still angry at Jesusita—not so much that she left him—but for the way people afterwards joked about it."

Lucas is quiet for a while, before saying, "And besides all that I am a Gringo who married one of their women—and with whom I am likely to sow a couple of blond-headed kids."

"You know these people better than I do Candelario—what do you suggest I do?"

Candelario' expression turns grim.

"You still haven't heard the half of it—an acquaintance of mine from San Juan made a special trip all the way up to the cave to tell me to tell you that the drug cartel does not want an American living where you do."

"I don't know whether the message was the work of Gavino—he possibly having a friend or relative who works for them—or whether it originated within the cartel itself."

"In any case the drug thing is turning nasty Lucas—for some time now—here in the Sierra and in much of Chihuahua—the Sinaloa cartel has controlled the municipalities and their *presidentes* and police—but now other cartels have come in—and they are all warring for territory—two days ago the *comandante* of the police in San Juan and also the assistant to the *presidente* were both assassinated in broad daylight—the people are terrified."

He stops—goes on.

"I don't think they are liable to kill an American—it would be very bad for business—but they have many other ways of getting at people—for example they could say that that you are backing some of the growing—that that is why you are here in this remote part of the Sierra."

"At the snap of a finger they can bribe witnesses—buy off the judge—and you would rot in a Mexican jail."

"Yes—being an American with ears and eyes—I will ultimately wind up knowing far too much—and the cartels hate Americans anyway—for financing the effort to exterminate them—well what else?—like maybe a big time earthquake is heading this way?"

"Right on Lucas—Mexico is *perdido*—lost—bigger and bigger money is making the dog dance like never before.

"These narco people are not a group of villains apart from the others—they are melted right into everything that is Mexico—not just municipal presidents—but governors and all the way to the top—and those not in some way directly involved have relatives who are—no one can be trusted or believed."

Lucas says softly, "Some very big financial interests run my country too."

"Right on again Lucas—because it's not about just Mexico or drugs—it's about this new fancy modern life—and that what were once good people have learned that for money it is perfectly okay to do absolutely anything to anyone."

"It's a force more powerful than an earthquake—even living in a cave away from it all—I feel something I can almost touch shaking me like a rag doll."

Lucas says, "What you've told me is more than my brain can process right now—let's drink some of this coffee—Felipa ground the beans I bought on her *metate*."

"Mother said that people are saying that you are going to take Marta to the United States—and Reyna too—and that when the moon is big you are married to María."

"I heard the police talking—they are going kill you and me—hang us from a tree and feed us poison—and stick long knives into us—and then call the Devil to take us away and bury us in his grave yard—where no living being has ever set foot."

She then switches to Tarahumara and rattles on for almost an hour, he sitting nearby—waiting for her disturbed physiology to wind down.

When she does, he says, "People say and repeat and believe anything—how could it possibly be true that I am going to go off with two other women when in just a few days you I will be taking you to the border—to my house on the Rio Grande?"

"Because you are a bad man."

"But how could I possibly have spent even a single night with María when I spent every one of them next to you?

"Because you are a *brujo*—and your soul goes to her when I am asleep."

That night she sleeps just far enough away from him so that he cannot reach over and touch her.

In the morning she tells him that although she has told her mother they would be over for breakfast, she is not hungry, and does not want to go.

"I just want a nice cup of coffee."

Soon the fire is blazing and the shiny coffee pot over it.

"I scrubbed and scrubbed and tried to make the bottom clean and shiny too—like it was when you gave it to me—but couldn't"

"At my house we will have a gas stove—and you will be able to keep all the pots clean."

He could see she did not understand how that would help.

"When are we going?

"As soon as we can—in a few days—first I want to say goodbye to Candelario—and to a few others."

He pours coffee into two cups, sets the coffee pot back over the fire—and they sit down against the rock wall shoulder to shoulder to drink it.

"Is it very far?"

A crack like thunder makes the coffee pot fly from its rock support and bounce clattering across the ground before coming to rest against the base of an oak.

Lucas grabbing Jesusita drags her around the corner of the rock house and pushes her down onto the ground against the wall—she screaming. Twisting and breaking free, she runs off into the woods howling her familiar howl.

He stays put. Stares at the wreckage of what was once a coffee pot.

Finally—he goes over to it. The shot came from a high caliber rifle. He turns, and sighting across the still-burning fire picks out the rise from which the bullet must have come from.

He finds Jesusita at the other house with Chalelo, Felipa, and Zenaida.

Chalelo says, "I don't think Gavino has a rifle—and if he got hold of one I doubt he could hit a coffee pot at the distance you said it was probably hit from—of course he may have a friend."

"Or it could be the cartel just wanted to make sure you got its message—I didn't tell you this—but they recently asked my permission to plant marijuana in one of my fields—saying they would pay me well—I told them no."

"A few days later I found one of my cows dead—slashed with an ax."

Felipa wraps an embroidered cloth around a stack of tortillas smeared with mashed beans and hands the small bundle to Jesusita who sticks it into the white plastic grocery sack at her feet which already contains a skirt, blouse, kerchief, and a comb with some missing teeth.

Felipa shakes Zenaida who is asleep in a corner.

Lucas finishing his cup of laurel tea, stands up, slings his bedroll across a shoulder. Then he and Jesusita, the white grocery sack in her hand, go outside into the damp coolness of the morning—followed by Chalelo, Felipa, and Zenaida.

Lucas and Jesusita head out across the green muddy corn field, stepping uphill from the top of one furrow to another between the almost head-high corn. Goats baa in the pole corral. There are already a few puffs of cloud in the blue Sierra sky.

Chalelo, Felipa, and Zenaida standing together at the door, hands hanging at their sides, continue to watch Lucas followed by Jesusita as the two of them ascend the steep slope, leave the corn field, and arrive at the crest of the ridge.

Watch Lucas—and then as a red skirt, a yellow and white blouse, and last of all a blue kerchief disappears down the other side.

24

Only His Fear

Almost in the blink of an eye the bus had left the curves and pine forest of the Sierra, and had begun zooming along a straight stretch of highway across the grassland plains of the Mennonites. Jesusita, her nose pressed to the window, was enthralled by the countryside so treeless except for the occasional mile-long apple orchards thickly hung with yellow apples.

In spite of her illness and her never before having ventured further than San Juan, she had so far moved through the Chabochi world as would have any other Tarahumara—full of curiosity, yet timidly, and sometimes a little scared.

When Lucas had taken her to a restaurant in San Juan, to eat fresh fish from the coast, she wanted to squat with her feet planted on the seat of the chair. Fumbling with her fork, she ended up breaking up the fish with her fingers and putting it on a tortilla along with a chile.

In their hotel room, shown the toilet, she again wanted to squat, with her feet on its rim. The flushing terrified her and she always asked him to do it.

The hotel having Internet access, Lucas on an impulse decided to submit an application to the American Consulate in Juarez for a border crossing card for Jesusita so that she could accompany him as a visitor to the US whenever he went over to Buena Vista for his mail or to El Polvo to see Jesse and Javier.

That night the queen size bed with its crisp sheets felt so strange to her that they slept on the floor.

They were now on their way to Juarez for the photo, finger printing, and interview that would complete the application process

Tonight they would stay in Chihuahua City, and in the morning ride another bus northward to Juarez which was across the Rio Grande from El Paso, Texas. Then they would have to return to Chihuahua City and take yet another bus again northward, but this time to La Junta which was also on the Rio Grande but more than a hundred miles downriver from Juarez.

Lucas was acutely aware that probably no one had seen a couple like them before. Yet so far not a single person had appeared in any way interested in them—the opposite of what would have been the case were he with an American woman.

Saying goodbye to Candelario and Carmen, Candelario had said, "The ones who think of themselves as so white and uppity—and resent Gringos besides—and that means almost all of them—will hate what you two represent—but never say it to your face."

That night at their hotel in Chihuahua City Jesusita asked for beans and some corn tortillas. And slept for the first time in a bed.

Earlier at another hotel whose parking lot was almost empty he had been informed at the desk that all the rooms were occupied.

In the middle of the night Lucas woke up wondering whether they would actually be able to pass without mishap through what could well turn out to be for them a fire-breathing dragon-infested Wasteland lying between the remote Sierra Tarahumara and the equally remote piece of desert to which they were headed.

In the morning the first thing Jesusita said was, "The corn tortillas from the clattering machines of the Chabochi are thin like paper—and taste like paper too."

Yesterday they had taken care of the finger printing and photo.

Now they are standing in a long line waiting their turn to enter the American Consulate, a huge sleek fortress-like building around which swarm an army of military police in berets.

Ten minutes ago, walking around the side of the building, he had stopped on the sidewalk to check some documents and was immediately approached by two of them, who after asking him what he was doing instructed him to move on.

They obviously took their jobs much more seriously than the Mexican soldiers that had boarded the bus just outside of Juarez, and whose perfunctory manner of supposedly searching for drugs actually made him smile. Such as when one of the soldiers fished out or Jesusita's plastic grocery sack the comb with the broken teeth and then studied it carefully for a moment before putting it back.

Almost everyone in line is well-dressed and middle class. Having either businesses or good jobs in Mexico, they are here to demonstrate to the State

Department that they are not desperate for work and also that they have a compelling reason to return to Mexico—and not, once across the border, disappear into the underground of Mexicans residing illegally in the United States.

Some possibly came from as far away as Chiapas and Quintana Roo. And to there they would have to return to await the arrival of their visas which if granted would arrive by courier in several weeks.

There was no other way for any of them to legally visit a family member living in the United States—to step across the tightest international border in the world.

Lucas followed by Jesusita enters the building. At the body scan machine his plastic ball point pen is confiscated. They follow the signs to an outdoor waiting area of folding chairs under a large awning. He knows that lawyers are not permitted to accompany the visa applicant to the interview—but then he is no longer a practicing lawyer.

Jesusita's number appears on a screen. They leave the waiting area and enter a room where a man behind a window says, *Buenos días* and asks them to sit down. They too say, *Buenos días*, as they sit down, Jesusita having first pulled her chair back a ways.

The man scans some papers before him—then types into his computer.

"Are you the husband referred to in this application?"

"Yes."

"Does she speak Spanish?"

"She speaks very simple Spanish."

"How many children do you have Jesusita?"

There is silence. And it immediately occurs to Lucas that she probably does not know whether Zenaida—raised as she was by Felipa and Chalelo—is her child or theirs.

Lucas says, "Excuse me—why not ask her how many children she has given birth to—and where they are?"

"My job is to interview her—and not you—without a Tarahumara interpreter I cannot do this interview."

"She doesn't need a language interpreter—she needs a cultural interpreter—that's why I am here—the Tarahumara do not respond to questions in the way you or I might."

The man turns away and enters some information into his computer.

"I have to deny this visa application—here—this explains my decision."

Lucas goes over to the window where he is handed a slip of paper. A checked box states: The applicant failed to demonstrate any compelling reason for returning to Mexico.

And at the bottom the slip is the statement: This decision cannot be appealed.

Lucas followed by Jesusita walks out the door.

He will need to approach acquiring the border crossing card another day. And in quite another way, since he now sees that the interview process is structured in such a way as to automatically deny a visa to any truly indigenous person—and to anyone else who is poor, unschooled, and has a limited comprehension of contemporary modern life.

The interviewer only acted as would have any efficient and model State Department employee representing a country that has an almost paranoid fear of an influx of Mexicans ruining what it terms its quality of life.

As for the State Department, whose mission has always been to maximize American dominance and control abroad, neither in Southeast Asia or the Middle East nor anywhere else has it ever demonstrated anything resembling cultural understanding and sensitivity. All of which has a lot to do with why its foreign embassies resemble armed fortresses.

Again and again in its foreign policy statements to the American public and to the world it has demonstrated itself to be the consummate master of misrepresentation—the most antithetical to the authenticity and innocence of an Arctic seal that anything can get.

He is angry. Just as millions of Mexicans, and others are also angry.

Glad to be out of the building and back in the noise and congestion of Juarez and glancing at his watch he sees it is still early enough for them to get to La Junta tonight. He negotiates a price for the taxi ride back to their hotel and from there to the bus station, and they get in.

He looks over at Jesusita who has become withdrawn. It was made very clear to her that she was not wanted in his country. And most likely she is also aware of his preoccupation—and still lingering anger.

At the hotel they grab their few things, and get back into the waiting taxi. On the way to the bus station Jesusita turns from withdrawn to black—abruptly moves as far away from him as possible.

"It wasn't that important—instead of us visiting my friends across the river—they will come visit us instead."

But it seems that she did not even hear him, much less understand.

Amidst the noise and confusion of the bus station he needs to steer her by the arm onto the bus and to their seats. The bus pulls out for Chihuahua City. When a man comes up the aisle selling burritos and soft drinks he asks her if she is hungry or thirsty. And she does not answer.

He has never seen her like this.

Was it more than just being denied the visa? The stress of three days of travel? The impersonality and strangeness of Juarez and of the visa process? All of that together?

Why the anger, and specifically at him?

The bus passes through desert and more desert. From out of a television come the roars, screeches, and crashes of a high speed car chase. Jesusita removes her huaraches.

She begins to unbutton her blouse. He reaches over, stopping her at the fourth button, and buttons the other three back up, she not resisting.

She seems totally—gone.

She not really knowing the difference between the United States and Mexico, might she have thought that they were applying for a visa to go to his house, and that that having been denied, they were now returning to the Sierra?

And that it all having been associated with him it was he who was responsible—again, not unlike the process by which the horse sees the bridge as being the cause of the rattlesnake on it?

And maybe even in her withdrawn state she can tell that yes the direction in which they are headed at the moment is indeed back toward the Sierra.

"Jesusita—listen to me—tonight—or at the latest tomorrow morning— we will be at my house—at your new house."

But it was too late. Nothing that he said any longer entered into her, except for perhaps his fear—his fear that he might lose her, has already lost her.

The bus slips into its stall at the bus terminal in Chihuahua City.

Lucas with his bedroll draped across a shoulder and Jesusita's huaraches, their thongs tied together dangling around his neck, and carrying the plastic grocery bag in one hand, with the other hand steers the reluctant barefoot

Jesusita off the bus. She takes a few steps and immediately sits down in the middle of the vacant adjacent bus stall, as if it were a clearing in the forest.

"Get up Jesusita—that's where any minute a bus is going to park—and try to hurry a little—the bus for La Junta will be leaving very soon."

She continues sitting there, immobile, dazed. He goes over to her and pulls her up and over to the revolving turnstile leading into the ticket counters and waiting area—the two of them going through together. She is resisting with her feet as he pulls her toward the ticket counter. He hears a sharp voice, "Hold it—what do you think you are doing?"

Lucas stops, turns around, and sees a uniformed security guard, he already pushing some buttons on the radio in his hand.

"I have a loco American here—who was forcing an Indian woman to go where she obviously does not want to—five minutes?—good."

"She's my wife—she's mentally ill—and was sitting down where the buses pull in—she possibly wanted to go to sleep there."

"You can explain all that later."

When the four police arrive and one of them asks Lucas whether he had been forcing this woman to go somewhere against her will, he tells them what he had told the security guard.

When they ask Jesusita whether she wants to go with the American, she looking over at Lucas in a strange way, only says, "He wants to take me with him to the United States."

There is silence.

He is asked to turn around and to put his hands behind his back. They handcuff him.

"Both of you—come along with us."

By the end of his first half day in jail, Lucas had concluded that Javier was right. The view from behind bars was a valuable one that everyone should experience.

He had known that no explanation by him at the police station would serve to abolish what the woman who interviewed him referred to as his act of physical aggression—that only a judge could do that. She told him she would call the *comandancia* in San Juan and have one of their people go up to Tónachi to check whether as he claimed Jesusita had a history of serious mental illness, and also whether she was in fact his common law wife.

If his story was corroborated he would be held for 36 hours which was the longest she said they could hold him without him appearing before a judge. He decided that unless something changed he would not bother with a lawyer.

Jesusita, her anger toward him gone and clutching his arm and being told to come this way, had been led off by a woman guard up a corridor—she submitting to prison authority in a way she had not to his. He was told that she had been charged with vagrancy.

He surrendered his bedroll and the huaraches still dangling from his neck, as well as his documents, watch, cash, and belt. Then he was faced against a wall and searched, and after that put into a bare cell with only a toilet in back. A neatly-dressed, amiable-looking man was sitting against a wall. A guard poked a plastic bottle filled with water between the bars. Men were yelling in the other cells, some occasionally clanking the bars.

His cell mate asked him what he was in for and Lucas told him.

He was Rodolfo and the owner of a hydroponic-greenhouse business in a town outside of Chihuahua City. As he told it, he had made it clear to his wife who was on medication for bipolar disorder that he did not want her sister who was an alcoholic coming around the house.

Yesterday when the sister showed up drunk and became obnoxious, he removed her forcefully from the house.

He told Lucas this was a low security prison and that the two of them were sharing a cell for those having perpetrated domestic violence and that there were other cells for drunks, vagrants, those having committed robbery, and for those having committed more serious physical assault.

Lucas ran in place for half an hour and did some pushups. After which, like his cell mate, he sat against a wall.

The lights always on, one told time in the windowless building by the changing of the guards, the coming of the food wagon, and when once a day someone entered the cell to mop and to pour a bucket of water into the toilet to flush it.

He had more than enough time to think.

He thought of gorillas and zebras in the zoo, and caged birds, and pythons in glassed cases, and horses in their stalls. Of the Consulate employee who had interviewed him stuck for most of his waking hours in his booth. Of young people confined to years of sitting at their desks in a classroom.

And he thought of the old time Australian aborigines beginning the day when it suited them and freely wandering the desert in all directions and sitting down in the shade of some bushes also whenever it suited them.

And he thought about how the illusions and the fashions in thinking comprising the bulk of daily human existence give rise to prisons of the mind.

Nevertheless, the dominant image that would not let go of him was the infinitely more vivid one of an ill and bewildered barefoot Tarahumara goatherd from the remote canyons, in her red skirt and blue kerchief—she staring off into the distance at the blank walls of a jail cell and subjected to prison procedures.

Her one possible solace being that special place of solitude her brain had created for her.

A man came by pushing a food wagon, spooned a watery greasy broth with bits of potato, carrot, and onion floating in it into two plates, and slipped them under the door along with some paper-thin tortillas.

After he and Rodolfo finishing eating he thought some more.

The fear of the wrath of God or of the penal system does not inculcate morality or make people good people—only embitters and alienates them even more from society. Nor does it in any way address the society's underlying social pathology and the hopelessness of so many.

The impersonal Apparatus—with its laws, bureaucracy, guns and prisons, along with the cleverness and trickery of its imposed ideology—may more or less serve to hold a modern society together, but only in such a manner that dehumanizes absolutely everyone in that society.

His country may pride itself on being a Nation under Law—which however is entirely different from being a nation in which all the people respect one another, look out for one another, and count.

In Chile, under the military junta, and in other countries, the government has brandished the slogan Law and Order to justify torture and even genocide.

Throughout recorded history most of what has been legalistically correct has for the most part served an elite. Law students predominated at the first mediaeval universities, to then serve the landed gentry in consolidating its power. It was mostly wealthy lawyers who drew up the American constitution and provided the means by which an elite would control the government and the laws by which the System would operate.

And to this day, the elite, now a global elite, still believe that the people are incompetent for judging or determining what is best for humanity and that it is thus necessary for the rich and technologically sophisticated to control the world—while at the same time upholding the illusion of democracy.

Benjamin Franklin had pointed to the Iroquois Confederacy as a model for genuine democracy, one of those Iroquois having said, "We are born free and united Brothers, each as much a great lord as another."

Rodolfo as he was escorted from the cell invited him to stop by his greenhouse for some tomatoes and melons, and wished him good luck.

Several hours later when it was his turn he was taken to a desk where he signed some papers he did not bother reading, and where his belongings were returned to him.

"Where is my wife?"

"I don't know—I believe she was released about eight hours ago"

"She's mentally ill—there is absolutely no way she can manage in Chihuahua City by herself—she'll wind up raped—or in an institution or back in jail."

The man not appearing concerned picks up a phone. Dials a number, and then another number. Talks for a minute or so, before returning the phone to its receptacle.

"We don't have any idea where she is—only that someone from a government office came to get her—most likely from the Coordinadora Tarahumara."

"Where is that?"

The man scribbles an address on a slip of paper, and slides it towards him. When Lucas asks which way is out—the man points.

25

A Soft Grey Mist

During his taxi ride across Chihuahua City, amidst the roar and horn blasts and passing first a Kentucky Fried Chicken, and then an Auto Zone, and Wal-Mart, Lucas tries to assimilate what some call Progress, and a few unbridled materialism—but what he himself has come to see as possibly the derailing of the human psyche.

That vast shopping emporium—extending all the way to Bangkok, and from there continuing onward back to Chihuahua City.

With its sea of human beings, all of them frantically scurrying every which way and pushing each other aside in an attempt to grasp what they consider indispensable for their conception of a proper life.

One that never lets up on demanding more and more to make it just right.

Suddenly he finds himself with his head stuck out of the last window of the last car of a passenger train winding through the green forested Sierra. He glimpses a Tarahumara woman with a baby in her *rebozo* watching the train go by.

And then as the train coming out of a curve begins to cross a high trestle bridge spanning a deep canyon, he watches as the locomotive careens, and careens some more, and plunges downward into empty space—followed by one car and then another and another.

"This is it—the offices of the Coordinadora Tarahumara."

Lucas pays the taxi driver and gets out.

Inside no one knew anything about a mentally ill Tarahumara woman. Some phone calls were made. Just as he was about to go a secretary suggested he check the Albergue—she describing it as a kind of shelter, a free place for Tarahumara from the Sierra to stay for a while should they find themselves in the city seeking medical care or on other necessary business.

He flags down another taxi—that takes him to the Albergue. Stepping out of the taxi he hears the music of *Onward Christian Soldiers*.

He passes through a large portal, its two iron doors swung wide open, and steps into a courtyard along three sides of which about twenty Tarahumara are seated on benches. Several Mestizo men in black pants and white shirts are milling about a podium. He immediately stops—the music still playing.

Two nicely-dressed young Mestizo women are going around passing out what seem to be lollipops to the Tarahumara who accept them without looking up at the women.

One of the men positions himself behind the podium, and the others on either side. The music ceases. The man taps a microphone. And then begins to speak to what to Lucas seems to be a more or less captive audience

"Jesus is here with us today—you cannot see Him—because He left his earthly body and is now Spirit—the tingle each one of you can no doubt feel in the air—if you open your hearts—is Him—and He has come here to help you—all of you who are His children—and to repair what is troubling your lives—"

Lucas passing in front of several of the seated Tarahumara heads towards what appears to him to be the office.

"Did a mentally ill Tarahumara woman show up here—possibly sometime this morning?"

"I wasn't here this morning—ask over in the women's dorm—it's the green building."

He passes in front of some more Tarahumara, no one appearing to even notice him—this gringo in their midst—just as no one appears to be listening to the speaker.

He anxious and distracted almost bumps into one of the women handing out lollipops—she not offering him one.

He enters the dormitory. A Tarahumara woman is sitting on one of the beds.

"*Kwira.*"

The woman hesitates, then murmurs a barely audible, "*Kwira.*"

"Is there a woman here who may have come this morning—and is mentally ill?"

"There is someone in the other room—I don't know anything about her."

He goes into the adjoining room but sees no one—nor a body under a blanket.

Turning to leave he sees something red under the table in a corner—the red skirt of who must be Jesusita, crouched there. He goes over to her.

"*Kwira*—it looks like you've found yourself a good place to hide from what is going on outside."

Seeing him she remains immobile—not giving the least sign that she recognizes him. He takes hold of a hand and gently pulls her up from under the table, and sits her down on one of the beds. Sits down beside her.

"I am very glad I found you—it was not easy—it's very good to be with you again—many times I was sure I had lost you for good."

They sit there on the bed for a while. Outside, an electronic device is spurting out words in Tarahumara.

"It looks like you are still not well enough to go anywhere—to go out onto the street—so I am going to talk to the people in the office and see if I can stay here with you until you are a bit better—and if they can give us our own room—I'll be right back—does that sound okay?"

She does not respond—only staring down at the pink running shoes on her feet.

He talked to the manager of the Albergue. There were more phone calls. Yes he could stay with her in one of the rooms for married couples while she recovered. But after ten days he would have to go.

From a kitchen worker he got an orange. The evangelicals were leaving. When he gave the peeled orange to Jesusita she wrung it for a moment between her hands, and then plastered it against her mouth, its juice running down onto her blouse.

She began to say a few occasional phrases although so softly that he always had to ask her to repeat them. She told him that the woman who had brought her here had given her the shoes.

They shared a room with a Tarahumara couple who had two huge plastic garbage bags of used clothing by their bed. Jesusita exchanged a few sentences with the woman in Tarahumara and told him there was a building nearby where one could go in and take what one wanted. She said that they being from the Tarahumara Alta she could not understand the woman very well.

She did not want to go with him to the evening meal, and neither did she want him to go and leave her.

He explained Jesusita's condition to the Tarahumara couple and asked if they would bring them back something to eat. But they did not.

Jesusita went to sleep early, a radio blaring in the courtyard.

It was still dark when someone woke them both up saying that it was time for them to join the crew sweeping and mopping down the courtyard. He explained why Jesusita would not be able to participate.

He talked her into going to breakfast. Entering the dining room she became fearful, and then even more so sitting down among the other Tarahumara. The food was better than he had expected—tortillas, beans, eggs scrambled with onion, tomato, and chile, and coffee. Jesusita sat with her plate on her lap eating with her fingers, pieces of food falling onto the floor, and eating very little.

After breakfast she went over to a corner of the courtyard near to where the cement scrubbing troughs for washing clothes were. And squatted down there. Where she remained—immobile, and as if in a trance.

He sat on an unoccupied bench across from her. A few Tarahumara were sitting on other benches, they too passing the time just sitting, which they did so well. Now and then someone went out through the portal and into the city on some errand.

When he went over to her and suggested she change her clothes and wash those she had on which were now conspicuously dirty and that he would help her, she did not answer.

When he went over again and this time told her he was thinking of going to a store to buy some mangos and bananas, both of which he knew she loved, a terrified look came to her eyes.

"Stay here."

"Come with me then—the store is very close by."

"I am afraid."

When an hour later he came over to her yet again to see how she was she became furious at him.

"I am going to tell everyone that you are a bad man—that you beat me and that is why I hurt all over—and that you killed a woman."

The perversity of her smile startled him.

All that now remained was for her to do her disappearing trick by heading down the street and into the waiting maw of this city and just like that she would be gone forever.

He turned away from the perverse smile, and went back to his bench.

He picks up a Chihuahua newspaper, turns its pages, reading here and there.

And suddenly laughs as he reads about an American who was apprehended and jailed for attempting to abduct a Tarahumara woman—the notice having gotten his name wrong.

A voice out of nowhere speaks into his ear:

"What are you laughing at Lucas?—they only printed the truth—a touching human interest story—about a barefoot goatherd from the canyons—a delicate wildflower that you managed to rip from the earth—only because she was not well and had no means for resisting you."

"Tell me—how was that all that different from what the southern slave owners continually did."

Lucas sticks his fingers in his ears.

"Shut up—I've got enough to deal with—that train that flew off the tracks to Kingdom Come—wasn't just civilization—it was also me—Lucas—sitting as far back as I could get—minding my own business—and trying my best to stay out of trouble."

"Me—Lucas—just trying to do a few things another way—damn it."

As the days went by, Lucas could see that Jesusita was becoming perfectly content in her inner place, her needs taken care of and wanting nothing. She squatted all day against one or another wall, unresponsive and inaccessible, safe in the here and now, and in a world where the future and what was beyond the Albergue did not exist.

Whenever he brought up the possibility of leaving for his house or going back to the Sierra he could see she did not know what he was talking about.

"In a few days they are going to tell me I have to go—and eventually they will not let you stay here any longer either—and they will put you in another place that is much uglier than this one."

But the future and future consequences were meaningless to her.

He remembered the time they were climbing up out of the *barrancas,* and how midway she plopped down at the base of some cliffs and for whatever reason would not go on, wanting to sleep right there, unable to comprehend the threat of rain and that in a few hours it would turn bitter cold.

Since other Tarahumara spent hours just sitting she did not come off to them as all that odd.

Not one of them had taken the slightest interest in her or made any effort to be nice to her—which he felt would have helped her condition considerably and like nothing else could have. Here there was no Antonia. Only these Tarahumara far from their forests and canyons and who did not talk to each other either.

For him it was yet another example of how sharing a language and a culture, or interests, did not necessarily serve to connect people.

A Tarahumara had come over to him, a little drunk—the same man who always woke him up in the dark to take part in the cleaning—and informed him, at the same time giving him a little kick, that Americans were not permitted to stay here and that if he did not leave he was going to report him to the police.

"When you find us in your country you stick us in jail to punish us—and then finally toss us back to Mexico so you do not have to feed us any longer—like garbage."

That afternoon, sitting together on the bed in their room, he mentioned to Jesusita that she must feel very disappointed in him not having been able to take her to his house.

"Maybe that is why you are sometimes so very angry at me."

She said nothing.

Bending over the plastic grocery bag at her feet, she pulled out her extra skirt and blouse. And left the room, he following her to the door, where he remained, watching her as she went over to the women's bathhouse. He sat down on one of the benches.

She came out dressed in her change of clean clothes, barefoot, her hair stringy and wet, and took the dirty clothes straight over to one of the outdoor washing troughs. Where slapping them like a wild woman on the concrete, she scrubbed them clean.

Afterwards she put on her huaraches.

At supper she finished her entire plate of food. And in the middle of the night, even with the other couple in the same room, the two of them at one point almost rolled off the bed together.

In the morning, although she still would not go to the store with him, she let him go. And so he was able to bring her mangos and bananas—which not only she but he too devoured.

That evening he persuaded her to leave the courtyard with him. And from then on—that was what they did every evening, once the day had cooled.

She would venture down the sidewalk away from the portal for about thirty feet. But no further. And there she would stand pressed against a wall of a building watching the traffic and the passing people—though perhaps not so much watching as simply absorbing the interplay of shapes, colors, motions, and sounds.

Should an ice cream or fruit juice vendor peddle by, bells jangling, or some outlandishly-dressed woman pass by in front of her, she did not appear to notice.

They would go back inside at nightfall, just before the two portal doors were swung shut.

Given her sometimes bizarre behaviors and unpredictable sudden angers toward him he always felt themselves particularly vulnerable on the street. Once, she having tugged on her skirt to make it hang low, began rubbing her belly, and he had to lead her back into the courtyard.

Lucas knew it was time to leave the Albergue. Jesusita was much better. But still she would not go—neither forward to his house on the Rio Grande, nor back to Tónachi or anywhere else in the Sierra Tarahumara.

"Everywhere is so very far away."

Two days before he knew he was supposed to leave, a woman from the Coordinadora Tarahumara came to see him and introduced herself by explaining that she was the person who had picked up Jesusita at the police station.

"I suppose she has told you that on the way over to the Albergue we stopped by to see a psychiatrist."

"No—she did not mention anything like that."

"After about a two minutes in the office with him she yelled something about a black devil wanting to grab her—and fled out the door—and would have been gone except that she turned down the wrong corridor."

"The doctor unequivocally recommended hospitalization—have you considered that?—because that's what I have come to talk to you about."

"Given who she is—and so Tarahumara—I think it would only make her worse—and make her lose all trust in me besides—forever."

He pauses. Sees Norma pulling herself up by the bars, trying to peer out.

"Make her so much worse—she might never come away from there."

"They say the new drugs are very good."

"Yes that is what they say—because the pharmaceutical companies have spent countless millions convincing the doctors and the public of that—and also in influencing the direction and results of the scientific research."

"As I see it—the drugs while they may be appropriate in certain situations—are not always a solution."

"It is unfortunate for Jesusita that you have such a closed mind on this matter."

"She is very Tarahumara—and I very much doubt that the psychiatrist understands what that means—by which I mean the very indigenous mind."

"I just talked to her—she does not want to leave—for you to take her away against her wishes—you would need medical certification of her condition—and also legal custody."

"Yes—and all that could take a very long time."

"So what are your plans for her?"

"I'll have to think about it."

In the evening Lucas leaves to buy some bananas. When he returns, Jesusita says, "You were gone a very long time."

"I know—and I'm sorry—but they were out of good bananas—and so I had to go to another store—let's eat some of these out on the street—it will be dark soon."

Sitting on the curb in front of a parked white sedan they each eat a banana. And continue to sit there together some more, it now almost dark and the traffic and the people having thinned out.

Lucas says, "We'd better get back—the doors will be shut soon."

He taking hold of her hand they get up.

As they pass the door of the white sedan Lucas with his free hand swiftly opens it wide and then with both hands shoves Jesusita inside. Slamming the door shut, he darts around the front of the car and enters it and pushes the screaming Jesusita against the other door, she now beating with both fists on the closed window.

Lucas drives around the block and is soon in heavy traffic in a direction out of Chihuahua City.

Jesusita stops beating on the window—and begins howling her coyote-like howls.

"Stay cool Lucas—no speeding—no stupid little thing that might get you pulled over."

Otherwise, he feels safe—the only precarious moments having been the few seconds it took to get Jesusita into the rented car and driving off. But all of which is now ancient history.

He glances into the rear view mirror. Receding in back of them in the now dark night, eerily lit up by the glow of the city, he sees it, in all its ugliness—a monstrous black building with faces peering out from behind tiny barred windows.

The faces shouting at him to take them with him too.

He again looks into the mirror.

But now at an even blacker and uglier structure. Which he can see by its towering turrets and the moat around it—is clearly a castle.

And standing on top of the tallest turret, he wearing a long, red-spotted yellow mantle, and waving both arms at the sky, is the crazy wild-eyed Wizard.

That caster of charms, spells, and enchantments. Who for thousands of years, had kept captive for his personal pleasure and other nefarious uses—the most beautiful princess in the land.

A land in which one day the winds gave their last gasp—and blew no more. So that almost all life died.

The howling stops—the princess now asleep with her head against his leg.

The image in the mirror recedes some more—as the castle with its turrets and moat is swallowed up in a soft grey mist that blows in on what seems to be the gentlest of breezes—a soft grey mist that, as it spreads out and covers the entire land, is much more powerful than all the Wizard's waving and enchantments.

The highway now two lanes and the traffic down to almost nothing, Lucas drives out into the openness of the desert. He passes a flashing neon sign:

Welcome to the Chihuahuan Desert—
Home Of
The Center For Independent Thought
For A Better World.

Lucas says aloud, "What the hell might that be?"

After two more hours of driving, he turns off onto a narrow sandy track that heads off into nowhere. Follows it, creosote and thorned, stick-like ocotillo scraping the sedan, for about a mile—and stops. Turns off the engine and the headlights.

And sits there a while—soaking as if in a hot springs in the waters of his exaltation.

He wakes up Jesusita. Shows her how to open the door. Grabs two bananas and his bedroll from the back seat. And they both step out into the warm desert night with its almost overpowering rich smell of creosote bushes.

A night of intense quietness and intense stars. And a night of an equally intense but very different kind of love making—one for dispelling past terrors.

As well as for dispelling whatever fire-breathing dragons may have eluded the soft grey mist.

They now mere, barb-tailed, scaly, behemoth lizards, serenely ambling about, and breathing out nothing more dangerous than the primordial creative energy that fires the Universe.

When Lucas and Jesusita open their eyes, the sky in the east is blotched with crimson—like the blood accompanying something being born.

Lucas watches Jesusita stand up, adjust her blue kerchief, rub her eyes. And then watches as she turns ever so slowly around looking in each direction at the flat endless expanse, broken here and there by an isolated clump or ridge of high sierra.

Nowhere a single house. Or cornfield—or tree.

"Where am I?—what wonderful new world is this you have brought me to?"

Again she turns around slowly, bathed in the crystal air and crimson of the sky.

"I was right—you are a *brujo*—an audacious and powerful one—and not at all like Don Corpo."

26
Already Containing Everything

Jesusita did not want to sit in the chair that Manuel brought out for her, preferring the cottonwood log alongside the house. So Lucas went to sit by her there.

Manuel says, "What a miracle you have come back—we in Las Palomas still talk about you—as if you were one of us."

Counsuelo says, "We knew that one day you would have to come by for your truck and other things—but no one—and I mean no one ever imagined you might then stay to live here with us—with us poor burros on this side of the river."

"I felt that Jesusita would do better away from the Sierra—and that here along the river might be as good a place as any for her—it's peaceful here—and I have some good friends."

Consuelo goes over to the large red plastic bowel that is set in the middle of them and takes it into the house. And comes right back out with it filled with more slices of yellow watermelon. Goes over to Jesusita, who takes one of them.

"And how do you like it here Jesusita?"

"It's very nice."

"After dinner I will go with you and Lucas over to your place and clean it up a little—it's just like Lucas left it—except that in the spring the winds can blow so hard that sand and dust seeps inside all our houses through the tiniest cracks around the windows and doors."

Manuel says, "Sometimes the sky turns black and even the desert disappears—it's like the end of the world."

He gets up and takes a slice of watermelon.

"And might I ask you Lucas—what kind of little business it is exactly you have in mind—in such desolate and sometimes fierce place—and so away from everything?"

"I haven't a lot to say only because I haven't thought it all out yet—but basically I'm thinking of taking small groups of Americans—say four at a time—out into the desert between here and Barranco Azul and beyond—on foot and for maybe a week or so."

"We would make our camps at some of the old Indian sites—and the point of it all being for the desert to show them another world—and for it to teach them what it can."

"And I was also thinking—if it was okay with you—of starting the trips here at your place—so the people can get to know you—see what old time desert folk were like."

"Count us in—but do keep it at four—more than that would make us feel like we were in a museum."

Consuelo says, "And cooking enchiladas for any more than that would turn me into an enchilada factory."

"It's like this Gregorio—I heard and saw the many things that blew in on me from the four directions—thought and thought about all of it—what began to appear as everything under the sun—adding to the almost incessant clatter that started up in my brain the day I first crossed the border into Mexico."

"And that kept on getting louder and louder—until my head hurt."

"And so what finally happened was that I left all of it there in the canyons—to be carried off by the torrents of the summer monsoons and down the big swollen rivers out into the Pacific Ocean."

"There was too much—more than the rivers could handle—but then one day a soft grey mist came by—and kindly sucked up what was left."

"Anyway that is why there is no story—only what you see before you—me and this very fine Tarhumara woman."

"But Lucas—this is incredible—a Gringo and a Tarahumara—that is all the story I need—the two of you will soon be more famous up and down the river than Polo."

Gregorio goes over to the table and puts more chile macho on his bean and cheese burrito.

"Would you like more on yours too Jesusita?"

"Yes—a lot."

He puts the bowl of chile sauce next to her.

"There is a popular Mexican folk song called *Pajarito Barranqueño*—Little Birdie of the Canyon—I'll have to work some to come up with a title as good as that one."

"By the way Gregorio—what is this about a Center For Independent Thought for a Better World?"

"It's Javier's creation—he said he got tired of sitting behind a rock waiting for the ill winds to stop—and that now it was time to face them like a man—he says it's time for people to again be people—and to stop letting what he refers to as Big Brother manage their lives and brains."

"He told me that what prompted the turnaround is that he was sitting behind his house reading a book—when a drone surveillance missile flew over his head—and very low—in order to frighten the people of El Polvo—so low that when he gave it the finger he thought it may have wiggled."

Luca smiles.

"When I asked him whether human beings—so easily bamboozled into believing almost any story and into doing almost any crazy thing—once they own a nice house and are eating roast beef really cared about what was happening beyond them—he—with that strange look he sometimes gets in his eyes—said that that was precisely what the Center was all about—to help snap them out of their delusional stupor."

"As soon as Jesusita and I finish visiting everyone on this side of the river I plan to go over to see him—and Jesse too—as well as some of the others in El Polvo."

"You know what Lucas?—maybe we don't need that *corrido* after all—because the two of you together are like a bean and cheese burrito with chile macho—already containing everything—to which nothing more really needs to be added or said."

Polo standing by a wire grill placed over red mesquite coals, a can of beer in one hand, and a long-tonged fork in the other, flips over one of the steaks.

"Darn it Lucas—you managed to rob for yourself what must have been the prettiest woman in the entire Sierra."

Hermelinda speaking from the other side of screen door to the house, says.

"And you Polo—stop looking at her."

Lucas also with a beer in his hand and standing next to Polo, says, "It's okay Hermelinda—everyone likes her—is fascinated by her—even the women—but I think it's because she is so different—in her flowing flowered skirt and kerchief—the tire-tread huaraches—and squatting like she is now off to one side and sipping her can of beer."

Hermelinda with a baby cradled in one arm steps out onto the porch.

"You could be right—she is not like anyone I could have even imagined—and you are right that it's much more than just being pretty—or her dress—it's something—well like an aura—that takes one in—that made me feel as if I were her sister."

Hermelinda fusses with one of the baby's shoes.

"And believe it or not Lucas—Polo no longer looks at women the way he used to—it could be because he's getting old."

Polo flipping another steak, says, "Or it could be because of you—dimwit."

Polo pokes Lucas with his beer can, and says, "Better believe it Lucas—that woman of mine is something else too."

Hermelinda comes over to the grill, and says, "This is little Lucas."

Lucas stares down at Lucas—who has a white floppy cowboy hat tied with a blue bow to his pudgy chin.

"Well my goodness—dey hey bey to the both of you—let me go inside to fix some lemonade—and I promise you that it will have just a little sugar in it and nothing else—so please—each of you find yourself the most interesting patch of shade to sit down in—and then—why sit down—ha la la."

As they sit down on some old leaves under the cottonwood tree, Jesusita says, "What an odd Chabochi—she is a little like a Tarahumara."

Petronila returns and hands a glass of lemonade to Jesusita and the other to Lucas. Pivots on one foot and skips back inside—and comes back out with hers. Sits down on the ground facing them, arranging her long green skirt, and then her thin legs into a cross-legged position.

"I saw right off and from a distance that whoever or whatever you are—you are not Lucas—thank goodness—and lucky for this sweet woman too—ha la la—and amen."

They sip their lemonade.

"I already know what you've told a few people—but are you sure you want to live with such an unusual woman right in the middle of Las Palomas—and across from the school besides?"

"For as old as you must be you have a buzzard's eye—I've been wondering the very same thing myself—knowing what neighbors can be like—even friendly ones."

"What do you mean old?—if time is an invention—how can there be young and old?"

"And as for the neighbors—I say diddly dee about what they think—but to be sure they can be extremely dangerous—and so it is always wise to take cautious measures against them."

"If they cannot even begin to comprehend the intensity of my love for the moon and the sky—and for the trees and all the wild animals—how will they ever comprehend an American and a Tarahumara goatherd living together?"

"They seeing her or me with a skirt hiked up—watering the Earth—or whatever—will report it in a minute—pointing a finger—and slobbering with glee—and shouting, Burn her at the stake."

"But excuse me—there I go being bitter again—and I assure you—that when the wintry blasts of decay finally beat me down—I have no intention of sinking back into the Earth Mother as a bitter hag."

"Only as sweet-smelling compost."

"So forget what I said—because what I meant to say was that it seems that everywhere—night and day—the devious Prince of Lies is at work—filling good decent people with very strong opinions about the only way life should be."

Lucas says, "I've noticed how very upset even nice people can get even when Jesusita does not sit herself down in a chair—or when she shows up barefoot."

Petronila finishes her lemonade with a slurp.

"Such a very beautiful straightforward and sacred world—and now all so backwards and upside down—so every which way—that not even all the king's men can put it right again."

"But you—Whoever or Whatever You Are—listen carefully—I have a sister who lives by herself and is finding it hard to get around on a bad leg and so wants to move to La Junta—hers is the last house up Arroyo Grande—all by itself—facing toward the Sierra Rica—and that has a few acres in alfalfa that are irrigated with water from the canal."

"Jesusita can put some goats out into the alfalfa—and at other times herd them in the desert behind the house—ha la la—and Tonantzin—as she flits through the forest up there on her mountain—and floats across the sky—will help you keep watch over her. "

"Petronila—you are truly a magician—tell your sister I'll buy it."

And then he shouts, startling himself and Jesusita too, "Dey hey bey."

❖ ❖ ❖

Anita and Ricardo burst through the door.

Mara their mother asks Anita, "Why are your sleeves rolled up—and where is your hat?"

"I gave it to Jesusita—she is wearing it on top of her kerchief—I want the sun to bake me dark like her—we couldn't keep up with her—she moved up and down through the rocks with the goats just like one of them—except that instead of bounding like they do—she sort of glides."

Ricardo says, "From way off—she hit a rabbit with a stone—but only its ear—so it got away."

Mara asks, "And where may I ask is she?"

"As soon as we finished putting up the bars to the corral—she ran over to the edge of the arroyo—and squatted down there—looking up it toward the Sierra de la Mula."

Chapo laughing, says, "Lucas—that woman of yours—after just two days—is already much more a part of this land than any of us who have lived here in Barranco Azul all our lives"

Lucas says, "That could be because everywhere—anywhere she is outside in nature—and free to roam and do as she pleases—is her home."

Chapo says, "And possibly too she can sense that this in the middle of nowhere place—where so much water flows as if by magic out of the ground— has been an Indian encampment for one group or another for thousands of years."

Anita says, "Lucas—can I ask you something?"

"Anything you want to."

There is a long pause.

"Ricardo and I want to work for you and Jesusita—take your guests to some of the other houses and to the dinosaur bones and anywhere else you'd like us to."

"If that's fine with your mom and dad—you're both hired."

"Hey guys—do you see what I see below us heading down the arroyo?"

"Yeah—it's Lukie—on his way back to Las Palomas—with his kerchiefed woman wearing a cowboy hat on top of her head walking along behind him— who is so dark and Indian that even if you dressed her in jeans and a T shirt and cowgirl boots—she could never even begin to pass for a *Mestiza*."

"Hey you down there—you—Luke the Duke."

Luke glances upward at the four buzzards hanging high in the sky above him. Keeps on walking.

"Congratulations—you brought back a real Indian woman—someone other Mexicans see as coming from the sludge at the bottom of the diesel barrel—and you even picked one considered by her own people to be the least among them—someone they probably considered no better than a buzzard."

"You now know that we smelly, ungainly black buzzards are majestic beings—who along with our equally smelly javelina cousins are much smarter and tuned in—when it comes to right living—than you humans."

"Did you hear Lucas?—we said congratulations."

Lucas and Jesusita are both sitting near to Norma under the cottonwood tree that she has always sat under.

When he had explained to Jesusita how he had come to know Norma, he had right away seen she did not understand, especially when she asked, "Was she one of your wives?"

Now and then Jesusita speaks something to Norma in Tarahumara—already having spoken to her more than she has so far to anyone else along the river.

To Lucas the two of them appear to be very much in tune with and at peace with the day—and with the peculiar worlds they each live in.

Norma's mother comes out onto the porch and Lucas gets up and goes over to her. And says, "Norma seems remarkably more relaxed and less fearful—I'm glad to see she no longer needs to be on that blue and yellow tether."

"It is still hard—but yes—a few things have changed for the better."

"The cake will be ready soon—as soon as I heard you were back I bought some eggs and a mix."

They sit on the porch watching the two women now sprawled on the ground like carefree gypsies.

White clouds beginning to billow up above the Sierra Rica—Lucas catches a fleeting glimpse of who could only have been Tonantzin.

Although Jesusita still sometimes howled or cried, still railed in Tarahumara at imagined adversaries, and sometimes at Lucas too, and still occasionally ran off a little ways and hid, the frequency of these crises had diminished. When they occurred, Lucas tried to react to them as he would have to another's sneezing.

By now he fully accepted Jesusita in all her herness. Anything too different—would no longer be her. He knew the best he could do for her—and maybe for anyone—was to leave her utterly free to be who she was.

One night he said aloud to the desert, "How can one possibly hold in the heart something like challenging a Supreme Court Decision—or engineering a space station—or being rich—or being highly thought of?"

In Las Palomas, El Valle, and as far away as Barranco Azul—people became a little happier, and their lives took on a more meaningful tint—even the buzzards seeming to float more benignly across the sky.

But no one had the slightest idea why.

"Javier—when I first heard of The Center for Independent Thought for a Better World I thought it might be some new government program for engineering public consent."

Javier laughs. Says, "Yeah I know—or even one advocating the overthrow of the government."

"In my rushes of blind enthusiasm I do stupid things—I've already changed the name to *Las Voces del Polvo*—Voices From Out of the Dust."

"It's like this Lucas—how can this country point itself in a new direction if the only stuff inside people's heads is the propaganda pumped into them by the government and corporations who control the media, the schools, and the experts?"

"Tell me Lucas—why should those addicted to power and money know how the Universe works and know what they are doing and what is best for the world any better than anyone else—when they are probably even more out of touch—more in a tunnel than the rest of us?"

"And yes I know Lucas—getting people to think for themselves is not easy—especially when they are being bombarded by loud music, novelty, and fashionableness—are doing everything in a rush—are preoccupied with a million things that they see as more important—and are talking on their cell phones at the same time."

"Nevertheless—I hope to make a start—with people from along the river—who aren't so caught up in the craziness of things—with Jesse, Carlos, Gregorio—and the women too—letting anyone say some words about what would make a better more harmonious world—but only if what they have to say is sincere and heartfelt—and is not being heard and repeated all over the place."

"Simple ideas from simple ordinary people—those that the founding fathers of this country referred to as the rabble—who will not let their concept of what is a quality and dignified life for human beings get mired in the diversionary issues and mud of foreign policy, financial strategies, elections. and corporate profits."

"Maybe put the best ones in a blog—and eventually bring in people from other places—but no experts in anything—or big names—since the big shots got to be who they are by saying the socially and politically correct things."

"Whew—long winded Javier—I do sometimes get wound up."

"So what do you think Lucas?—do you want to speak?"

"I don't know—these days words seem to come to me from further and further away—and then I have to work to fit them together—that's one of the reasons why I am thinking of bringing a few people to the desert—and having it and not me do the talking and teaching."

"Like long ago it used to—along with the mountains and forests and rivers—and the animals—and the sun and moon and the stars."

"You should call your business Cosmic Encounter."

"I was thinking of something more earthy—like Javelina Expeditions—or Buzzard Works."

"That reminds me—a Pizza Works just opened in Buena Vista—when Jesse and I come over to meet Jesusita—we'll bring one with us."

"Great—but don't act surprised when she cuts her slices into small pieces and rolls them up along with a chile in a tortilla."

"But Lucas—that's what Voices From Out of the Dust is all about—coming at life from who one really is—and from all directions—and then some."

Javier pauses, and then says, "Maybe she should be the one to raise a voice from out of the dust—and not you."

"Yes—my new wife is a Tarahumara Indian—a goat herd."

Mary for the first time ever is at a loss for what to say.

And Donald without his appropriate quip from the realm of modern physic stands there like a plucked duck. Who regaining somewhat his composure, manages to come up with, "Well—congratulations."

And Mary says, "Yes—congratulations Lucas—but why didn't you bring her?"

"Because this country won't let her come here—she's too Indian."

He first heard the crack, and then saw the earth split downward, opening up a chasm between those two and where he was standing just wide enough that not even with a running start could anyone jump across.

"You will need someone with some burros to carry water and a few other things—and to take anyone who drops from the heat or exhaustion—or gets bitten by a snake or scorpion—to the nearest house."

"Someone like me, Lucas—who grew up with rattlesnakes—herding goats in that country—and knows every rock and rabbit hole."

"It's a deal Jesse—I'll try to get the first trip off about the end of September—when the sun's not so high anymore."

"Perfect—that will give me time to buy a second burro."

Lucas says, "And me time to trade my pickup for something more suitable for shuttling people and their gear from the airport and back again."

Jesse is quiet for a moment, as if thinking hard.

"Lucas—you and I will guide them not just over the sands and gravels and stones of the Chihuahuan Desert—but try to sneak those city people up as close as we can get them—to the Source."

"And with luck—if it all sort of works out—maybe some of them will go back home having left their old worn-out skins—as sometimes some snakes do—dangling in the thorns of a catclaw bush."

"We'll see how it goes, Jesse—we'll just have to see how it goes."

"Let me tell you a story Lucas—Javier and I were sitting around one night—and he began telling me about the Desert Hermits—who he said back a long time ago went out to live in the North African desert in order to hear more clearly the voice of God."

"He told me that for them to accomplish that—they first had to learn to bow to and be subservient to other men—and to give up women—even all thoughts of them."

"And then Javier said—with that wild look in his eyes—Be ye as marshmallows and ye shall know God—and suddenly laughed so hard in his beer that some of it blew in my face."

Lucas smiling, says, "You and I will revel in the virile independence and freedom and toughness of the desert nomads—and just like them—with daggers gripped between our teeth—we will defend all that—along with our women and children—with a vengeance."

"That's what I was just about to say too—that that is what life has always been about."

"Tell me Jesse—I've been wondering—how is the Wall thing going?"

"I gave up on the Wall—because I now see that what civilization is— is walls—walls around individuals, groups, things—around everything—and with everyone thinking that only with a wall around it does anything exist."

"What you and I are going to find out Jesse—is whether maybe the winds and silence of the desert can help weaken those walls—crumble some of them back into good old desert sand—that you can run through your fingers."

"I'm with you Lucas—I'm with you—all the way."

When Jesusita left Lucas asleep in their bed in the middle of night and fled into the desert, this time it was not out of any sudden uncontrollable anger or desperation—but rather to talk to the Moon.

"Moon—it must have been in another life that I last talked to You—a life with days on end with only the tinkle of a goat bell—and at night the howling of the coyotes—and sometimes the shriek of a jaguar."

"But even as very far away from all that as I now am—You are the same big round Moon—all which makes me wonder whether I am still the same me too—in spite of so much that has happened."

"Except that here—where there seems to be so little of anything—You seem so much grander.

"And that which I can't see but feel is flowing through both of us—and is so comforting and soothing and connecting—feels so much stronger."

"So powerful and overwhelming that I can feel myself being drawn up to You—or You down to me—I do not know which."

"Many things I am unable to tell Lucas—he not understanding Tarahumara—and it could even be that Norma—in her silence—understands better than he does."

"I tried to tell him about feeling I was grander than just a Tarahumara— in the way that You are grand—though of course not as grand as You—who are the Moon."

"Though maybe I could not make him understand because I do not understand it myself."

"I feel less fearful—here by this river that flows so wide and beautiful through the desert—and everyone has been very nice—but I still cry—especially because I still can't do everything I once used to—and at other times too when I don't know why."

She remains silent for a while, feeling herself being bathed in a cleansing sea of what is more than just moonlight.

"My periods of crying—and anger—and sometimes the tortillas I make—embarrass me terribly."

"Lucas told me those things were not important—he is very good to me—like Pancho was—and like Carmen says Candelario is."

"I see that here it is the same world as the Tarahumara world—only different—Juarez and Chihuahua City too—only they even more different—and with a cloud of ugliness hanging over them—like when the soldiers came."

"I have been thinking of asking Lucas—the next time we go to La Junta—for a cut of brightly flowered cloth for another skirt—and for a brand new kerchief to replace this faded blue one—but then too maybe not—because really I already have everything."

"Except of course I will need some clothes and a blanket for what sometimes kicks so hard inside my belly."

"Do I talk too much?—I know the Tarahumara do not to talk to You in this way—and that who taught me that was my Grandfather Benito—explaining to me how the Padre often talked to You—even when it was day and You were not up in the sky to see."

"Grandfather Benito said the words were not important—but rather telling them to You—to someone who listens to where the words came from—and who more than anything—cares."

"Then too—maybe I do not need to tell You anything—just be with You—knowing You are there—and that that is how it should be with Lucas also."

"But now Moon—it's time to go back to Lucas—I will be very careful to not wake him up—and so make an effort to hold my tongue until morning—before telling him I suddenly feel much better."

Those who went with Javelina Expeditions although they spent much of their ten days talking about such things as what makes a good hamburger and what they needed to do as soon as they got back home—nevertheless appeared to enjoy themselves immensely.

Jesse when he returned from having taken the third group back across the river to Buena Vista and from there on to the airport, told Lucas, "I get to listen for two hours to their non stop yakking—and do you know what I now think?—that it is not only the desert that may have changed them just a little—but also they having gotten to know you and Jesusita."

"Especially how much you care for her—and how you take care of her the way you do."

Jesse twiddles with an ear for a moment, before saying, "But what I think they are least likely to forget is Jesusita herself."

"All of them leave enchanted by her—I think she opens their eyes to the reality of the world being somehow far different from what they thought it was."

Katrina was with Lucas when the baby came. And it was she who cut the cord, cleaned him, and handed him wrapped in a towel to Jesusita. Who saw right away that he was as white and foreign-looking as Lucas.

That same day a soft grey mist enveloped the Rio Grande country—and all through the night a fine drizzle fell. And on into the next day.

A week later, out in the desert, the tips of the tall, bare, spindly spiny sticks of ocotillo bloomed with bright clusters of small red flowers.

Lucas chose for their child the name Tamo. Which some rural Mexicans would know is the chaff that is discarded when grains or beans are winnowed—the very least among things.

At first Lucas had to constantly remind Jesusita, "He's crying—put him to a breast."

Since it took her months to realize that this strange-looking Tamo was truly hers—and not just another clever deception of the Chabochi Devil.